PRINCESS OF THORNS

ALSO BY STACEY JAY

Juliet Immortal

Romeo Redeemed

Of Beast and Beauty

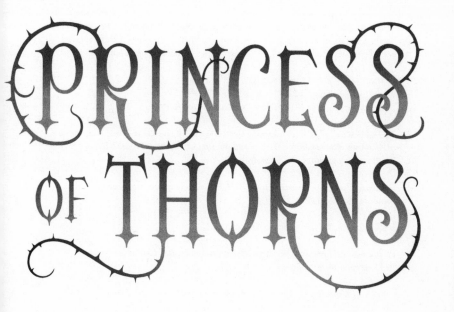

PRINCESS OF THORNS

STACEY JAY

DELACORTE PRESS

Text copyright © 2014 by Stacey Jay
Jacket art copyright © 2014 by Nick Chao
Map art copyright © 2014 by Jennifer Redstreake Geary

All rights reserved. Published in the United States by Delacorte Press, an imprint of Random House Children's Books, a division of Random House LLC, a Penguin Random House Company, New York.

Delacorte Press is a registered trademark and the colophon is a trademark of Random House LLC.

Visit us on the Web! randomhouse.com/teens

Educators and librarians, for a variety of teaching tools, visit us at RHTeachersLibrarians.com

Library of Congress Cataloging-in-Publication Data
Jay, Stacey.
    Princess of thorns / Stacey Jay. — First edition.
        pages cm
    Summary: After ten years of exile among fairies who teach her to use her magically-enhanced strength and courage, Sleeping Beauty's daughter Aurora enlists the help of Niklaas, eleventh son of King Eldorio, in the fight to reclaim her throne.
    ISBN 978-0-385-74322-8 (hc) — ISBN 978-0-307-98143-1 (ebook)
    [1. Princesses—Fiction. 2. Princes—Fiction. 3. Adventure and adventurers—Fiction. 4. Inheritance and succession—Fiction. 5. Fantasy.] I. Title.
    PZ7.J344Pri 2014
    [Fic]—dc23
    2013026324

The text of this book is set in 11.5-point Sabon MT.
Book design by Stephanie Moss

Printed in the United States of America
10 9 8 7 6 5 4 3 2
First Edition

For M,
my partner in all adventures

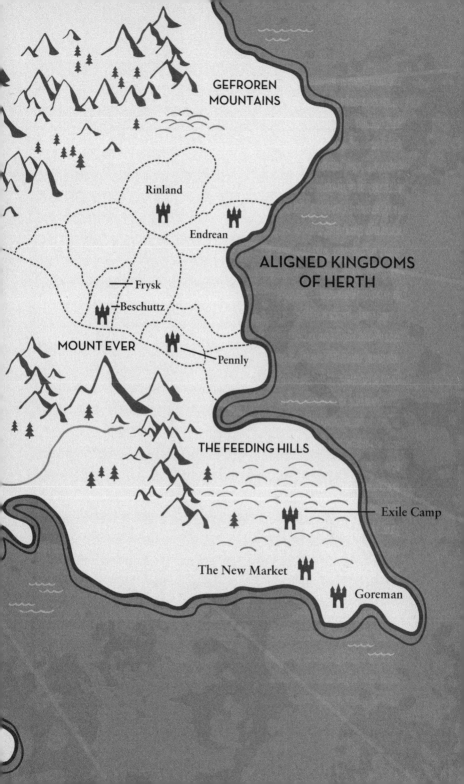

Once upon a time there lived a
prince and a princess

with no happily-ever-after. . . .

THE PAST . . .

In my youth, longing for immortality gave me many sons.
Now it sows the seeds of their destruction.

—Eldorio III, Immortal King of Kanvasola

Having discovered the secret to eternal life, and jealous of his throne, the immortal king summoned a witch to the castle and ordered her to curse his eleven sons, ensuring none would live past their eighteenth birthday, the age at which a Kanvasol prince may become a king.

But the witch was a gentle woman and so tempered her curse with kindness. The princes still in line to inherit on their eighteenth birthdays would not die, but would be transformed into a lamentation of swans.

Years passed and ten sons were transformed, but the eleventh, the prince Niklaas, raged against his fate and vowed to break the spell.

The past, sadly, is immortal. No child is born innocent.
                              —ROSE RONCES, "THE SLEEPING BEAUTY"

After years of marriage, the Sleeping Beauty longed to travel beyond the fairy briars surrounding her castle, but Prince Stephen's stepmother was an ogre, who the prince feared would imprison their two children if she was to learn of their existence. And so Rose remained hidden, until the day her new maid let slip that the prince's other wife was not nearly as lovely as the beauty.

Doubting her husband's fidelity, Rose rode to the capital, where she met the prince's barren first wife and his stepmother, Queen Ekeeta. As Stephen had feared, Ekeeta ordered his children locked away. The prince begged for mercy, and Rose was given a home at the edge of the city, where she and the children were guarded at all times.

Years passed, and Stephen came to believe it was safe to leave his family for several months at a time. The night after his departure to the wars in the east, Ekeeta's soldiers came for Rose and the children. They were imprisoned, and Rose was sentenced to death.

Knowing the end was near, the Sleeping Beauty embraced her eldest, Princess Aurora, and wished for the girl to be granted fairy blessings. But it was not for grace, or beauty, or the gift of song that Rose wished. . . .

CHAPTER ONE

AURORA

Prophecy foretells that in the last days of the Long Summer, the Age of Reaping will dawn with the rise of the living darkness. The four kingdoms will dwell in shadow, and the souls of man feed the First One's hunger for a hundred years.

And when the land lies barren, and not a single man remains upon it, the gates of the underworld shall open and all souls—human and ogre—descend to dwell in peace with the Lost Mother for all eternity.

Only a human child, briar-born, can usher in the Final Age. And so such children must be collected and held captive until the coming of the Long Summer.

Any citizen found to be sheltering or aiding in the escape of such a child will be sentenced to death.

—Royal Proclamation, 20th of Sunswane, 1458

"It's time, button," Mama whispers. Her voice is like lines of music—delicate bars that trap and hold me prisoner on the floor before her.

I am so terrified that I can't move, but I love her too much to run, even if I could. Even if there were somewhere to run to, some way out of this cell where Mama and Jor and I have been brought to await our moment to die. The queen said Jor and I would be spared and allowed to live out our lives in the dungeon, but Mama doesn't believe her.

Neither do I.

Queen Ekeeta will finish with the nobles and judges and merchants loyal to my father, and then her guards will come for us. Before nightfall, she and the ogres who came in the black ships from across the Winter Ocean will magic the light from our eyes, drink our spirits down, and throw our soulless bodies into the sea.

I have seen our fate.

The sun was rising when the guards forced us along the wall walk five mornings past. I saw the waves crashing far below the keep. I saw the ladies in their fine dresses and the men in their shining armor washing in and out on the tide, their limp bodies knocking against the rocks like dolls some spoiled child had thrown away.

I realized they were dead—all the human members of my father's inner circle, every one dead and gone—and I screamed. I screamed and thrashed and kicked until the guard pulling me along had to pick me up and tuck me under his long arm to carry me to the dungeon. I fought for my freedom, but I was too small. Too weak. I am only seven years old.

I will never be more than seven years old.

"As soon as it's over, take Jor and go down the waste chute," Mama says.

The waste chute? I look up, lips parting, but Mama pushes on before I can protest.

"There is no other way. It will be tight, but you will fit, little button." Mama smoothes my hair from my face with her soft hands.

We've been in the dark with the biting beetles, the filth of the prisoners who slept here before us, and the sour water leaking down the walls for five days, but her hands still smell like spring blossoms.

Mama always smells like flowers. Daddy says it's because she is as beautiful as a flower, the most beautiful woman in the world. The fairies made her the most beautiful when she was only a baby. Mama wouldn't let the fairies bless me when I was born—she said it was too dangerous, that fairy blessings, no matter how well intended, too often become curses—but she's going to bless me today. She's going to give me the fairy magic hiding inside her. Time is running out, and there is nothing left to lose.

"Are you ready, Aurora?" Mama cups my cheek.

"Will it hurt?" I try not to cry, but fail. Hot tears spill down my cheeks, and my body shakes hard enough to wake Jor, who has fallen asleep with his head in my lap.

"Ror," he mumbles. He pats my face with one pudgy hand. He turned four last month but still has a baby's hands.

I love his baby hands. I love my little brother. I can't imagine a world without him. But we are both briar-born— children birthed within the circle of enchanted fairy briars— and Mama says the queen will kill us if we don't escape. Even

5

if Mama is wrong, and the queen sincere in her promise to hold Jor and me captive until the long summer of the ogre prophecy, a life lived in a cell is worse than no life at all.

I am Jor's only hope, which makes me even more afraid.

"Don't cry, Ror." Jor sounds near tears himself as I settle him on the floor beside me and tuck his blanket beneath his cheek.

"It's all right, biddle bee. Go back to sleep." I sniff away my tears and rub his tummy until his eyes drift closed, trying to be brave the way Mama wants me to be.

But I'm not brave. I am so frightened that *frightened* is too small a word to describe the feeling crushing my heart to liquid inside my chest. I need a bigger word, a word with fangs and blood dripping from its chin, but I haven't learned a word like that yet, and now I never will. I will die tonight. I know it. I can't do what Mama asks. I'm too little, so small people often mistake Jor and me for twins when we go to visit the castle with Father. I will never be a hero, not even with the help of fairy magic.

"There is no more time, love. Be my brave, strong girl." Mama plucks the long knife from the floor. "I know you will make me proud."

One of the prison guards smuggled the knife in with our breakfast this morning. He is loyal to Ekeeta but can't bear to see two innocent children killed. Mama believes we can trust him to take Jor and me to the fairies, and that the Fey will protect us until it is safe to return to Norvere.

"I love you both so much," Mama says, her voice breaking as she begins to cry. "Tell Jor how much. He's so little he might forget. You must help him remember."

I've heard Mama cry before—when Daddy would leave our estate with bags full of gifts, bound for some secret destination in the east—but I've never heard her sound this sad. Despite everything she's told me, and the hours spent discussing her plan, it is only now that I realize she truly intends to do it, to take herself away from us. Forever.

I clutch her soiled skirt in my hands. "Mama, no, I—"

"You and your brother are the brightest lights I've ever known," she says, trembling as hard as I was a moment ago. "You will shine for this kingdom. You will grow up strong and brave and clever and kind, and you will make everything right. I know it." She pulls in a desperate breath. "And I will always be with you in your heart, button. Always."

"Mama, don't! Please!" I throw my arms around her waist, press my face to her chest, and hug her tight, but Mama doesn't hug me back. She tenses and her body jerks.

Moments later, I feel it—something hot and wet rushing over my forehead, sticking my hair to my skin, running down my cheeks. Even before I wipe my face and bring red away on my fingers, I know what it is.

Blood. *Mama's blood.* Because fairy magic will only leave a body in blood, when a human chooses death in order to pass the power to another.

Mama is dead. I am alone. *Alone!*

I open my mouth to scream for Mama to come back, to beg for help, but before words can escape something flickers within the hollows of my bones and a transformation begins deep inside me. Deeper than blood or sinew, deeper than this dungeon, deeper than the sea crashing against the rocks below the keep or the world the ogres believe exists beneath ours. A place so secret and deep I had no idea it was there until the light of Mother's magic fell into the darkness and lit me up.

But now it has, and I know I am more than a frightened little girl; I am a briar-born child, beloved by the Fey. I am a daughter and a sister and a princess, and as fierce and strong as I choose to be.

And I *choose* to be strong. I choose to fight, even if I am small and alone. I choose to be the hero my mother wanted me to be.

Without a sound, I ease Mother's body back onto the stones and hurry to the pallet we've shared since the morning we were brought to the dungeon. I use our thin covers to clean my face and hair as best I can, then lay the blanket gently over Mama, refusing to look too closely.

I will not remember her as a corpse. I will remember her smile and the way her eyes danced when she built castles of pillows for Jor and me on days when it was too cold to go outside. I will remember her stories and songs and the way she never let a day go by without whispering "I love you" in my ear. I will remember the flower smell of her clothes when she hugged me tight and her laughter when we would sneak out to dance in the rain without Jor, because rain dancing was our secret, just between Mama and me.

I will remember her, and I will avenge her.

"Goodbye, Mama," I whisper, ignoring the stinging in my nose. There will be time to cry later, when Jor and I are safe.

Being careful not to wake him, I scoop my brother into my arms and carry him to the dungeon's waste chute. He is tall for four and I am short for seven, but it's easier than I thought it would be to hold him to my chest as I shuffle across the stones. I'm glad. It will be better if Jor doesn't see Mama again, and if he doesn't realize he's falling until he's halfway to the bottom.

The waste chute empties onto a street outside the castle walls. The kind guard promised to have a cart of straw waiting there to break our fall, but even if he's changed his mind about helping us, there's a chance we'll survive the thirty-hand drop to the stone road, a better chance than we'll have if we stay here to await the coming of the ogre priest.

I saw Illestros yesterday, his long white robe dragging along the filth-caked floor as he came to fetch Father's spymaster from the cell next to our own. He is even taller than the other ogres, with dozens of tiny coin-shaped tattoos marking his large bald head. Queen Ekeeta wears a wig to cover her hairless skull and looks nearly human—though taller than a mortal, with larger eyes and mandrill fingers Mama said are left over from a time when the ogres consumed more than human spirits, when they would pry between our bones for each tender piece of meat—but the priest makes no effort to hide what he is. He flaunts the tattoos that show how many souls he's captured inside of him; he bares his pointed teeth when he smiles.

He is a wolf, and Jor and I are rabbits he means to devour, but he will not have us.

Ignoring the putrid smell, I ease Jor into the waste chute and give him a push. He wakes as he falls and begins to scream, but I am already climbing into the chute, muffling his cry with my body, keeping it from the ears of the guard at the top of the stairs.

The longer our departure goes unnoticed, the better the chance we'll reach the woods where the fairies will be waiting.

I count to ten—knowing I must give Jor time to land and hopefully be pulled out of the way—and then I flatten my body, lift my arms, and slide down the chute. My spine knocks painfully along the slimy stones for a few moments, but after a fall of a dozen hands, the narrow passage joins a larger tunnel where rushing waste water carries me along more gently, gaining speed as the channel dips sharply toward the ground.

Less than two minutes later, I am born into my new life in a rush of filth and wet.

I land with a grunt in the sodden, stinking hay of a farmer's cart and turn to look for Jor. I find him clinging to the neck of the guard with the dark eyes and the single brow scribbled across his broad forehead.

When he sees me, the guard's breath rushes out, his eyes widening as he takes in my bloodied hair and face. "She's dead, then? Lady Rose?" I nod, and he hugs Jor tight before whispering, "The gods rest her beautiful soul."

"She didn't believe in the gods." I brush the hay from my dress. "She believed in good people. She told me to tell you thank you with all her heart," I finish in a voice I scarcely recognize.

I sound like a grown-up. A girl who will become a queen.

I *will* be queen. Father is dead, and he had no children with his first wife. He named me his first heir and Jor his second. I will go to the fairies now, but one day I will return with an army and reclaim my kingdom from those who have stolen it, and I will start gathering my allies now.

I come to my feet in the cart, putting myself at eye level with our savior. "When I am queen, I will grant you forgiveness for pledging yourself into Ekeeta's service, and land of your own, if you're still alive to work it."

The guard nods, but I see the pity in his expression. When he looks at me, he sees a helpless little girl. He doesn't know that I have Mama's magic inside me. He doesn't know that I will *never* stop fighting to avenge her, not so long as there is breath in my body.

"Come, Princess. My horse is tied in the alley. You and your brother will both fit on the saddle in front." He shifts Jor to one arm and reaches for me with the other. "Think you can hold the little man tight as we go?"

"I can." Ignoring his hand, I vault over the edge of the cart, landing lightly on the stones, my bones vibrating pleasantly from the impact. I feel as if I could leap the entire road, run for miles. As if I could lift the heavy sword hanging from the guard's belt over my head, storm the castle, and knock every ogre inside it into the sea. I've never felt so strong or fearless or full of life.

Even before we meet the fairies in the shadows of the woods—before Janin, the Fey healer who will become my second mother, places her hand on my chest to take the measure of my new magic—I know that Mama has wished something very different for me than the beauty or grace or lovely singing voice the fairies granted her in her cradle. When I learn that I will walk through life with enhanced strength, a brave spirit, a merciful mind, and a heart no man I love

11

will dare defy, I am pleased that Mama wished so well for me, that she gave me such fine tools to help me reclaim our kingdom.

I don't dream for a moment that she has cursed me as surely as she's blessed me.

I am only a child, too innocent to realize that there is no salvation without sacrifice, no light without darkness, no triumph that doesn't carry the seeds of its own destruction bouncing in its pocket.

CHAPTER TWO

Ten Years Later

AURORA

The immortals are wrong; the golden god the humans say comes to fetch their spirits at the end is real—far younger than they've imagined, and neither wrinkled nor bearded, nor possessing a third eye in the center of his forehead—but real all the same.

Real, and *divinely* beautiful.

Sleep tugs at me, but I struggle to keep my eyes open, not wanting to miss a moment of my death.

I wonder how the god will summon my soul from my body, and if it will hurt the way it does when ogres steal a soul. I wonder if he will take my spirit to the Land Beyond, curse me to the Pit, or force me to live out another mortal existence, this time as a vulture, or a Carn fish, or a maggot, or something equally miserable in order to pay for the mess I've made of my human life.

"A fifty-fifty chance and I get the wrong one." The god

laughs bitterly as he runs a hand through his shaggy hair. "Should have flaming known."

I try to ask what he means, but all I manage is a moan.

"Waking up, then, are you?" He glances down at me where I lie, wrists chained to a metal ring the Boughtswords drove deep into the ground. "How you feeling, little man?"

His voice is deep and softened by an accent I know I should be able to place, but I can't remember the language of round vowels and soft *R*s. I can't even remember the names of the four kingdoms. There is no room in my thoughts for anything but the god's terrible beauty—his golden hair falling in waves to his shoulders, his bee-stung lips, his eyes as bright and blue as the sea stone I stole from Janin's treasure box.

He is . . . magnificent.

The god snaps his fingers between my eyes, but I'm too numb to flinch. "Can you understand me?"

I reach up, patting his cheek before running a buzzing finger over his impossibly perfect mouth, surprised to find his lips as solid as the chains knocking against my arm, real and warm and a tiny bit chapped, which for some reason makes me giggle.

"Sleep-drunk bastard," he mumbles, knocking my hand away. His expression is kind enough, but I see the disappointment in his eyes.

But then, he is a god, and must see straight through me to the secrets of my black heart. He must know that I have lied, thieved, and betrayed my only friends, and all of it for nothing. I am dying, and soon Jor will join me in death and the Ronces line will reach its tragic end.

"Forgive me," I say, but the words come out tangled. My

tongue is thick, my mouth dry, and my head full of smoke and shadow.

The leader of the Boughtswords set four braziers of Vale Flowers burning in my tent, determined to keep me too sleep-sick to damage any more of his men before the caravan reaches the slave market. Instead, I will soon be dead. I try to take satisfaction in the fact that he will lose the small fortune even a scrawny, Fey-trained warrior would have fetched at market, but I'm too muddled to focus on any one thought for long.

Even Golden God, the great and beautiful, with his lips like a love poem, has begun to lose my interest to the dragon-shaped shadows flickering on the roof of the tent until he takes hold of my shoulders and gives a shake.

"Focus, boy." He pinches my ears before tapping my forehead with his thick finger. "If I free you, can you stand? It'll be easier to get you outside on your own feet."

Outside? Outside the tent? Outside my body? Outside . . .

My eyes begin to burn from being held open too long. I try to blink, but my lids slide shut and stay that way, no matter how I fight to open them. My lashes are made of stone, my lids weigh more than the leather armor lying heavy on my bound chest.

The armor is stolen, too. I snatched it from Thyne's cot the morning I left, though I knew he would give it to me if I asked. Thyne would lie down and let me use him as a carpet if I told him to, though, of course, I never would. What's the point in walking on a broken man?

What's the point in walking on an unbroken *man?*

The thought confounds me, making my head ache even

more than it did before. What *is* the point in walking on an unbroken man? Is the question nonsense or a riddle I must answer in order to gain passage out of this limbo world inhabited by gods and monsters and the ghosts of all the people I've failed in my seventeen years of life?

Failed, when I was so certain . . . so determined . . .

I'm dimly aware of the god patting my cheeks, but it's too late for him to draw me out. I am sinking into myself, back into the mists of my mind.

I run down a red mud road, past Janin, my fairy mother, who cradles Thyne in her arms, mourning the son who might as well be dead after what I did to him. I run past my mother, covered in the wasted blood she used to bless me. I run until I reach the outskirts of Mercar, and then on through the abandoned city, down roads where ancient buildings have begun to crumble beneath a bruise-black sky.

I throw myself through the castle gates into the royal garden, where the sacred Hawthorn tree's leaves flame crimson red. I hear my brother scream from somewhere deep within the castle and run even faster. Faster and faster, but I can't remember the way to the throne room where Ekeeta conducts her rituals. I can't find Jor, can't free him, can't do anything to right my many wrongs.

It should be me, I think as I race down one empty hallway after another, alone but for the sound of Jor's tortured cries.

I'm the one Mama blessed. I should have done more to protect my brother. I should have insisted we put an end to our twice-yearly visits, no matter how careful we were when traveling under the cover of night. The entire point of being raised in separate corners of the world was to prevent both of Norvere's heirs from being killed or captured at once. I should have insisted we stay apart. I should have listened to the fairy elders and married the king of Endrean and his navy of five hundred ships. I should have heeded Janin when she warned that there is a difference between bravery and pride, but I didn't, and now my pride will be the ruin of the world.

I finally turn the corner to the throne room, only to find the doors locked against me. I push and shove. I slam my fists into the etched metal where my father's family seal—thorns lifting a red-sailed galleon from the sea—still marks the door, but all I receive for my efforts are broken bones. Something cracks in my right hand and pain blooms in my fist. I fall to the ground, clutching my arm to my chest as Jor's screams cut off with a terrible suddenness.

My brother is dead.

I know it the way I know the sun is hot and the seas are blue. Jor is dead. My sweet brother, my best friend, my last living family member and the only person it is safe for me to love, is gone. He will never grow into those extra inches and broad shoulders he sprouted this year. He will never be a man or a beloved or a father. He will never celebrate his fifteenth birthday.

"I'll kill you!" I scream, ignoring the tears that run down my cheeks. "I'll cut your heart out!"

"You'll do no such thing, child." The queen is suddenly in the hall before me, staring down at me from her great height.

She is sixteen hands if she's a finger, a long, lean column in her ivory dress with the gold trim. Her face is as taut and firm as it was when I was a child—youthful and pretty in its gaunt way, though I know she is close to two hundred years old—and her bald head is concealed by a mass of golden curls. The wig looks like her own hair, but it is not. It is a lie, as everything about the false queen is a lie.

I leap to my feet, determined to kill her with my one good hand, but when I reach for her my arm goes limp, falling to hang useless at my side. I cannot use deadly force except to defend myself. My mother's fairy gifts do not allow me to be merciless, even to the one being who deserves no mercy.

"Give yourself to me, Aurora," Ekeeta says. "There is nothing left for you to live for."

"Stuff yourself," I growl, wishing I could sink a dagger into her heart.

"It's a shame." Ekeeta leans down until her eyes are level with my face. Her thin lips stretch, but she doesn't show me her sharper-than-human teeth. "One would think your mother would have wished for intelligence for you along with your other gifts. But Rose wasn't known for her thinking, was she? Poor, pretty . . . dead thing."

With a howl, I lunge for the ogre queen's throat, but the moment my clawed fingers touch her flesh she vanishes, leaving nothing but a pile of biting beetles behind.

The beetles tumble over each other as they scuttle along the floor, fleeing the boot I bring down upon them again and again. I stomp them to juice, panting with panic born in my days in the dungeon when I woke with beetles nesting in my hair, crawling along my throat, creeping beneath my skirt to leave bite marks up and down my legs.

The last of the insects disappear beneath the throne room's door and I collapse against the wall, covering my face with my hands, weeping in a way I haven't in years. I weep *for Jor and Thyne and Janin. I weep for the people of Nor-vere, who will never be free of the tyranny of ogre reign.*

I weep for what feels like years and am still crying when I'm plunged into a world of cold, where there is no air to breathe.

My eyes fly open and I suck in a lungful of water as I'm pulled to the surface. I see bleary gray sky and my own boots sticking out the end of a watering trough, and I cough loudly before a rough hand covers my mouth and a voice hisses in my ear—

"Quiet, little man. These ragers are drunk, not dead."

I shove the hand away and spin to face the voice, sending water sloshing out onto the grass in the process.

Behind me, squatting with his thick arms crossed atop the rough wood of the trough, is the young god, looking far less godlike in the thin morning light. He's still the most stunning thing I've ever seen—which is saying something for a girl raised among fairy boys so lovely they can break a human heart with a glance—but he's not divine.

A god wouldn't have a faint bruise staining one cheekbone or the beginnings of a mangy beard with patches where the whiskers have refused to grow. A god wouldn't have dust on his clothes or smell like a mix of campfire and barley liquor. And a god certainly wouldn't wear a full-sleeved gray shirt of the style popular only in southern Kanvasola.

Worship of all gods, human and immortal, has been forbidden in Kanvasola for years, ever since the Immortal King Eldorio decided to live forever and ordered his country to worship him instead.

"You speak the language of Norvere?" the boy asks,

hesitating only a moment before asking me the same question in Kanvasol.

"Who are you?" I ask in my native tongue. I know a bit of Kanvasol, but not enough to carry on a conversation. "What do you want?" I shiver but make no move to step out of the water. My head is clear and my stomach settled for the first time in days, and the cold is at least partially responsible for banishing the haze of the Vale Flowers.

"I'm Niklaas of Kanvasola, eleventh son of King Eldorio," he says with a grin and a slight bow of his head. "And you are Jor, the lost prince of Norvere."

I shake my head. "No, I—"

"I gave a priceless suit of armor and a piece of my soul for a charm to help me find a briar-born child." He reaches into the front of his shirt and pulls out a pendant shaped like the spokes of a wheel. It is made of flat, unremarkable gray stone, but as soon as it is free of his shirt it rises of its own accord and strains toward me. I'm certain if Niklaas took it off, the charm would glue itself to my face. "Seeing as you and your sister are the only two such creatures left, I know exactly who you are."

"What do you want?" I reach up to squeeze the water from my hair, grateful that my warrior's knot is holding strong atop my head.

I look boyish enough with my braids down—it takes more than long hair to make me easily recognizable as female, especially when I'm dressed in a Fey warrior's clothes—but I'm grateful my hair won't be in the way if I need to fight. I can't imagine what a Kanvasol prince wants with a briar-born child, but I'm certain he's up to no good.

"Relax, boy, I mean you no harm," Niklaas says, obviously reading the distrust in my expression. "I'm going to help you escape, and in exchange you're going to help me find what I'm looking for."

My first thought is to tell him to take his "help" and shove it so far between his ass cheeks he'll waddle down the road—I stopped speaking like a princess the day I began training to be a warrior—but I bite my lip. I came to the Boughtsword camp alone, certain the Fey gem in my pocket and the promise of more once Jor was freed would be enough to secure an army.

Instead, the gem, which in my naiveté I hadn't realized was far too valuable to be used as a token payment, was stolen and I was taken captive. I wounded a dozen or more men before I was locked away, but still . . .

"How did you get the chains off?" I ask, rubbing the chafed skin at my wrists.

"Picked the locks." Niklaas pushes to his feet and reaches a hand down to help me from the trough. "It's a skill best learned early in my family."

I ignore Niklaas's hand and allow my eyes to flick up and down his long body, considering the eleventh son of the immortal king. He's tall and strong, with thick muscles obvious beneath his gray shirt and dusty brown riding pants. I imagine he could be dangerous-looking if he would smile less. And he can pick locks and sneak unnoticed into Boughtsword camps and no doubt has many other useful, real-world skills.

I'm a well-trained fighter, strengthened by magic, light on my feet, and nearly fearless, but I've been too isolated on my fairy island. I need an ally who knows the ways of the mainland in order to secure an army, and I need to find that ally quickly. I must free my brother before the Hawthorne tree in Mercar Castle's courtyard turns crimson. If I don't, Jor will die come the changing of the seasons. Janin saw his death in a vision, and her visions are rarely wrong.

Rarely, but not never. Mortal interference can change the course of fate.

Janin foretold that my mother would live a long, happy life once her hundred years of sleep had passed, but my father fought his way through the fairy briars to wake the Sleeping Beauty twenty years early and changed all that. I have to believe I can change Jor's fate as well. If I move quickly.

Summer is lingering this year, but the crisp in the air this morning warns it will not last forever.

"Come on, then," Niklaas says, frustration creeping into his voice. "The camp will wake soon, and I'd rather you stay alive. At least until we locate your sister."

"What do you want with Aurora?" I eye the sword at Niklaas's waist, gauging my chances of taking it from him. Ekeeta put a bounty on my head as soon as she realized I had escaped her dungeon. If this prince means to find "my sister" and deliver her to the ogre queen, I will be better off finding another ally.

"I want to court her. What else would a prince want with a princess?" Niklaas asks with a grin I'm certain has convinced more than a few girls to tumble him without the benefit of sacred vows. "But sadly, my charm was magicked only to take me to the nearest briar-born child and won't work a second time."

"That is sad," I say in my flattest tone.

"Could be worse," he says, still grinning like the rat that

gave the cat rabies. "I'm sure your sister will be pleased to learn I saved her baby brother from the slave market."

He pats my cheek; I slap his hand away. "Perhaps. If your father weren't Ekeeta's *only* ally." I glare at him, not bothering to hide my suspicion from my alleged suitor.

Suitor. Ha! This pretty lion-boy would gag on his own tongue if he knew *I* am the girl whose hand he hopes to win. A girl who has no trouble passing as a boy, with not a whisper of the beauty her mother was so legendary for.

"Exactly." He winks. "Nothing could make my father angrier than his son shaming him before the queen. So I mean to marry your sister, assuming she'll have me." He braces his hands on the trough. "Now let's go, little man, before we lose our chance."

He's lying. No one within spitting distance of his right mind would marry the most hunted girl in Mataquin simply to irritate his father. I have no idea what Niklaas's true motives are, but it doesn't matter, not so long as I get what I want before he realizes he's been played for a fool.

"All right. I'll take you to Aurora, but first I'll need your help securing an army." I stand up, wincing at the sound the water makes as it pours from my clothes.

I glance around at the camp. The only movement comes from two buzzards circling high in the leaden sky and a wispy ribbon of smoke rising from the remains of last night's cook fire. The brown tents remain tightly wrapped, and even the animals are still asleep.

"An army, eh?" Niklaas watches me struggle out of the trough and squeeze the water from my overshorts with an assessing look. "Better be a flaming big one, boy. Even then, you may be able to take the capital, but *holding* it will be another thing."

"I appreciate your concern, but I don't require your advice." And I don't require an army big enough to take Mercar. I only need an army big enough to distract Ekeeta and her ogres long enough for me to sneak into the castle and free my brother.

"Require it or not, you're going to get it," Niklaas says with an arrogance that makes me blink.

But I shouldn't be surprised. Human princes take for granted their right to bully anyone smaller or less powerful than they are. Princes like my father, who lied and deceived and stole the things he wanted without stopping to consider the lives he destroyed in the process.

"Reclaiming your sister's throne will take more than a few thousand men," Niklaas continues. "You'll need ships to defend the coast. Without them—"

"I'm raising an army," I say as I wring out the sleeves of my linen undershirt. "If you want to meet my sister, you'll keep your thoughts to yourself and help me find one."

"Cocky thing, aren't you?" he asks, eyebrows lifting. "Well, big britches, you've already failed to secure the one army for hire this side of the Gefroren Mountains, so how exactly am I—"

"I hear the people in the Feeding Hills might be willing to fight for me."

"The Feeding Hills?" Niklaas chuckles. "I'm not going to the Feeding Hills."

"What about you, then?" I ask. "Do you have an army? One I could . . . borrow?"

"You want to borrow an army?" His lips curl at the edges.

"Yes," I say, pinning him with a look I hope makes it clear how little I enjoy being the object of his amusement. "If you plan to marry my sister, then *your* army will be *her* army sooner or later, now, won't it?"

"*Hers,*" he says, still grinning. "Not yours."

"My sister and I are very close." He has no idea *how* close. "She would want you to lend me your aid."

"I bet she would." His smile sours as he runs a hand through his hair. "Too bad for the both of you, I don't have an army. I'm an eleventh son. Eleventh sons are lucky to have a horse and a sword and a copper pot to piss in, and I lost my copper pot to the witch who sold me this charm."

I try not to let my disappointment show or to give in to the urge to ask Niklaas what the devil he has to offer an ousted princess if not an army to help her reclaim her kingdom. I can't afford to scare him away. He might still prove useful as a guide, if nothing else.

"All right." I cross my arms, sending water streaming from beneath my vest. "Then you will escort me to the Feeding Hills in exchange for an introduction to my sister."

"I'm not taking you to the flaming Feeding Hills," he says with a strained laugh. "They're halfway across the world, and I—"

"They are an eight-day journey. Less if the horses are traveling light," I say. "And you'll take me where I ask."

"Now see here, boy—"

"And I am not a *boy* or a *little man*," I snap. "I'm fourteen years old."

He snorts. "You look on the weaning side of twelve."

"And you look like a prince who'll have no princess to pester if he doesn't do as I say."

"Listen, *boy*," Niklaas says in a harsh whisper, his blue eyes growing darker. "I can put you back in that tent as easily as I plucked you out. Maybe you should think on that before you start giving orders."

"Then leave." I sit down on the edge of the trough, calling his bluff. "Good luck finding my sister alone. She's been hidden for ten years, and unlike me, she's very good at staying out of the way of dumb princes with no armies, who think they—"

"All right then, you cursed little . . ." Niklaas's grumble ends in a sigh and a forced smile, a grimaced baring of his teeth that would be amusing under different circumstances. "We have a deal. Do you know how to ride?"

"Of course I know how to ride. And how to fight." I draw myself up to my full height, but the top of my head is still barely level with Niklaas's shoulder.

Jor takes after my mother—tall and long-boned, with white-blond hair and blue eyes. I take after my father—short and delicate, with hair the color of a dusty yellow dog and flat gray eyes as mysterious as spring drizzle. Without berries to paint my lips and burned nutshells to stain my lashes black, my face is as interesting as a lump of dough.

If Ekeeta had birthed a child who had lived past his cradle days and I were no longer the rightful heir to the most powerful throne in Mataquin, I wouldn't have to worry about kings or princes wanting to marry me. I wouldn't have to dread the day I'll be forced to bind myself to a man I don't love, a man I will destroy the moment his lips meet mine.

"All right, runt." Niklaas claps my shoulder hard enough to make me stumble. "We'll see if we can find you a sword on our way out, as well as a horse."

"I prefer a staff," I say, rubbing my shoulder. "I'll fetch my pack and staff from the treasure tent and we can be on our way." I turn to cross the camp to where the Boughtsword prostitutes sleep amidst the mercenaries' other stolen treasures but am stopped by a hand clutching my elbow.

"Are you mad?" Niklaas asks, his eyes wide.

"My gold is in my pack."

"I've got gold enough for the both of us."

"And my staff is fairy ironwood and sized for a small fighter," I say. "I'll never find another so perfectly suited to me."

"Then you'll make do with one a little less perfect," he says through clenched teeth, clearly on the verge of losing his temper. "If you go prancing around the camp, you'll be caught, and we'll both be killed."

"I won't *prance*. And I won't be caught." I break his hold, freeing my arm with a twist of my elbow learned while training in hand-to-hand combat with Thyne. "And if you're captured, you won't be killed. Pretty oafs fetch a good price at the slave market."

Niklaas shoots me a menacing scowl—confirming my suspicion that he can look suitably dangerous—and lunges for me, but I anticipate the move and sidestep at the last moment.

His momentum sends him tumbling to the grass with a grunt that makes me grin as I dash away, the only sound a soft squish as water oozes from my boots.

CHAPTER THREE

NIKLAAS

Flaming son of a demon. Arrogant, briar-born slog. Stuffed and trussed, barely teat-weaned, fuzz-faced baby man!

I call the Brat Prince every foul name I know and a few I make up on the spot as I follow the slip of a boy across the sleeping camp. I move as quickly as I can with my head drink-fogged and not an hour of sleep the entire night, but I can't catch up with Jor before he reaches the treasure tent and slips inside.

He's a spare thing—shorter than my sister, Haanah, and narrower, too, with pigeon legs covered in linen pants sticking out beneath his brown leather overshorts and his scrawny chest swimming in an armored vest two sizes too big—but he's wretched fast.

And wretched foolish.

He's scrapped our easy escape and practically delivered us

both into Boughtsword hands. Now we'll have to fight our way out of the camp and hope the mercenaries are still too drunk to prevent us from stealing their horses and getting far enough down the road to avoid an arrow in the back.

"Cheek licker," I mutter as I pull back the tent flap.

I reach for my sword—expecting to find the little man already snatched up by mercenaries—but once my eyes adjust to the murky light, I see his boots sitting on a carpet a few hands away and the prince silently picking his way across the body-littered ground in his stocking feet.

It seems more than a few of the Boughtswords stumbled to the treasure tent after our drinking games to visit the pleasure girls and never made it back to their own beds. Men and women in various states of undress lie snoring on straw pallets on the ground, blankets and pillows strewn about, ripped and leaking feathers, as if a battle was fought with the bed things before the revelers passed out for the night.

The tent stinks of garlic and onions and barley spirits, with a hint of soured milk that makes me wager someone couldn't hold their drink, but beneath the stink are the sharp tang of gold and silver and the smoky scent of magic, the smell of treasure drifting from the crates stacked on the far side of the tent.

The Boughtswords are primarily concerned with increasing their stores of hard currency, but they traffic in magical items as well. It was my enchanted charm, which I assured them would lead them to the legendary pirate Swain's lost treasure, that earned me their welcome last night. We were still debating the price for the charm when the Boughtsword leader passed out before the fire, giving me the chance to go hunting for the briar-born captive I suspected was being held in his camp.

I managed to stay conscious after the final Boughtsword fell, and I have Usio to thank for it. My brother and I built up quite a tolerance to spirits in the months before the curse claimed him. Knowing that our debauchery helped me avoid being robbed and taken prisoner makes me even more determined to see this adventure through. I have to succeed in my quest, if only to live to tell Haanah she was wrong and that my days spent drinking and wenching my way through half the kingdom weren't a tragic waste of time.

I *will* succeed. Three weeks remain until my eighteenth birthday; three weeks to find the lost princess, convince her to marry me, and escape my brothers' fates.

Finding her will be the hard part. I've yet to meet a girl who can refuse me when I crave her favor, and I've never wanted a girl the way I want Aurora of Norvere. I will find her and marry her and Haanah and I will finally be out of my father's depraved shadow, and the Land Beyond help this reckless prince if he thinks he can deter me from my course.

The woolly-headed boy is now across the room, climbing a stack of crates like a ringtail. He reaches the top and balances on one foot as he paws through the weapons in the uppermost crate and pulls out a fairy staff more slender than my wrist. It hardly seems sturdy enough to last a sparring session, but it's tougher than it looks. When the boy jumps from the crates—aiming the staff at a clear place on the floor and using it to leverage his body up into the air before giving a shove that sends both him and his weapon sailing over the sleeping mercenaries to land in a silent crouch ten hands from where I stand—the wood doesn't even creak, let alone crack.

The boy looks up, meeting my eyes with a satisfied grin before padding across the carpet to stuff his tiny feet into his boots.

"Madman," I mumble, but I can't keep a grudging smile from my face.

Prince Jor is a runt and a brat and lacks the sense the gods gave a blind goat, but he is an agile thing, I'll give him that. I'm not sure how much good he'll be in a fight, but at least it seems his staff will help keep him out of trouble.

I cock my head and hold the tent flap open to let the boy pass, but instead of ducking under my arm he lunges forward, jabbing his weapon into the air behind me. I hear a deep groan and spin to see a bleary-eyed mercenary with a mangy red beard drawing his weapon.

I reach for my sword, but the prince is already slipping around me, staff flying. He brings the wood down on the mercenary's hands hard enough to make a cracking sound and, when the man drops his sword, goes for the bastard's head, batting at one side of Red Beard's face and then the other—back and forth, back and forth, sending the man's head rocking before finishing him off with a final slam of the staff atop his skull.

Red Beard sinks to the ground, gripping his head with a pitiful moan.

Before his knees hit the grass, Jor is turning to run.

"The horses are this way," he says as he flies past me, swift as a river rushing over slick stones.

"I know where the horses are," I say in a harsh whisper.

I glance back at the man curling into a ball in the damp grass, wondering if I should kill him to keep him from alerting the rest of the mercenaries to our escape, but I decide it isn't worth bloodying my sword and run after Jor.

Jor and I are traveling light, we'll have a head start, and I know the secrets of these borderland woods as well as any Boughtsword. Usio and I explored every inch of Kanvasola and the surrounding borderlands, from the Locked Forest to the sea caves at Sivnew to the dying volcano high above Eno City—any adventure to keep us away from my father. I'll have no trouble finding a safe place to camp come nightfall and will have avoided committing the ultimate crime against my fellow man for another day.

I have yet to take a life. My father has killed enough people—enemies and friends, criminals and innocents, mortals and immortals—for the both of us. I am determined to be his son in no more than name, and that not any longer than I can help it.

It's customary in Norvere for the wife to take the husband's family name, but I'm planning to break with tradition. I look forward to being Niklaas Ronces. I will have my new initials engraved on a seal and use it to close the letter I'll send to my father telling him to go straight to the Pit and rot there.

The thought makes me smile as I jump the remains of last night's fire and race past the Boughtsword leader, still senseless on the ground beside it. He's snoring, openmouthed, where I left him, making me feel that much better about our odds of escape.

By the time I reach the remains of an ancient stone wall where the horses are tied, Jor has bridled a handsome bay with an ink-black mane and matching stockings and is swinging up to ride the beast bareback.

"Saddles are in the tent at the far end of the wall. I suggest you get one, unless you want to be thrown before we leave the woods." I hurry past him to where Alama is tied—already saddled, bagged, and ready—a few horses down.

She snorts and tosses her white head as I approach, glaring at me with accusing brown eyes that seem to demand to know what I was thinking when I saddled her and walked away.

"Poor girl," I coo, smoothing a hand down her throat as I untie her. "Saddled and left to stew."

I had the sense to saddle my own horse before allowing the charm to lead me to where Jor was being held captive. Unfortunately, I was too drunk to have the forethought to saddle a second horse for my newly liberated companion.

Truth be told, I'm still half in my cups. We stopped shooting barley brown less than two hours ago. I didn't drink as much as the other men, but I made a good show of it. Now I wish I'd dumped my cup's contents on the ground. I've got the beginnings of a rager headache, a sour stomach, and a parched throat I know I'll have no chance to ease for hours. We can't risk stopping to refill my skins until we've put distance between us and the mercenary camp.

"Hurry up, big man. We haven't got all morning!" Jor shouts as he rides past, urging his horse into a canter with a squeeze of his legs.

I see he's ignored my advice to fetch a saddle, and curse

the boy, then curse him a second time as he turns his horse east and gallops off down the main road, racing away beneath oak trees' tangling fingers above the dusty lane.

"We're not taking the main road, you fool!" I shout after him, but he's already too far away to hear.

"Blasted twit," I mumble as I swing up onto Alama's back and urge her after the latest burr in my britches.

As we gain speed out of the camp, she lets out a harsh whinny that I take as an agreement with my assessment. She's a clever horse, after all, and knows a pain in the arse when she sees one.

⤙ *In the Castle at Mercar* ⤚

THE OGRE QUEEN

We do not relish torture, but we are not above it.

We cannot be above it, when so much is at stake.

We lift our arm, signaling for our soldier to turn the wheel another revolution, tightening the ropes pulling at Prince Jor's arms and legs. The boy cries out, squeezing his eyes shut as his already pale skin blanches a sickly white. His pain aroused our pity in the beginning.

Now we loathe him for drawing out his suffering. And our own.

"You have the power," we whisper, leaning close to his sweating face. "Reveal your fairy blessings and the pain will stop."

The boy doesn't answer, but his eyes open, his gaze fixing on the ceiling with silent determination. It has been three days and nights and still he refuses to reveal the nature of his fairy blessings, knowledge our brother must possess in order to conduct the ritual to fulfill the prophecy.

We have tended to the interrogation personally, certain we could break the boy, but the child has proved exceptionally strong. Exceptionally enraging. Our patience is at an end, our desperation too great to allow any room for mercy in our heart.

"Again." We snap our fingers and our man turns the wheel. This time the boy's wail lasts several moments, becoming a howl more fitting a beast than a prince blessed with fairy magic. It is a satisfying sound—one we hope carries to our brother's divining room a floor below the dungeon—but it is not enough. Not nearly enough.

"Tell us," we hiss into the prince's ear. "Or your suffering will never end. You will not be allowed to take your own life. We will not allow you the mercy of death."

Jor presses his lips together, muffling the whimpers escaping from the back of his throat, still refusing to speak, as if he knows his silence is more infuriating than words of defiance could ever be.

We are the queen. We are the vessel of the prophecy. We have been trusted with so much and will fall so far—so very far—and we will not be ignored by a boy barely old enough to grow whiskers!

"Tell us!" we shout, bringing our fist down on the board beside his head.

"My queen." Our brother's voice reaches our ears a

moment before his hand alights on our shoulder. "Come away from the boy."

We shiver as we turn, meeting Illestros's gaze. He is disappointed in us. We have failed our brother, the most powerful prophet the world has ever known, at the moment when our success means everything to our people.

We shiver again.

"Release him." Illestros motions for our man to ease the tension on the ropes. "Take the prince to his cell and give him a restorative to drink."

"We will try again later," we whisper.

"There's no need." Illestros watches with pitying eyes as the soldier unstraps Jor and leads the limping prince from the room. The boy casts a glance over his shoulder as he goes, his expression filled with a chilling mix of hatred and resolve. He may never confess, no matter how we torture him, and what will we do then?

"But we had no answer," we say, shamed by our admission. "We must try again."

"It would do no good, my queen. The boy has no answer to give." Illestros strokes our back, soothing us with his touch before soothing us with his words. "He is not the fairy-blessed child. It is the girl."

The girl. *Aurora*. We never imagined Rose would choose her daughter as her champion.

"A hawk brought word from the Locked Forest this morning," Illestros says, handing over a small scroll. "The Boughtswords believe they have captured the lost prince of Norvere and are demanding his ransom be paid."

"But the prince is here," we mutter as we read the missive.

"We know this, but they do not," Illestros says. "You were wise to keep the boy's capture a secret. They say a boy dressed as a fairy attempted to hire them to attack the castle, and when they refused he put up such a fight twelve men were injured before he was contained."

A frown tugs our brows together. "It could be a Fey boy. Surely the princess—"

"They sent a lock of hair," Illestros says. "My divinations confirm it belongs to one briar-born."

"Then it is the girl." Our relief is tinged with only a hint of fear. "And she is blessed with strength in battle. Will this knowledge be enough?"

"Perhaps." Illestros takes our hand, drawing us across the room and up the stairs, out of the blackness of the dungeon. "If not, there is still time to discover her secrets. I have sent word to Keetan and his men. They aren't far from the Locked Forest. They will have her in hand by tonight."

The Locked Forest. Only two days' hard ride from the castle. We could have as little as two days left. We do our best to believe it will be enough.

CHAPTER FOUR

NIKLAAS

I catch up with the boy a field before the splitting of the road and force him onto a deer trail in the woods. Thankfully, he doesn't seem compelled to argue for argument's sake and allows me to lead the way through a grove of southern beech trees and into the denser forest on the hillside.

We are halfway up the hill, barely out of sight, when the sound of hoofbeats pounding across hard dirt rumbles through the trees.

I motion for Jor to stop, straining for a sign that a rider has turned off to follow us. There wasn't time to conceal the hoofprints leading into the woods. If the mercenaries are watching the ground, one of them will spot the place where we left the road.

But the hoofbeats soon fade, replaced by the silence of watchful woods. Jor lifts a pale brow, but I raise my hand, motioning for the boy to wait. Finally, when one bird and another resume their song, I urge Alama forward, thanking the gods for a bit of luck. Jor and his horse follow behind, and we travel in blessed silence for close to a quarter hour. I thank the gods for that as well.

My headache has blossomed into a carnivorous flower determined to devour my brainmeats from the inside out. The last thing I want is to be forced to make conversation with the Brat Prince.

But sadly, no reprieve lasts forever.

"I assume we'll turn east when we reach the ridge?" Jor asks as the path grows steeper. His voice sounds even more feminine when drifting to my ears from behind than it did talking face to face.

You can tell the boy was raised among fairy folk, where the men and women act so much alike it can be hard to tell one from the other. The Fey have become reclusive in recent years, since Ekeeta placed a bounty on every fairy head, but I've run into enough fairy men to know that, despite their skill in battle, they're far more interested in singing and dancing and fussing over their ancient plants than in any respectably masculine pursuit.

The manliest thing about Jor is the scar above his left eyebrow, that puckered bit of skin the only part of his face that isn't smooth and pillowy. From his apple cheeks to his button of a nose to his smooth chin and mouth with the upper lip curving in a bow, the boy might as well be Fey himself. I've been called a pretty boy myself a time or two, but I was never as delicate as the boy behind me. Even my brother Valerio, who my father bitingly called his "firstborn daughter," had the shadow of whiskers by fourteen.

"Did you hear me?" Jor asks, that uppity note creeping into his voice again.

"I heard you," I grumble. Thank the gods I'm the youngest of my cursed brothers and accustomed to a certain degree of abuse. Nariano and Ninollo would have exercised their fists on anyone who dared to use that tone with their princely selves.

"And? Will we be turning east?"

"Considering turning west will take us closer to Mercar and people who want your head on a pike, I think east is best." I close my eyes for a moment, knowing Alama will keep to the trail. "Unless, of course, your sister is hidden somewhere to the west . . ."

"I told you, I'm not taking you to Aurora until you—"

"Your army. I know." I open my lids a crack and regret it immediately as the sun flickering through the canopy stabs its cruel rays into my eyes. "Have you thought of how you're going to pay for that army? I notice you didn't bother with your pack."

"I was trying to hurry," Jor says. "You said you had enough gold for both of us."

"I have enough gold to keep us in food and drink and pay for an inn once we get close enough to a village to find one, not to hire an army."

Jor sighs. "Well, I may not need gold. I'm told the people in the Feeding Hills are sympathetic to my cause."

I grunt. I would wager the cowards in the Feeding Hills are sympathetic only to their own cause. The entire population is composed of nobles who swore loyalty to Ekeeta and her ogres during the takeover of Norvere—watching those who stood against the queen robbed of their souls and thrown into the sea—only to sneak away in the night in the months following to hide in the one place the ogres wouldn't dare hunt them down.

The Feeding Hills are the birthplace of the ogres, the spot from which they emerged from the ooze to become the first beings walking the land. It is also said to be the location of their last surviving predators. The Feeding Trees atop the hills are as old as Mataquin itself, gnarled behemoths as big around as a farmer's hut, with trunks that reach through the clouds. No human alive has ever seen them do anything but sprout needles, sway in the breeze, and other trees-going-about-their-business sorts of things, but the ogre legends say the Feeding Trees house the spirits of the upstart gods who banished the Lost Mother to the underworld. In her last act of magic, the goddess transformed her enemies into trees.

Trees with a taste for vengeance . . .

Allegedly, the Feeding Trees use illusions to lure ogres into their trunks, where the creatures are digested over the course of a few hundred years. Fairy story or not, the ogres are spooked enough to leave the traitors living in the Feeding Hills alone, despite the fact that the exiles led repeated raids on Ekeeta's supply wagons and provided soldiers to help fight the last battle between Norvere and the Aligned Kingdoms of Herth, helping stave off Ekeeta's takeover of the ten tiny countries.

"The exiles were paid to fight for Herth," I say finally, knowing Jor needs to hear the truth. "Paid well. In gold and in betrothals for their children."

Betrothals that have severely limited my own ability to find an eligible princess.

Not that I would have had much luck if the princesses of Herth were unspoken for. My father is Ekeeta's ally, making him and his offspring the enemies of the Aligned Kingdoms of Herth. I spent months touring the countries of the north, but despite interest from the newly widowed Princess Gerace of Rinland and vows of undying devotion from the twin princesses of Pennly I didn't get within spitting distance of the altar. The mothers and fathers wanted no part of the immortal king's eleventh son.

Aurora is my last hope, the only unbetrothed princess who might see my lineage as a blessing rather than a curse. Norvere and Kanvasola were allies in her father's time, and her father's first wife was my aunt Ninia, a woman betrayed and slain by the ogre queen. We have a common history and a common enemy. A marriage between us could be a first step toward an alliance for the future of Mataquin.

"But the Kingdoms of Herth aren't the exile's homeland," Jor says. "I'm second in line to the throne of Norvere. Surely they'll be open to helping me out of loyalty alone."

"You realize you're talking about people who have a history of switching sides as easily as flipping a frying cake in a pan?"

Jor scowls. "One way or another, I will convince them to fight for me."

"Succeed or fail, it's no matter to me so long as you keep your end of our bargain," I mutter, guiding Alama toward the sound of running water. "But as your future brother-in-law, I wouldn't feel right if I didn't make it clear you're making a dicey choice."

"You're terribly sure of yourself." The path widens, and Jor urges his horse forward, pulling even with Alama. "My sister isn't some simpering fool to be swept off her feet by a pretty face and bulging muscles. She's clever and determined and—"

"And a girl."

Jor rolls his eyes. "Well, of course she's a girl."

"And that's all I need her to be. A girl with no father or mother standing in my way," I say with a grin that I can tell gets under the boy's skin.

Good. Let it. He'll be even more piqued when I have his sister in my bed before we've been acquainted a fortnight.

"You'll understand when you're older." I glance over at him, taking in his strong profile and clear skin. "You're handsome enough, and some girls actually prefer waifish, fairylooking boys."

Jor surprises me by laughing so hard and loud that the horses startle and break into a trot.

"Goodness." He soothes his horse with a stroke of its neck.

As much as I'd like to see him thrown simply so I could say "I told you so," he seems to have a way with animals.

"You're something, aren't you?" he asks with a grin.

"Laugh while you can, runt." I rein Alama in, not wanting her to twist an ankle on the increasingly rocky trail. "You'll see I'm right. Just as you'll see that the exiles will be harder to win over than you expect."

Jor's smile slips, banishing the dimples that had appeared on either side of his mouth. "At least they were once my people. I would have gone to them first, but I worried there wouldn't be time. The matter for which I need the army is . . . pressing. We'll have to ride long days and reach the Feeding Hills as soon as we can."

I grunt in response and swing off Alama's back. The creek is in sight across a bed of round gray stones she'll cross more easily without a rider.

"That's why I decided against the saddle." Jor slides off his horse. "No saddle means less weight for Button to carry."

"Button?" I shoot the animal Jor leads a pointed look. The horse's back is higher than the top of the boy's head. The beast is two hands taller than Alama, and she's one of the largest horses—especially females—I've ever seen.

He shrugs. "It was my mother's nickname for me. I hope it will bring me better luck than I've had so far," he says, casting his eyes down as we reach the stream and the horses dip their whiskery noses into the water.

For the first time since I carried Jor from his makeshift prison—him whimpering in the middle of some nightmare—I feel for the boy. Everyone knows how the Sleeping Beauty died.

My own mother died shortly after Haanah was born. I was not quite two and don't remember her at all, which I've always considered a cruel bit of fortune. But what would it be like to harbor the memory of your mother slitting her throat in front of your eyes? The boy must remember it. If he remembers his mother's pet name, he must also remember her suicide.

"Jor . . ." I clear my throat, wondering how one offers condolences for such an old wound. "I'm—"

"My Fey family calls me Ror," he interrupts, sparing me. "You can, too. It's more familiar to me than my given name."

I nod. "I would say you can call me Niki, but only my father does that, and I hate the man like toe rot and gangrene mixed together."

Ror glances up with a smile I return before handing him one of my waterskins and squatting to fill the other. I chug as much liquid as I can hold, hoping the water will help ease the aching in my skull. Ror stoops beside me, pulling his staff from the sling fashioned into the back of his armor and placing it within reach as he fills his own skin.

I don't think we'll have cause to fight out here in the middle of the forest, but I appreciate that the boy is making an effort. It seems unavoidable that we'll be traveling together, and I feel better knowing he has some instincts toward self-preservation.

"We'll try to reach the edge of the woods before we make camp," I say, wetting my sleeve and using it to wash the grit of yesterday's ride from my face. "If we pace ourselves and walk the horses now and then, we'll reach the petrified forest before nightfall. Assuming we keep putting in long days, that should bring us within a week's journey of Goreman."

"Goreman?" Ror wipes the water from his lip.

"It's the closest place to hire a guide to the exile camp. They're well hidden. We could wander the mountains for weeks and never find them." I cap my skin and secure it to Alama's saddle before reaching for Ror's.

Ror takes one last drink. "All right. I suppose I have no choice but to trust you."

"I'm flattered," I say with a sour twist of my lips.

"I'm not being rude, I'm being truthful," he says. "I've been in hiding with the Fey since I was four years old. I've lived my entire life on an island. I've studied Mataquin's land and history, but I'm ignorant of many things about the human world."

"Does that mean you'll listen the next time I tell you not to do something?"

He glances up at the limbs swaying high above us. "I will take it under serious consideration."

"That doesn't sound like a promise."

Ror's grin has a hint of mischief in it. "You noticed."

"I'm not as dumb as I look," I say. "And I'd like a promise. I need you to stay alive long enough to lead me to your sister, little man."

"How old are you, exactly?" he asks with a sigh.

"I'll be eighteen in three weeks," I say, and immediately wish I hadn't. Ror doesn't seem to have heard the rumors about my family—not many people outside Eno City have; my father tends to kill those who share his secrets—but it's best to be careful. I don't want Ror or his sister realizing how much hinges on my making marriage to Aurora a reality before my eighteenth birthday.

Desperation isn't attractive, and pity isn't the emotion I want to inspire in my future wife.

"Eighteen." Ror rolls his eyes. "You're barely four years older than I am."

I shrug as I lead Alama across the water to where the trail picks up on the other side. He's right, but I feel eons older than this naive boy who assumes the world will be on his side. "Life has left me feeling older."

"And why's that?" Ror asks. "Have you had a hard life?"

"Hard enough."

"My life with the Fey hasn't been hard, but I've lived through horrible things, and lately I've done . . . horrible things," he says, something in his voice killing the mocking remark on the tip of my tongue. "Most mornings, I wake up feeling a thousand years old and terrified that my sister or I will be captured and used to usher in an age of ogre rule."

"The ogres rule most of Mataquin already," I say, my jaded view of the current politics creeping into my tone. "The world won't be so different if the prophecy is fulfilled."

"The Fey know better." Ror leans his cheek against Button's glossy shoulder as he walks. "The world as we know it will cease to be. There will be no sun. Plants and animals and the Fey will die, and humans will live in terror. Once their reign begins, the ogres' sole purpose will be to consume the spirit of every human in Mataquin. They believe it's the only way to open the gates to the Underworld where their Lost Mother waits for them."

I'm silent for a moment, my drink-soured stomach clenching. The Fey are flighty, emotional, prone to dramatic gestures, and a dozen other things I've been raised to disdain, but they are also masters of foresight. If they say the ogre prophecy is something to fear, they are no doubt right. And Ror has awoken with this knowledge, and the fate of the world, weighing on him every morning since he was not much more than a babe.

I stop Alama and reach out to squeeze Ror's narrow shoulder. "All right then. You're not a child. I'll do my best to remember."

Ror's gray eyes go wide and his brows lift toward the warrior's knot atop his head, his shock so apparent I can't help but laugh.

"I'm not really a dumb oaf," I say, swinging up into my

saddle. "I admit it when I'm wrong. On the *rare* occasions when I am, of course."

"Of course." Ror shakes his head before jogging forward, using his staff to boost him level with Button's back. The horse sidesteps when Ror's feet leave the ground, but the prince is quick to slide his leg over Button's back and take his seat before the startled animal moves out of reach.

"There, there," he mutters, stroking Button's throat before glancing back to me. "Thank you, by the way. For rescuing me."

"Thank you for the whipping you gave the man creeping up behind me. But then, I wouldn't have had a man creeping up behind me if it weren't for you." I nudge Alama with my heels and she moves off down the path. "Practice being less foolish in the future, will you?"

"Only if you practice being less insufferable," Ror calls after me.

"Can't." I sniff. "Have to keep myself in prime condition for your sister. Girls like insufferable boys. It's the nice ones they can't be bothered with. Store that pearl away for your future, Ror, if you hope to fare well with women."

Ror grumbles something foul beneath his breath that makes me grin, and a weight lifts from my shoulders.

It isn't healthy for two men to talk soft to each other for too long. Better to leave the feelings to women and fairies and others who have the time for them. A man's energy is better spent getting his work done, and at the moment my work is to get Ror across Norvere as quickly as possible, leaving me ample time to woo his lovely sister.

CHAPTER FIVE

AURORA

My insufferable guide and I reach the ridge above the forest proper—where the trees are thinner and the unusually warm autumn sun is hotter on our bare heads—by midmorning and continue east.

We ride hard through the middle of the day, stopping only to water the horses and take a quick meal in the shade, sharing dried meat and crackers from Niklaas's pack, accompanied by hard, sour apples I gathered as we traveled.

Mercifully the ridge road is narrower and less trafficked than the road below. We see signs that someone has camped off the trail a few days' past but meet not a soul the entire day. The scarcity of travelers isn't surprising. The Boughtswords rule these woods, a state of being Niklaas says is encouraged by both Ekeeta and his father. The woods serve as a buffer between two kingdoms that have never entirely trusted each other, though they have been allies since before my grandfather's time.

"You've met Ekeeta, then?" Niklaas asks.

"When we were little, my father would take Aurora and me to court on festival days. Ekeeta would give us toys and sweets, but I remember being afraid of her. Even then. Why my grandfather chose an ogre for his third wife is something that was never explained to my satisfaction." I shift my weight forward on Button's back, doing my best not to wince in pain.

I don't want Niklaas to know how raw I'm feeling after so many hours of riding without a saddle. The fact that my britches were damp for the first several hours of the ride hasn't helped matters, but I would be feeling a lot less chafed if I'd taken the time to saddle Button before fleeing the mercenary camp.

"Well, Ekeeta is a beautiful woman," Niklaas says, pressing on, though the sun is sinking into the trees behind us, painting the forest in dreamy pink light. "All long legs and creamy skin and tits as pert as a girl's a tenth her age."

I wrinkle my nose at his crass description as I shift my weight again, still unable to find a comfortable position. "Maybe. But she has disturbing fingers."

"Disturbing fingers?" he asks with a laugh.

"Long and spindly, like spider legs. Not to mention that she's a monster who feeds on mortal souls. She may look human, but she isn't."

Niklaas chuckles again. "At least the ogres stopped eating our flesh. That's something, right?" He reins Alama in, giving Button and me the chance to pull even with them on the trail. "And a beautiful woman is a beautiful woman, disturbing fingers, questionable eating habits, or no."

I blink up at him. "You aren't serious."

"Why not?" He grins as he leans forward to stroke Alama's long white throat. "Men are fools when it comes to a pretty face."

"I'm sure there were prettier faces in the capital at the time," I say. "Prettier and *human*. Grandfather could have had his pick of any woman in Mercar."

"Ah, but he didn't want *any* woman. He wanted one *particular* woman." He glances over at me, that increasingly familiar "big brother about to impart wisdom to the youngster" look in his eyes, the one that makes it practically impossible to resist rolling mine. "Women fall in love a dozen times before their fifteenth birthday, but when a man falls, he falls heart, body, and soul, and no woman but the one who has captured his imagination will do."

"Is that right?" I lift a brow in his direction.

"It is," he says. "The poor bastard becomes obsessed. Every bit of sense he possesses flees his head to set up camp in his britches, and there's no reasoning with him until the spell is broken."

"Or until his imagination is *captured* by someone else," I add.

"Exactly." Niklaas laughs; I squeeze the reins tighter. He may find man's fickle nature amusing, but I don't. Mother was Father's second wife, but she may not have been his last. Father was gone more often the year before he was murdered.

51

I remember the servants whispering, wondering why he packed silk in his saddlebags if he wasn't going to court a woman.

Mama knew something was wrong, and it ate away at her, turning the last of her love for Father to hate. It was during one of his absences that she told me the true story of how she and Father met, of how he woke her from her long sleep and led her to believe she was his only wife, lying to her for years, until it was too late for her to escape him.

Human men can't be trusted, not even fathers.

"I was under a woman's spell once," Niklaas says as he turns Alama into the woods to the left of the road. I follow, hoping the change of course means we're near our camp for the night. "A girl's spell, anyway. It wasn't too awful. While it lasted."

"What broke it?" I ask, feeling no need to subdue my curiosity. Niklaas has done his share of nosing into my business. It seems only right to return the favor.

"My father married her." Niklaas snaps a branch off one of the trees and uses it to bat at the low hanging leaves. "She's been my stepmother for a year."

"Oh," I say, unsure how to respond. "That must have been . . . difficult."

He shrugs. "Regiene didn't love me; she loved being with a boy with ties to the crown," he says, not a trace of hurt in his tone. "As soon as she had a crown of her own, her true colors began bleeding all over the castle. She's been a terror to the other ladies, including my little sister, and I could never love a girl who treated my Haanah poorly."

I stare hard at his broad back, wondering if he's being sincere, the way he seemed to be when he promised not to treat me like a child. "That's . . . good of you."

"I'm a good, good man. You should tell your sister as much." He glances over his shoulder with a wiggle of his eyebrows. "And tell her I'm more than ready to fall under her spell. It's been too long since I've been stupid over a beautiful girl, and I mean to fall dumbly in love with my future wife."

I barely resist the urge to gag. I'm *sick* of listening to him go on and on about his future with my "sister," and we've only been traveling a day. By the time we reach Goreman, I'll be ready to cut his tongue out to spare myself the torture.

As if I'd ever marry a boy so arrogant he believes every girl he meets is tripping over her own feet in her eagerness to leap into his bed. Even if it were safe to lose my heart, Niklaas wouldn't get within spitting distance of snatching it away.

But it isn't safe. . . .

Thyne. It still hurts to think his name, though it's been over a year since it became clear that my fairy gifts have a dark side, a wicked side as black as an ogre's belly. Over a year that I've known I will never kiss a boy again, at least not a boy I love. It's too dangerous.

I didn't even love Thyne in *that* way. He was like a big brother to me, a best friend who taught me to fight and climb trees and sneak the last of the cocoa cakes from the kitchen while Janin was busy. He carved my first staff when I was nine and gave me my current weapon—blessed ironwood coveted by every boy on our island—for my sixteenth birthday.

That was when I kissed him. At first, a peck on the cheek, but then a brush of my lips against his, a brush that turned into something more, something . . . nice, but too strange to be a proper kiss. I expected us both to pull away and laugh, putting the possibility of something more than friendship behind us forever, but when the kiss ended Thyne wasn't Thyne anymore.

He was a lamp with the wick blown out, waiting for me to light him.

Janin told me long ago that my mother had blessed me with a heart no man I loved would dare defy, but none of us could have imagined the damage the blessing would inflict. I'm sure Mama didn't intend for my kiss to steal away the free will of the boys I love—especially not a boy I loved as a brother—but she said herself that fairy blessings have a way of becoming curses. . . .

My curse means that I will never know romantic love. Not all human men are wicked, and there are so many kind, handsome Fey boys I daydreamed about when I was younger, but I will never know what it is like to love one of them. I will never know what passion feels like. I will always be alone.

Sometimes it seems a small price to pay for my fairy gifts. Sometimes it makes my body ache with a loneliness so profound I fear my soul will forever be bruised. I am a prisoner in a cell of my mother's good intentions and I will never, ever escape.

"Are you all right?" Niklaas asks, startling me from my thoughts.

I glance up to find him studying me. "I'm fine," I snap.

"Don't bite me a third eye," he says, holding up a hand in a gesture of surrender. "Just trying to be 'good' is all. You look a little pale."

I take a breath and force my face into the expressionless

mask I've perfected in the past year. It has become my armor, a way to survive living side by side with the boy I destroyed and the people who love him. People too gracious to hate me the way I deserve to be hated, too honorable to banish the human girl who was never really one of them, too polite to watch when Thyne leaves the supper table to follow me to my cot, awaiting the chance to do my slightest bidding, to weep outside my window when I refuse to let him share my bed.

"I'm bone-weary." I swallow past the tightness in my jaw. "The Vale Flowers kept my head too clouded for rest. I haven't had a good night's sleep in at least three days."

"Then it's a good thing we're here."

We pass out of the last of the close-growing pin oaks onto a bald hilltop inhabited by the reclining corpses of ancient, hollowed-out trees. The petrified forest is smaller than I had imagined but lovely and peaceful, with a stunning view of the softly rolling grassland below. The golden grass beneath our overlook shimmers like a thousand mini-torches set fire by the sunset, while beyond the outlines of great blue mountains brood in the graying distance.

"Are those the Feeding Hills?" I ask.

"They are." Niklaas swings off Alama with a soft groan that makes me feel better about how damaged our ride has left me. He ties her to a dead tree's gnarled limb, leaving enough lead for her to graze on the short grass.

"They're bigger than I thought they'd be." I bite my lip to stifle the moan that tries to escape as I slide off Button's back.

"Meaner, too," Niklaas says, removing Alama's bridle and reaching for the belt of her saddle. "There'll be wicked snowstorms and avalanches up there come winter. It's good we're making the journey now. Though in a normal year we'd still be risking snow on the higher trails." He sets Alama's saddle atop the tree with a grunt and motions for me to bring Button closer. "Hopefully the fair weather will hold."

"It will," I say, limping as I hand Button over to Niklaas, who ties the horse next to Alama with an extra length of rope.

Button dips his head and begins to lip contentedly at the grass. At least he doesn't seem sore from our ride, but I didn't expect him to be. One of the few advantages of being a runt is knowing you won't give your horse an aching back at the end of the day.

"How can you be sure?" Niklaas asks. "The fairies tell you?"

"We're in the long summer of the ogre prophecy. We should have warm weather until Nonstyne. Or until the rise of the living darkness," I add in a sour tone. "Whichever comes first."

"What is the living darkness?" he asks, fetching his water-skin from his saddlebag. "I've heard of it, but I always thought it was more ogre madness."

I lean against the fallen tree and pull my overshorts lower on my hips, hoping to grant my tender parts a little relief. "No one knows, not even the Fey."

"But the prophecy says a briar-born child will usher in the Final Age."

I nod, accepting the skin he passes over. "Yes, but we don't know how. Aurora and I would never aid the ogres willingly, but it might be our blood they need for a ritual or . . . something. It isn't clear. Hopefully, we won't ever find out."

"Assuming Ekeeta doesn't get her hands on you or your sister."

I nod again.

"She doesn't have Aurora now, does she?" Niklaas asks, making me choke on my gulp of water.

"Of course not." I cough, cursing myself for letting my guard down. He's too close to the truth. "Why would you think that?"

"I don't know." Niklaas watches me with deceptive calm, but I can feel his gaze boring into me the way it did when I was half out of my mind on Vale Flowers and certain he could see through my skin. His eyes aren't merely beautiful; they're as crafty as a thief's. I'll have to be careful if I want to keep my secrets.

"I've been wondering why a prince in your position would need an army," he says, "aside from getting your sister's kingdom back, which we both know you're in no position to do without ships to secure the coast and an army five times the size of the one you may or *may not* secure in the Feeding Hills. You're not a fool, so you must have a compelling reason. Getting your sister away from Ekeeta would be a good one."

"Ekeeta doesn't have my sister, but she has someone . . . dear to me. A Fey friend who was captured while carrying a message to Aurora," I lie, grateful that Ekeeta has kept her capture of Jor quiet for whatever reason.

I have to tell Niklaas something if I want him to stop picking before he rips the scab off the truth. If he really wants to be introduced to the princess of Norvere as badly as he says, then telling him Ekeeta has "my sister" would gain his support for raising an army—but it could create other problems.

What if he went charging off to rescue the fair maiden himself, only to find a boy in the dungeon? I doubt he would save my brother out of the goodness of his heart, not after I'd tricked him, and it's far more likely that Niklaas would end up dead for his troubles. As irritating as he can be, I don't want to be responsible for his death.

"A friend," Niklaas repeats, clearly unsatisfied with my answer. "A friend you're willing to risk your life and your sister's kingdom for? Aurora will need all the help she can get if she hopes to stage a successful overthrow in the future. If you're dead, she'll have lost her only family and the ability to marry you off to some nice princess and strengthen her alliance with the countries of Herth."

"I know what my sister and I have to lose." I cap the waterskin and hand it over but keep my eyes on Button's shivering side, running my fingers down his dusty coat as he grazes, wishing I had a brush to curry him with. "I know what's worth fighting for."

"Aren't you a little young to—"

"Don't say it," I warn, close to losing my patience with his condescending attitude. "If you start preaching about my youth again, I'll have to beat some sense into you, no matter how sore I am."

"Sore, eh?" He hums low in his throat. "I know what'll make you feel better. Me too. I'm as sore as a newlywed's nethers," he says, thankfully letting the matter drop. "Feel like I've been beaten between the legs with a rolling pin.

Which, sadly enough, actually happened to my sorry self upon one occasion."

"Really?" I fall in behind him as he takes off into the trees, down a gentle hill.

"Really." He sighs. "One morning, not long ago, a baker off the coast of Eno City got up to set his loaves cooking and caught me asleep by the fire with his daughter."

"Whose loaves you'd set cooking the night before," I say, tsking beneath my breath.

Niklaas laughs as he spins around, treating me to a rakish grin I'm sure the baker's daughter is still dreaming about to this day.

"Maybe you aren't so young after all." He's still chuckling when he turns to leap atop a large stone and climb up the side of an even larger boulder blocking the path.

I scramble after him, determined to hold on to the light moment. Niklaas isn't all bad, and I can't deny that I'm anticipating whatever this is that will make us feel better.

The anticipation lasts until I reach the top of the boulder and see Niklaas already down the other side, bounding across two flat rocks toward a pool of steaming water, stripping his shirt off as he goes. By the time he reaches the edge of the smoking spring, he's shucked his boots and loosened the tie on his riding pants.

I realize what he intends to do, but before I can turn my back, his pants slide off his hips, and Niklaas, eleventh son of the immortal king, is as naked as the day he was born.

I freeze—jaw dropping, blood draining from my face— unable to tear my eyes away, though I know I should. But, warrior's clothes be damned, I'm a seventeen-year-old girl, and what seventeen-year-old girl could look away from a sight like *that*?

Niklaas may have the face of a golden god, but he has the body of a devil, a creature sent from the Pit to tempt a girl to abandon everything she holds dear for one night, skin to skin, with a creature designed for pleasure. The sort of pleasure that, since the day I kissed Thyne, I've known I must forever do without.

But now, as I watch Niklaas ease into the water, I wonder . . .

What if I didn't love the boy—not even friendly love, the way I loved Thyne? What if he didn't love me? Would my kiss still steal away his mind? Or would he retain his head so long as our bodies were the only part of our selves involved?

What would it be like to join Niklaas in the water? To show him who I really am and feel his hands on my bare skin, his lips at my throat? The thought is enough to make my pulse speed, until I remember who I'm lusting after and come to my senses with a shiver of disgust.

Even if it were safe, there's no way I'd give Niklaas the satisfaction of knowing that the girl he's determined to make his wife before he's even met her finds him even a lick interesting in *that* way.

"Come on, Ror," Niklaas calls, pushing the damp hair from his forehead. "It's a ball stinger for a few minutes, but after that . . . pure heaven."

His *wife*. I will never be this prince's wife, and once he knows it, he'll have no reason to keep helping me, even if I tell him that my brother's life, and the future of Mataquin, is at stake. No doubt he would refuse to accompany *any* girl on a hunt for an army, no matter what the circumstances. Human men aren't like Fey men. They don't believe a well-trained woman can fight, or lead, as well as a man. Niklaas already doubts my abilities because I'm small. Gods forbid he find out I'm female.

As soon as he realizes the truth, he'll leave. Or worse, kidnap me—to ensure my safety, if my judgment of his character is correct; to force me to marry him at sword point, if it is not and marriage really is what he's after—and Jor will die.

Niklaas can never discover my secret. I have to leave. Now. I should have run the moment his billowing Kanvasola shirt hit the bank.

"All right, little prince?" Niklaas asks, a careful note in his voice.

"I'm not accustomed to bathing with other people." I clear my throat and shift my gaze to a patch of sky visible between the leaves, wondering if my cheeks are as pink. "I'll go get the fire ready and come back later. It will be dark soon and a fire is . . . good."

"A fire *is* good," Niklaas says. "Build it beneath the trees. The wind should scatter the smoke, but just in case, the leaves will hide the fire. The Boughtswords might still be looking for us. We don't want to help them with the finding."

"Right." I risk a quick peek down to where Niklaas lounges in the pool, his thick arms stretched along the rocks, steaming water rising to his chest, watching me with a shrouded look that emphasizes the bright blue of his eyes.

Even in the shadows beginning to thicken the air, his eyes are aggressively blue, like a northern hunt dog meeting a stranger in the woods, debating whether to rip out the newcomer's throat. I feel exposed all over again, though I know there's little chance Niklaas has guessed what I was thinking a moment ago. He's convinced I'm a fourteen-year-old boy, and I'm not going to linger to give him reason to suspect otherwise.

Without another word, I slither down the other side of the boulder on my belly, ignoring my aching muscles, refusing to think about how nice it would feel to be soaking in the hot spring instead of hurrying back to the camp. I'll have my chance for a soak later. Alone. Without any insufferable princes lurking in the water.

"I'm not some baker's daughter," I mumble, dumping an armful of wood to the ground with more force than necessary. "And even if I were, I'd know better."

Across the clearing, Alama whinnies, her long tongue dangling lewdly from her mouth. I stick my tongue out in return, smiling when she rears her head and stamps the ground.

I have to put up with Niklaas and his nosy questions and pearls of wisdom and piercing devil eyes; I don't have to put up with being sassed by a horse.

My small triumph cheers me until a flash of black draws my eyes to the sky above the valley. There, dozens of vultures—crooked wings spread wide and bald heads craned toward the ground—drift in slow, relentless circles in the fading light, searching the world below for the ogre queen's prey.

CHAPTER SIX

NIKLAAS

When I arrive back at our camp—after a soak that has turned my toes to happy prunes and my aching back to mush—Ror is nowhere to be found. The horses are tied as they were and grazing peacefully, but I draw my sword anyway.

Better to find out the boy is off answering the call and not need a weapon than to be surprised by an enemy.

"Ror?" After a moment with no answer, I call a little louder, "Ror? Are you—"

"Shh!" comes a hiss from my left. "In here."

I turn toward the sound of his voice, but find . . . nothing.

"Inside the tree," he whispers. "It's hollow."

I circle around the petrified tree where the horses are tied and kneel down to peer inside. After a moment, my eyes adjust and I see Ror—a mad gleam in his eyes—crouched in the darkness ten hands away.

"I'm hiding," he says.

"I see that."

"Maybe you should hide, too," he says, scooting farther into the darkness. "There were two of them at the mercenary camp this morning. I was too muddled to think they might have been sent by the queen, but they could have seen us together." He waves an arm, motioning for me to join him. "Come on! I don't know how much they know."

"How much who knows?" I glance over my shoulder, poised to defend myself if whoever's spooked Ror is still near the camp. "Who did you see?"

"Not who, *what*," he snaps. "They're everywhere. Don't you see them?"

"See what?" I ask, not bothering to hide my frustration. If there's danger at hand, the boy needs to be less flaming vague!

"The vultures swarming above the blasted camp!"

I lift my eyes, but the sky is empty, save for the sliver moon rising above the Feeding Hills. "I don't see anything."

"But there were so many," Ror says, refusing to budge. "At least a dozen, and more flying in from the east."

I stand and turn in a slow circle. "Well, they're gone now. Vultures can't see much better in the dark than we can. They'll be off finding a place to roost. I suggest we do the same. If you want your turn at the pool, you'd better get moving."

Ror crawls from his hidey-hole, staff clutched tightly in hand. He still looks spooked, even after his own search of the sky reveals I've told the truth. "I'm not mad," he says, pointing a stubby finger in my direction. His hands are ridiculously wee, so precious I would be tempted to make fun of them if he weren't acting so strange.

"Stop looking at me like that," he says.

"Like what?" I ask, innocent as a lamb.

"With your careful eyes, and that careful voice, too," he says, glaring. "I haven't taken leave of my senses. My fairy mother says Ekeeta has enlisted carrion creatures as her allies. The queen throws them her scraps when she's done harvesting a soul. In exchange, they spy for her."

"Scraps, eh?" My empty stomach churns. "I thought they were giving the criminals who feed the ogres' hunger a decent burial these days."

"The days are changing." Ror tugs his ear as he searches the sky one last time. "Maybe they didn't see me. I hid the moment I spied them."

"Or maybe they were normal vultures and nothing to worry about," I say, unable to keep the mocking note from my voice.

"And maybe you're a fool," Ror snaps, but when he turns back to me he doesn't look angry. He looks worried, older.

For the first time, I notice faint wrinkles at the sides of his lips, lines that emphasize his soft mouth. The boy is pretty enough to be a girl. His sister must be even prettier. It wouldn't matter if she were the ugliest lump of troll dung ever birthed—it would be worth wedding a dog with an ass at both ends to live to see my nineteenth birthday—but I can't deny I'd enjoy a pretty wife more than a homely one.

Just as I'd enjoy a friendly relationship with my brother-in-law rather than a strained one. Best to humor the boy. There are worse things than being too careful, or too shy to take a bath with other men around.

"Go on, take a soak. You'll feel better after." I chuck Ror

on the shoulder, doing my best to put him at ease. "When you get back, we'll have a bite and you can get some sleep. I'll take first watch."

"All right." Ror moves toward the woods but turns back before he reaches the path. "I'm *not* crazy. Ekeeta does have animals spying for her."

"I believe you," I say, with what I hope is an encouraging smile.

"This isn't a safe journey," he says, tugging his ear again. "It's dangerous to travel with a briar-born child."

He takes a deep breath, dropping his eyes before glancing back up with an expression so pitiful it makes me want to give the kid a hug. He doesn't look old now. He looks like a child who has lost his mother. "Maybe you should leave me. I'll understand. I don't want you killed."

"I won't be killed," I say, pushing on when Ror opens his mouth to argue. "I understand the risk, and I'm willing to take it."

He blinks, and a furrow forms between his pale brows. "Why? For the chance to meet my sister? It doesn't make sense."

"Wanting to marry your sister isn't a passing fancy," I say, sheathing my sword. "I thought long and hard before I came looking for her. Aurora is the only match that makes sense for me. I'll do whatever it takes for the chance to win her. Even risk death escorting her brother across the country."

Ror bites his lip. "But there are other princesses. Princesses who have country and family and no price on their head. No ogre queen for an enemy."

"Ekeeta is everyone's enemy."

"You know what I mean." His head tilts to one side, studying me. "And why the rush? You're not even eighteen. My father didn't take his first wife until he was twenty-six. Wouldn't you rather wait until you've had a few more bakers' daughters?"

"I've already had my share of bakers' daughters," I say with a wink. "And farmers' daughters, and noblemen's daughters, and magicians' daughters, and a few fairy girls I met at a carnival who taught me the most amazing trick with—"

"I understand." Ror rolls his eyes. "You're terribly successful at convincing girls to sleep with you. I'm sure your country is very proud."

I laugh, but Ror doesn't join in. He folds his arms across his chest and his studying expression becomes scrutinizing. "You haven't answered my question. Why the rush? Why tie yourself to a princess with nothing to offer you but trouble?"

I sigh and run a hand through my damp hair. "I have my reasons."

"What kind of reasons?"

"Reasons I'll be happy to discuss with *your sister*," I lie, knowing I'll do no such thing. Hopefully Aurora will be of a less suspicious ilk than her nosy little brother. "Now go on and have a soak, will you? Maybe it will put you in a better temper."

"I'm in a fine temper. I only want what's best for Aurora."

"As do I. I mean her no harm." I hold out my hands, palms up, showing I have nothing to hide. At least not when it comes to treating his sister well. "I'm not a bad sort, Ror."

"I don't think you're a bad sort," Ror mumbles. "I just . . ."

"Just what?" I ask, growing nervous of this conversation.

If the boy backs out of our bargain, I'll be back where I started, with time running out and no idea where to find the one girl who might save me before it's too late. Finding the witch my father paid to curse his sons was a bit of pure luck—a drunken conversation in a bar by the sea led to another drunken conversation, which led to a woman living in an abandoned shrine my father hadn't gotten around to burning just yet.

The woman knew who I was at once and apparently felt guilty for what she'd done to my brothers and me, but not guilty enough to give me the charm to lead me to a briar-born child free of charge. She took my armor—the only truly valuable thing I owned, a gift from an ancient king of Norvere passed down through my brothers—and made me split the skin on my palm and press it to my forehead while she whispered a spell, banishing my memory of her appearance to protect her in case I decided not to honor my promise to keep our meeting a secret from my father.

If I lose Ror, I'm up a ladder without a basket. "Come on," I say, doing my best to keep desperation from my tone. "You can trust me."

"Said the spider to the fly."

"I'm not a spider."

"No, you're the fly, and you could be risking your life for nothing," Ror says. "I know my sister, and there is a very, *very* good chance she'll want nothing to do with you. At least, not as more than a friend and ally."

"Very, very?" I chuckle.

"I'm not joking."

68

My smile slips. "Well, that's a chance I'm willing to take. Now go on," I say, shooing him with both hands. "Have a soak and give the fretting a rest."

Ror sucks in his lips, biting them before giving a terse nod. "I won't be long." He starts to go, but turns back again. "Thank you. I appreciate your help. And your bravery."

Before I can respond, the prince spins and scurries into the forest. I watch him go with a sinking feeling in my stomach. There was something in his voice . . . almost as if he knows *without a doubt* that Aurora will want no part of me. But he can't, not for sure. Not even a brother can know all the secrets of his sister's heart.

Perhaps especially not a brother.

I certainly had no idea Haanah was carrying on with a castle guard before Father caught on and sent the man away. Greer was a decent sort but plain-faced and serious to a fault. I never imagined Haanah would give him a second thought, but she was mad for him. She spent a month mourning like an orphaned puppy when she learned he was gone.

Ror can't know Aurora better than I know Haanah. Haanah and I are practically twins, the only two children named after my mother's side of the family, just eighteen months apart and even closer than Usio and I were before his change. Aurora could very well surprise her brother the same way my sister surprised me.

Or so I tell myself as I start the fire and set about pulling together a meager meal from our rations. But my reasonable arguments offer little comfort. I need to know what Ror is hiding, what secret he's keeping tucked inside that warrior's knot of his.

I decide to get it out of the boy, one way or another, but the hour grows late—insects sing their night songs, and the world beyond the cliff is devoured by darkness—and Ror doesn't return. I wait as long as I dare, but finally decide he must have become lost and prepare to go hunting for him.

I've just finished fashioning a torch from a thin log and dry moss from the limbs of the pin oaks when I hear him scream.

CHAPTER SEVEN

AURORA

I wake to darkness so complete it swallows my gasp and stuffs it deep into its pockets.

I lift my head from the stones of the bank and shift my weight on the underwater ledge, stomach lurching. I can't believe I fell asleep—I'm lucky I didn't slip into the water and drown—but there's no other explanation for closing my eyes on a forest filled with moody gray light and opening them to blackness.

I pull my knees in and cross my arms over my chest beneath the water, feeling my nakedness in a new and uncomfortable way. Ever since those days in Ekeeta's dungeon, I have loathed the darkness with a passion exceeded only by my hatred of biting beetles, roaches, and anything else black and crawly with crunchy outsides and liquid innards.

My mother's fairy blessings have made me nearly fearless,

but not even magic can banish my irrational terror of tiny crawling things.

The thought of chancing upon a Skittery Small electrifies my nerves as I reach out to search for my clothes on the bank. But it's not a crawly thing racing across my hand that makes me scream, it's the brush of my fingers against stiff feathers and the guttural hiss that follows.

I scream and the creature *glock-glock*s and hisses again, a warning echoed from the rocks all around me. I kick to the center of the pool, heart slamming against my ribs, staring wide-eyed into the night. After a moment, I'm able to make out hunchbacked shadows, denser concentrations of black that pitch back and forth on the rocks, stretching their wings, bobbing their bald heads up and down as they grumble and hiss.

The vultures. *Ekeeta's* vultures. They have to be hers. There's no other explanation for why the creatures have tracked me down to keep watch on my bath. Normal vultures don't hunt people—they don't hunt at all, preferring to scavenge for their meals—and they roost at night. I knew that even before Niklaas reminded me that—

"They don't see well in the dark." The pulse racing in my throat slows.

If they can't see me clearly, that means Ekeeta can't, either. Ekeeta's magic allows her to see through the eyes of animals, but her spells don't give the creatures supernatural powers. These vultures can't see or hear any better than an unmagicked vulture, which means they can't be transmitting a clear picture of my location. There's still a chance Ekeeta doesn't know where I am, a chance that Niklaas and I can escape.

No sooner have I thought his name than I hear him calling mine.

"Ror!" He sounds panicked. He must have heard me scream. "Ror!"

"I'm all right!" I swim hard for the bank. Torchlight bobs beyond the rocks. Niklaas will be here in a moment, and I must be dressed when he does.

"Shoo! Get out of here!" I splash water at the creature closest to my clothes and it hops to the side with a nasty growl. Seizing the opportunity, I haul myself up onto the bank and fumble for my clothes.

My pants stick and cling to my wet skin, and the vulture I frightened away returns to peck at my legs as I bind my breasts, but by the time Niklaas appears atop the boulder overlooking the pool—sword in one hand, torch in the other, illuminating the vultures surrounding me like beggars at the royal gates—I am pulling my borrowed armor over my linen shirt and reaching for my staff.

"By the Lands . . ." Niklaas pauses to take in the alarming gathering before leaping off the rock and waving his torch at the nearest knot of birds. The vultures hiss and grunt as they hop away from the crackling flame, but they don't go far, clearly determined to stay by my side until their master orders them to leave.

"Get moving or I'll burn the lot of you!" Niklaas shouts.

"No, don't!" I knock two birds out of the way with my staff as I hurry to his side, bones aching with the fairy magic that compels me to choose mercy whenever possible, even when it comes to carrion-eating creatures. "They're innocent."

"Innocent?" he asks, keeping an enormous raptor at bay with the tip of his sword.

"They're only animals, loyal to the one who's fed and magicked them. They don't know any better." I snatch the torch from his hand and hurl it into the pool, plunging the woods back into darkness.

"What did you do that for!"

"It will make it harder for them to follow us."

"It'll also make it harder to find our way back to the camp!" Niklaas growls, sounding like the kinsman of the birds grumbling all around us.

"I can use my staff to keep to the path." I reach for him in the dark, finding his chest with my fingers and following his arm down to grasp his hand. His palm swallows mine, making me feel absurdly small, a fact I immediately resent.

"Come on. Let me lead you." I give his arm a tug. Thankfully, after a moment of resistance, he allows me to guide him away from the spring.

I tap the stones in front of us, using my staff to find the easiest route to the large boulder where Niklaas and I drop hands to climb over before linking up again on the other side. Behind us, much croaking and hissing and flapping of wings ensues, but none of the birds seem inclined to follow us just yet. Vultures don't care for flying at night. Hopefully that will buy Niklaas and me some time.

"What the devil happened back there?" Niklaas asks as I find the path and aim us back toward the petrified forest. "Did they all come down from the trees at once, or—"

"I don't know. I think I . . . fell asleep," I mumble.

"You *think* you—"

"I fell asleep!" I snap, cheeks burning. "And when I woke up there they were."

"You could have drowned," Niklaas says in his big brother tone, the one that reminds me of Janin when she chides me for forgetting that even a fairy-gifted human body has its limitations.

"I know," I mutter through clenched teeth.

"You could have been killed. *Killed* by your own bath before you—"

"I know! It was foolish. It won't happen again." I debate dropping his meaty paw and letting him find his own way back in the dark.

"It will be a miracle if I manage to keep you alive. Flaming ridiculous," Niklaas scolds, but the way he squeezes my hand makes it clear his temper is coming from a place of concern, and I feel bad for snapping.

"Thank you for coming to help me," I say softly.

Niklaas acknowledges my gratitude with a grunt. "I can't see a damned thing! Are we even walking in the right direction?"

"We are. We'll be back to the horses in a few minutes." I pick up my pace, relying on memory and the shadowy outlines of obstacles along the path as much as my staff. I have a good eye for ground and rarely forget a trail once I've traveled it. "There should be enough moonlight in the clearing to saddle Alama and gather our things."

"We can't ride now. The path to the grasslands is too steep to travel at night."

"We have no choice," I say. "An ogre battalion could be on its way. Ekeeta can communicate what her creatures see to her Captains of the Guard."

"More magic?"

"No, it—" I break off when my staff finds an obstacle in the trail. "We've reached the fallen log. About three hands in front of you." I climb over and wait for Niklaas to do the same before hurrying on. "It's not magic. Ogres of the same clan have a telepathic connection. That's why Ekeeta chooses her captains from her closest family members."

"I didn't know that."

"That's how she organized the takeover of Mercar," I say, my palm beginning to sweat. Niklaas's hand isn't only large, it's as warm as a fresh coal. "Her family's telepathic connection let her know the moment her kinsman killed my father on the west road, and her cousin waiting off the coast know exactly when the king's guard entered the chapel to pray for their prince. The ogre fleet attacked during the vigil. The only guards on duty were the ones Ekeeta had bribed into her service. The city fell within hours."

"So you don't believe your father was killed by bandits, then?"

"Does anyone?"

"No. Not even my father, though he'd never admit it." Niklaas drops my hand as we reach the clearing, where a small campfire burns and the moonlight has turned Alama's white mane to shining silver. "Put out the fire and conceal it as best you can. I'll saddle Alama."

I do as he says, hesitating only a moment to let the fire warm my fingers before scattering the burning sticks and stamping them out. I shiver as the wind rushes through my clothes, raising gooseflesh on the damp skin beneath.

It seems I'll be starting a ride in wet britches again, but at least they aren't as wet as they were this morning, and Button and I have had a couple of hours' rest. I just hope a few hours will be enough to keep the horses going. The farther we get from our current location, the better.

"Can you find the trail we were on earlier alone?" Niklaas asks when I join him by the horses.

"I can," I say, wondering if, now that the danger is real, Niklaas has changed his mind about staying with me.

Something inside me cringes with disappointment, but I should have known better than to place my trust in an arrogant prince I've known less than a day.

"Good." Niklaas presses Button's bridle into my hands. "We should split up. Give the ogres two trails and divide their forces. You take the road, and I'll take the steep path to the grasslands. I've ridden it before, and Alama knows the way. It would be more dangerous for you and Button."

I nod, ashamed for my thoughts a moment before. "Which way should I go?"

"Ride hard back the way we came. When you reach the stream where we watered the horses, give Button a drink and let her walk through the water for half a field or so. If they have dogs, that should throw them off your trail. Then start through the forest toward the low road," he says, lacing his hands together to form a step I use to climb onto Button's back.

"There's a trail near there," he continues, "but if you can't find it, Button should be able to pick the easiest way through the wood. When you reach the main road, head east until you reach an abandoned gristmill. About a field past, there's a grove of scorched birches. Hide there and wait for me until first light."

He swings onto Alama's back and reaches into his saddle-bag, pulling out something I can't see clearly in the moon-light. "If I don't join you by then, keep going on the low road. Choose the southerly branch for the first two forks before you turn north." He reaches out, dropping a bag full of coins into my palm. "Take my purse and—"

"No, I'll wait in the grove until you arrive." I shove the purse back into his hands. "It's smart to give them two trails, but we'll want to join up again as soon as possible. We'll both be safer."

"I agree," Niklaas says. "But I'm not sure if I'll make it to the bottom in time to lead the ogres north without being caught. Alama isn't rested, and those torches are moving fast."

"Torches?"

"Down in the valley, coming from the north." Niklaas pulls Alama a few steps to the right, giving me my first clear glimpse of the world below the clearing. There, still far enough away for their torches to resemble matchsticks deco-rating a harvest cake, a group of riders at least forty strong makes quick progress across the valley.

Ogres. Coming for us on their range horses, the ones they've bred tall and fierce and perfectly suited for their ab-normally long riders.

The hairs at the back of my neck stand on end and my hands squeeze the reins hard enough to make my knuckles crack. They're coming. The monsters who've taken everything from my family, whom I've feared my entire life, are close enough to hear the hoofbeats of their horses echoing through the valley.

"I'll try to lead them away and then double back and meet you in the grove," Niklaas says. "But if I'm captured, I—"

"You won't be captured, you'll be killed," I say. "*I'll* take the steep trail."

"No," Niklaas says, his tone as stubborn as my own.

"Yes," I insist. "I'm lighter and riding a bigger horse. Button and I will make it down to the grasslands faster and—"

"And be in greater danger, no matter how fast you ride." He captures Button's bridle in his fist and holds tight. "You're the one we have to protect. I don't matter."

"You *do* matter," I say, horrified by the thought of him risking himself for me, though I know he's right.

I can't be captured. If I don't retain my freedom and find some way to liberate my brother, it could mean the end of everyone, including Niklaas. But that doesn't mean he should take this risk. Using him to get what I want is one thing; letting him sacrifice his life for mine is quite another.

"Come with me. Please," I beg. "We can find somewhere farther down the road to split up. Someplace safer."

"No. Two riders are easier to track than one, and it's—"

"Please." I wrap my fingers around his arm, knowing the muscles there won't do a thing to protect him from ogre arrows, arrows poisoned with the monsters' own tainted blood. "I don't want you to die for me."

He sighs, but even in the dim light I can see the softening in his expression. "All right," he says. "We'll stay together as far as the low road."

"Thank you." I release his arm after a grateful squeeze.

"You obviously need a keeper," he says. "It's probably best if we stay together."

I bite my tongue, knowing better than to argue with someone who's given me my way.

"Come on," he says, nudging Alama forward. "If we're lucky, the ogres will take the steep trail instead of coming up through the woods and we'll have a nice head start."

Niklaas clucks his tongue and Alama takes off toward the ridge road at a trot, with Button close behind. I give Button his head—knowing he can see much better than I can—and concentrate on staying low over his back, avoiding being swatted by the branches that smother this portion of the trail.

I stroke his neck and tell him how grateful I am that he's ready to ride again after such a long day. He whinnies his appreciation and, by the time we reach the ridge, seems ready for more adventure, breaking into a canter to catch up with Alama.

He's a wonderful horse, much more amiable than Spirit, my horse back home. But Spirit is the offspring of a mainland horse and a wild island pony and has the feral, stormy blood of everything on the island of Malai, the Fey paradise hidden in the shadow of larger volcanic islands off the southern coast of Norvere. Everything on Malai—from the animals to the ancient fairy plants to the Fey who call the island home—is wild.

I know that's why I've grown up as untamed as I have. Back home, I'd think nothing of falling asleep near a jungle waterfall and waking up when it suited me—fairy wards protect the island from observation by the ogre queen, and there are no enemies or predators to worry about aside from a few scuttlebugs as big as my hand—but I'm not back home. I have to make smarter choices, and allowances for things like exhaustion. I'll be no good to Jor if I run myself into the ground. There is still time before autumn creeps in. At least three weeks, maybe more, and it's better to use the time I have wisely than to rush and make foolish mistakes.

"We'll both have a long rest as soon as we're safe," I whisper to Button, who pricks his ears back at me but doesn't slow down.

We ride for another half hour through the silver night, the cool light of the moon transforming the road into a more magical place than it was during the day. With the constellations spinning dreamily overhead and dew-kissed spiderwebs glistening amidst the leaves, it's almost impossible to believe that a battalion of ogres is pursuing us.

It seems even more unlikely that we'll meet anyone on the road, but not forty minutes into our ride I hear hoofbeats from down the ridge.

"Niklaas, wait!" I call out.

Niklaas pulls Alama to a stop, and I rein Button in beside her, pulling my staff from its sling. "Do you hear that?"

He nods but doesn't speak, his entire body tensed with listening.

"More ogres?" I ask, too anxious to keep still.

Niklaas waits another moment before shaking his head. "Not enough riders to be ogres; moving too fast to be innocent travelers."

"Boughtswords." I curse beneath my breath.

"That would be my guess." He turns Alama toward the

woods to the left of the road. "Follow me and keep moving. If they get too close, I'll send you ahead. If we're separated, go to the grove."

I follow him into the forest. There is no trail, only a steep decline and loose dirt where the plants of the forest floor have begun to lose the battle against the eroding hillside. Button hesitates, but I urge him on with a squeeze of my thighs, praying to all the gods my mother warned me not to believe in that our luck improves. If one of the horses falters or we meet more enemies on the low road, we'll be killed or captured for certain, and I will never be able to thank Niklaas for his help.

Or to insist he find another princess to dream about. I may admire his spirit—when he isn't driving me mad with frustration—but I will never be his girl.

I will never be anyone's girl but my own.

CHAPTER EIGHT

NIKLAAS

The darkness beneath the trees is alive with dangers—low limbs, hidden rocks, horse-crippling holes in the ground—and those are only the things I'm certain are there. There could be other perils as well, unseen enemies lurking in the night. I'm not sure how many breeds of carrion-eating creatures there are, but even three or four is too many.

The forest could literally be crawling with Ekeeta's spies.

I can't get the damned buzzards out of my mind, the way they crowded around Ror like Reformers at a witch hunt, ready to tear the thing they fear to shreds. It was unnatural. And those cursed things could be following us, flying overhead, keeping Ror in their mistress's sight, leading the ogres straight to our location.

We have to reach the low road. We have to make it to the next fork beyond the mill before riders—ogre or mercenary—block our way.

"Faster," I hiss, knowing Ror will hear me. He heard the riders approaching from down the ridge road before I did, he must hear that we've acquired a tail.

It's only a horse or two, but a horse or two with a skilled archer in the saddle is all that's required to put an end to us both. And only a horse or two behind could mean the rest of the Boughtswords are taking an easier path, aiming to be ready if the archers fail and we're spit out onto the road.

At least he isn't alone. I urge Alama to pick up her pace, though the tension in her neck leaves no doubt she thinks we're going plenty fast already. The only luck we've had is that we stayed together. At least if we have to fight, it will be two against ten or twenty.

Or forty or fifty, if the ogres take the low road, instead of the more direct route to the petrified forest.

"Come on, girl, come on," I murmur. Alama hits even ground and pours on a burst of speed, flowing like water over the obstacles in our path—leaping a fallen tree, crashing into a stream on the other side, and pushing on without a moment's hesitation, her sides heaving beneath my calves.

I stay low and hold on tight, grateful for my saddle, fearing any second I'll hear Ror lose his seat behind me. It's too dark for a ride like this one. I can't see what's coming in order to prepare for it. Only the barest moonlight penetrates the foliage, and the ground is shrouded in darkness. Alama's abrupt shifts in direction come out of nowhere. I have only a split second between feeling her muscles tense and the instant she springs into the air to prepare myself for her jumps.

By the time we reach the base of the ridge, I've nearly fallen more than once, but when we hit even ground, I no longer hear riders behind us. On the flats, Alama opens up, charging toward the low road as if she understands how much every moment matters. It's only then—with my horse devouring ground like a racing dog drugged on Elsbeth's Rose—that I relax for the whisper of a second.

A whisper is all it takes.

Alama darts to the left and I fly to the right. She shrieks as I leave the saddle; I hit the ground before I can make a sound, shoulder slamming into the dirt before I go rolling across sticks and stones. Something jagged rips through my shirt and blood runs from torn flesh near my hip, but I know instantly that the wound isn't bad. I'll survive, so long as I'm not run over before I get back on my feet.

Ror is close behind. If his horse doesn't see me, I could take a hoof to the head and die before I set eyes on Aurora, three weeks before my birthday, the gods' punishment for attempting to change my fate.

With a groan muffled by my startled ribs, I draw my knees to my chest, rolling over until my forehead is pressed into the dirt. I do my best to walk my feet beneath me, but I'm not even halfway there when hoofbeats rattle the ground. I try to call out, but my cry emerges as a croak I know Ror can't have heard.

I'm squeezing my eyes shut and gritting my jaw, bracing for impact and praying the beast will stomp me someplace survivable, when Button slows and the horse lets out a deeper version of Alama's startled whinny.

A moment later Ror is beside me. "Niklaas!" He grabs me beneath the armpits and heaves me upright, summoning

85

another gravelly cry from my throat as my spine protests the sudden movement. "Are you all right? Are you hurt?"

"F-fine." The word becomes a cough as my chest releases the breath it was holding captive.

"I thought you'd been shot. I thought—"

"Get Alama," I say, struggling to stand. "Before she runs off."

"She's stopped up ahead." Ror shoves his shoulder under my arm, helping me stagger to my feet before reaching back to grab Button's reins. "She's too sweet on you to run off."

I look up, searching the dark wood ahead. I hear Alama's swift breath but can't make out so much as her shadow. "You can see her?"

"She's there. By the double tree. Can you ride?"

"Yes. Help me over. Hurry, the other riders aren't far behind." I wince as Ror's hand wraps around my waist, brushing against where the skin has torn.

"You're bleeding," he says, sliding his fingers higher on my ribs. "Are you—"

"It's nothing. The bruises from the fall will be worse." I try to shift my weight away, but a flash of pain in my hip makes me reach for Ror again, wrapping my arm around his narrow waist.

He flinches and pulls my arm back to his shoulders. "It's easier for me to bear your weight this way. Watch your step. Big rock."

I stare at the ground but can't make out the rock's outline until we're on top of it. I can feel Ror's staff snug in its sling beneath my arm, so I know it isn't the stick he's using to test the ground, which begs the question "How did you see that? From so far away?"

"I don't know. Back home the girls always beat the boys at hide-and-seek when we played at night," he says, clearing his throat as we reach Alama's side. "But of the boys, I did the best. Do you need help getting up?"

"No, I can do it." But when I try to pull myself into the saddle I find my left side unwilling to cooperate with my right and my torso too stiff to bend.

"Let me help." Ror grabs me around the legs and shoves his shoulder into my rear end, giving me enough of a boost that I'm able to slide my leg over Alama's back with a pitiful groan.

"You'd better take the lead," I say, wincing as I reach down to rub Alama's withers in comforting circles, thanking her for stopping. "If we find trouble on the road, you're better equipped to fight. I'll do what I can, but—"

"If it comes to a fight, we'll lose, with your sword or without it," Ror says, vaulting onto Button's back. "Stay close, and I'll try to find a path through any resistance. The mercenaries have been riding all day, and the ogres breed their horses for sustained speed, not short sprints. If we can get past them, we should be able to outpace either group and find a place to hide."

"All right," I say, knowing he's right. The Kanvasola-trained fighter in me shouts that we should make a stand and fight to the death, regardless of our odds, but the survivor in me knows better. Honor is well and good, but sometimes it's more important to do what it takes to stay alive.

Ror leads the way, setting a swift pace, but not quite as swift as the one that led to my fall. Still, we stay ahead of our pursuers and, not twenty minutes from where I fell, emerge onto a clear stretch of the low road lit by blue moonlight. A glance in either direction reveals we are alone, with not an ogre or a mercenary in sight.

Ror glances over his shoulder with a relieved smile.

"Let's not put our good shoes on yet," I say, though I can't help but return his grin as I urge Alama into a gallop down the road. Every hoof-fall sends a jolt through my aching body, but breathing is easier and my voice carries clearly through the still night.

"We'll turn south at the fork and go into the water beneath the first bridge," I say when Button pulls even with Alama, the pair of them running side by side like they've been traveling companions for years. "The water should be low this time of year. We can walk the horses up the bank and slip past anyone on the road."

Ror nods as he leans forward, shifting his weight until he seems to hover, weightless, above Button's back. He adjusts so perfectly to the horse's movement that he becomes a part of the creature, like a centaur from the ancient stories.

Legends say the ogres hunted the centaur race to extinction in their lust for the creatures' flesh, enchanted meat that gave the ogres extended life, allowing them to survive until the race of man grew plentiful enough to feed their hunger.

In those times—so long ago man still spoke the language of the beasts—the ogres looked very different. They were giants covered in hair from head to foot, with sharp claws and sharper teeth and bulbous eyes that glowed at night, transfixing any man unfortunate enough to encounter them in the dark. But as centuries passed and humans gained power over fire and forged weapons with which to fend off their predators, the ogres began to shrink, growing slimmer and softer, coming to resemble the humans they hunted, to use deception to hunt their prey when brute strength was no longer sufficient.

And when that trick, too, began to fail them, they stole magic from the human witches they consumed and learned to feed on human souls, to leave a corpse behind and no blood on their hands, no way to prove it was an ogre who killed the one you love.

They are relentless in their quest for survival, and have already outlived every creature but the Fey by several centuries. Ror wasn't foolish when he ran to hide from the slightest hint of ogre presence today, but hiding was too little, too late. We both need to be more careful, beginning with making it more difficult for Ekeeta's creatures to spot the boy with the golden warrior's knot atop his head.

"Wait," I call as the bridge comes into sight.

Ror reins Button in, walking the horse back to where I've stopped, while I dig into my saddlebag and pull out my tightly rolled oilcloth cloak. It's not heavy enough to offer warmth—I bring it for protection from the rain—but it has a hood that should more than cover Ror's small head.

"Put this on before we go down to the river," I say, handing it over. "Cover as much of yourself as you can. Hopefully that will make things harder for Ekeeta's spies."

"I should have asked if you had something sooner." Ror wraps the cloak around his narrow shoulders. It's so large that it hangs past his waist to cover his knees and a good portion of Button's rump. "I had a cloak of my own, but I lost it at the mercenary camp." He pulls the hood forward, completely obscuring his features. "How's this?"

"You've got a black hole for a face. It's good." I nudge Alama forward.

Button falls in beside, innocent of the fact that his rider now resembles the headless demons said to bear the plague into villages in their saddlebags.

"What?" Ror tugs the hood even lower. "Is something wrong?"

"You're ominous-looking is all," I say. "Like a plague rider. Or Death's little brother."

"Really?" Ror's laugh drifts from the dark hole where his face should be, sending a prickle up my neck. "Are you scared?"

"Terrified," I say with a roll of my eyes.

"Don't be afraid, Niklaaaaassssss," Ror hisses in a voice that makes the hairs on my arms stand on end. "Death has not come for you tonight."

"Stop that." I shudder in spite of myself and urge Alama to move faster, past ready to be off the road and beneath the bridge.

"Why?" There's a wicked merriment in Ror's tone that makes his "Death" voice even more disturbing. "Death only wantssss to be friendssssss."

"There's something damaged in that head of yours," I say, leading the way down the rock-littered incline on the south side of the bridge, holding my breath as Alama skips through the loose gravel to land lightly on the hard-packed dirt and larger rocks of the riverbank. Come the winter rains, this sturdy blue clay will be underwater, but for now it is the perfect makeshift road. The clay is too hard to take prints easily and the rocks should help conceal any trail we do leave behind.

"But has Death not saved your life tonight?" Ror asks as Button dances onto the bank. "Did I not shove your immense backside into your saddle? I shouldn't scaaaaaare you."

"Keep it up and you're going to scaaaaare the horses," I say.

Alama nickers in agreement, making Ror laugh as we set the animals to walking north, giving them a rest from the breakneck pace now that we're off the road. We're not out of danger yet—there's always the chance the ogres will check the river—but it's obvious we both feel safer down here, with the low water burbling over round stones, muffling the sound of our passage.

"And my backside is hardly immense for a Kanvasol prince," I say. "*I'm* the runt back home. My brothers were all a hand or two taller."

"Were?" Ror finally abandons his Death voice. "Did something happen to them?"

I open my mouth to lie, but for some reason the words won't come. Maybe I'm too tired. Or maybe Ror has simply become enough of a friend that it feels wrong to lie to his face—even when I can't see it.

"I'd rather not talk about my brothers," I say. "It's . . . a painful thing."

We travel in silence for a moment, the only sounds the song of the river and the soft clop of the horses' hooves, before Ror says, "I was only joking, you know. You're not immense; I'm a runt, like you said. I'm only glad I was able to lift you."

"You're not a runt," I say, regretting the nickname.

"Yes, I am." He shrugs. "It's all right. I'm resigned to it. There are worse things to be."

"There are," I agree, thinking of the boys I trained with in Eno City when I was younger. They were as large and strong as my brothers, but not a single one would have stopped to put me back on my horse when their own lives were in danger. But then, they knew the truth. They knew I'm not long for this world, and hardly worth risking their own necks over.

"Thank you," I add after a moment. "I was sure I'd be the one pulling *you* up off the ground, but . . ."

"I find it's best never to be sure of anything," Ror says with a weary sigh that seems out of place coming from someone his age. "It's easier to avoid making a fool of myself that way."

"My pride is definitely more bruised than my body."

Ror pulls Button to a stop. "Your wound. I forgot. We should—"

"The bleeding has stopped. It can keep." I continue past him, around a bend in the river that grants a moonlit view of a long, lonely stretch of low water and wide bank. "Let's keep going for another hour or two. Then we'll find a place to sleep for a few hours before moving on."

"All right, but as soon as we stop, I'll clean you up," Ror says, falling in beside me. "I'll keep an eye out for Cavra leaves. The Fey use them to fight infection. I saw some on the road earlier. I should have grabbed them. You can never be too careful."

"I don't think either of us was being nearly careful enough," I say. "We'll have to change that if we want to live to see the Feeding Hills."

"I know. No matter how much I want to keep going, I'll need to rest as soon as it's safe. I'm exhausted and a danger to us both." Ror sighs another weary sigh. "If I hadn't fallen asleep in the pool, none of this would have happened."

"No, if I'd taken your worries about the vultures seriously, this wouldn't have happened." I take in the seemingly peaceful landscape, wondering what dangers are hidden just out of sight. "But after all these years, with the ogres feeding on criminals and leaving the rest of us alone . . . I'd forgotten what determined blighters they are."

"That's what they want," Ror says. "They want everyone to forget. Until it's too late and remembering won't make a bit of difference."

He mumbles something that sounds equally ominous, but I don't ask him to repeat himself. Whatever it is, I don't want to hear it. Not tonight. Tonight, I want to travel this seemingly peaceful road and hold on to the hope that it's leading to something better. If I give up that hope, there will be no reason to run from the ogres, no reason to keep putting one foot in front of the other, no reason to do anything at all.

Without hope, I might as well lie down in the river and let it wash my worries away. Forever.

Some day—or night, it's always harder at night, when the darkness outside makes the darkness within harder to bear—it may come to that, but not tonight. Tonight Ror and I are the lucky ones.

—❦ *In the Castle at Mercar* ❦—

THE OGRE QUEEN

We've lost them, my queen. Our cousin's voice comes to us from far across the land. His battalion is three days' ride from the castle, but we hear him clearly.

His panic. His rage. His . . . despair.

Illestros is listening as he readies the altar at the center of the hall. He shakes his head. I know what he's thinking.

Our cousin should know better than to despair. The Lost Mother guides our steps. To despair is to doubt her presence and her plan and to turn his back on her love.

We stroke the oiled feathers of the raven in our lap. The bird nestles closer, a rattle of pleasure vibrating its throat. Outside, the night air is warm, but within the stone walls of the throne room it is always cool. Our friend is grateful for our warmth, our affection. It is a simple creature without doubt or fear of the future. Its presence settles us.

In recent nights—when the weight of the souls depending on our success has bowed our shoulders like a mantle made of lead—our creatures have been our only comfort.

We will circle back to the Borderland woods, our cousin says, his fear making the words echo uncomfortably within our mind. *We will search every—*

No, Keetan, you will take your men to Goreman. We use our gentlest voice, earning a smile from our brother. *Our friends have shown us the princess and her Kanvasol protector. They travel northeast. Now that she has failed to hire a mercenary army, we believe she will appeal to the exiles.*

Then we will overcome them on the road, my queen, and—

You will allow them to travel in peace. We stroke the raven with a firmer pressure. *We feel the hand of the goddess in this. We will send a messenger, warning the exiles to expect the princess in disguise. We will grant them favors, and they will lure her in and take her peacefully, without the risk of harming the girl.*

Can the exiles be trusted, my queen? Keetan frets. *If the princess remains sheltered in the Feeding Hills, we may be unable to fetch her out in time.*

Do not doubt our wisdom, Keetan. We still our fingers, fighting a wave of anger. Illestros wasn't pleased that we let our anger get the better of us with the prince. Anger is beneath us, anger is *her* emotion, her weakness, and one day soon it will be her downfall. There will come a night when we will wrestle in the darkness with the princess and her anger for the forever crown, but that night has not yet come to pass.

We have been chosen by the goddess, we continue in a tone as smooth as altar glass, *and we carry a thousand souls within us.*

Yes, my queen. Keetan's shame is clear. He carries only fifty souls and possesses only a fraction of our magic and foresight. Every spirit held within us gives us power . . . along with great responsibility.

We must succeed. We must usher in the age of reaping and deliver every soul—ogre and mortal—into the paradise of the underworld. If we fail, it is not only our own life we will forfeit but the treasures held tight within us as well.

Go to Goreman and make your presence known. We stand, carrying our raven as we descend the steps leading to the dais. We will write a letter for it to carry to the exiles tonight. With its strong wings, the creature will deliver our message and return to us long before the princess reaches the Feeding Hills. *If you don't, the girl may suspect something is amiss. We will send word on how to proceed when we have received the exiles' acceptance of our terms. Good journey, cousin.*

Yes, my queen.

The pressure at our temples eases as Keetan severs contact. We cross the room to where Illestros stands before the altar, whispering sacred words over a goblet of mead. The golden liquid has already been blessed with a drop of the offering's blood.

Tonight, the offering is a young woman convicted of stealing milk from her neighbor's cow, an urchin who has not stopped whimpering since the moment she was brought in.

We look down at the peasant in her filthy brown dress, not surprised to see her cowering before us, tugging frantically at the chain binding her shackled foot to the floor. She is afraid, as they all are, but she needn't be. The prick of her finger was the only pain she'll feel tonight. The worst is over. After so many ceremonies, we are deft at teasing a spirit from its body. We will slide her soul away as easily as pulling a key from a lock and fit her neatly within us like a beloved book settled on a shelf.

Our pain will be worse. The traditional marking—the coin tattoo that represents the treasure taken—is etched upon the skin with a blunt bone needle. Illestros will drag it across our flesh when the deed is done, depositing umber deep beneath the surface. There is no room left upon our skull. Now the tattoos trail down our neck and onto our back and shoulders like sand stuck upon the skin after a day at the shore.

We sigh, remembering running naked on the beaches of Fata Madorna when we were young and alone in our body, no one to care for but ourselves, no worries but how long we would be allowed to stay out before Mother called us in for dinner. We ate the flesh of our father's human cattle in those days, ignorant of the great wrong we did. The prophecy had yet to be revealed, and the time of the enlightened transition was decades away. Our family was innocent of how soon our world would change and how great a role we would play in the goddess's plan.

Somewhere inside, at the core of ourselves, beneath the rustle of the souls filling us to the brim, beyond the murmurs and sighs, we are that girl still. We are simple Eke, too young to have earned the rest of our name. How ancient and silly the stories of the Lost Mother seemed to us then. Now, they are our only truth, and she our only comfort.

"My queen." Illestros lifts the goblet, bowing as he offers it to us.

The raven caws in protest as we set it on the floor and take up the cup.

"May you live and die in wisdom," Illestros whispers, "and always blessed be."

"Blessed be." We lift the goblet and close our eyes, focusing as we prepare to draw the girl's spirit into the altar glass.

"Please, please have mercy," the girl shouts. "Please, wait!"

We open our eyes, though we know talk will do no good. This human has been fooled into worshipping false gods and cannot fathom the paradise that awaits her soul when we lay our treasures at the Lost Mother's feet.

"What is it, child?" we ask.

"I stole the milk." The girl's grime-streaked throat ripples as she swallows. "But I only done it for the babe, muh lady. Mum says my milk won't come if I don't drink it while the babe's inside, and our cow died last winter."

We reach out to the girl with our magic, pressing past the layers of fear wavering around her like heat escaping from stone, until we sense the swift rhythm of her heart and, beneath it, the swifter pulse of the babe growing within her. It is a new life, not quite five months formed, but big enough that a spirit has come to dwell within it.

We close our eyes and send out a prayer of thanksgiving. Such bounty. Surely it is a sign that the Lost Mother blesses our plans.

"She tells the truth." We meet Illestros's gaze, nodding in answer to his unspoken question. He bows and turns to exit the throne room, going to fetch more ink. The umber pigment is a sacrament used sparingly. Illestros only ever brings enough for one coin. He will need more to mark me twice.

"Don't be afraid, child. Your babe will dwell in peace and joy in the kingdom beneath and you along with it." We sigh as we reach out with our magic, snatching the child's soul away as easily as plucking an apple from a tree. Having had so little time to grow attached to its body, it comes to dance in the glass quite willingly.

The girl, however, proves more difficult. She seems to sense the departure of the child's spirit, clutching her belly and moaning like the cow she thieved from. Her fearful whimpers become a wail of mourning, and then a scream of rage born of the love she felt for the unborn babe.

Love makes her stronger, and our task more difficult. She fights us bitterly, writhing on the floor, cursing us for long hours until her last breath shudders from her body with a ragged sigh and her soul flickers into the altar glass moments before we become too dizzy to stand.

By the time we draw the souls from the glass into the goblet, we are trembling with exhaustion, but as soon as the spirit mead flows down our throat, we are restored. The souls feed and sustain us, blessing us as surely as we will one day bless them.

We remove our wig, open our robe, and lie prostrate on the floor beside the empty body. We will lie here until Illestros returns to mark us and remain until the first light of dawn, meditating on the bounty and wisdom of the goddess. And when the sun rises, we will deliver the corpse to our creatures that dwell in our gardens and they will gather to feed and we will stroke their fur and feathers and hum along as they buzz and chitter and caw and take comfort in the nearness of good things.

Soon Aurora will be our captive, and the moment of the prophecy at hand. Soon the world will be transformed and our people will feed until the final human shell falls to the ground with the last sigh the air will ever hear and the Lost Mother is free to call her children home.

If Illestros speaks the truth . . . If this prophecy isn't false like the—

We banish the thought before it can reach its end. Illestros left the hall when he realized the girl's soul would take some time to claim and has yet to return, but he could be close. And if he is close, he could be listening. We are born of the same parents and share a connection even greater than that we share with our cousins. He knows our every thought, our every weakness.

It isn't safe to doubt our brother when he might hear. It is never safe to doubt the prophet. All who doubted are dead, slaughtered and thrown into the sea without the final sacraments, their souls cursed to dwell in the black depths of the ocean forever.

The memory of those dear ones drifting on the tide breaks the wall holding our thoughts at bay.

Better cursed than used. Better one woman damned than all the beauty of creation lost and nothing at day's end but destruction and despair. If this prophecy is a lie, there will be no descent into the underworld. If it is a lie, we are not a shepherd gathering her sheep into the safety of her flesh and bones . . . we are . . .

We are a murderer. We are a monster and the most tragic fool ever born.

We press our forehead into the stone floor. We cry out silently to the goddess for guidance, for some sign that our doubts are nightmare children born of our weakness, but she doesn't answer. She never does. She tests our faith with silence. She draws just close enough for us to feel her presence before flitting away, pulling the comfort we crave out of our reach like a sweet held too high for a child to snatch.

Illestros was never the sort of brother to play tricks like that, not when we were younger. When we were children, he would bring us treats and presents; he was always protective, determined to keep us safe.

These doubts are madness. Illestros wouldn't demand this sacrifice if the prophecy weren't a true one. He has betrayed others, but he would never betray us. We are different. We are special.

We shiver, but we do not reach for our robe. We relish the suffering of our body. We focus on our discomfort and will ourselves to believe we suffer for the salvation of the world. If we let our doubts take root and flourish, we will be lost.

It is too late for doubt. It is too late for salvation. We've come too far down this foreign road to ever return home.

CHAPTER NINE

AURORA

We ride until the horses begin to stumble and dawn stains the horizon an ugly brownish orange before finding a decent hiding place beneath the far-reaching limbs of two alders bending low over the bank. We tie the horses near a creek that dribbles down to join the river and lay our bedroll out in the deep shade of the trees.

I stay standing long enough to lay the damp Cavra leaves I gathered across Niklaas's wound—too exhausted to feel awkward about touching his bare stomach—before I plop down on my weary bottom and set to tugging at my boots.

Niklaas makes some vague noises about staying awake to keep watch, but I shush him with a finger in the air and a motion of my hand across my throat.

"What does that mean?" he asks with a chuckle that quickly reshapes itself into a yawn. "Someone has to take first watch."

"Sleep. Both. Useless without it." I throw my boots to the rocks with a grateful sigh. "Sleep. Now."

I point to the other side of the bedroll before turning and falling onto my half of our shared sleeping space. The bedroll will be big enough for two so long as we let our legs dangle off the edges, and right now I could share a hammock with a litter of baby tigers and have no trouble falling asleep.

I curl into a ball inside Niklaas's cloak with my head pillowed on my arm, and am asleep almost instantly. I have no idea whether Niklaas took my advice and got some rest as well, until I wake up hours later to find a wide, warm back pressed to mine, and a snuffly snore drifting through the air.

He snores. The realization makes me blush.

I've never known such a private thing about a boy before. I've never slept with a boy—in any sense of the word—but I certainly never imagined that simply *sleeping* at the same time in close proximity with one would feel so intimate. But it does. I am suddenly shy, unsure what to do next.

I lie still, blinking as the sunlit world beyond our shadowed hiding spot comes into focus. From the glare, I'm guessing it's at least noon, maybe later. We've slept six hours or more, but I'm still as tired as twice-boiled meat. I could close my eyes and sleep another hour or two easily.

I might have been tempted—it's peaceful in the shade and the gentle hum of insects and carefree calls of the river birds make me certain trouble is nowhere near—if my bladder weren't in serious need of an emptying. After a moment it becomes obvious that the tickling low in my body is what awoke me in the first place, and no sooner is the need obvious than it becomes *imperative*.

Moving quietly, I sit up and shove my feet into my boots, glancing over my shoulder when Niklaas rolls onto his back with a soft moan.

He's still dead to the world, his eyes closed and his lips softly parted. Despite the increasingly serious bald places in his increasingly furry beard, he looks sweet in his sleep. Younger. Innocent of the ways people find to use each other.

I remember that I have to tell him the truth—that my sister will never have a husband if she can help it, and certainly never ensnare a decent person like him—and my stomach lurches. I have to do it. He risked his life for mine last night. If he refuses to believe me, then I won't feel guilty about taking advantage of him, but if he does, this could be the first and last time I wake next to this prince. The notion is oddly disappointing, but my bladder is aching too fiercely to dwell on the feeling for long.

Pulling Niklaas's hood over my head, I scurry along the hard clay, past where the horses sleep, up the bank to a patch of dense brush. With one last glance over my shoulder to make sure Niklaas hasn't awoken and decided to follow me, I rearrange my clothes and squat behind a sticker bush, comforting myself by thinking how much easier it will be to relieve myself if I don't have to worry about being discovered.

I'll be alone and friendless again if Niklaas leaves, but I'll be alone and friendless and free to do my business like a girl whenever and wherever I feel like it.

"Small comforts," I mutter as I hitch up my britches and set off to the river to wash up.

By the time I scrub my hands and face, scrape the fuzz from my teeth, decide the messy knot on my head can last one more day before I need to brush, braid, and reknot it, and return to our hiding place, Niklaas is awake.

He's sitting cross-legged on the bedroll, thoughtfully gnawing a handful of jerky. He greets me with a squint of his eyes, which seem even bluer after his rest.

"Sleep well?" I ask, still a little shy for some reason.

"Like a stone. And woke up hungry to the spine." He smiles and holds out a piece of jerky. "There are blackberries across the way. I'll pick some once I get my strength up."

I take the offered jerky and gnaw the salty meat. Despite its leathery texture it's surprisingly delicious, even better than yesterday. Or maybe I'm half starved. I'm not sure which, but I know I'd give a toe or two for a bow and arrows to hunt with as we travel. A rabbit for supper would go a long way to renewing my faith in the future of this quest.

My stomach growls loudly enough to be heard over the rustling of the alder leaves, and Niklaas chuckles. "Should I fetch out the last of the crackers?"

"No," I say, knowing we have to ration the food. "Ignore it. My stomach's a spoiled thing. It's usually had two meals and as many treats by this time of day."

"Fairy food, eh?" he asks, brows lifting. "I thought humans who ate fairy food had to stay with the Fey forever or else they get all shriveled and ancient as soon as they leave fairy lands."

"It's true," I say with a serious nod. "I'm shriveled and ancient over most of my body. Luckily it's the part covered by my clothes."

He grins. "So that's why you wouldn't get in the spring with me."

I shrug. "I wasn't sure you were ready for the majesty of my raisiny bits."

Niklaas laughs, chucking his last piece of jerky at me. I catch it before it hits the ground and pop it into my mouth to hide my own smile.

"When we get to Goreman, I'm going to eat my weight in fish. Sweet corn and potatoes and fish and cold beer until my stomach explodes." He hops to his feet, wincing as he stretches his arms above his head.

"How is your stomach?" I motion toward where his gray shirt is stained black with dried blood. "Did the leaves stay on overnight?"

"I think so. It feels better, anyway." Niklaas lifts his shirt, revealing his wound. The leaves have fallen off, but the skin beneath looks calm and smooth. I step toward him and lean down for a closer look, probing the flesh around the wound with gentle fingers.

"There's no swelling or heat, and it has closed well," I say, ignoring the tingle in my fingertips as some girlish part of me notes how unexpectedly soft his skin is above the firm muscle beneath. "The risk of infection should be gone, but I'll keep an eye out for more leaves. It wouldn't hurt to keep that covered for another night or two."

"All right." Niklaas drops his shirt and I stand up, grateful for the hood that conceals my heated cheeks. "I'm going to pick some blackberries and wash up. I've got linen and mint and rosemary ash in the saddlebag. You should use it."

I make a sound somewhere between a laugh and a snort of surprise. "Are you saying my breath smells?"

"I'm saying it's important to take care of your teeth," he

says with a wink. "You'll never get a girl to kiss you if you've got a mouth full of rot."

My smile slips. "That reminds me . . . About my sister, I—"

Niklaas stops me with one hand over my mouth while the other makes a slicing motion across his throat. I recognize my exhaustion-crazed gesture from last night and grunt. "What's that supposed to mean?" I ask, voice muffled beneath his palm.

"It means I don't want to hear it," he says, removing his hand and smoothing his sleep-rumpled hair from his face. "I'd rather things stay the way they are."

"But—"

"We made a deal and I'm holding you to it."

"But—"

"Uh-uh!" He points an accusing finger at my face. "A deal's a deal. I honor my half, and then you honor yours."

"I'm not saying I won't *honor* it," I say, frustration rising. "I'm saying that—"

"Nope." He covers his ears and closes his eyes. "Not listening."

"But—"

"Not. Listening!"

"Fine!" I snap. "But don't come complaining when—"

"La la la la, la la loo-la lay." He takes off toward the blackberry bushes on the opposite bank, singing his ridiculous song loud enough for it to carry. I think about shouting for him to be still—we could still have ogres and mercenaries on our trail—but shouting would defeat the purpose, and I know there's no real reason to be quiet.

Last night, we forced ourselves to keep riding until we were in the middle of nowhere. We're fields and fields away from any of the main roads. The river is low now, but Niklaas says this entire valley is prone to dangerous flooding in the spring. As a result, the trail to Goreman was cut on higher ground to the north and all but the most daring farmers have built their houses in the foothills. The chances that there is anyone close enough to hear me shout or Niklaas sing are slim to none.

Out here, it's only the creatures loyal to Ekeeta I have to worry about, and so far I haven't seen any animals behaving strangely. There are no vultures circling or crows lurking in the trees overhead. No wild dogs or pink tails or swarms of corpse flies or . . .

I realize my knowledge of the creatures that feed upon the dead is probably incomplete and tug my ear as I fetch the linen and cleaning ash from Niklaas's pack. Hopefully, if I keep my face hidden until we reach the Feeding Hills, where no ogre soldier would dare follow, it won't matter.

I return to the river and attend to my teeth. Niklaas—still busy in the blackberry bushes—has switched to a different tune, a song I don't recognize about summer and lovely girls with long black hair. His voice isn't particularly pretty— fairy boys have lovelier voices, and Jor sings in a tenor as pure as spring water—but there's a warmth to Niklaas's tone that makes it special. His pitch might be off and his rhythm wobbly, but his song makes me feel something. It has heart.

Unlike you. You should have forced him to listen.

I ignore the guilty voice in my head. I tried to tell Niklaas the truth; it's not my fault he doesn't want to hear it. He's old enough to make his own dumb decisions, and so long as we steer clear of ogres, I might be doing him a favor, keeping him from hunting down a bride for a few weeks. Maybe it will give him time to come to his senses. He's too young to be married. He can't even grow a proper beard. What business does he have taking a wife?

"Get in there, Ror. That jerky mouth isn't going to take care of itself." Niklaas appears at my side with his own linen and snatches the ash from the rock beside me.

"You should shave when you're finished," I say, determined to give as good as I get. "You look like you've contracted mange."

"Don't be jealous, little prince." Niklaas laughs. "Your face should get prickly soon. Even fairy boys grow whiskers eventually, right?"

I want to tell him that fairy boys grow lovely whiskers, perfect whiskers that would never dare grow in looking like a half-burned field of grass, but I bite my lip. Boys don't go around admiring the perfect whiskers of other boys, or if they do, they don't admit it out loud. I nearly slipped last night when I mentioned girls seeing better in the dark when I used to play hide-and-seek. I need to remember that being careful includes watching myself around Niklaas.

"I'll shave when we reach Goreman." Niklaas spits into the river before rinsing his cloth. "No one to be pretty for until then."

Even the way he spits is overly confident. The boy is entirely too sure of himself. He deserves to be taken down a notch or two, and discovering he's gotten the worst of our bargain isn't the most terrible way to learn a lesson. Maybe once he's learned it, he will be less insufferable, and the next girl he goes after will like him better.

But even as I think it, I don't believe it. I imagine most girls like Niklaas just fine the way he is.

I sneak a peek at him from the corner of my eye to see a pained expression flash across his face. His wound must be hurting more than he let on.

"We can put more Cavra leaves on for the ride," I say.

"What?" he asks, not shifting his gaze from the treetops on the opposite side of the bank. I look up to see three white swans, a mother and two adolescents, flying east, their elegant bodies alabaster against the azure sky.

"You look like you're hurting," I say, shifting my attention back to Niklaas. "The Cavra leaves will help with the pain."

"I don't think so." He turns to me with a smile, but there's something sad behind it, and his eyes seem dimmer than they did before. "I'll be fine."

"Are you sure? It won't take—"

"I'm sure," he says with a wider smile. "You ready to get back in the saddle?"

"I wish." I moan, unable to conceal my misery at the thought of subjecting my aching muscles to another day of riding bareback.

"Should have taken the time to fetch a saddle." Niklaas sighs a put-upon sigh. "It's hard being right. All the flaming time."

"I can imagine," I say, rolling my eyes.

"Truly. Always right, always wise and sage, but no one will listen."

I throw my wet linen at him, but he dodges it easily.

"Say I was right," he says with a laugh.

I stick my tongue out in response, which only makes him laugh harder.

"Say I was right," he says, "and I'll let you have the saddle until we stop to water the horses."

"Really?" I ask, surprised by the offer.

"As long as I hear something sweet," he says, cupping a hand behind his ear.

"You were right." Forget pride. There are more important things, like being able to feel my bottom at the end of the day. "Absolutely right."

"That wasn't so hard, was it?" Niklaas throws an arm around my shoulders and knuckles my head before bounding off to where the horses are tied as if he had slept sixteen hours instead of six.

No, it wasn't hard, but I've had experience admitting I was wrong. Especially this past year, when everything I touch seems to turn to crypt dust beneath my hands. Admitting I've made a mistake comes easily these days.

I only hope it will be as easy for Niklaas when it's his turn.

CHAPTER TEN

NIKLAAS

Our second day on the road passes much more peacefully than the first—thank all the gods and goddesses and the little baby demigods in their downy cradles. The most dangerous creature we encounter is a snake that slithers across Ror's boot when the boy goes creeping into the woods to answer the call.

He's an odd bird—with his craving for pissing and washing up in private when it's only the two of us—but fourteen is a strange age. Usio stopped bathing for months around then, and I spent my fourteenth year sleeping in a hammock I'd hung above my bed because I was convinced sleeping in hammocks was good training for adventuring.

As if there were hammocks strung up in the trees along every roadside.

Fourteen-year-olds are idiots, but Ror proves himself less idiotic than most. When we ride beneath a swarm of crows near dawn on the third day, he is careful to keep his face covered, and when we rejoin the road and encounter the rare fellow traveler, he never speaks a word. He even obeys my order to stay hidden with the horses while I enter the one inn between the barrier woods and Goreman to take my evening meal alone before fetching out a dozen chicken legs and a sack of rolls for Ror.

Our third day ends in a cave a few fields from the road, where we find shelter just before a rain, and the fourth begins with leftover rolls shared between us next to the remains of our fire. The fifth and the sixth days pass in a blur of riding and watering the horses and getting off to walk the animals when they, or our own poor, abused asses, grow too tired for riding.

With each passing day, Ror becomes increasingly enjoyable company. His imperious, impatient side softens, and I learn that his crookedly clownish side is the more natural one for the boy.

We fall into a pattern of good-natured teasing, with the occasional sharing of something true about ourselves and our lives, and—by the time we awake on our seventh morning on the trail—I'm feeling positively affectionate toward the little bastard. I've never had a younger brother, but if I did, I'd want him to be like Ror: quick with a joke, slow to truly anger, loyal to his friends, skilled with his weapon of choice, gentle with his horse, and odd enough in his thoughts and habits to be interesting. I've come to like the idea of keeping Aurora's little brother under my wing, of having someone to bully and teach and adventure with the way Usio and I once did. I think my blood brothers would like that, knowing their legacy was being passed on and their stories told.

It makes me even more determined to prove that the gloom that fills Ror's eyes every time I mention his sister's name is a storm made of empty clouds and not a drip of rain. No matter what he thinks, I believe I will be able to win Aurora. I *must* believe it.

"Is that smoke on the horizon?" Ror asks, standing up in the saddle he won the use of in a vicious game of dice between us the night before. He pulls my hood back far enough for his nose to peek out and sniffs the air.

"It is," I say. "We'll reach the outskirts of Goreman by noon."

"We will?" Ror asks, excitement rising in his voice. "Then we may be able to hire a guide today instead of—"

"We'll reach the New Market, where the looters and slave traders sell their scraps, by noon, but I wouldn't stop there for a meal, let alone to make camp."

"How long until we reach where we *will* be staying?"

"The best inns are another hour and a half by horse, over Long Bridge, past the cathedral ruins, on the cliffs above the shore," I say, "but we'll settle for something clean in the city center, near the arena. It's always crowded there, and we should blend in with the other boys staying in the city for the blood tournaments."

"I thought blood tournaments were outlawed." Ror stretches taller in his saddle, as if he expects to be able to see all the way to the arena where young men risk their lives to win purses smaller than my monthly allowance. "My fairy mother said even Ekeeta signed the treaty."

I snort. "She hates to see a human die before she's claimed their soul, no doubt."

"No doubt," Ror agrees. "Still . . . I wonder if she knows the tournaments are still being held in a corner of her country."

"It's Goreman," I say with a shrug.

"It's still part of Norvere."

"A far-flung part that's always made its own rules. It's a feral place."

"How feral?" Ror asks, concern coloring his tone.

"The elder council maintains a militia that keeps the streets safe enough, but you won't see many women or children in the city, aside from the whores in their houses and the damaged things who sell themselves near the arena stables," I say, wishing I could banish some of the sights I've seen near those stables from my mind—the little girls with their right hands painted red, meaning that their tiny fists were ready to service any twisted monster with a coin or two; the crippled girl with her shriveled leg, using her walking stick to brace herself as some stranger lifted her skirts in full view of half the men drinking at the beer tents.

If it had been my choice, a single trip to Goreman and its infamous arena would have been more than enough, but Usio had a sick appreciation for the blood tournaments. He even competed on occasion, fighting like a boy who knew he had only a little life left to lose. He always won, but that didn't keep my heart from leaping into my throat and choking me half to death every time the arena announcer called his name.

"We won't linger long." I push my dark memories to the back of my mind. "Anyone who stays in Goreman more than a few days is asking for a knife in the gut."

"Then why should we stay even a night?" Ror asks.

"Because we're road-weary, filthy, and in need of a decent night's sleep," I say, resisting the temptation to slap the boy on the back of the head to knock some sense into him. "And a change of clothes and an extra bedroll wouldn't be a bad idea, either. I'll duck into the exchange and see about that and soap and razors and anything else we think we'll need, and then we'll find an inn where they won't ask too many questions."

"But we should still be settled before supper. That leaves several hours left to at least *start* looking for—"

"Several hours to take a long bath and have a leisurely shave."

"Even a long bath and a *leh-sure-lay* shave," he says, mocking the lazy vowels of my Kanvasol accent, "can't take more than an hour."

"I'll be washing my hair as well." I shove the ratty mess from my face. "I suggest you do the same. Your knot is getting ripe under that hood. I can't decide what smells worse, you or the saddle blanket."

Ror snorts. "How you can smell anything over the fried-onion reek of your own armpits and the cheese stink of your feet is what's truly amazing."

I laugh. "Then you agree we should spend the evening getting clean and fed and enjoying a well-earned rest after crossing half the damned country in barely a week?"

Ror settles back into the saddle with hunched shoulders. "Yes. Fine. All right."

"What was that?"

"All right. You're right," he mumbles in a dejected voice

116

that takes all the fun out of the words. "It makes sense to have a good night's sleep."

"It does. And it's only a few extra hours," I assure him. "We'll go looking for a guide first thing tomorrow. Should be easier to spot one in the daylight anyway."

"Why is that?"

"I'll tell you in the morning," I say with a grin. "Wouldn't want you rushing off to find one on your own and wiggling out of your half of the bargain, now, would we?"

"I wouldn't do that," Ror says, sounding genuinely hurt.

"There, there, little man, don't get sniffly, I was only joking."

"I'm not sniffly, and don't call me that," he says, his hands tightening on Button's reins. "I swear I'm going to bite your arm the next time you call me 'little' anything. Give you a scar in the shape of my *'wee tiny little'* teeth to remember me by!"

"All right," I say, surprised by how sensitive he's being. "I said I was sorry."

"No, you didn't."

"Well, I am." I guide Alama close enough to Button that I can lay a hand on Ror's shoulder. "Seriously. I was just taking it out on you, like usual."

Ror sighs and relaxes beneath my hand, but he doesn't say a word.

"What's wrong?" I ask. "You haven't seemed yourself today."

"I'm worried about my friend," Ror says softly. "About what might be happening to him. I put it out of my mind while we were traveling, but now that we're so close . . ."

I squeeze his shoulder, amazed again at how slight he is. No matter how I enjoy teasing him about his size, it's easy to forget how little he is. His personality comes off much larger than nine or ten hands. "Don't worry. We'll find a guide tomorrow and, if all goes well, be in the Feeding Hills by tomorrow night."

He looks up, the hood shadowing his features, making the hollows of his eyes look bruised with worry. "I know but . . . what if you're right? What if the exiles refuse to help? What if we've traveled all this way for nothing?"

"Then you'll think of something," I say. "I'll help, if you like, as soon as you—"

"Take you to see my sister." He shrugs my hand off with a roll of his shoulder. "You're like a parrot. A lazy parrot, who would only be trained with a single, stupid phrase."

Normally, I would laugh, but it's obvious Ror is still angry. "Being single-minded isn't a sign of laziness," I say in my most reasonable voice. "It's a sign of being focused on getting what you want. I would think you would understand that."

"I do," he says, some of the heat leaving his tone. "But sometimes you can't have what you want, no matter how you focus. Sometimes you have to give up and move on."

"Are you going to give up?" I ask. "If the exiles tell you no?"

He blinks, as if I've said something that makes no sense at all.

"Well, will you?" I press.

"Of course not," he says, brows furrowing with determination. "I won't give up trying to save him until I know he's dead. And then I still won't give up. I'll keep hunting for an army until I find someone willing to help me destroy Ekeeta for what she's done."

"Well then. Don't expect me to give up, either."

"Getting some girl to marry you isn't a matter of life or death, Niklaas," Ror says in his uppity voice, the one that reminds me of Haanah's when she used to chastise me for wasting my time adventuring with Usio when, in her esteemed, feminine opinion I should have been hunting for a way out of the curse.

She didn't understand how hard it was to *imagine* a way out, let alone go hunting for one. By that point, I'd seen nine brothers transformed, watched the painful shrinking of their bones and the obscene ripple of their flesh as their human skin was stolen away and replaced with a swan's feathers. My fate seemed inescapable. It took time—and a meeting with the witch who cursed the males of my line—for me to learn how to hope.

Haanah didn't understand that, just as Ror doesn't understand that it is impossible for me to give up the hope I've fought so hard to possess.

"You don't know what will be the life or death of me," I say in a soft voice. "You don't know me at all, so I'd appreciate it if you'd keep your opinions to yourself."

"I know more than you think," Ror says, ignoring my request.

"Is that right?" I don't bother hiding the challenge in my voice.

"It is," he says, a cunning note in his. "I know you're not as happy or carefree as you pretend to be. And I know you're kinder than you would have people believe."

"I'm not kind," I say. "I'm self-interested."

"That too," Ror agrees, guiding Button close enough to crowd Alama to one side of the road. "And fiercely secretive when you want to be. That's how I *also* know that you're *never* going to tell my sister the truth about why you want to marry her, no matter what you say. If you won't tell me, you're certainly not going to tell her."

"You're mad." I give Alama a squeeze with my legs, urging her to pull ahead, deciding I'd rather not ride beside Ror for the next leg of the journey.

"Am I?" He nudges Button with his heels until the larger horse keeps pace. "I hear the way you talk. You think the girls you care for should be coddled and protected, the girls you lust after charmed until you grow tired of them, and none of them told what's really going on in your head."

I flinch, unnerved by how hard he's hit upon the truth. It's not as devilish and manipulative as he makes it sound, but still . . .

"And so," he continues, "whether you decide to care for my sister or to lust after her, it won't matter. You still won't tell her the truth."

"And how have you worked that out?" I ask with a bemused look in his direction.

"Well, if you care for her, you'll lie to protect her from whatever it is you're hiding." I chuckle, and Ror pushes on with a stormy look. "And if you lust after her, you'll seduce your way into getting what you want."

"And seduction is a lie, too, I suppose?"

"Of course it is," Ror says, sounding angrier by the minute. "Unless you mean the sweet things you whisper, seduction is the same demon wearing different clothes."

"Or no clothes at all," I say, but the joke falls flat. I'm not amused by Ror's assessment of my character, and he's obviously not amused by me.

"And if you neither care for her nor lust after her," he says, biting out the words, "then you'll look straight past her. Like a shadow on the ground."

"That's ridiculous."

"It is not. I've listened to the stories you tell," he says, that wounded note creeping into his voice again. "It's obvious that any girl who isn't bound to you by blood or affection—or *busty* enough to catch your eye—isn't worth your time."

"I couldn't care less about the size of a girl's bust," I say, forcing another smile I don't feel. "I prefer a shapely back end and pretty feet and soft—"

"Ugh!" Ror growls. "You're impossible!"

"I'm not impossible," I snap, close to losing my patience as well. "And I'm not the criminal you're making me out to be."

"I never said you were a criminal, I said—"

"This world preys on the weak," I interrupt, tired of Ror's preaching when he's far too young to sit at the front of the chapel, let alone occupy the altar. "I'm bigger, stronger, and used to dealing with the rougher parts of life. I'm *obligated* to protect the women I love from the misery that awaits girls who have no protector. I can imagine what would have happened to Haanah if I hadn't put myself between her and my father. I was happy to shield her from what misery I could.

Why should she suffer? Why should any woman learn how wretched this world can be if they don't have to?"

"Because they are strong enough to know the truth, and proving that to themselves will make them stronger." Ror sits up straighter in his saddle. "And perhaps, if men were brought up to be gentler people, women wouldn't have need of protectors. Have you ever thought of that?"

I shake my head. "Men aren't going to change, Ror. Men are what they are."

"And women are more than you allow them to be. Women can be strong, Niklaas. If given the chance, they can handle the world, maybe even handle it *better* than a man."

"All right." I snort. "If you say so, Ror."

"I *do* say so."

I look straight at him before I roll my eyes, wanting to make sure my opinion of his opinion is abundantly clear. "Maybe you've met girls like that in your many travels around your enchanted fairy island, but that's not the way it is in the real world."

"It isn't, is it?" he asks, his hands beginning to tremble.

"No, it *isn't*."

"It *isn't*," he repeats with a strained laugh. "Well *you* wouldn't know *real* if it came riding up to you and cut off your stupid, thick head!"

Ror digs his heels into Button, sending the horse bolting forward with a whinny of surprise. Button leaps down the road, breaking into a full canter toward the mouth of the canyon a few fields ahead. I give Ror a good head start before I nudge Alama, urging her to pick up her own pace. Whatever has crawled up Ror's wee bottom and died has left him unfit company. I'll happily let him lead the way and rejoin him when his snit has worked its way out. I'm not sure what provoked him, but I'm more certain than ever that his time among the Fey has made him daft when it comes to human affairs.

Still, his rant has given me new reason to hope. It's clear he doesn't understand normal, human women, and maybe not even his own sister. Aurora might want to be protected, to be sheltered and cherished and, yes, *lied to,* when necessary. She might appreciate the line of defense a man can offer from the harsh realities of the world.

And if not—if she wants to ride a horse astride and teach me wicked kissing tricks like a fairy girl—then I will make sure she knows I can appreciate that as well.

Ror is wrong on one thing for certain—Aurora will never be a shadow for me to step on; she will be the light at the end of my long, dark night.

CHAPTER ELEVEN

AURORA

I should slow down and let Niklaas catch up, but I'm too angry.

Pointlessly, *stupidly* angry.

Niklaas is the way he is, and I like him fine that way—so long as I'm Ror and not Aurora—and by the time he finds out I'm *not* a boy, I will be on my way to war and have no energy to waste being angry with anyone but the queen. I shouldn't waste my energy with pointless anger now, but that doesn't stop me from pushing Button to run faster.

We easily outdistance the other riders on the road, kicking up dust that swirls around the tired horses and heavily burdened carts trundling through the pass toward Goreman. Hard-faced men and boys stare as I charge by, the wariness in their eyes making my skin prickle. It's not smart to attract attention, even if my face is concealed, but I can't seem to stop. It feels like I'm running away from something bigger than

Niklaas or the pigheadedness of human men or even my own anger, something as inescapable as my skin that lurks within me, a weak, mewling thing curled behind my ribs with its head ducked beneath its paws.

There's a part of me that longs to tell Niklaas the truth, naively hoping he'll remain the same when I'm revealed to be the prey he's hunting. I don't want to lose my new friend to my true self, I don't want to look into his eyes and see a rake intent on seduction in the place of my companion or a liar determined to "protect" me.

With every day that we've traveled, Niklaas has impressed me more. He is insufferable at times, but he is also a good, brave person with a kinder-than-average heart. I want him to truly be *my* friend, *Aurora's* friend. A person Aurora can tease and confide in the way "Ror" has. I want to tell Niklaas the truth about Jor, and how vital it is I secure an army to free my brother. I want to tell him what it's like for a girl to grow up with no one telling her she can't be strong or wise or fierce. I want to tell him about Thyne and how I destroyed my best friend and how broken my heart is now, so broken that it will never—*can* never—be put back together again.

I want him to know that I've deceived him, and forgive me for it.

I want him to . . .

I want him . . .

I grit my teeth and push Button even harder, until we're racing along so fast there's no room in my head for anything but clinging to the reins and keeping my seat as Button strains toward the end of the pass. I refuse to let my thoughts take a single step down that road. It is a road to nowhere, with a cliff at its end and a long fall to crash against the jagged rocks of Things That Can Never Be.

Never, never, never, I chant inside my mind, but still my heart beats faster, that canny thing realizing the truth no matter how determined the rest of me is to deny it.

By the time I reach the exit through the pass, it feels as if my chest will explode.

Button and I emerge from the narrow canyon, and the land opens up like an enchanted storybook. The three hills of Goreman appear on the horizon, each one topped by tall stone buildings and taller onyx ruins that stab toward the sky like the crooked spine of a sleeping beast. Below the hills, the city folds down toward the sea, its bridges and towers and dozens of piers deceptively tame-looking from a distance. Even the arena—a stone hollow at the base of the first hill, a hole so perfectly round it's as if a confectioner took a pudding scoop to the land—is a tidy, ordered thing.

Beyond the city, the Feeding Hills loom like giants, dwarfing even the largest of Goreman's hills. They are monsters in dusty white hats, dressed in humorless gray robes of evergreen trees, Feeding Trees—some young and relatively new, some tall enough for their trunks to stretch fields above the rest and old enough to be the stuff of ogre legend.

I long to aim Button toward those trees and ride until it's safe to throw this cloak from my shoulders, to let my hair down to blow as I ride, to be free of Niklaas and my false self and the confusion twisting my insides into knots. Instead, I give Button's reins a tug. He obeys with a snort and a twitch of his heaving sides, slowing to a walk as we reach the edges of the market.

As my horse catches his breath, I peer out from beneath the safety of my hood. The market is not as rough a place as I expected, but it's rough enough. The hard men on the road look positively friendly compared to the adamantine men—and few women—occupying the stalls spreading like an inky rash across the flat land to the left of the road.

All the stalls are black. Black pens contain half-starved animals, black shelves hold food and drink and potion bottles like the ones Janin keeps locked in her trunk back home, and black canvas stretches over the tops of the stalls to keep the rain out.

The air is as dry as it has been for days, but it must have rained recently. The market has been pitched for a while—there is dust on the potion bottles, the shelves holding baskets of potatoes have sunk unevenly into the dirt, and the one-eyed woman squatting behind a table covered with fate cards looks as if she lives in her filthy stall—but the canvas has a shine to it, a glisten that gives the market sharp, dangerous edges.

The New Market looks like a good place to catch a curse or a knife in the ribs. Or maybe simply to have your purse stolen. If you're lucky.

I've decided to keep going and wait until I reach the other side to let Button graze and Niklaas catch up, when I see the banner strung above a pen at the back of the market:

PRACTICE RING. BATTLE TILL FIRST BLOOD.

TRY YOUR WEAPON BEFORE YOU GIVE YOUR LIFE.

A GOLD PURSE FOR EVERY FIGHT.

The pen sits farther off the road than the other stalls but not so far that I can't see the two men going at each other within its confines—one with a sword, the other with a staff like my own. The man with the staff is winning. The swordsman is giving his best, swinging his weapon with the strength and enthusiasm of the young and newly trained, but he can't get close enough to put his blade to use. After only a moment, I'm wagering on the staff for first blood, though judging from the shouts coming from the crowd circled around the pen I'm guessing most of the red-faced men screaming and waving bet slips put their money on the sword.

Just like that, I know. I know I've found a way to release the frustration building inside me and earn some coin in the process. It won't be enough gold to tempt the people of the Feeding Hills—winnings from a practice ring won't hold a candle to the purses at the blood tournaments, let alone the fairy jewel the mercenaries stole from me—but it should be enough to buy a pack and rations, things I will need to continue alone if the exiles refuse to help me and I must leave Niklaas behind.

And if I play it right . . .

Visions of a saddle of my own dance before my eyes, whispering sweetly to my aching backside, banishing the last of my hesitation.

After checking the sky and ground and finding no carrion creatures in sight, I untie my borrowed cloak, roll it up, and shove it into the saddlebag. I muss my hair, widen my eyes, and slouch as I turn Button toward the ring. It will go better for me if I look as small and defenseless as possible. I want the odds weighed decidedly in my opponent's favor before I place my bet. I don't have money of my own, but Niklaas won't mind if I borrow a few coins, and surely he'll be able to figure out where I've gone. No fourteen-year-old boy with "Ror's" skill with a staff could resist a prizefight.

But in case he rides through without seeing the banner, I pause by the fate reader's tent, clearing my throat until her one rheumy eye fixes on me.

"What do you want, boy?" she asks, her voice as gritty as the riverbed we left behind days ago. "You don't look old enough to have a care for your fate."

The pale blue eye is blanketed by a layer of milky white, cloudy with age and too much peering into realms where humans are better off not poking their noses, let alone their eyes. Still, she seems to see me well enough. Surely she'll be able to spot a sun god parading through the market on a great white horse.

"My companion is behind me," I say, nodding toward the pass. "A tall blond boy of nearly eighteen years riding a white horse bareback. If you'll tell him I've gone to the practice ring, I'll have a coin for you on my way back through the market."

"How about a coin now?" She holds out a palm crisscrossed by miniature rivers of dirt. "I'm an old woman. I forget things, I do. A coin would help me remember."

With a sigh, I fish a gold piece from Niklaas's purse and slide off Button's back. There's no time to waste bargaining. The staff fighter has indeed won his match and acquired a new opponent, a monster of a man I wouldn't mind being pitted against in the name of terribly weighted odds, but I want to be in the ring before Niklaas arrives. Niklaas has seen me use my staff once, but once might not have been enough to convince him that a "boy" of my size can handle himself against fully grown men.

"You'll tell him, then?" I ask, dropping the gold into the woman's palm.

"Aye, young master. I . . ." She trails off, then tilts her head and lifts her thin brows, as if listening to someone whispering over her shoulder. As she moves, the ratted bun pinned atop her head falls to one side, revealing an ear with part of the lobe chewed away, and a neck with bite marks scabbing the wrinkled flesh.

Before I can walk away—I know enough about dark spirits that feed on humans in exchange for supernatural favors to realize this woman is drowning in black magic and no one is safe in her presence—she draws her arm back and flings the coin at my feet.

"I don't want your gold." Her hands tremble as she sets to picking at the wounds on her neck with a jagged nail. "I'll tell the boy, but you'll need the gold. You'll need that and more if you hope to make it in time."

I stoop to pick up the coin. I know I shouldn't say a word, but I can't keep from asking, "What do you mean?"

"You'll lose that horse and need another, and horses don't usually come for free, do they?" She barks with laughter before narrowing her cloudy eye in Button's direction. "You won't be lucky enough to *steal* one next time."

I shiver, feeling naked beneath her all-seeing eye, and lay a hand on Button's throat, hating the thought of losing him.

Unfortunately, there are bigger things to lose.

"You said something about making it in time," I say, so desperate for assurance I stay put though every sensible bone in my body screams for me to run from this woman as fast as my fairy-blessed legs will carry me. "Will I? Will my brother live?"

"It remains to be seen." She swallows something she must have had stored in her cheek before continuing. "There will be a choice. You must make the right one."

"What choice? What must I—"

"A difficult choice. That's all we see." Shadows move behind her eye, and I suddenly feel even more watched than before. Watched by this woman, and by whatever dark forces dwell within her. "To look closer will draw her attention."

The queen.

The fate reader nods as if I've spoken aloud. "Soon she will hunt you in earnest. You must be in green hills, near a bewitched stream, before that happens." She begins to chew again, this time with her mouth open enough to catch a flash of inky flesh—flesh too black to be living yet still squirming as it's crushed between her few remaining teeth.

I swallow hard, suppressing the revulsion tightening my stomach. "Please. Is there nothing more? I cannot fail. So much depends on my success."

"Aye, it does. Not even the darklings will survive if the prophecy is fulfilled. Not even my beautiful darklings." She seems to shrink, burrowing into her filthy purple robes. "Trust in the gifts your mother gave you, princess. If you don't, it may be the end of us all."

My heart races as I glance from side to side, terrified that someone has heard her use my title. But there is no one close. Even the roughest men seem content to give this booth a wide berth.

"Go to the ring," she says, gathering her cards in a gnarled hand. "I'll tell the boy where to find his *friend*." She smiles, a wry baring of her teeth and gums. "Some prince," she mutters. "Doesn't recognize a princess when she's sleeping curled up beside him."

"Don't tell him." I adjust my grip on Button's bridle, deciding I will look smaller if I walk to the ring leading a giant horse than riding one. "It is my secret to keep."

"And his to discover." The fate reader chuckles and the shadows behind her rheumy gaze writhe, as if they, too, are amused. "Sooner or later those pretty gray eyes will give you away, girl."

I don't respond. I won't think about what my eyes might betray. I won't think of anything but my brother and how desperately I need gold in my pocket. I will draw first blood before my opponent has a chance to lift his weapon. I can practically taste victory, hot and salty on my tongue.

CHAPTER TWELVE

NIKLAAS

The ancient fate reader who called my name from the side of the road points to where Ror has gone to seize the destiny she foretold for him.

I follow her crooked finger in time to see the boy entering a makeshift battle ring, looking like a doll plucked from a toy house compared to the man across from him. His opponent is a monster with a long black braid, a jaw hacked from a hunk of rock, and a bluish tinge about him, like all people raised in the extreme north. His veins are dark streams visible beneath his pale flesh, angry rivers pumping blood from forearms as big as Ror's waist to shoulders twice the width of my own.

The fool's going to die. He's going to flaming die!

The thought is barely through my head before I'm digging my heels into Alama's sides and she's off, charging through the crowded market.

Shoppers leap out of my way with angry shouts and threats to my life, but I don't rein Alama in. I have to reach Ror. The fights in the practice rings are supposed to end at first blood, but first blood can too easily become lifeblood. One firm jab in the wrong spot with the sword the northern man is lifting could be enough to end Ror's life.

"Ror, stop!" I shout.

Ror turns at the sound of my voice, and the northerner seizes on the boy's momentary distraction.

The giant rushes forward and the world slows. My pulse lurches in half time as Ror faces his opponent, crouching down and sweeping his staff in a low circle across the dirt. The giant's feet tangle in the wood and he begins to fall, but manages to keep his sword aimed at Ror's chest, preparing to drive the blade through the boy's leather armor with a single shove of his massive arms.

My insides seize, my mind already imagining Ror's body split in two, when he dives forward. He rolls beneath the giant's knees heartbeats before the other man falls to the dirt. The northerner is quick to recover, but not quick enough. Before he can turn, Ror brings his staff down on the man's temple, hitting where the skin is thinnest, bursting the delicate flesh, drawing first blood.

I suck in a ragged breath as an enraged shout rises from the crowd, but the northerner doesn't seem to realize he's lost. He surges to his feet with a bellow, swinging his sword around in a hacking motion that would have sliced Ror in half if he hadn't leapt backward like a circus performer a second before.

Ror's hands reach for the ground as his feet flip over his

head—once, twice, three times, with his staff somehow still in his grasp—until he's at the edge of the pen. He turns to leap over the side, but the men there grab the boy and throw him back in, straight into the path of the blue monster.

I decide then and there that if Ror dies, I will kill those men. I will slit their throats and watch their blood soak into the soil, without a moment of regret.

"Let the boy out! He's drawn first blood!" I vault from Alama's back and charge the pen, grabbing spectators and hurling them to one side with growls that send most stumbling away even before they turn and see that I'm a good head taller than they are.

Aside from the beast bringing his sword down to clash against Ror's staff with an angry *thwack,* I'm the largest man near the practice ring. I flinch, expecting the staff to break, but it holds strong for several blows, long enough for me to part the crowd and jump the fence, drawing my sword as I enter the ring.

"Leave him alone!" I shout.

The northerner turns to me with a roar of outrage. I take advantage of his split focus, grabbing Ror by the back of his armor and shoving him behind me.

"The boy drew first blood!" I lift my sword, preparing to meet the northerner if he refuses to admit defeat. "It's running down your face, man. You've lost your bet. This boy's death will serve no purpose."

The man's forehead wrinkles, but I'm not certain he's understood me. I've begun to worry that he doesn't speak the language of Norvere and that this will end badly because I was too lazy to learn more than two of the Herth languages before abandoning my studies, when he lifts his hand to his temple and swipes his sausage fingers through the red running down his face. He stares at the blood for several long, tense moments before finally lowering his sword.

Still, I don't dare pull in another breath until he trudges to the edge of the ring and climbs out of the pen, rejoining a group of his northern brothers. Only when I'm sure he's gone for good do I snatch Ror up by the arm and drag him in the opposite direction.

"I won the match!" Ror shouts, digging in his heels. "I have to go again. I said I'd fight until I lost."

"I don't care what you said," I growl through clenched teeth.

"I'm doing well. I drew first blood. I—"

"You're lucky you weren't killed!"

"At least let me collect my winnings!" Ror wrenches his arm free with that uncanny move of his, the one that feels as if he's broken his arm in two only to reconnect it a second later.

I grab for him, but he's already across the ring with his hand under the bet keeper's nose. The weasel-faced man glares at Ror, his close-set eyes shining with rage, but he's a more honorable sort than the men who threw Ror back into the ring. He has a business to run, one that will not continue to profit if it's heard that the ringmaster refuses to pay out on occasions when a fighter wins against extraordinary odds.

The man counts off an impressive number of coins before dumping them into a small burlap sack and throwing them at Ror. The bag hits Ror in the chest, but he doesn't flinch.

He only clutches his winnings and inclines his head before turning to pin me with a look cold enough to freeze even the northerner's frost-resistant skin.

"*Now* we can leave." Ror crosses the pen and leaps the railing, shouldering his way through a cluster of men clearly not pleased to have lost their bets but unwilling to attack a boy who bloodied a man twice his size in thirty seconds flat.

Ror collects Button from where the horse is tied, while I fetch Alama and lead my good girl—she didn't move a hoof from where she stood when I dismounted—over to join him. I dispense my own hard looks to the men glaring holes in Ror's back, and by the time I reach the boy, most of the spectators have had the good sense to look away.

Ror waits until I'm close, but not too close, before leading Button out of the market. I follow, biting the inside of my cheek to keep from beginning my dressing-down before we've reached the road. It's best if these men see Ror and me as united companions with no anger between us, but as soon as we're out of earshot . . .

We mount up and set the horses toward Goreman proper at a brisk walk, but we're barely a field from the market when I let go, unable to control myself a second longer.

"What the devil were you doing back there?" I demand, shocked by how enraged I sound. I can't remember using this tone with anyone, not even Regiene when she announced her engagement to my father. "Do you have a death wish?"

"I was acquiring more gold for the journey." Ror pulls my cloak from the saddlebag and shrugs it around his shoulders. "I was told I'd need it."

"Told you'd need it," I repeat, breathless with anger. "By

some mad fortune-teller who thought it would be amusing to see a kid get his guts spilled!"

"It wasn't like that," he says, still utterly—infuriatingly—calm. "She knew things she couldn't have known without real insight into the future."

"It doesn't take insight into the future to know—"

"And even if she was mad," Ror pushes on, "I didn't need a fate reader to know the odds were good that I would win."

"Against trained warriors two times your size? With decades of fighting experience? You thought *those* were *good*—"

"Yes, I thought those were *good* odds," he says, tugging his hood up over his head with a sharp jerk of his arm. "You saw me fight. I won. I drew first blood easily, and I would have done it again if you'd let me keep going to the next round."

"Are you out of your head?" My voice cracks with disbelief. "Were you fighting the same fight I was watching? Those people threw you back into the ring. They would have kept throwing you back until the northerner killed you if I hadn't—"

"If you hadn't distracted me, I would have been better prepared to begin the fight in the first place," Ror says, heat finally coloring his tone. "And if you hadn't stuck your sword in where it wasn't needed, I would have kept at that man until he was unconscious or dead. I didn't enter that ring intending to kill someone, but if he had given me no choice, I would have been able to defend myself. Until the death, if I had to."

I shake my head, mumbling beneath my breath.

"Just say it," Ror says. "I'd rather fight than hear you mutter for—"

"Maybe you'll want to enroll in the blood tournaments, then," I snap, the words making my chest ache. Ror is safe, I shouldn't be so angry and afraid, but I am. "If you're so eager to take a life, you'll find ample opportunity there."

"I'm not eager to take a life," Ror says with a sigh. "I didn't say that, I said—"

"My brother Usio fought in them." I grit my jaw, remembering the way Usio would laugh when I begged him not to fight. Laugh, and then go to the ale tent right before his match to rub my concern for his life in my face. "Several times, no matter how I tried to convince him not to."

"Why? You didn't think he could handle himself, either?"

"No, I thought he was better than that," I say, my voice revealing my hurt no matter how hard I try to hide it. "Better than our father and Ekeeta and other people who fight and kill when they don't have to. I thought *you* were better than that, too."

"Niklaas, be fair," Ror implores, his tone gentler than it was before. "I didn't say I *wanted* to kill someone. Of course I don't, but—"

"Then you shouldn't have set foot in a ring, even a practice ring." I turn, deciding I might finally be able to look him in the eye without wanting to grab his shoulders and shake some sense into him. "Anytime you pick up a weapon, there's a chance you or someone else could be killed. I think your sparring match back there made that clear."

Ror stares up at me from the shadows of his hood, a hint of regret tightening the skin around his eyes. "I know, but I assumed . . . I didn't know it would be like that."

"There's a lot you don't know," I say. "By the gods, you're

fourteen years old! If you want to live to see fifteen, you have to be more careful."

"I *was* being careful," he says. "It was a calculated risk. I know what I'm capable of, Niklaas. Truly I do. Can't you trust me? I'm younger and smaller than you, but it doesn't necessarily follow that I'm more foolish."

"You risked your life for gold when I have more than enough to get us to the Feeding Hills!"

"But what about after? What will we do for money if the exiles turn us away?" he asks, making enough sense for me to pause to consider the question. "And even if we had enough gold, *you're* risking *your* life for an introduction to a girl you've never met. I know you have your reasons, but you have to realize how foolish that seems to me."

I don't say a word, not wanting to admit he's right, not wanting to start another argument about his sister or girls or marriage or anything relating to the three.

"But I trust you, regardless. You've earned my trust," Ror continues. "I think I've earned the same benefit of the doubt. I've been nothing but cautious and reasonable since we escaped the ogres that first night."

I grunt. "Luring me into a false sense of safety. I should have known better than to let my guard down. Fourteen is a dangerous age."

"I will be dangerous at any age," Ror says, a teasing note creeping into his voice. "I think that was apparent from my time in the ring as well, don't you?"

My lips curve and my shoulders relax, my body ready to let go of anger even if my heart isn't there yet.

"Come on, Niklaas," Ror wheedles. "I was good, you can't deny it."

"Maybe." I shrug one shoulder.

"Maybe?" He guides Button closer and puts a hand on my shoulder, sending a rush prickling along my nerves. It's an odd . . . *aware* feeling—one I wouldn't normally associate with being touched by a friend—but I thought the boy was going to die. It makes sense that my nerves are out of sorts. "Were you watching the same fight I was fighting?"

I shrug his hand off with a laugh. "You were good," I concede. "Like a boneless monkey."

Ror smiles. "I'll take that as a compliment."

"Where did you learn your tricks? I've seen Fey warriors spar, but nothing like that."

"My friend Thyne taught me, starting when I was only eight," he says, his dimples vanishing. "The island fairies are all fond of tricks, but Thyne was the first to add them into training with the staff. He's an amazing fighter."

"The only person who can out-monkey you?"

"No. I could beat him. If I wanted to." He sounds too sad for the words to be a boast, but when he looks back up at me, he's smiling again. "I have an idea."

"Sounds dangerous."

He punches me, his grin growing bigger. "Let's celebrate tonight."

"Celebrate what?"

"Making it to Goreman, surviving the market, having enough gold to buy a second saddle." Ror shrugs. "Take your pick."

"A second saddle sounds worth celebrating."

"Then I'm buying dinner," he says, patting his new purse. "As much fish and corn and beer as you can stomach."

"And potatoes with onions," I add, mouth already watering. "I can't have fish and corn without potatoes and onions."

"And potatoes with onions," he says, "though I think I'll skip those. Smelling your pits day in and day out has killed my appetite for onions."

"All part of my plan," I say, clapping Ror on the back. "Now I'll be able to eat your portion as well."

"Devious," he says.

"When it comes to food? Always, my friend."

Ror's laughter makes his eyes light up and his cheeks dimple, transforming his face into something a little too lovely. For the first time since seeing him in the ring, I appreciate what a clever thing he did, using his appearance against people who assumed a soft boy with a pretty face would be unable to hold his own.

"What were the odds against you?" I ask, wondering how many coins are in his burlap purse.

"Twenty-five to one," he says. "I bet five of your gold pieces on myself."

"You should have bet twenty."

His eyes widen. "Twenty?"

"You were sure you would win."

"Mostly sure." He fidgets with the strings on the purse. "But I didn't want to wager too much. Just in case."

"You were already wagering your life. Money is nothing compared to that." I wait until he glances up and hold his eyes. "Next time, if you're betting your life, feel free to bet as much of my gold as you like."

Ror is quiet for a long moment before giving a curt nod.

"But there won't be a next time, right?" I ask with a pointed look.

"I'm not the sort who goes looking for a fight, Niklaas."

"Yes, you are," I say. "You're spoiling for a fight, anywhere, anytime, any way you can get one. I know you better than you think, too, you know."

Ror's mouth quirks up on one side. "You think so?"

"I know so," I say, nudging Alama into an easy canter. "Come on. There's a saddler near the mercantile. My ass says a saddle should be the first item on our list."

Button picks up his pace and Ror and I ride into Goreman side by side, crossing the final bridge into the town center, where the city of fighters, fisherman, and thieves is already bustling with preparations for the night's tournaments.

I spy more than a few pairs of brothers bargaining for new leather chest plates at the armory and standing in line to have their swords sharpened by a peddler with a whetstone and am grateful that Ror and I will be staying far away from the prize fights.

It will be a relief to spend a night in Goreman without worrying that someone I care about is going to have their blood spilled before morning.

CHAPTER THIRTEEN

AURORA

Niklaas and I finish our shopping and find a simple inn on the hill above the arena with stalls for the horses and two rooms to let—I insist on two, refusing to pass up what might be my last chance for a bath for only the gods know how long—and spend the rest of the afternoon soaking the aches and pains and filth of the road away.

I wash my body three times and my hair twice before wrapping up in a towel and pulling the room's wooden chair in front of the fire to comb out my tangles. I had the inn's boy light the fire after he fetched up water for the bath. With the endless summer dragging on, it's too warm for a fire, but I need the flames to get my hair dry enough to rebraid before supper. I've twisted it up wet before, but the weight gives me a headache, and I don't want anything to distract me from enjoying my last night with Niklaas.

I've decided to tell him the truth tomorrow, as soon as

we hire our guide, and let him decide whether a journey into the Feeding Hills is worth his time once he's in possession of all the facts. I trust him not to abduct me, the way I once feared he would. He might still consider it, but my performance in the ring today should leave no doubt that if I decide to fight for my freedom, it won't be a fight that's easy for him to win.

And despite his size and strength and stubbornness, Niklaas is a peacemaker. He looks for the path of least resistance, he doesn't go charging in with fists raised unless he has to. Like today—he only lifted his sword when he felt he must fight to save his friend.

I didn't require his help, but still . . . it warms something inside of me to know that Niklaas values my life more than his gold.

"Values Ror's life," I mutter as I run my fingers through my long hair, holding segments up to the fire to dry.

Once Niklaas knows the truth, he might have reasons aside from the revelation of my true identity to change his good opinion of me. I have lied to him. I have lied to him every day for seven days that feel like seven months. Our journey has brought us closer than two people usually would be after knowing each other only a week. It has made lies even more unforgivable. Niklaas hasn't told me his entire truth, but he hasn't deceived me, and if he had I would be livid.

He may hate me come tomorrow.

"All the more reason to enjoy tonight," I mutter, wiggling my bare toes at the fire, considering my squat little feet, wondering if Niklaas would find them pretty.

I banish the thought immediately, but the shame of

thinking it lingers, making my cheeks hot for reasons that have nothing to do with the fire.

"Fool." I tug hard on a tangle, sending pain zinging along my scalp, knowing I deserve that punishment and more.

I am a fool, and maybe I can't help thinking foolish things, but I can help being cruel. I will *never* be cruel to Niklaas. I will never give him a reason to believe I'm curious, let alone that curiosity might develop into something more. I care about him, and I wouldn't damn a man I hated, let alone a friend, to be my husband. I've already destroyed one strong, clever, beautiful boy. I won't destroy another.

By the time I've pulled on my things—new gray linen pants and a gray undershirt with my freshly oiled leather overshorts on top—I am Ror again, firmly back in my boy skin and no longer thinking anything about Niklaas except how awed he'll be when I'm able to eat more fish than he can.

I reach for my armor but decide to wear the new leather vest I purchased at the mercantile instead. The temptation of an evening without armor weighing on my shoulders is too much to resist. I've bound my chest beneath my undershirt, and the vest reaches my hips and will conceal my curves. I will look boyish enough, and if Niklaas hasn't questioned my nature in the past seven days, it's doubtful he'll start tonight.

I finish by pulling my mostly dry hair atop my head with a fresh strip of leather, working the waist-long strands into three braids and wrapping the braids into a tight warrior's knot that I secure with more leather.

When I finally leave my room two hours after going in, I

find Niklaas sitting in a patch of setting sun outside my door, his blue eyes slitted and a lazy smile on his face.

He's wearing his new clothes, too—a cream shirt that emphasizes the gold of his skin and tight brown pants that cling to his thighs more than his other pair, leaving no doubt that Niklaas's lower half is as well muscled as the top. His hair has dried a lighter shade of lion mane than it looked when covered in dust and lies in shining waves to his shoulders. His cheeks and chin are freshly shaven, and his full lips once again dominate his face, drawing my attention no matter how I try to pull my eyes away.

"Ready to eat?" I ask, my voice thankfully less breathless than I feel.

"Past ready. I've already bathed, napped, checked on the horses, and put out the word to a trusted friend that we're looking for a guide into the Feeding Hills." He springs to his feet and claps me on the back hard enough to make me cough. "You, meanwhile, have wasted the afternoon away."

"The hair." I motion to my warrior's knot. "It takes a long time to dry."

"Then cut it." He sets off toward the stairs and the tavern below the inn.

The traditional Goreman meal—fish, sweet corn, and potatoes with onions—is on the menu tonight, which I suspect is the main reason Niklaas chose this inn over the others we passed, though he made a great show of inspecting several stables and declaring them unfit for his horse.

"Fey men never cut their hair. Everyone knows that." I bound after him, so much lighter in my new vest that I feel I might float away. It makes me hopeful. Hopeful that there will come a day when I will be back in my fairy dresses, with nothing but whisper-soft skirts to weigh me down. "They'd no more trim their hair than cut off a finger."

"You're not Fey," he says over his shoulder. "You're human, and human men don't waste two hours fussing with their hair."

"Human men also smell like wild hogs and relieve themselves in the street. I prefer the Fey ways, thank you."

"Let's see if you say that after your meal tonight," he says with a laugh. "Not even the Fey make food like this."

He pauses at the bottom of the stairs, reaching back to catch my arm and pull me behind him, sheltering me with his body as he scans the room. I stay where he's put me, knowing he must be checking the tavern for possible spies, and try to ignore the heady soap and spice and . . . Niklaas smell of him.

No matter how much I teased him about it, he never smelled of onions, but he *had* begun to stink of the road. Now he smells like summer, like warm skin, tall grass, and the breeze off the ocean. He smells like adventure and safety, the familiar and the unknown, woven together, making me long to press my face against the back of his shirt and breathe deep.

Against my will and good sense, I'm beginning to lean in when he turns around.

"The company looks harmless, and there's a table in the corner so far from the windows it's nearly night over there already," he whispers, close enough for his mint and rosemary breath to warm my lips. "Assuming they don't have a rat problem, we're safe."

"Good." I duck my head. "Let's go," I say, voice cracking as I try to move past him.

"You all right?" he asks, stopping me with a hand on my shoulder.

"Fine. Why?"

"You sound a little . . . strange."

"Just starved to the bone." I shrug off his hand and punch him lightly in the stomach, but for the first time the chummy gesture feels awkward. I force a smile, praying Niklaas hasn't noticed. "Come on. Let's sit. I'm going to eat my age in fish."

Niklaas snorts. "Just don't drink your age in beer and we'll be all right."

I follow him with my eyes on the ground, doing my best not to attract the attention of the patrons already taking their dinner. Niklaas is right: the group of boys in ratty battle gear commanding the large table at the center of the room and the two old men sharing potatoes near the window look harmless, but it's best to be careful.

We arrive at the table Niklaas has chosen, and I agree it's perfect—shoved into the shadows at one end of the bar, with only a tiny, flickering candle to light it and no way for anyone, or *anything*, to spot us from the street outside. It's probably the safest place we've been in days, and the perfect spot to tuck into my first hot meal in over a week.

My stomach growls. "Let's eat like it's our last meal," I say as I pull out my chair.

"Like condemned men," Niklaas agrees, motioning to the innkeeper's wife.

And eat we do. And eat and eat, gorging ourselves on butter-smothered whitefish so tender it melts on the tongue, fresh sweet corn bursting with juice, and Niklaas's much-adored potatoes and onions. By the time we're finished, my stomach is a hard knot at the center of my body, my heartbeat sluggish with the effort of digesting it all.

"I feel like a tick," I say, sipping my beer. I'm still on my second mug. Niklaas is on his fifth but doesn't seem any worse for it. As big as he is, it probably takes more than a few beers to make him drifty.

"A happy tick." Niklaas holds up the empty bowl of potatoes, motioning for the innkeeper's wife to bring another.

"You've got to be kidding," I say. "You're having more?"

"I am," he says. "Anything else for you? Another beer?"

I shake my head. "I'm already drifty. I should stop."

"You're a better man that I was at your age." Niklaas sits back, stretching his hands high over his head, as if doing so will make more room in his stomach. "The night I had my first beer, I had my eighth and ninth. I was sick as black magic the next day."

"I've had beer before," I say with a smile. "And wine and spirits. I like wine best, especially the sweet ice wine at the Marrymeet festivals."

"I wouldn't recommend the wine here," Niklaas says. "Probably closer to vinegar. Goreman isn't known for its wine." He shoots his mug a critical look. "Or its beer, for that matter. Too dark and bitter. The beer in Kanvasola is much better."

"It doesn't matter." I wave a hand in the air before resting it on my too-full belly. "No room for wine anyway. My stomach's on the verge of rebellion."

"Then you'll just have to watch while I finish up," he says, grinning at the innkeeper's wife as she delivers the potatoes. She is old enough to be his mother, with gray streaks in her auburn hair and lines creasing the sides of her mouth, but she still blushes and giggles when Niklaas thanks her for the wonderful meal.

"And here's another beer for yeh," she says, placing a sixth beer in front of Niklaas as she stacks our dirty dishes. "No charge for that one. Just a thank-yeh for taking yer meal here with us tonight."

"Thank you, my lady." Niklaas grins one of his wicked grins, the ones that seem to melt women from the inside out.

"Aw, now," she mutters, "call me Nell. All the boys do. We're like family here. Somebody's got to keep an eye on all these young ones so far from home."

"You're as sweet as your cooking, Nell." Niklaas caresses her name with his voice, while I try not to roll my eyes. "I'm Niklaas, and this is my friend Ror."

"Nice to meet yeh both," she says, though she doesn't spare me a glance. "Enjoy yer night and keep out of trouble, boys."

"We will." Niklaas's naughty wink is in direct conflict with his words, making Nell giggle again as she turns from the table.

"Ugh." I shake my head as the woman scurries away, watching her peek back at Niklaas as she collects the dirty dishes from the other tables. "You're terrible."

"I'm charming."

I grunt. "Charming or not, you certainly have an effect on the fairer sex." My nose wrinkles as I remember the way the whores flung themselves into the street as we rode past their

151

houses, caressing Niklaas's leg, begging him to frequent their establishment while in town. It was all I could do not to bat their grabby paws away with my staff.

"Jealous again?" Niklaas asks, jaw working as he digs into his potatoes.

For a second I'm startled speechless, until I realize he means jealous of *him,* not the other women.

"Not in the slightest," I say with an exaggerated roll of my eyes. "It must be exhausting, having women swooning at your feet all hours of the day."

"It is," he says with a put-upon sigh that makes me snort. "Pity me, Ror."

"I'm serious," I say, though I can't help smiling. "How can you be expected to think of women as anything other than giddy things with fluff between their ears when they're always acting the fool for you?"

"I'm serious, too. I really do wish you'd pity me." He bats his lashes, making me wonder if he's feeling those beers after all. "I'm tired of being a wanted man. I'm ready to be married. I swear I will be a good and faithful husband. Won't you consider putting in a kind word with your sister for me, my good, good friend?" He stabs another forkful of potatoes and shoves them into his mouth, somehow managing to make even chewing look tragic and pitiable.

A part of me wants to laugh away his request, but the other part . . .

"Even if I did, it wouldn't matter," I say, my full stomach beginning to ache. "I've tried to tell you, Aurora will . . . She'll *never* agree to marry you."

"You can't know that for sure," he says around a mouthful of food.

"I can." I stare at the flickering candle, dreading revealing myself tomorrow morning more than ever. "Trust me."

"No, you can't." He drops his fork to the table with a clatter that pulls my eyes from the flames. "You're her brother, and it's obvious you love her, but you can't know *everything* about her. Just like you can't know *everything* about me. Maybe I'll surprise you. And her. And you," he says, brow wrinkling. "I already said 'you,' didn't I?"

"You did. I think maybe you've—"

"No, listen to me, Ror. Listen. I'm going to tell you some truth." Niklaas shoves the now-empty bowl of potatoes away. "I know I've never met Aurora, but I think your sister and I will understand each other. In a way that's special. That's different than just boy and girl and kiss and talk and blah blah blah."

"Is that right?" I ask, curious though Niklaas is obviously a little drunk and this entire conversation pointless.

"Listen, Ror," he says, pointing a finger so close to my nose that my eyes cross.

"I'm listening," I say, trying not to smile.

"My father? He's a terrible man. Really. Terrible, terrible." The misery in his voice banishes the urge to grin. Janin knew the Kanvasol princes would never be contenders for a marital alliance, and so my studies of Kanvasola lagged behind the rest, but I've heard enough of Niklaas's childhood stories by now to know he would have been better off being raised by wild dogs than the immortal king.

"Like a devil from the Pit," Niklaas continues, "hovering over me since the day I was born, cursing every moment of my life." He scowls before washing the words down with a long swig of beer.

"Niklaas, don't you think you've—"

"Aurora knows what that's like." He sets his mug back on the table with a thunk. "She knows what it's like to live in the shadow of a monster, with the beast itself lurking around the corner, ready to pounce and rip her apart. *She* knows and *I* know and I think we'll . . . get along," he says, a hopeful note in his voice that makes my heart ache for him.

"Niklaas—"

"And maybe . . ." He swipes a hand across the back of his mouth. "Well . . . maybe together we'll prove that prophecies, and curses, and kings and queens with nothing but evil in their souls aren't as powerful as people helping each other. People tying their hearts and minds together and telling fate to go stuff itself."

I watch Niklaas drain his beer and think about what he said. He may be drunk, but he's also right. I *do* know what it's like to live in the shadow of a monster. I *do* know what it's like to long for a connection with someone who understands, someone who might help me prove that good people can win in the end, even if their enemies are bigger and stronger and better equipped in every way. But knowing Niklaas and I have more in common than I've already assumed only makes the reality of our situation harder to bear.

I try to remind myself that Niklaas would never be interested in a girl like me—a girl so plain she has no trouble passing as a boy, a girl who speaks her mind and fights for what she wants and doesn't need anyone, male or female, to protect her—but the arguments don't feel as convincing as they once did. Niklaas likes Ror. He could come to like Aurora, to care about her and laugh with her. And isn't caring and friendship what makes a marriage work, what makes you wake up years in the future and smile to see your friend's graying head on the pillow next to yours?

You'll never know. You will never know that sort of love. And if you do, all you will bring to your marriage bed are shadows and despair.

I squeeze my eyes shut. It's true. It doesn't matter if Niklaas could come to care for the real me. It doesn't matter that I'm beginning to feel something more than friendship for him. My mother's curse is all that matters, it's all that will *ever* matter.

"Aren't you going to say something?" Niklaas finally asks.

I open my eyes to find him staring intently into his glass, as if it is a crystal ball that might reveal his future. "I think my mother would have liked you," I say, knowing it's the least painful truth I can tell.

He looks up, his eyebrows lifted. "Really?"

"She believed what you believe. She thought people working together were the only hope for our world," I say, remembering the way she held my hands and explained to me how important it was for me to choose kindness whenever I could. "She said it was the love of everyday people that worked miracles."

"It's nice that you remember her. I can't remember a thing from when I was four. Or five . . ."

"My sister helps. She's always told me stories." I hate to

155

lie to him. I know it's only for one more night, but still . . . This doesn't feel like a moment for lies.

His brow wrinkles again. "I don't remember much of six, either, except for the time I fell asleep in the carpenter's shed and was locked in for the night. I was so afraid. I was certain the axes would come to life and cut my head off if I went back to sleep."

I smile. "You had quite an imagination."

"Still do, I suppose." He sighs and an unfamiliar lost look creeps into his eyes.

For the first time, he looks like the boy he is instead of the man he's about to be. I see fear in him, and worry, and how desperately he wants someone to help him banish them both. And for a moment, I wish I could be that person, that I could take him in my arms and kiss his furrowed forehead and tell him that everything will be all right.

"Am I imagining things again, Ror?" he asks. "Am I imagining that you and I might be brothers in more than spirit one day?"

Brothers. It confirms what I've been feeling since our third day on the road, that Niklaas and I could be more than good friends, that we could be family if we chose to be. With the exception of Jor, all of my family is chosen family, people I have no relation to by blood, but who I have chosen to love and let love me in return.

I could love Niklaas. But that's the problem. I could love Niklaas, but I could also *love* Niklaas. I already care too much to consider risking a kiss the way I did that evening by the hot spring. I'm too close to him now, and if I let myself, I could get even closer.

Dangerously close. At least for him.

"I'm sorry," I say, my throat tight and an unexpected stinging in my nose. "But we will never be anything more than good friends."

Niklaas brings his fist down on the table, making me jump and a feminine gasp escape my throat. Thankfully, he's too drunk and/or angry to notice. "I won't believe it," he says. "I won't believe it until she tells me to my face. To my face!"

"Niklaas—"

"You don't unner-stand," Niklaas says, his words beginning to slur. "She's my lass chance. I'll die without her."

"You won't die." I roll my eyes, his ridiculousness helping lighten the moment.

"I will. I'll die," he moans, burying his face in his hands. "Or as good as. And then I'll never get Haanah away from our father."

"You'll be fine, and you'll find a way to help your sister." I dig into my vest pocket and drop a few coins on the table before pushing my chair back. "Now let's get you to your room before you're too drunk to climb the stairs."

"You're mad." He glares at me beneath lids drooped to half-mast. "I can outdrink men twice my size. I'm not drunk."

"You're not sober, either." I take his arm. "Let's go."

"No. I want more potatoes," he says, jerking his arm free.

"If you eat more potatoes, you'll explode." I reclaim his arm and tug him out of his chair. He pulls away again, only to stumble into the empty table next to ours, sending one of the chairs tipping over.

"Uh-oh," he says, staring at the chair with wide eyes.

"Come on." I tuck myself close to his side and wrap my arm around his waist. "Lean on me. I'll help you."

"Maybe I *am* a little drunk," he says, dropping a heavy hand on my shoulder and allowing me to lead him toward the stairs.

"Maybe a little," I agree in a mild voice, grateful no one seems to be paying us any attention. But I'm sure young men stumble drunk from this room all the time. Half the boys in armor were tripping over their own feet by the time they left for the tournaments, making me hope none of them planned to fight in that condition.

"Sorry, Ror. Didn't mean to." Niklaas weaves slightly as we reach the first landing. "I never get drunk. *Never.* Iss the beer's fault. I'm strong, but that beer must be sssssstrooo-oooong."

"You are strong," I say, urging him up the last flight of stairs.

"I *am*," he says, sagging against me until I grunt beneath the added weight.

"I know. I'm agreeing with you." I half drag him down the hall, desperate to get him into his bed before he's unconscious. If he passes out in the hall, I'll never be able to carry him to his room.

"You say that like a joke," he says, "but it's not. I am very, *very* ssstroong."

I resist the urge to laugh, but just barely. "Yes, Niklaas. You're a massive, manly beast. Now where did you—" My words end in a squeal as Niklaas grabs me—one hand gripping the back of my neck, one clasped high on my thigh—and heaves me into the air above his head. I lift my hands to keep my face from smashing against the beams, but thankfully Niklaas's arms are too short to lift me all the way to the ceiling.

"See?" He lifts me up and down, up and down, as if I'm a log at a strongman contest.

"Put me down, this second!" I hiss, wary of drawing the attention of anyone already locked in their room. There are a dozen rooms along the hallway, and the innkeeper said all of them would be filled.

"And I could lift someone heavier." Niklaas spins in a circle so fast it's hard not to squeal again. "You're too light, Ror. Like a girl, all hollow inside."

"Girls are not hollow inside." I slap my hands behind my back, aiming in the general direction of his big, drunken head. "And you're going to be very, *very* dead if you don't. Put. Me. Down!"

"All right, don't get snappish," he says, setting me down so suddenly that the world spins and I grab onto the front of his shirt to steady myself.

Unfortunately for us both, at the moment Niklaas isn't the steadiest port in a storm. I tug at him and he staggers, and a moment later we hit the floor in a tangle of limbs—his elbow knocking my forehead, my knee slamming against his, and his heavy body pinning me to the ground beneath him.

"Ow!" he groans. "What you tackle me for?"

"I didn't tackle you." I grunt, shoving at his chest. "You fell over, you insufferable, drunk—"

"Don't start calling names." Niklaas brings his hand down on my chest as he tries to right himself, his fingers brushing against the bandages covered only by the thin linen of my shirt.

"Get off!" I snap, knocking his hand away.

He hums beneath his breath. "What's that? Are you—"

"Get off of me!" I push at his chest until my arms tremble, trying not to panic. I planned on telling him the truth tomorrow anyway, but I don't want him to find out I'm a girl like this, with his hands on me and his mouth perilously close to mine. In his drunken state, he might decide to kiss his newly female friend and doom himself to a fate worse than that death he's so worried about.

"All right, all right," he says, coming to his knees before rocking back to sit with his shoulders braced against the door of his room. He's breathing heavily by the time he's upright but not panting the way I am. "Whass wrong? You hurt?"

"I'm fine," I say, struggling to catch my breath as I scoot away from him.

"But your chest." He points at my stomach before closing one eye and adjusting the height of his finger. "I felt bandages."

"It's a fairy thing." I think fast, hoping he's too drunk to see through a lie. "We wrap our chests to keep our shoulders strong. When we . . . fight."

Niklaas frowns. "Never heard of that."

"There are a lot of things you've never heard of. You're only seventeen years old," I say, throwing his words from earlier back at him as I come to my feet. "If you want to make it to eighteen, you should start drinking less."

Niklaas's frown becomes a pout. "Serrsly, Ror. Haven't

been drunk since I was fifteen. Don't know what . . . It's . . . strange . . ." He yawns and his eyes begin to slide closed.

"No you don't," I say, shaking his arm. "No sleeping until you're in bed. Where's your key?" I pat his cheek. "Niklaas? Niklaas! Where is your key?" I give up patting and slap his cheek. Hard.

"Ow!" His eyes fly open. "You hit me!"

"You picked me up and then fell on me like a sack of bricks," I say, no longer in the frame of mind to be amused by his idiocy. "Now get up!"

"I didn't crush you, did I?" he asks as I haul him to his feet, worry replacing the outrage in his tone. "I'd feel turri-bull if I crushed you."

"No, you didn't crush me," I groan. Not yet, anyway, but he's getting heavier by the moment, and if he falls on me again . . .

"Thas good." He pats me on the head like a puppy before letting his arm go limp, jabbing me in the eye as his arm falls back to his side. "I don't want to crush you, Ror. You're a decent little bass-turd."

"Give me your key, Niklaas." I blink tears from my jabbed eye as I tighten my grip on his waist. "I need to get you into bed before you do one of us lasting damage."

"In my pocket," he says, fumbling at the front of his shirt.

I snatch the key from the pocket near his heart and slide it into the lock. The door falls inward and Niklaas and I stumble inside, half walking, half falling across the room to his bed, where I deposit him with an "oof" of relief.

I stretch my arms above my head to get the crick out of my spine before reaching for his feet.

"Thanks, Ror," he mumbles as I tug off his boots, his eyes already closing again. "See you in the mmmumm . . . ing. . . ."

"See you in the morning, you rager." I sigh as I heave his legs onto the bed.

I consider trying to take his pants off to make him more comfortable but decide that's better left alone. He's going to find out I'm not a boy tomorrow, and I don't want him knowing I've undressed him. He'll already know that I've seen things I shouldn't have that night at the spring. That night when he was standing in front of me as naked as the day he was born and I stared a little too long . . .

He's not nearly as attractive tonight, but I have to admit not even sloppy-drunk-and-snoring-like-a-moose completely disagrees with him.

"Pity you," I mutter, tugging the blanket up to his waist. "You should pity the women of the world. We're defenseless against you."

He lets loose with an especially long snore, making me giggle as I brush the hair from his eyes then tug at the strands that have found their way into his parted mouth. The moonlight through the window falls on his face, accentuating the hollow above his upper lip and the proud angles of his cheekbones. He looks more serious without his dimples but younger, too, no longer a golden god but a boy standing at the gates of the Land Beyond, staring into the blue light from which no human has ever returned, wondering what awaits him on the other side.

"Whatever it is, you won't find out for years and years to come," I whisper, tracing the line of his jaw.

I don't know what has made Niklaas so certain his death is close—his father or some other monster—but I wish he could see himself the way I do. He isn't just a prince, he's a hero, the sort of person even death is hesitant to approach without a nod.

"You will live, and you will change your fate." I should pull my hand away, but I let my fingers brush across his lips instead. "I will help you, if you'll let me."

Niklaas mumbles in his sleep, and I take a guilty step back. We've slept on the same bedroll for a week, but I've never felt like I was invading his privacy the way I do now. I shouldn't be touching him. I haven't earned the right, and I never will.

With one last check of the room—making sure the window is locked and a glass of water placed by Niklaas's bed for when he wakes up with a mouth full of cotton—I let myself out, taking his key and locking the door behind me, figuring I'll be up before he is and he's better off locked in.

Outside in the hall, I place my palm against the door, wishing I hadn't asked for two rooms, wishing I didn't feel so reluctant to crawl into bed alone, without Niklaas's back pressed to mine and his irritating sleep sounds waking me in the night.

Sad to miss a night of snoring. I *must* be losing my mind.

With a sigh, I tuck Niklaas's key into one pocket and pluck my own from the other.

"Surely you're not going to bed already." The voice—and the low growl that follows it—comes from not ten hands behind me, making me jump and reach for my staff, cursing myself for letting my guard down for a moment.

CHAPTER FOURTEEN

AURORA

I spin to find a girl in a red cloak leaning against my door. A shaggy white dog big enough to ride crouches beside her. The creature's blue eyes narrow and its growl turns even more menacing as I point my staff at its lady.

"It's all right, Hund." The girl runs her fingers idly back and forth along the beast's back. "This boy won't hurt us."

"I wouldn't be so sure," I say, tightening my grip on my staff.

"Easy, now. We only want to be friends." She tosses her head, sending curls the color of hot chocolate tumbling around her shoulders.

Her dark eyes consider me with a hungry look, while lips stained a deep red push into a pout every bit as seductive as Niklaas's. She is his feminine counterpart, a girl so striking it's impossible to believe she's a mere mortal. She would turn heads dressed in an oat sack, but in her red cloak and tight black dress—displaying what I, for one, consider an aggressive amount of cleavage—with the scarlet leather belt at her waist, she might as well be parading around with a court trumpeter by her side.

"You'll want to hear what I have to say." She brings a hand to her hip, emphasizing her curves, drawing my attention to the small axe hanging from the leather at her waist. It's an unusual choice of weapon but a dangerous one, assuming she knows how to throw it. "I have a proposition for you."

A proposition, eh? I lift my eyes from the axe. This girl must have been sent by one of the madams, a treat to tempt the handsome boy on the white horse.

I'm suddenly very glad Niklaas decided to drink too much. I wouldn't want to see the way he'd look at this girl. I'd enjoy seeing him pull her into his room even less.

"I'm sorry," I say, trying to sound it. "But I'm not interested, and my friend is too drunk to . . . um . . . perform."

"Perform?" Her eyebrow lifts.

"Yes," I say, blushing despite myself. I've heard about prostitutes and seen them at the mercenary camp, but I've never spoken with one. I'm finding it more awkward than I would have thought.

What must it be like? To sell something so sacred? To have men look you over like a menu at a tavern and decide whether or not to . . . consume you?

"You're . . . you're beautiful. Really." My blush becomes a burning in my cheeks. "But we don't have money to waste on . . . companions."

"Companions . . ." Her brow smoothes. "Oh my!" She throws her head back and laughs, displaying her flawless white throat before ducking her chin and tossing her hair.

Her mane is like a luxurious fur, so glossy and thick and soft-looking that it begs to be touched. Even *I* wouldn't mind twirling it around my finger, and I couldn't be further from her usual customer. She must do quite well with real boys.

"I see." She presses two fingers to her lips in a gesture that does nothing to conceal her delighted smile. "You think I'm a whore. How sweet."

I blink. I wouldn't call someone who had confused me for a whore "sweet," but to each her own.

I grip my staff, on guard once more. "If you're not a whore, then who are you? And why are you standing in front of my room?"

"I just want to talk," she says, ambling down the hall.

The dog makes to follow her, but she stops him with a pointed finger and a sharp command in a language I don't recognize. I've studied the major languages of Mataquin, but I can't recall anything that sounds so guttural. She must be from the extreme north, even farther north than the man I fought today.

A wave of uneasiness passes through me. Beyond the countries of Herth, on the far side of the Gefroren Mountains, mountains so tall the bodies of ancient giants are said to be buried beneath them, lies the last refuge of human witches, men and women born with magic in their blood instead of borrowed from the Fey or bartered from dark spirits, like the fate reader at the New Market.

Centuries ago, human witches were hunted by the ogres,

who gained a portion of the witches' magic when they consumed their flesh. The ogres, craving more power, eventually turned their efforts toward stealing magic from the Fey, but not before they decimated the witches' numbers and drove the few remaining men and women into hiding. The last of their people are a fiercely secretive and vengeful tribe, who only venture from their arctic home to kidnap children and pillage the harvests of Herth's farmers. They can clear an orchard in a night, leaving behind only a few crystal-filled stones most farmers are too terrified to touch, let alone sell for profit.

I wouldn't be surprised to learn this girl is a witch. There is something . . . not right about her. She wears her beauty like a costume, something false she could shed at a moment's notice. It isn't a part of her, it's a tool, a weapon every bit as dangerous as the axe at her waist.

"Don't come any closer," I warn.

"Don't be afraid." She keeps walking, hips swaying. "I want to be your friend, little prince."

"How do you know me?" I ask. "Who are you? Tell me or I'll put you down."

"Threatening a woman?" The girl lifts her hands in the air, but she doesn't seem frightened and doesn't pause until I stop her with the end of my staff against her chest. Her dog growls, but the girl silences him with another guttural command.

"This is no way to behave," she says, turning back to me with wounded eyes. "You'll have me trembling all over in another moment."

"I've asked you once," I say in a humorless tone. "I'll ask

once more, and then I'll knock you unconscious. Who are you, and how do you know me?"

Her eyes widen further, but she looks more excited than frightened. "I'm with the exiles. I heard you were looking for a guide to the Feeding Hills."

The guide. Niklaas did say he had put a word in with a friend.

"If that isn't true, I'll be on my way," the girl says, drawing my attention back to her pouted mouth. "There's no need to threaten me with your . . . weapon." She reaches up, running her hand up and down my staff in a way that leaves me feeling vaguely ill.

I pull it out of her reach. "We *are* looking for a guide," I say, mentally cursing Niklaas. Couldn't he have found someone else? Someone less . . . busty?

"Then I am at your service. My name is Crimsin," she says, sidling closer.

"Jor," I say, withholding my nickname. I don't want this girl getting hold of any intimate part of me. Or Niklaas.

"That's what I thought." Crimsin smiles. "So what do you think, Prince Jor? Should we adjourn to your room for a chat? See if we can't work out an arrangement?"

She reaches for my warrior's knot, but I stop her with a hand around her wrist. She's not much taller than I am, but she's thicker. My fingers barely wrap around her arm.

"Tough, aren't you?" Crimsin asks. "How old are you? Twelve? Thirteen?"

"Fourteen," I say through gritted teeth, not liking the look in her eye.

"Fourteen." Her eyebrows lift. "Then you know what to do with yourself, don't you?" Before I can move away, her free hand darts out, quick as a snake slithering out of the grass, to grab the front of my britches.

I knock her arm away and take a step back, suitably shocked at having been fondled by a stranger. She takes a mirror step back, apparently equally shocked not to have found what she was looking for in my pants.

"I'm so sorry," she breathes, the huskiness vanished from her tone. "I didn't know—the messenger said . . ." She takes another step back. "Princess?"

"I'll answer questions when I have answers," I say, though I have to admit to feeling less threatened now that she's not trying to seduce me. "Shall we go to my room?"

"Ye-yes. That would be best." She takes a long look down the hall. "I don't like to be seen with the travelers who hire me, and I especially don't want to be seen with a Norvere royal. There was an ogre battalion in the city center yesterday. They've promised to kill anyone who even *thinks* about helping the lost prince reach the Kingdom in the Hills. I'm sure they'd be equally eager to capture the lost princess."

Ekeeta knows no one will be helping the "lost prince," but this must mean she's still keeping the identity of her prisoner quiet, which is good. I'll have the chance to meet the exiles as Ror instead of Aurora and get a feel for them before revealing myself.

Assuming I can convince this girl to keep quiet about her discovery . . .

"Thank you for risking your safety to come here," I say,

deciding it's not too soon to attempt to win her friendship and hopefully her cooperation. I start down the hall toward my room but hesitate as I near her animal.

"Don't worry, Hund's harmless." She snaps her fingers, signaling for the dog to stand behind her as I unlock the door. "At least so long as I want him to be."

I glance over my shoulder, debating whether to allow the dog inside. I know I can handle myself against Crimsin, but I'm not accustomed to fighting animals.

"Honestly, Princess, you have nothing to fear from me or Hund or the other exiles," she says, reading my expression with uncanny accuracy. "We are your only friends on this side of the kingdom."

She moves into the room, motioning for the dog to lie down by the fire, which Hund does, rolling onto his side and resting his massive head on his paws. "Any other person in this city would sell you to the ogres in a heartbeat," she continues. "Your bounty makes the purses at the blood tournaments look like a night's drinking money."

"You said the ogres threatened to kill anyone who helped me reach the exiles." I lock the door and lean my staff against the wall. "How do they know where I'm bound?"

"Where else would you be bound? To raise an army to take back your sister's crown? Or *your* crown, rather." She rolls her eyes as she flops down onto the floor by her beast, seeming so much younger now that she's moving like a girl and not a seductress. "I'm so embarrassed. I was sure I was going to bed a prince tonight. What you must think."

"My brother really *is* only fourteen. Isn't that a bit young?" I ask, raising a brow.

Her shoulder lifts. "I'm only five years older, and a prince who would take me with him when he heads off to war isn't a prince I'd let slip away."

"You're so eager to go to war?"

"I'm eager to live in the capital," she says with a crooked grin. "To live anywhere but the outer reaches of the land that time forgot. It is dreadfully boring up there, Princess. I'm sure our young men will knock each other over in their rush to sign up to fight. Anything to escape the damned hills."

"I don't have money to pay now," I say, a part of me refusing to believe this will be so easy. "But I'll have a small fortune for anyone who helps—"

"The counselors won't want your fortune, Princess, and I'll settle for an introduction to your brother." She wiggles her eyebrows as she scratches Hund's neck.

I snort. "You'd scare him half to death."

She cocks her head. "You think?"

"I *know*." My poor brother would turn twelve shades of red and hide in the privy for a week if a girl grabbed him between the legs. Before he was captured at the beginning of the summer, we used to chat nearly every day via the enchanted waters behind Janin's cot. He'd only just begun to talk of a fairy girl who'd caught his eye, let alone pursue her, or be ready for *her* to pursue *him*.

"I've never had a boy turn me down. At least, not a real boy." She laughs as she looks me over from head to toe. "I can't believe I was fooled. You even stand like a girl. You should spread your legs more, pretend you've got something between them interfering with your ability to get through life without making an ass of yourself."

I return her smile. "I do, when there are people to fool. But you know my secret."

She rolls her eyes again. "I do, and again, I'm sorry. I hope you won't tell the counselors. They'd have my hand cut off."

"Of course not," I say, seeing my chance to win a promise of my own. "And I hope you will keep my secret. I would prefer to meet your counselors as a prince. Sometimes it's easier to get a straight answer as a boy."

"I believe that," Crimsin says with a sigh. "I'm lucky to get crooked answers, and those I have to tickle out while men are staring at my chest."

"Then you won't tell your leaders the truth?"

"I am your subject, Princess. I will do as you command. You'll see the rest of my people are the same," she says, a warmth in her voice that makes me want to believe her, to relax and let relief flood through me, but I can't. Even if Crimsin is right, this is only a single step forward. There are still fields to go to free Jor. And after that . . .

I haven't allowed myself to think beyond making sure my brother is safe, but I know Jor and I can't slip back into hiding for the rest of our lives. My subjects are suffering under Ekeeta's rule—half their crops are seized for taxes, and their loved ones sentenced to feed the ogres' hunger for the slightest crimes. I owe it to them to fight for my throne. Even if I rescue Jor and we escape to Malai, sooner or later we will have to raise another army and fight. But at least we will be able to fight side by side and die with a weapon in our hands and our souls our own.

"But I would suggest we leave soon." Crimsin bounces back to her feet. "It will be easier to get out of the city unnoticed in the dark. I'll send Hund ahead with a message for the counselors to expect us."

"I can't leave tonight." I silently curse Niklaas for drinking himself into uselessness. "My companion really is drunk. I doubt I could keep him *awake* for longer than a few minutes, let alone mounted on his horse."

"Then we leave without him. You can write him a note saying goodbye." She crosses to the bedside table, pulling parchment and a stick of charcoal from the pocket of her cloak as she goes. "I'll rip my paper, and you can have half. It's better if my message is brief. Easier to fit inside the hole in Hund's collar."

"I can't," I say, though for a moment I'm tempted.

How much easier would it be to leave without saying goodbye? Without having to see Niklaas's face once he learns I've deceived him?

But we've made a deal, and Janin raised me never to give my word lightly. A broken promise breaks something inside of you, leaving less of you than there was before. Besides, I have a feeling Niklaas would hunt me down if I left without honoring my half of the bargain. He is insanely determined to meet my "sister."

"Don't tell me the Kanvasola prince can't read," Crimsin says, her attention focused on scratching out her message. "I've heard he's a pretty, lazy thing, but really . . ."

"He can read," I say. "But I made a promise. If I leave without him, I won't be able to honor it."

"But we're women," Crimsin says with a conspiratorial grin. "According to men, we have no honor. We can't really be expected to keep *all* our promises."

173

"I can't do that," I say, uncomfortable with her suggestion. "I honor my promises, and I hope you will honor yours. Can I trust you, Crimsin?"

Crimsin stands, the smile vanishing from her face. "Of course you can, Princess. I would never break a promise to a woman, especially you. And I respect that you have an honorable heart, but it really is best if we leave tonight. Who knows if the passage into the mountains will still be unguarded come tomorrow?"

She crosses back to her dog and crouches to slip her rolled note into his collar. "The queen hunts for you and your brother, and there are others who hunt for the Kanvasol prince. It's dangerous for you to remain his traveling companion."

"Who's hunting Niklaas?"

"His father, of course," Crimsin says. "The prince is about to turn eighteen, and that isn't allowed in Kanvasola."

"What do you mean? How do you forbid someone from having a birthday?"

I haven't spent much time studying Kanvasol law—Janin assured me my hours were better spent studying the Herth customs—but surely not even a king who believes he's eaten enough infant whales to become immortal can be *that* mad.

"Eighteen is the age it is legal for a son to inherit the Kanvasol throne." Crimsin fetches the pitcher on the washbasin and sloshes water into the bowl meant for washing up before putting it on the floor for the dog. "And so, not one of King Eldorio's sons has ever lived past his eighteenth birthday."

"You mean . . ."

She nods and mimes shoving a knife into her own gut. Mine twists in response.

So that is the beast lurking in wait for Niklaas. Suddenly his fear of an early death, and his refusal to speak of what happened to his brothers, makes terrible sense.

"That is . . ." I shake my head, at a loss for words.

"Wicked?" Crimsin supplies.

"Unbelievably wicked," I say, my heart breaking for Niklaas. What must it be like to grow up knowing your father intends to kill you before you become a man? To see your brothers slain, one by one, while every year you grow closer to sharing their fate?

"How does the king get away with it?" Loathing rises inside me, making me certain I could come to hate Niklaas's father as much as I hate Ekeeta. "Surely his advisers and his people don't—"

"His advisers are snakes, and his people are afraid, like we in Norvere are afraid," she says, stroking Hund's head as he laps water from the bowl. "But from what I hear, the king is careful not to make what he's done too obvious. His sons' bodies are never discovered, but everyone knows when a prince's bed is found empty on the morning of his eighteenth year that it will never be slept in again."

I imagine Niklaas, his throat cut in his sleep and his body dumped into some Kanvasol sea, and shiver. Silently I vow not to let him out of my sight until I can be sure he is safe from the monster who sired him.

"That's all the more reason for him to stay with me," I say. "I won't leave him behind. We'll have to wait until morning."

Crimsin sighs and her dark eyes flash with irritation. "Please, think this through. The ogres won't follow us into the hills, but King Eldorio's men have no fear of the Feeding Trees. If they find out the prince has left Goreman in our company, they will follow us and punish my people for sheltering their fugitive."

"But your camp is well hidden, isn't it?"

"It is, but—"

"And none of the other guides would lead King Eldorio's men to your location."

"There are no other guides in Goreman. They left two days ago, when the ogres arrived. I'm the only one who'd rather risk a run-in with ogres than crawl back into the wretched mountains to hide," she says with no small amount of pride.

She's either brave or stupid, or a combination of both, which is probably the most dangerous, but unfortunately she's also my last chance at securing a guide.

"Then we won't have to worry about the king's men being led to your settlement," I say, "and surely you have defenses in place to protect your people if by some miracle Eldorio's men find it on their own."

Crimsin wrinkles her nose. "Yes, but the counselors won't protect a Kanvasol prince. They'll hand him over if it will send the king's men away."

"But he's an innocent. How could they—"

"We were all innocent once, but the ogre queen stole our innocence. The counselors won't weaken our position when we're so close to overthrowing her. They will kill the prince themselves first." She crosses her arms and shoots me a hard look. "We are loyal to you and your brother, Princess. That boy means nothing to us."

"He means something to me." I meet her hard look with one of my own.

She lifts one perfectly arched brow. "Well, now . . . it's like that, is it? I suppose you'll be making us a batch of royal babies before too long, then?"

I roll my eyes as if the idea is absurd and hope my performance is enough to convince her. "He's a friend and an ally, nothing more."

"Right." Crimsin's lips curve. "That's why you were mooning about outside his door."

"I'm worried about him. That's all."

"Of course." Crimsin nods in an exaggerated fashion.

"Truly, we're just friends," I say, though I'm starting to sound absurdly defensive. "He doesn't even know I'm a girl."

Crimsin wryly lifts a brow. "So he doesn't know you've got a tender spot for him."

I roll my eyes again but know better than to keep arguing. Anything I say will only make things worse. "Tender spot or no, I'm not leaving without him." I pull off my boots and stretch out on the bed, hoping she'll understand that's the end of it. "You're welcome to stay here tonight if you'd like."

"You want to sleep?" she asks. "It's not even ten o'clock."

"We might as well. That way we'll be ready to leave early in the morning."

Crimsin sighs and runs a hand through her hair. "Very well, but I'm going down to the tavern. We won't be leaving early. We'll be lucky to get the prince up and about by noon. I put enough Vale Flower seeds in his last beer to put a stallion to sleep for a week."

I bolt into a seated position. "You *drugged* him?"

Crimsin shrugs. "I paid the innkeeper's wife to drug him. I knew it would be easier if he was asleep when we left." She snorts again. "He's a massive thing, isn't he? But not as handsome as the stories would have a girl believe. I was expecting a god with lightning shooting from his fingertips the way the whores talked about him."

I drop my legs to the floor, hands shaking as I squirm my feet into my boots.

"Decided to come for a drink?" Crimsin asks.

"I'm going to check on Niklaas," I say, barely concealing my anger. I need this girl, but right now I want to ball up my fist and punch her in her lying, drugging mouth.

"He's fine." She waves a breezy hand in the air. "He'll sleep like the dead but—"

"Unless the seeds make him sick," I say, a harsh note creeping into my voice. "If he gets sick while he's unconscious, he could choke to death."

I pluck my key from my vest pocket and throw it across the room. It lands near Hund's paws, summoning a growl from the creature that I answer with a glare. Let the beast come for me. It would feel good to fight something other than my own rising panic.

"I'll stay with him tonight," I say, transferring my attention to Crimsin when the dog lowers his head, evidently deciding he doesn't want to bite a chunk out of me after all. "You can sleep here. I'll fetch you when Niklaas is fit to travel."

"Princess, please." Crimsin hurries across the room,

laying her hand on the door before I can open it. "I wasn't thinking. I never meant to put your friend in danger. I'll keep watch over him. You stay. You're fresh from a long journey and need your rest."

I freeze, hairs on my arms prickling. "How do you know I'm fresh from a journey?" I turn, fingers tightening on my staff. "I could have been at this inn for days."

Crimsin's eyes dart to the left before sliding back to my face. I know she's going to lie before she opens her mouth.

"I don't *know*," she says, her gaze carefully blank. "I only assumed. Have you been here for days?"

I look up at her, but not too far up. She is, as Niklaas would say, a "wee thing" like me, a hand shorter than the average woman, soft and feminine-looking and so beautiful I'm certain she's accustomed to people thinking she's equally harmless, but I won't make that mistake. This girl isn't harmless. She's unpredictable and dangerous and not someone I'm inclined to trust. I will be sleeping with my weapon in my fist for as long as Crimsin is a part of our company.

"I want to believe you're not a liar," I say. "But I don't."

She looks up with a startled expression before dropping her eyes back to the floor. "That's . . . honest of you."

"I am honest when I can be and kind as long as I am allowed to be. Niklaas and I need you to guide us into the mountains, but if you betray us . . ." I pause, waiting for her to look up before I reach for the door again. "Sleep well."

"And you, Princess," she murmurs, her sober tone leaving no doubt she understands that if she betrays me, things won't go well for her. "Tell the prince I'm sorry when he wakes up."

I slip out the door and down the hall, hurrying to Niklaas's door, my pulse leaping with worry, but I know he's alive before I let myself into his room.

Even from the hall, I can hear him snoring.

I close the door behind me and lock up before padding over to where Niklaas lies sprawled as I left him. I watch him snuffle, unreasonably happy to be facing a night filled with his dreadful racket, before helping myself to his rosemary and mint ash, shedding my boots, and placing my staff within easy reach of the bed. Then, with a muffled groan, I roll Niklaas onto his side and lie down beside him.

His snores remain long and deep throughout the entire process. He really is dead to the world. I should have realized this was more than a case of having a few too many. I should have trusted him to know better than to drink too much.

"I'm sorry," I whisper, wedging my back more firmly against his to keep him from rolling over in his sleep. "I should have listened to you."

Niklaas doesn't say a word, of course, but the heat of his body is soothing all the same. After only a few moments, sleep creeps into my limbs, relaxing my shoulders, and I know I will pass a better night here than I would have in my own room. I've become accustomed to Niklaas. Even in sleep, he comforts me, making me feel calmer and safer than I do when I'm alone.

"I will keep you safe, too," I say, my whisper becoming a yawn. "I won't let anyone hurt you."

I won't. I will protect Niklaas the way he's protected me, but to do so I must keep him by my side. I can't risk telling him the truth. He must go on believing I'm a prince leading him to his princess for as long as it takes to make sure he is beyond his father's reach.

A quiet voice inside me whispers that I should feel terrible about continuing to lie to him, but the rest of me is relieved to have an excuse not to confess. I'm not ready to lose my friend. I need him too much, and he needs me.

I close my eyes and drift, prepared for the fears that come to torment me in my sleep, but tonight I don't dream of the crumbling castle or my brother's screams. I dream of a picnic in the meadow behind Mother's old house, of a blanket beneath the trees and honeysuckle thick in the air. I wear my white fairy dress with the silk flowers at the neck, and Niklaas is asleep with his head in my lap, while our friends play wickets in the meadow beyond.

It is the most beautiful dream. I fight to hold on to it, to stay asleep even as the birds begin to sing and sunlight warms the bed. I fight until I hear Niklaas moan and the day begins with a hellish smell and the splatter of sickness.

CHAPTER FIFTEEN

NIKLAAS

Despite my aching head and foul-tempered stomach, I manage to pack my things and drag my wretched body out of the inn by ten o'clock. Ror, our new guide, and I reach the gates at Goreman's northern edge an hour later.

Two ogres with soul tattoos etched onto their gleaming bald heads guard the gate, but Crimsin—in her second skin of a dress, minus the red cloak that would give her away as an exile—distracts them while Ror, the horses, and I slip out of the city along with a group of lumber wagons bound for the lower forests.

Ogre men are as susceptible to feminine charms as their human counterparts, and Crimsin certainly isn't lacking in "charms." If she hadn't drugged me into the worst bout of sickness I've experienced since the night Usio and I ate bad oysters off the coast of northern Kanvasola, I'm sure I'd have a hard time keeping my eyes off her bosom.

At the moment, however, I'm having a hard time resisting the urge to wring her pretty white neck.

As Ror and I guide the horses into the trees beyond the city, another wave of sickness grips my midsection. I force it down with only the softest moan, but Ror seems to have especially keen ears this morning.

"Try to make it a little farther," Ror says, fussing over me like he's done all morning. "Let's get up the mountain. Then we'll stop and you can have more water while we wait for Crimsin to catch up."

"I don't want more water," I say, forcing the words out through a clenched jaw.

"You need to keep drinking," he says. "If you don't, you'll never work the poison through. I could find some wild mint to calm your stomach if you think—"

"Quit fussing. I'm fine."

"You're not fine. You've been—"

"Leave me be, Ror," I warn, voice rough from all the retching I've done since sunup.

Blasted poison, blasted girl. If Crimsin weren't the last guide in Goreman, I swear to the gods I would have kicked her out of the inn with a boot in her shapely backside.

"I will not leave you be." Ror pulls at Button's reins, stopping the horse in the shade of two young Feeding Trees. "If you're not able to keep water down, we shouldn't have left the inn. It's not safe to be—"

"I'll drink the raging water! But only if you'll shut your flap for ten minutes at a time!" I snatch the waterskin from my saddle and tear off the cap, chugging as much as my miserable stomach can hold before plugging it with a glare in

183

Ror's direction. "I don't know what's worse. The sickness or your damned mother-henning."

Ror's eyes tighten in an expression so wounded I immediately feel even worse.

I sigh, running a trembling hand across my mouth, hating how weak I feel. "I'm sorry. I'm not myself. Thank you . . . for fussing, and for not leaving me behind."

"Of course I wouldn't leave you," Ror says, guiding Button closer. "I told you this morning, Niklaas. I want to help you. I want to keep you safe."

I grimace as my guts clench. My stomach quivers beneath my ribs, debating whether or not to send the water back the way it came. I hate feeling ill, but I hate Ror knowing the truth—even if it's only a shadow of the truth—even more.

Apparently, people on this side of Norvere believe that my father murders his sons and that he's sent assassins to Goreman to seek me out before my eighteenth birthday. That's the story Crimsin told Ror, anyway, and the reason the guide gave for feeling it necessary to drug me and leave me to sleep off the poison while she led Ror to the exiles.

Perhaps the story is true. Perhaps my father does intend to kill me for the crime of attempting to change my fate. I don't know how he would have learned of my quest or my new hope—Haanah is the only one who knows I found the witch who cursed our family, and she would never say a word—but he has his spies, as Ekeeta has hers. They may not be numerous, but they are clever and loyal and desperate to please their king, lest they end up dead like the men who have failed King Eldorio before them.

"I consider you a friend," Ror says, hurt still clear in his tone. "I would never leave a friend in danger. Deal or no deal."

"I consider you a friend, too." I lay a hand on his back. "And I *am* sorry. You're like a brother to me, runt, I told you that last night."

"You remember that?" Ror asks.

"I do, though I admit everything after climbing the stairs is a blur. I have a vague recollection of lifting you over my head . . . but I'm hoping that was a dream."

Ror grins. "No. Not a dream. But I—"

"Aren't you two delightful?" Crimsin's voice drifts through the trees, making my shoulder muscles bunch and my head ache. I pull my hand from Ror's back to rub the tops of my eyes. "Is there anything sweeter than two boys in love?"

"We're friends," Ror snaps, shooting Crimsin a look I don't understand. I get the feeling something uncomfortable happened between the pair of them last night, though Ror insists they only spoke briefly before he came to watch over me in my sleep.

"Forgive me, *Prince,* I was only teasing." Crimsin's lips push into a pretty pout.

She's the most beautiful thing I've seen in years, but I don't feel the slightest pull toward her, and not simply because she drugged me. There's something false about Crimsin, something secretive in the way of water with sharp rocks lurking beneath the surface that makes me wish we'd been able to hire anyone else but this girl.

"Now, what do Your Royal Highnesses think?" Crimsin stops between the horses and tilts her head up, providing a scandalous view down the front of her dress. "Should I ride

185

with Ror or with you, Niklaas?" she asks, hand coming to rest on my knee.

"You'll ride with me," Ror says, anger simmering in his words. "My horse is larger, and Niklaas still doesn't feel well."

"Maybe I could help him feel better." Crimsin leans into my leg, pressing her body against my thigh. For a split second, I consider retching down onto her soft, shining hair, but decide the pain of being sick again isn't worth the petty revenge.

"Ror seems better able to tolerate you," I say, nudging Alama forward with my heels, pretending not to notice when Crimsin has to scramble out of the way to avoid being stepped on.

"Charming," Crimsin says as Ror swings her onto the saddle behind him. "No wonder you were without a woman to warm your bed last night, Prince Niklaas."

I turn to tell the girl to keep her mouth shut unless she has something guide-worthy to say, when I see them—six sea-foam-colored Kanvasol horses surging through the gates of the city below, each one mounted by a knight wearing the blue coat of arms of my father's innermost circle. They're still a field away, but there's no doubt the men have spotted us amidst the trees. They draw their swords as they spur their mounts forward, flashing steel promising a swift death to the last human prince of Kanvasola.

It seems Crimsin was right, and I a fool for setting foot outside the inn while too weak to defend myself.

"Go, ride ahead with Niklaas!" Ror slides to the ground,

giving Button a swat on the behind. The horse leaps forward, making Crimsin squeal and clutch at the reins.

"No!" Crimsin pulls the horse to a stop, the playful lilt vanishing from her voice. "You can't fight them alone. They'll kill you, and I—"

"There's no time!" Ror slaps the horse again, harder, sending Button dashing off through the woods.

Ror turns to me. "Follow her. I'll find you later. You're not fit to fight."

"No, I won't—"

"Go!" Ror shouts. "You'll only distract me if you stay. I can take them. Go! Run!"

I reach for my sword—I don't care what he says, I'm not leaving Ror alone against six armed men—but before I can draw my weapon, Ror whacks Alama on the rump and she bolts with a squeal, leaping after Button.

I haul at the reins, but by the time I regain control and turn Alama around, Ror has already knocked three of the men from their horses and is using his staff to leverage his body into the air to avoid being trampled by the animals pressing in behind. I dig my heels into Alama's sides and barrel down the mountain, heart racing as a sword swings within inches of Ror's head, close enough to make his warrior's knot bob as he kneels to swipe his staff in a wide arc, tripping a fourth horse and sending the man atop it sailing from his saddle.

My swift pulse clears my head, and by the time I meet the last mounted man, my arm is strong. Our blades collide with a dull clang, a sound made familiar by days spent training with Father's men. It makes me wonder if this knight was one of my teachers, or one of the boys who trained beside me. His armor conceals his face, but there's a chance I know him, that the blood I'll spill is the blood of a former friend.

The thought should make me hesitate, but it doesn't. I have to get to Ror, I have to save his life before he dies trying to save mine.

I see a weakness in my opponent's defense and seize upon it, sliding my sword into the unarmored place beneath his armpit, sending a rush of red spilling onto his blue surcoat. He drops his weapon; I lift my foot from the stirrup and kick him in the chest, sending him sliding off his horse with a strangled cry. I hesitate long enough to make sure he won't be getting up to fight before urging Alama farther down the hill to where Ror is, miraculously, finishing off his final opponent.

Three men lie unconscious on the ground while Ror bats at the last man, knocking his armor from his head before finding the same vulnerable place I found with my sword and shoving his staff inside hard enough to make the knight cry out as he drops his sword. After that, it's only a matter of seconds before Ror sends the man crumpling to the ground with a sharp rap of his staff upside the unfortunate bastard's skull.

He watches the man fall and spins my way, only relaxing a fraction when he sees I'm not the enemy.

"Are you all right? Where's the other one?" He races up the hill so swiftly Alama dances nervously to the side. "There were six. I took four and you took the fifth, but—"

He's interrupted by a scream, a terrified cry that makes me feel something besides contempt for Crimsin for the first time since we were introduced over a chamber pot filled with my vomit.

I reach a hand down and pull Ror into the saddle behind me. Alama moves quickly up the mountain, not seeming to suffer from the addition of Ror's weight, but by the time we reach Crimsin, I fear we're too late. The sixth man has her on her back, a blade pressed to her throat.

I move to dismount before Alama comes to a stop, but Ror is even faster. He leaps from the saddle, landing with a hop that sends him into a front roll and back to his feet without breaking speed. He knocks Crimsin's attacker to the ground before the man can turn to see who's behind him, and a few blows later my father's final assassin falls to the dirt with a miserable groan.

Only when the man is unconscious does Ror drop his staff and reach for Crimsin. "Are you hurt?"

"I'm all right." Her words end in a sob as she clutches Ror tight. "Thank you."

"You don't have to thank me," Ror says, smoothing the girl's hair from her face.

"No, I do. I couldn't get to my axe and he . . ." She swipes at the tears on her cheeks with a fist. "You risked your life for me."

Ror takes her hands in his. "You're one of my people. It's my duty to defend you."

The girl blinks. "You really believe that?"

"What's the point of having a ruler if he or she doesn't protect the people?" Ror asks. "I know that's not the way it's been since Ekeeta took control, but—"

"That's not the way it was before, either."

"What do you mean?" Ror asks, a wary note in his tone.

Crimsin bites her lip, hesitating a moment before she whispers, "I had an older sister. Fifteen years older." She swipes at her damp cheeks again. "Gernin was . . . perfect. Beautiful and kind and always helping people. We thought she'd take over as the healer for our village one day, but then, the king came . . . and took my sister away."

"The king?" Ror gives a small shake of his head.

"Your father." Crimsin watches Ror, a cautious expression on her face. "He tried to win her at first, giving her silks and promising gold for her family if she would become his third wife, but it's not the way of our people to have more than one wife and Gernin didn't love him. She told him no." Crimsin's eyes shine, but when she speaks again her voice is flat, emotionless. "His men came to our house that night and stole her away. I never saw her alive again."

"You're . . . That's the truth?" Ror squeezes Crimsin's hands. "You swear it?"

"I swear it on my eternal soul," Crimsin says with enough conviction that even *I* believe her. "The king took Gernin, and a few months later . . . she was dead."

Ror is quiet for a moment before he says, "I'm sorry."

Crimsin's lips part. "You believe me?"

"I do. My mother suspected . . ." Ror lets Crimsin's hands slip through his fingers. "Mother didn't know my father was already married until after I was born. Father kept her hidden in the woods for years. She still loved him after she found out the truth, but she hated him, too. I know she longed for another life."

Crimsin curses softly. "I didn't know."

"No one did. Mother didn't want people to feel sorry for her, or her children." Ror cocks his head. "Are you sure your sister is dead? Is there a chance my father could have hidden her away as well?"

"No." Crimsin rubs her eyes. "They found her body by the road a week after the king was murdered. No one knew what had happened. After . . . Mother was never the same. She sold everything we had to pay the king's treasurer to take me with him when his family fled Mercar. She had nothing left. She died the next spring."

"I wish I could take back what my father did to your family," Ror says. "I wish I could make things better for you."

"You already have." This time, the passion in Crimsin's voice has nothing to do with seduction. "I believe now that you will be a different sort of ruler. That's why I can't—"

A howl sounds from higher up the hillside, seeming to emerge from the guts of the mountain itself.

"Hund," Crimsin mutters as she struggles to stand, a fearful look in her eyes. "He shouldn't be here. The settlement is hours away."

"What's wrong?" I ask, clutching my sword as I urge Alama over to where Ror is springing to his feet beside Crimsin, deciding it's time the pair of them remember I'm still here.

"They must have sent an escort." Crimsin shakes her hands in obvious panic before turning to Ror and grabbing him by the shoulders. "You have to run. Now!"

"What?" Ror asks. "But we—"

"Please." Crimsin takes Ror's hand and pulls him toward where Button is grazing. "Go northwest into Frysk, to the village of Beschuttz. It's a hidden place, but I'll send Hund with word to expect you. My mother's sister, Gettel, watches over a valley there. She's a powerful healer and magic-worker. She'll keep you safe."

"But what about the boy's army?" I demand. "We haven't come all this way to—"

"Please! You must leave these woods!" Crimsin turns to me, desperation written plainly on her face. "It isn't safe for Ror here."

"Come with us, then," Ror says, vaulting into his saddle.

Before Crimsin can answer—or I caution Ror to think this through—the mountainside opens as if by magic, and mounted men in red exile cloaks spill from between two gray rocks. There are twenty riders, maybe more, each one heavily armed. They move between the trees with confidence as the stones ease closed behind them, sealing the hidden passage into the mountain.

My jaw drops. It's a *gate*. A gate formed by slabs of granite as big as a fisherman's ship. I know the exiles brought great wealth with them when they fled Norvere, but even with all the gold in the world, I can't imagine how they constructed such a thing. The sight of those shifting stones makes me wary, though the men have yet to draw their swords or bows.

What other marvels might the exiles have at their disposal, and how could those wonders be used against us?

I drop my sword to my side but keep it tightly in hand. If Ror and I are to be forced to fight ten times our number, I'll take any advantage I can get, even if it's only the seconds it will take to draw my weapon.

Alama fidgets beneath me as the squat mountain horses

stream down the tree-littered mountainside, led by a swarthy man with tightly curled silvering hair on a shaggy mount larger than the rest. The man wears heavy leather armor and a hack sword designed for making men into cuts of meat, but beneath his neatly trimmed beard a welcoming smile graces his dark face.

"We've found you!" he shouts, pulling his horse to a stop. "We hoped we would catch up before the hour grew too late." His gaze alights on the unconscious Kanvasola soldier and his eyes narrow. "Looks as if you ran into trouble."

"Nothing my new friends couldn't handle," Crimsin says in a light, teasing voice as she skips across the dirt toward the silver-haired man, her panic from a moment ago vanished without a trace.

"We've found heroes in these princes, Lord Heven." Crimsin clutches his leg with the familiarity of a girl embracing a beloved uncle before motioning back to me with one hand. "Allow me to introduce Niklaas, the eleventh son of King Eldorio and protector of our prince. And Prince Jor Ronces of Norvere, second in line to the throne."

"Your Majesties." Heven smiles at me before inclining his head in Ror's direction. "It is our honor to meet you both, especially you, Prince Jor. I am Lord Heven, former head of the treasury for your late father and leader of your exiled people. Our hearts, minds, and weaponry are at your disposal, my prince."

"Thank you, Lord Heven," Ror says with a regal nod my father would approve of. "Finding friends among you means more than I can say. I look forward to working together to take back what was stolen from our people."

"As do I, my prince," Lord Heven says. "But first we must ensure your safety. Our settlement is only a few hours' ride. When we are secure behind our protections, we will feast in your honor and discuss how we may best serve you."

"That sounds wonderful," Ror says, still displaying no sign that he was ready to run from these people a few minutes ago.

"Excellent." Lord Heven reaches a hand down to Crimsin and hauls her onto the saddle in front of him with a theatrical groan. "This one is a lot heavier than when I first took her into these mountains."

He smiles as he lifts one arm, motioning for the horses behind him to turn. "I helped Crimsin escape western Norvere when she was little," he says as Ror and I pull our horses alongside his. "She was eight, but so tiny I could hold her in one arm and still have room left over for a loaf of bread." He chuckles as he urges his mount forward. "She slept most of the way, drooling on my arm like—"

"Please don't embarrass me, my lord," Crimsin says with an exaggerated pout. "I've convinced the princes to go swimming with my friends and me tomorrow morning. If you keep telling tales, they'll decide they don't want to come."

"There won't be much time for entertainment, Crimsin," Lord Heven warns, affection still obvious in his voice. "There are serious matters to be discussed."

"But surely you can spare the princes for an hour. I'll take them to the swimming hole to the northwest," she says, her eyes sliding my way. "It's a magical spot."

Northwest, the direction she told Ror to run to meet her witch aunt.

I nod in recognition of her warning, my stomach beginning to clench all over again. Of all the words I've heard Crimsin speak, her insistence that these hills weren't safe for Ror were the few that rang true. She was honestly afraid for her prince's life.

She's either crazy and should be locked away to spare the world her madness . . . or Lord Heven isn't the kindly man he's pretending to be.

The possibility makes a knot of foreboding tighten in my chest as I pull Alama to a stop next to Ror, awaiting my turn to be swallowed by the Feeding Hills.

CHAPTER SIXTEEN

AURORA

There isn't enough air to breathe.

The passage through the mountains narrows and the ceiling drops so severely that the men must dose the torches and file along one horse at a time, pressing onward through suffocating darkness. The utter lack of light weighs on me like a coat made of iron, making my bones ache and my breath wheeze in and out. I do my best to control my terror, but inside I feel like a child again, a seven-year-old girl trapped in a cell beneath the castle, with beetles tearing at my skin and Mother's tears wetting our shared pillow.

I'm not a child, of course, but I might as well be. I've allowed myself to be drawn into danger like a babe who grips the finger of anyone who reaches into its crib. I'm not safe here. I feel the danger lurking beneath Lord Heven's silken promises. I didn't miss Crimsin's second warning. I understood what she meant when she mentioned the northwest swimming hole. She meant that—no matter how at ease she seems—I am in danger, and that I must flee to her aunt in Frysk at the first opportunity.

The opportunity doesn't come.

Even after we emerge from the tunnels, the trail is a perilous thing, a dusty scratch between a rock wall and a cliff so sheer the world seems to disappear beyond the brown grass tufted at the edge of the trail. There is nowhere to run. Even if I were to abandon Button and attempt to escape up the mountain, the exiles could easily pluck me from the rock wall before I climbed too high.

I have a feeling they would, too. Lord Heven has stayed close. Very close. So close Niklaas and I haven't had the chance to exchange a word without being overheard.

I long to ask him what he's feeling, if his gut is screaming for him to run the way mine is, but I can't even shoot him a look without being observed. And so I ride and smile and do my best to pretend I am among friends, and wait. . . .

We reach the settlement—a gathering of cottages on the far side of a waterfall that rushes over the cliff with dizzying abandon—by midafternoon. The exiles cut off the flow of the water so that we may pass over the slick stones of the riverbed, but I'm too far back to see how the feat was managed, and there is no way even a sturdy horse could pass through the rushing water without being swept over the side. Once the water is allowed to resume its flow—again via means I can't determine—Niklaas and I are truly caught. Trapped. The settlement is built on a promontory cut off from the land around it by the river on one side and sheer drops into a cavernous gorge on every other. There will be no way out except the way we came. Should the exiles decide to allow it.

I'm careful to conceal my rising panic as Niklaas and I are shown about the settlement and assigned rooms for the night. I smile and make polite chatter throughout the feast, and put on a show of being grateful for the armed men Lord Heven assures me will be ready to march on Mercar within a few days' time. I don't allow myself to fully experience my dread until I am alone in my room long after dark.

I lie fully clothed on my mattress, shredding a piece of paper from the writing table into pieces, wondering when the men in the common yard will go to bed and it will finally be safe to slip across the settlement to Niklaas.

They couldn't have put our rooms farther apart. I am in a spacious suite at the back of Lord Heven's home, while Niklaas sleeps in a cabin three fields up the mountain, where the unmarried men live in small homes perched along the cliffs, separate from the family dwellings on the main level of the settlement. The exiles are purposefully keeping Niklaas and me separated. I wasn't even seated near him at the banquet.

I was placed to the right of Lord Heven, while Niklaas dined at the far end of the table, near Crimsin and a mob of giggling girls. Crimsin was dripping all over him like melted candle wax by the end of the meal. If I hadn't felt the truth in her warning, I would have believed she was a girl without a care in the world aside from convincing a handsome prince to warm her bed.

Warm her bed.

I wish Niklaas were warming *my* bed. It's freezing in this room, even with all my clothes on and a quilt pulled up to my chin. I haven't felt this chilled since I visited Jor in the mountains two Harmontynes ago, when a blizzard trapped the mountain Fey and the island Fey together in the great hall and an epic forty-eight hours of drunken gaming ensued. Jor lost his entire allowance in three hours, while I took so much gold from a pair of mountain brothers that Janin made me give it back when everyone sobered up. But then, I've always been lucky at cards.

If only I could say the same about quests.

"Please," I mutter to the shadows on the beamed ceiling, willing my luck to change. Being taken captive by mercenaries was bad enough, but if I'm taken captive by my own people . . .

I have to find a way out and take Niklaas with me. I can't leave him to be ransomed to his father. We must both escape. Tonight. Together we'll find a way through the Feeding Hills and cross over into Frysk, with or without our horses.

If only the exiles would go to sleep and give me the chance to fetch him!

But Crimsin was right about the young men of the settlement. They're thrilled out of their minds by the prospect of going to war. They've been drinking to it for hours, singing battle songs and hurling Feeding Tree cones into a bonfire in the middle of the common yard, shouting like naughty children when the pods explode with a sizzle of sap.

They're ridiculous . . . and saddening. I've never been to war, but I know it won't be the adventure they're imagining. Even if I believed Lord Heven's promise to hand over his army, I wouldn't want those boys joining the campaign. We'd be better off with a smaller force of older, seasoned warriors.

But at this point, it seems I'll have to make due with no military force at all.

My eyes slide closed, and a pained sound vibrates in my throat. No friends in the Feeding Hills means no army. It means Janin's vision will come to pass and my brother will die come the changing of the leaves.

"No," I whisper into the darkness. There is still time. It's cold in the mountains, but it's still summer in the west. I could have weeks before the leaves turn, and I will make the most of every day. I will find allies, I will secure an army, even if I have to—

The knock on the window shatters my thoughts.

I throw off my quilt and jump out of bed, staring hard at the shadow outside. I recognize the outline of Niklaas's shoulders and my breath rushes out in relief.

"I was waiting to come to you," I whisper as I open the pane.

"Are you alone?" he asks, peering past me into the room.

"Yes." I motion him inside. "Did they see you crossing the common?"

"No, I climbed down the cliff from the cabins." Niklaas shoves his pack through the window and then follows it, dropping down to crouch on the floor in a pool of moonlight. I squat beside him, not bothering to close the pane. If I have my way, we'll be going back through it in a few moments.

"I couldn't wait," he says. "The sooner we leave, the better."

"I agree," I say, relieved he won't require any convincing.

"I don't trust Crimsin—she's too changeable—but something isn't right. The young men seem to think we're going to war, but Lord Heven and the other counselors are hiding something. I can feel it."

"I feel it, too. In my gut." Niklaas presses a fist to his stomach. "There were Vale Flowers in my drink again."

"What?" I curse myself for not warning him to be careful. The counselors have hardly paid him any attention, but he's still a prince with a price on his head.

"Are you ill?" I ask, searching his face in the dim light. "Can you travel?"

"I'm fine," Niklaas says with a grimace that betrays his words. "Crimsin spilled the glass before it was half empty and warned me to fake a true poisoning."

"I assumed the stumbling was an act," I say, fetching my pack from beneath my bed and dragging it to the window. "It wasn't nearly as convincing as the real thing. Better stick to princing. I don't see a future on the stage."

Niklaas doesn't smile. "Crimsin was the one who drugged me. She was told to make sure I wouldn't be up and about tomorrow. The counselors don't want me interfering when the ogres come to collect you."

My lips part. "But the ogres wouldn't dare come here."

"The exiles sent men to lead them in through the tunnels and keep them safe from the trees they're so afraid of. Ekeeta thought this was the best way to capture you alive."

"But why would they help her?" I ask, pulse speeding. "By the gods, what could Ekeeta have promised that—"

"She's promised the Feeding Hills and the fertile flatlands to the east, all the way to the sea," Niklaas says. "The exiles are to be recognized as their own nation, provided they turn you over to her general tomorrow morning."

I shake my head, too numbed by betrayal to know what to say.

"This is my fault." Niklaas grips my shoulder, a strained look on his face. "I knew the exiles were traitors. They change their allegiance like stockings. Probably *more often* than they change their stockings. I shouldn't have let you come here. I should have found another way to your sister."

"You couldn't have known." I cover his hand with mine. "According to everything I've ever heard, the exiles and the queen are enemies."

"That's the other thing. . . ." Niklaas pulls away with a sigh.

"What other thing?" I ask, not sure I can take more bad news.

"We weren't as good at evading Ekeeta's spies as we thought. Crimsin said the queen was watching our journey through her creatures the entire time." He turns to dig in his pack. "That's how Ekeeta knew to send word to the exiles, offering her deal and telling them to watch for us in Goreman."

I sit back hard enough for the floorboards to bruise my bones through my thick overshorts. But the pain is a welcome distraction from the misery filling my heart. If this is true . . . If Ekeeta has been watching us all along . . .

Then there is no hope, no chance I'll be able to outwit her and save Jor.

I cover my mouth with my hands, holding in the moan

that tries to escape as I squeeze my eyes shut and curse every soul on this mountain. Everyone knows that the ogres require a briar-born child to fulfill their prophecy.

How could the exiles do this? How could they damn our world in exchange for lands that will be worthless when the ogres plunge all nations into darkness?

"They don't believe," I mumble into my hands.

Like Niklaas when we first met, the exiles must consider the ogre prophecy a mad legend. It's the only explanation, unless . . .

Unless the exiles know Ekeeta has Jor and figure they might as well give the ogre queen a matching set, seeing as she already has one briar-born child locked in her dungeon. But even then, I can't understand why they'd give up and await their own destruction rather than rage against it.

"They don't believe," Niklaas says, pulling me from my thoughts. "Or they simply don't care. Either way, we need to be gone before morning." He pulls a wad of cloth from his bag and tosses it into my lap. "Crimsin gave me something she thinks will help."

"What's this?" I lift the fabric between two fingers.

"It's one of Crimsin's dresses and a shawl. You're about the same height. If you wrap the shawl around your head, it should hide the fact that you're not her."

I blink, drop my eyes to the dress, and blink again. "You want me to—"

"I want you to put on the dress," Niklaas says. "And *Crimsin* and I are going to go for a walk. She's gone swimming after dark before. If anyone sees us bound for the road, they shouldn't question us, and if they do, you'll look at the ground and giggle and let me do the talking. We'll have to leave the horses, but this is our only chance."

I'll be a girl . . . pretending to be a boy . . . pretending to be a girl. The thought alone is enough to make me dizzy. "But how will we get across the falls?"

"There's a lever set into a stone by the road that diverts the water. Crimsin described it well enough. I'll be able to find it."

I bite my lip. "You trust her?" I ask, hesitating. There's no way I'll be able to conceal my true identity from Niklaas wearing Crimsin's dress. The plunging neckline will reveal my bound chest. I don't have nearly as much to bind as Crimsin, but without my shirt to conceal the bandages, it will be obvious I'm a girl.

"Of course not," Niklaas says, nervously running a hand through his hair. "But what reason would she have to lie about this?"

"None that I can think of."

"I believed she was afraid for you when she told you to run. She didn't want you trapped here," he says, waiting until I look up before he continues. "You got to her. You made one of your subjects love you. Now get changed and let's get out of here before you lose the chance to win over the rest of them." He stands, moving to the window.

When he turns back, I'm still on the ground, the dreaded dress puddled in my lap.

"This is the only way we'll get past the guards, Ror," Niklaas says. "It's a dress. It won't bite."

"I know." But I don't move. I'm frozen, rendered immobile by the force of my indecision. It's not only that I hate for Niklaas to find out the truth this way. This is dangerous for Crimsin, as well. If someone sees me in her clothes, she'll be implicated in our escape. But I can't leave dressed as myself, and there's only one way out.

"There can't be only one way," I mumble, letting the dress fall to the floor as I join Niklaas at the window, staring out at the cliffs and the mountains beyond.

"What?" Niklaas asks.

"There must be another way out. The counselors wouldn't trap themselves here with only one avenue of escape," I whisper, scanning the world outside.

Lord Heven's cottage is perched on the edge of the promontory and has the best view in the settlement. There is nothing between my window and the wide expanse of snow-sifted mountains and dark valleys, but half a field of rock and an outhouse built of the same glossy wood as the lord's cottage.

"If there's another way, Crimsin didn't mention it." I hear frustration in Niklaas's voice, but I don't turn to look at him. I can't pull my eyes from the outhouse. There is something strange about it, something . . .

"And we don't have time to waste," Niklaas continues. "Either put the dress on, or—"

"But there's a privy at the left of the cottage," I say, wondering why Lord Heven would need *two* privies when he no doubt has servants to empty his chamber pot.

"What's wrong with you?" Niklaas growls beneath his breath. "Grow up and put the damn dress on, Ror. I'd wear the flaming thing myself if it would fit, but—"

"Come with me." I snatch my pack from the ground,

205

stuffing the dress into the top before slinging the strap over one arm and claiming my staff from against the wall. "I want to look at something. If my instincts are wrong, I'll put the dress on and we'll go."

Right after you finish losing your mind when you realize you've been deceived.

Before Niklaas can argue, I lift my leg and climb out the window, landing softly on the ground outside and turning to look up. The windows on the second and third floors of the cottage are dark.

With a deep breath and a wish for luck, I pad silently across the rocks to the outhouse. As soon as I get within sniffing distance, I know it's not what it appears to be. There's no odor lingering in the air, only the cold, conifer-scented breeze blowing in from the mountains on the other side of the gorge.

"What are you doing?" Niklaas hisses as I tug open the heavy wooden door, revealing a circular staircase leading into the rock below our feet.

"Finding the other way out." I glance back at Niklaas with a smile, a smile that vanishes when a lamp flares to life on the third floor of the cottage.

CHAPTER SEVENTEEN

NIKLAAS

"Niklaas!" Ror grips my sleeve. "There's a light in—"

Before he can finish, the bell atop Lord Heven's home begins to ring, a deep, resounding *gong, gong* that foretells the end of the world.

Or the end of our escape, and of Ror's life come morning.

"Go!" I shove him down the stairs ahead of me. The front of Lord Heven's house is guarded and the common beyond teeming with people. There will be no chance of slipping by them unnoticed now. We'll have to hope Ror's gut is right and this staircase leads to a way out of the exile settlement, because if it doesn't . . .

I won't think about what happens if it doesn't. I won't think about Ror dead or worse because I was too focused on saving my own skin to consider how dangerous a journey to the Feeding Hills could be for the prince of Norvere.

Ror rushes down the stairs carved through the mountain's

crust with his usual speed, moving so swiftly he seems to hover over the ground. I lose sight of him before we've spun around twice. By the time I reach the bottom, racing through an archway onto a ledge where kite-like contraptions sit in rows facing the gorge, Ror is across the field-sized expanse, throwing his pack to the ground before meeting two exile men with his staff.

I drop my pack and draw my sword, but before I reach his side Ror has knocked one man unconscious and sent the second sailing off the edge of the outcrop. The exile screams as he falls, a cringe-inspiring cry that seems to go on forever, leaving no doubt how deep the chasm is between this mountain and the next.

Ror stands staring over the side, breathing fast. "I didn't mean to," he says, turning to me with frightened eyes. "It was an accident, Niklaas. It was an—"

I grab him by the back of the neck and bring my face even with his. "It's all right," I say, willing strength into him, knowing there isn't time for him to dwell on his first killing. "Don't think about it. We have to escape, or it will be for nothing."

Ror clenches his jaw and nods. I race back across the ledge, snatching Ror's pack and my own in one hand before sprinting to the nearest oversized kite.

"It's a glider," Ror says. "We should be able to fly it off the edge."

Fly it. That's what I'd assumed, but still . . . By the gods . . . *Fly.*

Up close, the contraption is larger than it first appeared, with a wooden seat big enough for two and a basket underneath for luggage. The basket isn't big enough for both packs, so I shove Ror's beneath the seat and toss mine to the ground, knowing he has more gold in his purse than I do.

"Send the others over the side." I move past Ror, slashing the ropes binding the machines to the ledge. Ror hurries behind me, hurling the contraptions, some even larger than the one we've chosen, over the side with surprising strength. But then fear makes everyone a little stronger, a little faster.

I pray it will make us fast enough.

I help Ror hurl the last glider into the gorge, and in a few minutes we've cleared the ledge, ensuring none of the exiles will follow us off of it.

"Take a seat, I'll push off," I say, sheathing my sword as I jog back to the remaining glider, relieved to see the archway leading to the stairs still empty.

"No," Ror says. "We have to—"

"Enough arguing!" I turn back to him, my scowl digging into my face like claws. "Do you *want* to die here?"

"No, but I don't want to die on that thing, either!" He shoves his staff into its harness and reaches for the rope tying the glider to the ground, glaring at me as he tugs it free. "You don't *sit* on it, you lie on your stomach to keep the weight balanced and give you access to the controls."

"You've steered one before?" I ask, anger vanishing in a wave of relief.

"Not one so large." He motions for me to help him lift the machine by the bar above the seat. "But the mountain Fey have gliders they use to travel from mountaintop to mountaintop. I've watched one being steered more than twice."

"Watched?" I ask, backing up with Ror as he steps away from the ledge.

"Watched closely."

"How closely?" I ask, pulse speeding.

"Closely enough . . . I think," he says, blowing a breath out between pursed lips. "We'll need to get a running start and then—"

Footsteps sound from the archway. The exiles are on the stairs, and we're out of time.

"Run!" I shout, forcing myself to charge toward the edge.

Ror launches into motion beside me. "Reach for the lever on your side after we jump," he pants. "The levers control the wings. I'll tell you when to shift yours."

I glance up, finding not one but two levers below the bar we're holding. But before I can ask Ror what the extra lever is for, we're taking our last step on solid ground and hurtling out into the breathless void.

I land on my stomach with a sizzle of nerves, like lightning skittering across water. My belly pitches and my throat squeezes tight, and then our momentum runs out and we begin to fall. The nose of the machine tilts *down, down,* aiming into the gorge while my muscles scream and my heart punches my chest like a fist. My mind's eye flashes on the man Ror killed—bloodied lips peeled into a smile as he reaches dead arms out to greet me—and my vision swims, terror twisting my insides so fiercely I forget how to breathe.

"Pull the lever!" Ror slaps my hand, and I reach for the lever, yanking it toward me, sending us into an even steeper dive,

down,

down,

down, so fast the wind stings my cheeks as the glider

picks up speed, hurtling toward the rocks below, and I know it's over, all over, and Ror and I are dead and there's nothing left to do but pray to—

"Put it back and pull the other one! The other one!" Ror screams, straining to reach past me. "Pull it, Niklaas!"

I reach for the controls, but my hands are stupid with fear, my fingers shot through with aging stiffness and bound in winter mittens. It takes an eternity to shift the lower lever back into its previous position and a second eternity to drag the upper level down, sending the glider soaring up and over the gorge.

Up, by all the merciful gods, *up.* I'm so grateful I can taste it, feel it stinging up my throat and into my nose, making my eyes water with relief.

As my heart lifts and my stomach shudders, I look down, expecting to see the treetops brushing my dangling legs, but the trees are still far below. We lost less than a field in the dive and are now sailing briskly along on an updraft, the nose of our glider aimed at the opening between two mountains.

"This one is different," Ror says, sounding as breathless as I feel. "Your levers are up and down. Mine are left and right." He adjusts one and the glider shifts to the left, centering us on the passage between the mountains. "We'll be all right. We'll be fine from here on out," he says, though I'm not sure who he's trying to comfort—me or himself.

"The ogre queen will have you!" Lord Heven's shout carries clearly through the cold air, lifting the hairs on my neck. "She will, child. One way or another! Return and make your capture worth something to your people!"

"Go sit on a flaming pole and burn," Ror mutters, but he

211

doesn't turn to look at the man who would have bartered his prince's life for a kingdom of his own.

"How long will we stay up?" I risk a glance over my shoulder to where Lord Heven stands on the ledge, surrounded by armed men. One exile pulls an arrow into his bow, but Heven stops him with a hand, confirming that the queen must want Ror taken alive.

"I don't know," Ror says. "It depends on the wind."

"They aren't shooting at us," I say. "But I'm betting they'll be sending a party through the mountains to meet us. The farther we get on this thing, the better."

"Well . . . we'll definitely get farther than we would have on foot."

"Yes, we will." I silently send up a thank-you to whichever god is responsible for our getaway. "We were lucky."

"About time," Ror mumbles beneath his breath.

I sigh in agreement. It *is* about time. Until a few moments ago, this quest has seemed as cursed as all my father's sons. "How lucky depends on how far we fly," I say, willing the wind to hold strong. "We'll need a generous head start to make up for the fact that the exiles will be on horseback and know the secret ways through the mountains."

"I'm sorry," Ror says. "I'll get Alama back for you. If I can."

"The horses are the least of our worries." I know it's true, but I can't help the pang of grief that tightens my chest when I realize I will never see Alama again. Since Usio was transformed, Alama has been my oldest friend.

"The fate reader said I would lose Button and need money for another horse," Ror says. "I hate to lose such good animals, but at least we have enough gold to purchase new ones, though we may have to go without saddles if we can't make a tight bargain."

"What else did she say?" I ask, shivering. I tell myself it's the crisp air blowing down the neck of my shirt that's responsible, but I can't help thinking of the reader's rheumy eye and the black scabs pocking her skin. She was in communion with dark forces, and a part of me fears what it means for her predictions to be coming true.

"She said I would be safe in green hills," Ror says. "By a bewitched stream."

I grunt. "Obviously, she was wrong. Or lying through her rotten teeth."

"I don't think so. You said the exile's waterfall was controlled by a lever. It was an invention. Men made it. Bewitching is the work of magic, not men."

"Crimsin said her aunt was a magic-worker. We'll have to see if the hills are green and the streams bewitched in Beschuttz."

Ror sighs. "I suppose we have no choice but to seek refuge there."

"Crimsin saved your life, so . . . Beschuttz seems like the most logical course."

For you, anyway. The most logical course for me would be to demand Ror tell me where Aurora is hidden and start seeking the princess as soon as we land. My time grows too short to be swept up in anyone's quest but my own.

But I'm already part of Ror's quest, and obligated to protect him, at least from the dangers I'm responsible for introducing into his life. I knew better than to take him to the

Feeding Hills, and I know better than to think he'll last long without me watching his back. He's like a headstrong little brother to me now. I could no more run off and leave him than I could have abandoned Usio to face sunrise on his eighteenth birthday alone.

"You're right," Ror says. "It's just getting so hard to trust . . . anything."

"You can trust me," I say, hoping I'm telling the truth, and that I will continue to make honorable choices when I can count the days I have left to live on one hand.

Perhaps Ror can sense my doubt, because he doesn't respond, he only pulls in a breath and holds it as we drift between the two mountains and come out the other side, sailing over a wide valley with more giant trees shooting up from the ground like whale spray rising above the ocean.

"Pretty," I whisper.

"Beautiful," Ror agrees. "Though I doubt we'll find it pretty after being lost in it for days."

"We won't be lost. See that mountain?" I point to the tallest of the Feeding Hills, a behemoth already covered in a dusting of snow. "That's Mount Ever. I had a view of it from my guest room while visiting Pennly's princesses in their summer home last Sunstyne. If we head straight for it, then around the left side, we won't lose our way."

"How many days until we reach Beschuttz?" Ror adjusts one of the levers on his side, aiming the glider for Mount Ever's left flank.

"We'll make it through the hills in two days, three at the most." I gauge the distance between our glider and the mountain with a critical eye, knowing distances appear shorter when viewed from above. "From there it will be another day to the borders of Pennly, and we should be in Frysk a day after that. I'm not sure where Beschuttz is, but the country is small. We should find it fairly quickly."

"That's assuming we're on foot the entire time," Ror says. "We can purchase horses in Pennly. If you have friends there, maybe we—"

"I didn't say I have friends there." King Thewen would welcome me back with a stint in his dungeon if he knew I'd returned against his orders. "In fact, it's best if I'm not seen in Pennly."

"Why's that?"

"The king's daughters cared more for me than he would have cared for them to. We parted on . . . less than friendly terms," I say. "I was advised to leave his lands and never return. The twins cried for a week afterward. Or so I heard."

"Twins?" Ror snorts. "Did you ravish both his poor darlings?"

"Of course not," I say, offended, though I suppose I shouldn't be. I've done my share of ravishing, but never sisters. And certainly never twins. The thought is vaguely repellent, in fact. "I was trying to convince the firstborn, the one named to inherit, to marry me, but her sister couldn't seem to help falling for me right along with Priscelle."

"But Papa didn't approve of the match."

"To put it mildly."

"Because of your father?" Ror asks, his tone softening. "Because of what he does to his sons?"

"He didn't know about that. I was surprised Crimsin did," I say, uncomfortable again. I hate the pity in Ror's voice

215

when he mentions my father. "No, King Thewen was still angry that Kanvasola refused to come to his aid during the war." I shrug. "It doesn't matter. I'm glad it didn't work out. If I'd married Priscelle, I wouldn't have met you or enjoyed all these wonderful adventures."

Ror snorts again. "At least the dinner in Goreman was good."

"It was. And Priscelle and I weren't a good match. She smelled of vinegar, refused to ride a horse, and had an unnatural love of cats."

"Cats?"

"She had six. Kept them in her bedroom," I say with a mock shudder. "Long-haired cats, short-haired cats, even a bald bastard with wrinkly gray skin and yellow fangs." I smile as Ror laughs. "Scariest thing I've seen in years. I never would have slept easy with that thing curled at the end of the bed like a goblin escaped from the Pit."

Ror's laugh becomes a giggle that reminds me that—no matter how determined or skilled a fighter he is—he is still so young. Now perhaps he'll have the sense to go back into hiding until he has the chance to grow up.

"I'm sorry," I say, watching his profile in the pale light of the half-moon. "I know you had high hopes for the Feeding Hills."

"It's all right." Ror stares down at the trees drifting by beneath us. "Surely one of the rulers of Herth will be willing to aid an enemy of Ekeeta's."

I pause, momentarily speechless. "You're joking."

Ror glances up, his gray eyes silver in the moonlight. "No. There's still time. I can't give up."

"And what about the ogre queen?" I struggle to keep my anger in check. "Do you think she's going to stand back and let you roam around Herth hunting an army?"

"I know it will be difficult, but—"

"It will be *impossible*. You'll be captured within a week," I snap. "Your only hope is to find a place to hide, whether that's in Frysk or back on that island you came from or wherever else the Fey can find to conceal you."

"I can't hide forever," Ror says. "My friend—"

"Your friend will have to die."

"Don't say that," Ror whispers, expression darkening.

I curse beneath my breath, amazed that he can still shock me with his stubbornness. "You're out of your mind! I can't believe the fairies let you out of their sight in the first place."

"They didn't. I crept out when they weren't watching," Ror says, heat in his tone. "And I'm *not* out of my mind. What if it were your sister in Ekeeta's dungeon? Would you give up on her so easily?"

"It's not my sister. And it's not yours, either." I pause as a terrible suspicion worms its way into my mind. "Or were you lying to me? Is Aurora—"

"No, it's not Aurora," Ror says, but there is something coiled behind the denial, a secret lurking like a rat in the flour.

"Then tell me where she is," I say. "You owe me an answer. I honored my half of our bargain. Now it's time for you to honor yours."

"Are you ready to go our separate ways, then?" Ror asks, voice trembling.

"I'll see you to Beschuttz, but I want to know where your sister is hiding. I've earned the truth from you."

"All right." Ror's hands tighten around the wooden bar. "I'll tell you tonight. As soon as we find a place to rest."

A part of me wants to keep pushing, but the wiser part advises to bide my time. What's a few hours? I've waited a week, I can wait a little longer.

Ror and I fall silent except for the occasional word when a lever needs to be pulled, and after a time I find myself enjoying the flight. The vast expanse of trees is soothing, like a calm ocean stretching before the prow of a ship, and the sharp, herbal smell of the Feeding Trees refreshing. We drift long enough that our sail takes us a day closer to Mount Ever, when the wind gives out and the glider drifts toward the ground.

"We should put down on that lake." Ror points to a horseshoe-shaped patch of black ahead. "We could make it farther, but we'll risk being ripped apart by the trees when we land."

The foliage surrounding the lake is thick, and the moon too low to light the surface of the water. The thought of landing in that inky black isn't much more appealing than taking our chances with the treetops, but Ror is right. Wrestling a Feeding Tree would be a good way to break a bone or three, and we can't risk it. We have to be ready to keep moving as soon as we hit the ground.

"Can you reach my pack?" Ror asks. "I'd rather be wearing it when we land."

"I'll wear it." I grab the pack and swing it over one arm. "I was born on the coast and practically raised in the water."

"I was raised on an island and swim almost as fast as I run." Ror sounds crankier than he has in days. "Drop the lower lever a few fingers when you're ready."

"Aye, aye, *little man*."

"You know, it's good we'll be together a little longer," Ror says, ignoring my jab. "I'll be able to protect you for a few more days."

"*You* protect *me*?" I ask, nerves vanishing as I laugh. "I think you've forgotten who fetched your wee ass from its sling tonight."

"I think *you've* forgotten who taught *you* to steer a glider."

"And you've forgotten who told you not to go to the flaming Feeding Hills in the first place," I say, my words ending in a gulp as the surface of the lake grows close enough to smell the mineral and moss scent of the water.

"We'll be all right," Ror says. "Get out from under the wings and swim for shore. Dump the pack if you have to. You're worth more than the gold inside it."

I realize Ror has paid me a compliment—and was likely provoking me to keep my mind off our landing—and then the lake is thirteen . . . ten . . . *two* hands away and we hit. We *hit,* toes sliding across the ice-cold surface for half a field before the last of our forward momentum runs out and we sink like knives through rotten fruit.

I hear Ror gasp as the water soaks into his clothes and then we are both under and I'm shocked still, paralyzed by snow-fed water so cold it stops every thought in my brain. My head throbs and my blood slows and for a moment I forget where I am, forget everything but the cold chilling my skin and bones, creeping icy fingers in to wrap around my heart.

But finally, after who knows how many frozen seconds, a stinging, aching, burning in my chest reminds me I have arms and legs and ought to be doing something with them. Fighting the sluggish feeling in my limbs, I kick for the surface, struggling against the added weight of the pack, my boots, and my sword tugging at my waist, breaking through just as my lungs are turning inside out with the need for breath.

I suck in air and cough through teeth that clack like hooves on cobblestones, echoing across the otherwise silent lake.

"R-r-ror?" I shove at the water, fighting to stay warm. "Ror? Ror, where—"

His gasp as he breaks through the surface is positively girlish, and his voice when he calls my name is an octave too high. "Niklaas?"

"I'm here. This way." I would tease him about sounding like his stones have crawled inside his body if I weren't losing sensation in my joints. Nothing is funny in water this cold, and I doubt we'll feel much warmer out of it. If we want to avoid dying of the quick chills, we'll have to get out of these wet things.

I crawl onto the shoreline, sword dragging across the stones, vaguely sensing the sharp edges of rocks and shells beneath my hands, but too numb to be bothered by them. Once I'm a safe distance from the water, I shrug the pack off my back and pry it open. The dress Ror shoved into the top is soaking wet, but below it Ror's second set of clothes, wrapped in the oilcloth cloak we purchased in Goreman, is relatively dry.

"He-here." I clap him on the back as he crawls—coughing and shivering—onto the bank beside me. "Change your clothes. I'll wrap up in your cloak."

"N-n-no. I'm fine." Ror bites his lip.

"You're not fine, and neither am I. We'll die of the quick chills if we don't get dry." I pull at my shirt, wrestling the sodden fabric over my head. In the dry mountain air, my skin dries instantly. Almost as quickly, I begin to feel a little warmer.

"Hurry." I pull the oilcloth cloak around my shoulders, grateful they didn't have a size small enough for Ror at the mercantile in Goreman. The cloak is tighter than my own, but it will provide enough cover to keep me warm while my clothes dry. "We should start moving north, cover more ground before we stop."

"F-fine," Ror says, inexplicable anger in his voice as he drops his staff and tugs his oversized leather armor over his head, flinging it to the ground with a huff.

"I'll turn my back if you like," I say, remembering Ror's penchant for privacy. "No need to get your britches in a . . ."

I freeze halfway around, every chilled muscle in my body pulling tight as I get an eye full of the woods beyond the shore, woods as dark as midnight in the Pit, lit up by yellow eyes shining like constellations of stars amidst the blackness. Even before I smell fur and musk, I know what the creatures are.

Wolves. More wolves than I've ever seen together at once, enchanted creatures sent by the ogre queen to hunt her prey.

"Stop," I say in a calm voice, knowing no good will come from allowing fear into my tone.

"I'm getting my shirt on," Ror says, his voice muffled by fabric.

"Get ready to run," I say. "There are wolves in the woods. Fifty. Maybe more."

Ror's breath rushes out. "No."

"On the count of three, grab your staff," I say, feet itching. "I'll get the pack."

"And then what?" Ror asks in a steady voice. The boy is braver than most men twice his size, I have to give him that. "I can't overcome that many. I couldn't if they were men, and I'm used to fighting people, not wolves."

"We'll only fight if we have no other choice. Until then, we'll run."

"We'll never outrun them," Ror says. "They're too fast."

I curse beneath my breath, knowing he's right.

"But maybe . . ." Ror's words trail away. "Follow me." Before I can tell him to wait, he snatches his staff from the ground and races down the shore, summoning a series of growls that ripple through the darkness seconds before the wolves burst from the trees.

"What happened to three!" I sling the pack over my shoulder and take off after Ror, running faster than I would have thought possible with sodden boots and wet britches sticking to my legs like a second skin. But then, it's amazing how motivating a pack of snarling wolves can be. After a few moments, I find myself pulling even with Ror, keeping pace as he races for a Feeding Tree down the shore, a beast so ancient it must have been planted before humans had language.

I understand he means to climb the thing and have a split second to wonder how in the Pit we're going to manage it, and then he's jumping into the air and I'm jumping along with him and somehow, my fingers find holds in the thick bark and my feet gain purchase and I'm scrambling up the scaled wood behind Ror, reaching the first giant limb and climbing on top just as the wolves leap for us, jaws snapping at the air.

"By the gods," I gasp, crouching beside Ror on the wide limb, lungs full of salt and razors from our sprint. "Give me some warning next time."

"Sorry," Ror pants, peeking at the wolves snarling in frustration below our refuge. "I just thought . . . this way we'll be able . . . to keep moving." He points along the limb, which stretches through the surrounding trees for half a field before narrowing to a point too thin for a man to walk on. "The trees are close enough to jump from limb to limb, but we'll get farther faster if we stick to the oldest ones."

I squint into the darkness beyond the trees clustered around the lake. "We'll need a torch. Once we get deeper in, it's going to be too dark to see where to jump."

Ror nods. "The flint is in the front pocket of my pack." He stands, looking frailer without his leather armor covering his linen undershirt and his sodden warrior's knot flopping to one side like a crooked hat. "I'll see if I can find a dead limb to—"

There is a sudden whistle and Ror's words end in a startled gurgle, but it isn't until he falls to his hands and knees and I see the arrow protruding from his arm that I recognize the whistle for what it was—an arrow cutting through the air, followed by more arrows with raven feathers for fletching and ogre blood staining their tips.

Ogres. They're here. In the Feeding Hills.

I realize the truth, realize how desperately Ekeeta must desire Ror's capture if she's willing to send troops into Mataquin's most unholy place for the ogre race, and wince against the violent clenching of my gut as it insists there is no way Ror and I will leave this wood free men.

Chances are we won't leave the hills alive.

No. I won't die here. Not now, when I'm so close.

Ignoring the growls from the wolves, shouts from the ogre soldiers, and arrows whizzing by too close for comfort, I grab Ror and drag him closer to the trunk of the tree, staying low to take advantage of the cover the wide limb provides. I have to get the arrow out before we try to escape. The ogres tip their arrows with their own blood, black fluid poisonous to humans. If left untreated, exposure to ogre blood will kill a man within days, and the longer the thing sits beneath Ror's skin, the more poison he'll absorb.

"Ogres." Ror looks over his shoulder with wide eyes. "What will we—" His question ends in a pained cry as I rip the sleeve from his shirt. I do my best not to disturb the arrow, but the shaft still tilts a bit, digging the tip deeper into Ror's pale flesh.

"Let's get this out of you first," I say, heart racing as I evaluate the wound.

The good news is that the arrow hit the meat and muscle of his upper arm, doesn't seem to have struck a bleeding vein, and is in so deep it should be easy to push it through.

The bad news is it's going to hurt like the bottom level of the Pit on the way out.

"It has to go through." I snap off the fetching and lay a hand on Ror's back, offering what comfort I can even as I wrap my fingers around the arrow's shaft. Ogres tend to do a better job of attaching their arrow tips than human archers. I can only hope the angle will stay true when I apply pressure.

There isn't time to go hunting for a knife to use instead. We have to get deeper into the forest. Darkness is our only hope. We won't be able to see where in the gods' green lands we're going, but the ogres won't have the moonlight to help them get a clear shot, either.

"Niklaas, wait," Ror says, his voice already thin and breathless.

"On three," I say. "One . . . two!" I push on two, jabbing the arrow through with a sharp thrust. Ror's entire body tenses, but he makes only the softest mewl as the arrow comes free.

"You're a fierce thing," I say, breath coming fast as I fling the bloodied arrow to the ground. I catch Ror as he slumps forward and pull him upright, only to have his head roll limply back against my arm.

He's fainted, which is a blessing when it comes to his pain but may end up being a curse on his life.

I grit my teeth, fighting a wave of panic. "At least you're small." I reach for the sleeve I tore away and wrap it around Ror's wound, staunching the flow of blood, trying not to be distracted by the arrows that continue to whiz within hands of where we're hunched on the limb. It's only a matter of time before the ogres overcome their fear of the Feeding Tree we've taken refuge in and climb up to fetch us. We have to move. Now.

"I'll carry you if I have to," I mutter. "Don't worry, little man." I shift Ror in my arms, balancing him on one knee while I tie his makeshift bandage, causing his torn shirt to gape open, revealing the bandages binding his chest.

I stare, frozen.

I can't . . . I never . . .

I am . . . I am an *idiot,* so devoid of sense I might as well be blind, deaf, and dumb.

I have a fleeting memory of feeling those bandages under my hand, a hazy recollection from the night Crimsin drugged me, but I don't dwell on it. There are too many other memories rushing in, little morsels from the moment I woke a giggling Ror in the mercenary tent to the moment he burst through the water with a girlish gasp, a hundred clues I was too stupid to catch until this very *female* bound chest was laid bare before my eyes.

Ror, my hound's ass. It is *Aurora* unconscious in my arms. I've had the princess sleeping next to me for over a week, and I never even *paused to consider* that my traveling companion wasn't a small, soft-cheeked pretty boy of fourteen, but a *girl.* A flaming *girl!*

"Fool!" I growl, angrier than I can remember being in my life, shaking with it, sweating with it, wishing I could smash something with the hand balling into a fist behind Ror's—*Aurora's*—head.

I'm furious with her, with myself, with every minute of my life before I met her, every experience that made me so certain a girl could never pass as a boy, never fight like a boy, never do half the things Aurora does every day without thinking twice.

The realization that it was a *girl* of seventeen who shoved me into my saddle when I was hurt, who bested that monster of a man in the practice ring, who took out five Kanvasol soldiers and is stubbornly bent on raising an army to march on Mercar hits me fully, sending my thoughts stumbling like headless chickens until an arrow shoots past within a breath of my neck and my ability to focus returns. Thank the gods.

There's no time to dwell on my stupidity. I have to get the princess of Norvere out of danger before she's captured by ogres and the entire world damned to darkness.

I reach for the pack with my feet, dragging it close enough to dig into the top with my free hand. I find Aurora's purse and shove it into the back of my pants before tucking the flint and waterskin in the pocket of my borrowed cloak. If we manage to escape the ogres, we'll need fire, water, and, soon after, gold. The rest of the pack is weight I can't shoulder while carrying Aurora.

Still, I know there's one other thing I can't leave behind.

I lay her on the tree and come onto my toes, squatting low. Tensing, I kick the pack over the side, taking advantage of the ogres' surprise as it falls to dash back to where Aurora was shot, snatch her staff, and hurry back toward the shelter of the trunk.

I'm less than ten hands from Aurora's side when the tree begins to vibrate, the limb beneath me shaking hard enough to knock me off my feet. I fall to my belly, clutching at the thick bark with clawed fingers as a quake rocks the Feeding Tree, sending Aurora sliding closer to the edge of the limb.

Closer . . . closer . . .

Going . . . going . . .

CHAPTER EIGHTEEN

AURORA

I'm on a glider, soaring through a starless sky. Below, fields wither and people weak with hunger run from ogres come to herd them into cages and I know the living darkness has come to pass.

I watch through tear-filled eyes as an old woman is dragged by her hair into a pen intended for animals and the ogres fall to feasting on her like wolves, forgetting their "enlightened transition" and their vows to forego human flesh, knowing they need not fear retribution now that the world is theirs.

I see the old woman's head snapped from her body and draw in breath to scream, but before I can make a sound, the glider vanishes and I am falling, tumbling through the air toward where the ogres feed for a heart-stopping moment before—

My eyes fly open with a howl. I scream before I understand why and then scream again as I realize I am dangling in midair by my injured arm, swaying back and forth while the Feeding Tree shakes like a dog out of water.

"Please!" I shout, too dizzied by agony to do anything but beg for mercy. I can't think how to end it, can't explain what's happening or how I came to be hanging here, watching the bark of the tree peel from its trunk like lips curling from a giant set of teeth.

Rotten teeth, so sticky with black sap it looks like the bark is oozing decay as it moves apart, opening a passage into the midnight hollow at the behemoth's core.

With one last shudder, the tree's shaking ceases and the wood falls silent. The ogres don't shout or run; the wolves cower with their heads tucked. Even the wind seems to hold its breath.

"Aurora. Take my other hand!"

I recognize Niklaas's voice and realize he must be the one holding my arm, but I can't tear my eyes away from the tree's mouth. Wisps of black smoke drift from within, spreading out to touch the ogres, twining between their thin legs, caressing their bald heads, beckoning with graceful smoke fingers until, one by one, the ogres' eyes slide shut and their weapons fall to the ground. And then, slowly, stumbling like sleepwalkers, the soldiers shuffle into the impenetrable darkness at the Feeding Tree's heart.

I catch a smell, like ancient dust and heat rising from long-baked bones, accompanied by the tang of sap nearly turned to syrup before the wood groans and the passage into the tree's belly begins to shake closed. It is nearly a human sound, that groan, a mixture of vengeance and relief, succor and restitution that makes me shiver. It's a cry of satisfaction after being too long from what you crave, a feast after too many months of famine.

Or years . . . or centuries . . .

Who knows when this tree last had a meal, but if the legends are true, it should have a few human lifetimes to enjoy tonight's spoils. The Feeding Trees are said to take centuries to digest, leaving their ogre prey alive for a hundred years or more before the hardy monsters finally succumb to starvation.

The thought is almost enough to make me pity the ogres who shot me. Almost.

"Aurora!" Niklaas calls over the moaning as the tree rearranges its bark, sealing itself so completely no one would guess there had been a gaping hole at its center a moment ago.

I look up, blinking into his worried face, my heart racing though the ogres are gone and the wolves crouched in the shadow of the tree, whining in shock and confusion. My arm has begun to go numb, and the pain that was overwhelming is now a manageable misery, but for some reason I'm still afraid.

"Take my hand," Niklaas demands, reaching his other hand down for mine. "I need it to pull you up."

"Niklaas." I gasp his name as I reach for his hand, as confused and panicked as I was a moment ago. Something is wrong, something—

"Don't worry," he says. "I've got you, Aurora."

Aurora. *Aurora*.

He *knows*. I don't know whether to be outraged or terrified, to weep with relief or demand that he keep calling me Ror, that nothing be allowed to change now that my secret has been revealed.

But that would be stupid, pointless.

Everything has changed. I can hear it in Niklaas's voice, feel it in the careful way he pulls me up and over the edge of the limb.

The skin below my bandaged chest scrapes against bark as I slide, revealing what gave me away. As soon as Niklaas releases me, I clutch my torn shirt with my good hand and pull it up, for modesty's sake. It's too late for anything else. Too late to tell Niklaas the truth the way I wanted to tell it, too late to make him understand that not everything between us was a lie, that he is still my friend whether I am a prince or a princess.

"Here, take this," he says, untying my cloak from his shoulders and swinging it around my own, leaving his chest bare.

"No, you need it. It's cold," I say, clearing my throat as I realize there's no need to drop my pitch. "You'll need it," I repeat in my natural voice, a high, floaty thing that feels unfamiliar after so long pretending to be someone I'm not.

Niklaas's breath rushes out as he shakes his head. "I can't believe I didn't see . . . You must have had a good laugh, eh?"

"No." I reach for him, wincing as the muscles shift in my wounded shoulder, but he pulls away like my fingers are made of fire. Or feces. Fire and feces mixed together.

"No," I repeat, ignoring the tightening in my ribs, the panic that courses through me at the thought of Niklaas hating me. "It wasn't like that. I was going to tell you the truth so many times."

"But what? You were having too much fun making a fool of me?"

"No! I . . . At first . . . I was afraid," I confess, voice quavering.

"Right." Niklaas's laugh is bitter. "Afraid of what? I've seen you fight, *Ror*."

I flinch at the venom in the last word. "I wasn't . . . I was afraid you wouldn't help me. Ekeeta has my brother," I say, relieved to finally tell Niklaas the truth. "Jor was captured on his way to visit me. He and the mountain Fey made the journey safely every summer, but this year Ekeeta had ogres waiting at the port near Sifths. We don't know how she learned they would be boarding a ship there, but . . . She took Jor and killed the fairies who fought to protect him.

"Not long after, Janin had a vision of Jor's death. When the Hawthorne tree in the courtyard at Mercar turns red, Jor will die. Unless I change his fate." I swallow the lump rising in my throat, dropping my eyes to the bark beneath my crossed legs. "I thought if I raised an army and marched on Mercar, Ekeeta might be convinced to give up Jor in exchange for my withdrawal. And if not, I planned to send my forces to attack the gates, while I crept into the city to free my brother myself."

Niklaas grunts.

My throat squeezes tighter. "At first I didn't trust you enough to tell the truth, but then . . . I was afraid if you knew I was a girl, even a girl fairy-blessed with skill in battle, that you'd tell me to forget about saving my brother. And I was afraid that once you knew . . . once you learned I would never agree to marry you that—"

Niklaas's laugh is so sudden it makes me jump.

My eyes dart back to his face and I watch nervously as he

laughs and laughs. Laughs until his breath comes in a rhythm more akin to a sob, until his eyes shine and he covers his face with his hands and draws a long, ragged breath. "What a joke."

"I'm sorry," I whisper.

"Me too." He grins as he swipes the wet from his cheeks. "You were my last chance and now . . ." His grin grows wider as his eyes grow colder. "Now I wouldn't marry you if your fairy mother came begging for me to take you off her hands."

I blink against the tears pressing at my eyes and fight to keep my lips from trembling. Niklaas has the right to be angry, and it's good that he's giving up his dream of making me his wife, but still . . . it hurts. It hurts to have him look at me with revulsion, to feel his disgust fouling the air between us.

I suck my top lip between my teeth and bite down as I nod.

Niklaas snorts, and for a moment I'm afraid he's going to resume his nerve-mangling chortling, but instead he jumps to his feet and prowls to the edge of the limb.

"Doesn't look like the wolves are going anywhere," he says, cursing. "We'll have to stick to the trees. Unfortunately, I threw the pack down when I thought I'd have to carry you. All we have left are the flint, the waterskin, and a bag of gold that won't do us a damned bit of good until we reach a village."

I struggle to my feet, careful of my arm, not knowing whether to be grateful or disappointed that Niklaas seems ready to stop fighting.

At least for the moment.

"I'm fine to walk," I say, "but I'll need help climbing when it's time to move to another tree." I slip my wounded arm through the cloak's sleeve, swaying as a fresh wave of pain makes me gasp and my eyes squeeze shut.

Niklaas steadies me with a hand on my good shoulder. My eyes open on his bare chest, a sight that sends a different sort of pain worming into my heart. He is as beautiful and untouchable as ever, but knowing I would never press my palm to his skin and feel the rhythm of his heart didn't hurt this badly before. When I was Ror, I had Niklaas's affection and friendship and respect. Now . . . I have nothing but his contempt.

"Can you walk? Tell the truth." Niklaas sighs as he realizes what he's said. "I mean . . . I can carry you. I *will* if you need me to. We have to move quickly. The arrow was tipped with ogre blood. We only have a few days to get you to a healer."

I look up and see the kindness behind the hurt in his face, and my composure slips. "Please don't hate me," I whisper, eyes filling. "I care about you, Niklaas. That part was real. You're one of the best friends I've ever had."

"You were a friend to me, too," he says in a strained voice. "When we were landing I kept thinking . . ."

"Thinking what?" I ask softly, not wanting to ruin this opportunity to mend the rift between us.

"That you were like a brother to me. A *brother*," he says with a miserable laugh.

"We can still be like brothers," I say, trying to believe it, though the words feel like the worst kind of lie. A lie to myself, a lie my head is trying to sell my heart.

"No, we can't." Niklaas's hand falls and his features firm

up, shutting me out once more. "You're not who I thought you were. I don't know who you are."

"Yes, you do! I'm still the same person."

"No, you're not. And neither am I. That Niklaas had hope. I have none, and you are to blame for the loss of it." He clears his throat. "Now can you walk, or can't you?"

I lift my chin and take a deep breath, refusing to cry or beg or make any more of a fool of myself than I have already. It wouldn't do any good—Niklaas is too angry to listen—and he's right, we have to get moving.

"I can walk. For now." I pick up my staff with my good hand, silently vowing to find some way to convince Niklaas to forgive me. "I'll let you know if that changes."

He nods. "Maybe we'll have some luck and the wolves will be too spooked to follow us."

My breath rushes out as I remember we're standing on the arm of a monster. "Did you see that?" I ask, pointing toward the trunk. "The way the tree opened up and the ogres simply . . . walked in?"

"It would have been hard to miss," he says, crossing his arms at his chest.

"I wonder what drew them in?" I peer over the edge. "Do you think they saw something we didn't? Or maybe it was that smoke, some toxin in it that only ogres—"

"I'm a dumb oaf, Aurora, too dim to know a girl from a boy. What would I know about Feeding Trees?" he asks, obviously not in the mood for talk. Or forgiveness.

With one last glance at the wolves cringing before the Feeding Tree, bellies scraping the ground, I turn and start down the long limb, walking until it grows as thin as a canoe bed, then a horse's back, then the ridge of a roof.

A part of me wants to keep going, to see how far I can get before I lose my balance, but I am fairy blessed, not immortal. A drop from this height could end badly, and I'm sure a broken leg would probably hurt more than the wound my pride will suffer from asking for Niklaas's grudging assistance.

Probably.

I stop, waiting for Niklaas to catch up and help me climb into the arms of another Feeding Tree, a baby monster with limbs barely long enough to deposit us onto a third branch leading deep into the forest. Beyond that, we rely on touch to find our way. It is too dark to see the trees or the ground or anything aside from the branches of the canopy shining silver in the moonlight.

It's too dark to see Niklaas's broad back when he moves ahead to lead the way, or judge his expression when a fever begins to burn beneath my skin and I grow too dizzy to walk, necessitating being thrown over his shoulder. Too dark to see my hands gripping Feeding Tree bark when the ogre blood reaches my belly or to see if there is worry in Niklaas's eyes when he asks if I am strong enough to hold on to him as he climbs down from the trees.

Once on the ground, I stumble on for another hour or more, leaning heavily on Niklaas, keeping my leaden feet moving through force of pure stubbornness alone. I manage to keep my eyes open long enough to see the sun rise beyond the hills and to hear Niklaas promise that we are within a day's walk of a village before fever claims me.

I slide into a sleep like a shallow grave, my rest all too easily disturbed by the world above. Time passes in a blur of heat and pain and nightmares of the ogre queen leaning over my sickbed, spilling horrors into my sheets from her open mouth.

I wake to Niklaas dribbling water between my lips and force myself to swallow before the fever pulls me under again. My eyes close on the needle-carpeted forest floor and open on a sky filled with vultures. They dive down to bite and claw at Niklaas's back as he holds me on the saddle in front of him. He shouts for the horse beneath us to run faster, urging it on with heels digging into its sides.

I struggle to keep my eyes open, determined to find my staff and help him, only to find I can't move my hands. They have drawn into claws against my chest, the bones and muscles petrifying as the ogre venom continues to work its evil upon my body.

"Nik . . . ," I murmur, wanting to thank him for trying so hard to save me. To tell him I'm thankful and sorry and that he is a good friend, no matter what happens, but I can't get enough breath inside of me to make the words I need.

He glances down, seemingly relieved to see my eyes open. "We're nearly to Frysk. Don't you die before we get there. Don't you dare." His arm tightens around me, pressing me closer to a rough gray shirt he must have purchased with our horse.

I am momentarily frightened by the knowledge that I have missed days of my life and further terrified by the worry in Niklaas's shadowed eyes, but soon oblivion comes calling, and I can't resist taking his hand as I tumble into the dark.

This time, there is no ogre queen waiting behind my closed eyes, only a tall, faceless man dressed in shadows who dances me across a field of stars, spinning me closer to a halo of light, whispering in my ear, assuring me it's okay to dance away if I am tired of the pain.

I look up and the shadows covering his face part, revealing gently wrinkled skin, a golden beard, and kind brown eyes. Three kind brown eyes, two in the usual places and one blinking in the center of his forehead.

The golden god.

I realize who he is and my heart jerks. "I can't die," I whisper, not knowing if this is a dream or something more, something real, a dance to a place from which I might never return.

"You can, and you will. Everything does. Even gods." The man smiles. "But you are young. There are adventures to be had beyond this pain. If you're willing."

"I have to save my brother," I say.

"You have to save yourself," the man corrects, swinging me in a circle.

"No." I strain to focus on his face. "Jor is in Ekeeta's dungeon. I have to—"

"Trust your gifts," he says, spinning faster.

"I don't understand." I squeeze my eyes shut, finding it makes the dizziness easier to bear. "What do you mean? I don't—"

Before I can finish, he releases me and I go flying, spinning into the void, the halo of light growing farther and farther away until it blinks out like an enormous eye.

THE OGRE QUEEN

The souls within rage like a tempest that will shatter us from the inside out. Our mind reels, our heart burns with a cold fire that leaves us trembling on the floor of our chambers, shivering as Illestros covers us with a blanket, but the blanket will not warm us. We are lost, staggering in the blinding light of an eternal dawn, alone with our failure and our shame.

The girl has vanished from our sight, ventured into some bewitched country to which our creatures cannot follow and our soldiers cannot find. Vanished, with poison in her blood and her precious life slipping away.

"If the fools were not dead already, we would kill them!" we shout, moaning as our souls churn within us. They will not remain settled when we are like this, but how can we cultivate peace when we have lost her, the prize so great there is no price we wouldn't pay to have her safe within our walls?

"They suffer a far worse fate," Illestros says, stroking our bare head.

We tore our wig off and threw it to the ground long ago, that first night, when through our wolves' eyes we saw Aurora shot and realized one of our soldiers had forgotten to replace his bloodied arrows with bare ones.

Fool, wretched fool!

We should never have given the order to wound the princess. We were infected with Keetan's desperation, tormented by doubt, and fearful of sending our cousins into the domain of the Feeding Trees. We lost faith and now redemption is lost to us.

Goddess, please forgive us! we beg, but the goddess is as silent as ever.

"This isn't your failure, my queen," Illestros says.

"It is. We are afraid," we confess, shoulders shaking as Illestros pulls our body into his lap. "We are afraid. Secretly. When we are alone. There are nights when we wish for this burden to be lifted, when we beg the goddess to spare our life."

"I know, my love." Illestros kisses my cheek. "She doesn't think less of you for it"

"But we—"

"Bravery isn't the absence of fear but the willingness to stay the course in spite of it." He shifts our body until we can look into amber eyes, so wise and filled with love. "You will have the chance to be brave. The princess is still alive."

"She is?" Our lungs draw a deep breath, but the souls within us refuse to settle.

"She is. You are the goddess's chosen daughter, and you may still prove you are worthy to sit at her right hand in the kingdom beneath."

We clutch our brother's hand, wanting to believe and not to believe at the same time. "We will capture Aurora?"

"We will," he says. "Do not doubt. You must stay strong in your faith."

We nod. The words are meant to warn as well as comfort. "Bless you, brother." We kiss the thin skin at the back of his hand, fighting to keep the dark whispers within our mind from solidifying into thought.

"Bless you, sister." He rises from the floor, pulling us with him. "Now, let us go to the boy and make good use of the time that remains."

We falter, hesitating. We do not wish to hurt the boy again, not when there is nothing to be gained from it.

"We must ensure his terror is real," Illestros says. "The prince's fear is the key to ensuring Aurora plays her part in the ritual. We must be ready as soon as she is in our hands. There was frost on the roses this morning. Summer will not hold much longer."

Then it's truly almost over. For better or worse.

"For worse?" Illestros stills, his body going motionless except for his eyes, which slide back and forth as he searches our face. We swallow and think of what gown to wear to the prince's chambers, how best to wring screams from his throat, but we know our brother isn't fooled.

"Is it only fear that plagues you, sister?" Illestros's voice is soft, dangerous, a peach soaked in poison. "Or doubt as well? Do you doubt the prophecy revealed to me by the goddess?"

"Of course not, brother." We force a gentle smile, ignoring the racing of our heart. "It is only for worse if we fail to capture Aurora, or to win her cooperation. You're right. We must make good use of the prince." We snap our fingers at the slaves lurking in the corner. "Draw a bath and repair our hairpiece. We cannot appear before the boy in this state."

"I will fetch the instruments and meet you in the prince's cell, my queen." Illestros kisses our cheek, seemingly ready to put the fraught moment behind us.

But we know better than to let our guard slip again.

We keep smiling. We smile as we are bathed and dressed. We smile as we glide into the boy's cell, baring our true teeth with no bone mouthpiece to give them human aspect. We smile as we strip the boy and lash him with a three-tailed whip before releasing the biting beetles to worry at the wounds.

"Please! Please, no! No!" The boy's shouts become word-less screams so sharp we can feel them lash at our own skin, but we stay and we smile, though his pain gives us no plea-sure, and our secret, soft heart weeps for the prince.

But Illestros is right. This is part of the Mother's plan, and even suffering is made holy in her name. It *must* be made holy. . . . Because if it isn't—

Our brother turns to watch us; we smile again.

"We struggle, but we will find the Mother's gentle dark-ness," we say, wrapping our arm around his waist. "We do not truly doubt. Do not doubt us, brother."

"Never, my queen," he whispers. "You will be the right hand of the goddess. And I will be your strength and comfort until the end."

The end. It draws so close we feel its fingers closing around our neck.

CHAPTER NINETEEN

AURORA

I awake on a bed, leaning over a woman's sweet-smelling shoulder. I am warm all over, a little damp, and absolutely naked. I try to pull away and cover myself, but I am so weak I can barely manage a pitiful moan of protest.

"Don't be afraid, sweetheart," the woman whispers, pulling a nightgown over my head and guiding my good arm through a sleeve. "You're safe in Beschuttz. No one will hurt you here."

I bite my lip, stifling a moan as she works my wounded arm through the other sleeve and lays me back onto the bed. I rest my head on a pillow that smells of lavender and watch the smiling stranger pull the nightgown down my legs before covering me with a heavy down blanket.

"I'm Gettel," she says. "It's nice to finally get a good look at your eyes. You have lovely eyes."

Gettel is the one who's lovely, with dark hair, sun-kissed

cheeks, and a wide smile that crinkles the skin around her eyes. She has a motherly warmth about her that reminds me of Janin. She reminds me of someone else, too, but I can't seem to remember . . .

My mind is sluggish, my thoughts tangled, but at least my head is blessedly cool. My fever has broken. I'm going to live. I can feel it in my weary bones, no longer aching from ogre poison but simply utterly exhausted. I am so tired, all I want to do is close my eyes and sleep for a thousand years, but before I do, I have to know—

"Niklaas," I whisper, my voice scratchy. I lick my lips, working up the energy to ask where he is, if he's safe, but Gettel spares me the trouble.

"Niklaas is well, and eager to see you," she says. "But rest first, poppet. When you wake, I'll bring you milk with something in it for the pain and bread to eat."

Eat. The thought makes my stomach snarl and Gettel smile, but I am too tired to return her smile, or to stay awake . . . another . . .

NIKLAAS

I sit in a chair by the window of the sickroom and watch Aurora sleep, her cheeks pale now that fever no longer flushes her skin, her hair liberated from its warrior's knot, free to spill in a yellow wave across the pillowcase and over the side of the bed.

Gettel washed Aurora's hair the day we arrived, three days past, when Aurora was still burning up and submerging her in tepid water was the only way to keep her cool. The fever broke yesterday, but she hasn't remained conscious for more than a few minutes at a time. Gettel says she's out of danger, but I won't believe it until I look into her eyes and see something in them besides fever madness.

And so I sit, and wait, and watch, comforted by every peaceful breath she takes.

I was too close to losing her before I could tell her that I forgive her. I can't forget, and I can't stop wishing that things had ended differently, but I can forgive.

I owe her that much before I go.

She sighs and shifts her arms, but she is still asleep when she shoves her blanket down, revealing the top of her white nightgown and the gentle curves beneath. She's not the scrawny rail she appeared to be in her boy's clothes. She dips and swells in all the girlish places, though she's still on the runty side, even for a female. But with her chest unbound, her hair free, and lace at her throat, it is impossible to believe Aurora ever passed as a boy. She's not simply feminine, she's . . . pretty.

I know I should look at her and feel something—curiosity, attraction, appreciation at the very least, but I don't. I don't feel anything but the concern I'd feel for a friend, or for Haanah if she were lying there looking like a rough wind could shatter her into pieces. I feel protective, of course, but that will fade once Aurora is recovered. I know she's more than capable of fighting her own battles. As soon as she wakes up and drills me through with that determined gaze of hers, the protective feelings will be banished by the force of her . . . Aurora-ness.

She is unlike any girl I've ever met, a foreign creature in every way, too strange for all the pieces that make her up to be held together in my mind at once. I'm not sure what to call the emotion I feel for her, but it isn't what a boy feels for a girl he wants to marry. I can't imagine trying to seduce her.

My lip curls at the thought.

"What a . . . pretty face." Aurora's voice is breathy but amused.

I look to the bed, relief spreading through my chest when I see her eyes open and her gaze clear, clever, and rested. "Thank you." I grin. "I'm *feeling* pretty today. The sun is out, the skies are clear, and you, my friend, aren't dead."

Aurora smiles, but I see the uncertainty in it. "No, I'm not. Thanks to you."

I wave my hand. "Think nothing of it."

"I won't think nothing of it," she says. "I don't remember much of the journey, but I know it was dangerous. You risked your life. I'll never be able to repay you."

Four days ago, I would have told Ror to put a good word in for me with his sister and we'd call it even. Now I only force another smile and assure Aurora, "You don't have to repay me. You would have done the same if our positions were reversed and you big enough to haul me over your shoulder through the mountains."

"I would," she says, her eyes troubled. "I'm glad you believe that."

"Yes. Well . . . I've decided to . . . forgive you," I say, the words sounding awkward aloud, not matter how many times I've practiced them in my head. "I came close to losing a good friend and I . . . didn't like it. So . . ."

"So there is a good part to almost dying." She smiles her first real smile, the one that dimples her cheeks and brings mischief to her eyes. She looks like Ror when he was teasing me, looking for a fight.

But then, she *is* Ror. Or Ror is *her.* Or . . . something.

Dammit. If only this were less *confusing.*

"I suppose." I shrug, nervous for some reason, unsure how to behave with Aurora now that I'm not angry with her or afraid for her life.

"I know." She smoothes a stray hair away from her forehead, seeming a little nervous herself. "How long have I been ill?"

"Five days. Three here and two and a half on the road," I say, grateful to put the feeling talk behind us. "Two and a half days chased by every kind of nasty creature the ogre queen could send to haunt our footsteps, but no ogres, thank the gods. She must not have had men close enough to reach us before we hit the border of Beschuttz. If she had . . ." I don't finish the thought. Aurora knows what would have happened if we'd encountered an ogre battalion. I'd be dead and she'd be waking up in Ekeeta's dungeon.

"Still, Ekeeta must know where we are," Aurora says, worry creeping into her tone. "It's only a matter of time before she finds this place."

"No, we're safe here. Gettel has magical protections set over the valley." I point out the window where green willow trees wave in the breeze next to the stream behind Gettel's house. "Ogres can't see Beschuttz, and even if they could, they couldn't set foot in it. Gettel's wards keep strangers—human and ogre—out. If Crimsin hadn't sent her beast with a warning to look out for us, we never would have found a way in. The village isn't even on the map."

"But what about Ekeeta's creatures?" Aurora pushes her hands into the mattress, sitting up with obvious difficulty.

"Nothing touched by ogre magic can enter the valley." I cross to the bed, rearranging her pillows before she leans back. "You should have seen the rats that tried to follow me across the river. It was like they hit a wall halfway across."

"Rats?" Aurora shudders. "I'm glad I missed that. I'm not a lover of rats. Or bugs. Biting beetles in particular."

"Afraid of bugs. You're such a girl," I tease, perching on the mattress beside her and nudging her thigh with mine.

She laughs, a high, sweet sound that makes me smile. "I *am*. And I'm not sure you should be sitting in my bed." She prods my leg with a teasing fist. "It isn't proper."

"Proper, my ass." I stretch my legs out on the mattress beside hers. "You're like my sister. Your virtue is *safer* with me in your bed. I'll scare off any boy brave enough to approach the princess while she is convalescing."

Aurora's laughter becomes a sigh. "I don't have time to convalesce. I've already wasted nearly a week. Jor doesn't have much time left."

I take her slim hand in mine, warming her fingers, hoping the gesture will make it easier to hear what I'm about to say. "There's no chance you'll be able to secure an army in time. You're going to have to let him go."

"I know it's too late for an army," she whispers, surprising me. I wasn't sure her stubbornness was tempered with any reason at all. "But there has to be another way. Jor will kill himself before Ekeeta can use him in her ritual. I can't let that happen."

"If you're caught, then it will be both of you lost." I squeeze her hand. "Your brother wouldn't want that. It would be a senseless waste."

Especially if he's already dead, I think. There has to be a reason Ekeeta is hunting Aurora. Her brother already dead and Ekeeta in need of a briar-born child for her ritual would explain the queen's determination to bring Aurora in alive.

"I know it's dangerous for me to go to the castle." She pulls her hand away. "But I could hire a champion, an assassin or a—"

"Assassins are skilled in killing people, not breaking them out of dungeons."

"A knight, then," she says, clearly frustrated. "Or a soldier or a daredevil or a circus performer who can scale the walls! Surely there has to be someone who will attempt a rescue if enough money is involved."

"Or if they have nothing left to lose," I murmur, unable to believe I've been so dim. Again. In my defense, I've been worried about Aurora, not her brother, but now . . .

"I could try my hand at it," I say. "I know my way around the castle. I visited Mercar when I was younger and Father still attended Ekeeta's midsummer celebration."

Aurora shifts on the bed. "What do you mean?"

"I could try to free your brother," I say, pulse speeding. Over the past five days, I've begun to reconcile myself to being transformed, but transformed and killed are two different things. Still, for all I know, I'd be better off dead than trapped in a bird's body, with everything that makes me human stolen away.

My brothers, in their swan skin, didn't care for me. They flew away the morning of their transformations, taking to the skies without a glance back at the family they left behind. Even when I tracked the swan Usio became to a remote lake near the center of Norvere and found him nesting with nine other birds—ten swans, the exact number of brothers I had lost—he didn't seem to know me.

None of them did. I was a stranger, a human who sent them flying away with angry honking when I approached their nesting grounds. As far as I can tell, they are completely animal now, creatures without hope or honor or memory or a thought in their head beyond foraging for their next meal.

Wouldn't I rather die a worthy death than become the same?

"I'll do it. I'll free him," I say, decided. "I'll at least try."

"No," Aurora says, shaking her head. "You've already risked your life for me; I won't let you risk it for my brother. He's my responsibility. This is my fight."

"It doesn't matter," I say. "I'll be gone soon anyway."

"No, you won't," she says. "Gettel seems kind. Surely she'll keep you safe from your father."

"I'm sure she would, but she can't keep me safe from his curse." I pull in a bracing breath, knowing the time has come to tell Aurora the truth. "Come sunrise on my eighteenth birthday, the curse will claim me, no matter where I try to hide."

Her brow wrinkles. "What do you mean? What curse?"

I tell her the story, watching her eyes widen as I describe the way my older brothers were transformed into swans as the sun rose on their eighteenth birthdays.

"That's why I needed to marry," I continue. "A few months ago I found the witch who cursed my family and learned there is a way out. The curse only applies to sons in line to rule Kanvasola. If I had removed myself from the line of succession by marrying a girl named to inherit a kingdom of her own, I would have been free. But now . . ." I shrug again, trying to feel as carefree as the gesture. "I might as well make good use of the time I have left."

Aurora blinks and I am shocked to see a tear slip down her cheek. "Why didn't you tell me?"

"I don't think you're in any position to be asking that question, *Ror.*" I pat her awkwardly on the knee beneath the covers, flustered by her tears.

She presses her lips together and nods. "You're right. I'm sorry."

"I didn't tell anyone." I cross my arms at my chest. "I didn't want a girl to marry me because she felt sorry for me. I wanted to win a wife based on my own merits, but now it's too late, so—"

"But it's not too late!" Aurora pulls one of my hands free and shakes it. "You're so beautiful it's ridiculous, Niklaas. Really. I thought you were a god when I first saw you."

"You were out of your mind on Vale Flowers," I say, shy for the first time in as long as I can remember. I know I'm nice to look at, but hearing it from Aurora is . . . strange.

"I was mistaken, not out of my mind," she insists. "You are the most stunning thing I've ever seen. And kind and funny and brave. There has to be a way for you to marry before your birthday. I mean, how could any girl *help* falling in love with you?"

"I don't know," I say with a strained laugh. "*You* seemed to manage just fine."

Aurora's eyes drop to the bed and she releases my hand. "Yes, but I . . . I'm a unique case."

"And why is that?"

She catches a lock of her hair and twines it around and around one small finger. "I ruined a fairy boy I loved once. I just . . . ruined him." She blinks faster, and I can feel how hard she's trying not to cry. "After that, I knew I'd never be able to marry. I don't even allow myself to consider it."

"How did you ruin him?" I ask, my heart going out to her. She's so hard on herself, even when there's no reason for it.

"I . . . I broke him."

I catch her chin in my hand. "You can't break someone who doesn't want to be broken," I say, willing her to believe it. "If he decides to recover, he will."

"No." Her gray eyes are as sad as storm clouds. "He won't. And it's my fault."

"Well, not every boy is like him," I say, realizing her stubborn mind is made up when it comes to her fairy boy. "The rest of us get broken and get right up, put ourselves back together, and go looking for someone to break us all over again."

"But I—"

"And sometimes *we're* the ones who do the breaking," I say, cutting off her protest. "But that's what searching for love is like. You keep pushing on, breaking and being broken, until you find the person you want to hold safe, the only one who knows how to keep you in one piece."

She sighs, studying me before she whispers, "I usually *hate* your advice."

I grin. "Usually?"

"You're so flaming smug," she says, rolling her eyes. "But that . . ." Her lips quirk on one side. "That was beautiful."

"I'm a beauty, inside and out," I say, fluttering my lashes. But Aurora doesn't smile or laugh. She simply stares up at me, into me, for a long moment in which I become aware of her leg warm against mine and only the covers between us, of her hair smelling like lavender and honey, and for a second, I wonder . . .

And then she says—

"I will marry you, Niklaas, but only if you swear *never* to kiss me."

—and I can't help but laugh, no matter how serious her expression.

"The thought is *that* repulsive, eh?" I laugh away her attempt to explain. "Don't worry, runt, I feel the same way. But thanks." I ruffle her hair the way I did when she was Ror and it feels good. Normal. The way things are supposed to be between Aurora and me. "It's good of you to offer, but we wouldn't work in that way."

"No?" she asks, a chilly note in her voice. "Why not? I'm still first in line to Norvere's throne."

"What's wrong?" I ask, still laughing. "You're not upset I turned down your romantic proposal, are you?"

"Of course not," she says, spine stiffening. "It's flattering to know you'd rather *die* than marry me."

"I'm not going to die. I'm going to be turned into a swan, a lovely white bird with a great long neck and—"

"Oh, shut up and get out of my bed." She shoves at my shoulder, wincing as she puts stress on her injured arm. "You're even stupider than I thought!"

Now it's my turn to stiffen. "You're right, I *am* stupid." I stand, brushing my hair from my face with a clawed hand. "And you're about as convincing as a member of the *gentler* sex as I am a sea cow!"

She glares up at me, her cheeks pale but for two bright spots of pink above her dimples. "It *is* stupid to give up when you still have time to find some ignorant girl to marry you."

"So *she'll* have to be ignorant, too!"

"And it's stupid not to consider my offer!" she shouts over me. "People get married for reasons other than love all the time, and saving a life is better than—"

"So the *incredibly* tempting offer still stands?" I ask, not bothering to keep the sarcasm from my tone. "You'd still marry the big stupid oaf to save his poor, dumb life?"

"Yes, you insufferable brat," she says through clenched teeth, her hands balling into fists. "And believe me, I have absolutely *no* desire to wed you or anyone else."

"Good, because I don't want your pity or your—"

"But I would do it!" she shouts. "Despite the fact that you are ridiculous and—"

"Ridiculous? Well, isn't that the donkey calling the ass a—"

"What's going on?" Gettel opens the door and hurries in, sloshing milk from the glass in her hand onto the floor in her haste. "What are you two shouting about?"

"Nothing," Aurora and I say at the same moment, earning me another glare from my would-be bride.

"It didn't sound like nothing." Gettel casts a stern look in my direction. "Really, Niklaas. Aurora is in no shape for a lovers' quarrel. You know how ill she's been."

At the words *lovers' quarrel*, I see red. Red with pointy black daggers dancing about and battle horns blaring in the background. I hurry to excuse myself, aiming my body out the sickroom door before I wring Aurora's scrawny little neck or say something I'll regret to the woman who saved her life.

At the moment I'd be happy to ride away from Aurora and never look back, but I happen to like Gettel.

"That's right, run away!" Aurora shouts after me. "That's what cowards do!"

I want to spin around, storm back into the room, and demand to know how I went from being brave and clever to an infuriating coward in the span of ten minutes, but I don't. I pound down the stairs and through the kitchen, where Gettel's assistant is stirring sharp-smelling medicine on the stove, and out into the end-of-summer day.

There is a hint of autumn in the air, a bite to the breeze that carries the sour scent of leaves ready to change through the valley. I break into a run toward the barn, focusing on the sun on my face and the hills still green with summer grass, refusing to think about Aurora or autumn or the fact that the fifteenth of Nonstyne is only eight days away.

CHAPTER TWENTY

AURORA

"I'm sorry." I glance at Gettel as she unlaces my nightgown to take a look at my arm. "I didn't mean to cause trouble."

Gettel laughs. "Don't worry, pet. I just didn't want you hurt. I understand what it's like to be young and in love. Things don't always run smoothly, do they?"

I feel my cheeks heat and am glad it's only Gettel in the room. "Niklaas and I aren't . . . We're friends."

"Of course you are," she says, unrolling the bandages covering my wound. "All the best lovers are friends."

My cheeks burn even hotter. "No, I mean . . ." I clear my throat. "He thought I was a boy until a few days ago. He doesn't . . . It's not like that."

"Ah . . . well then . . . that's interesting . . ." She hums beneath her breath as she probes the skin around the place where the arrow punctured my flesh. It aches a bit, but the pain isn't nearly what it was. "You heal too quickly, my girl. What exactly are you fairy-blessed with? If you don't mind my asking?"

"With enhanced strength, among other things. It aids in healing." I crane my neck to get a look at my wound, wrinkling my nose at the jagged black scab marking the skin on my arm. "That looks awful."

"It should look much, *much* worse, my doll." She pats my back before pulling my sleeve up and over my shoulder. "I don't even need to re-dress it. If you keep mending so sweetly, we should get you moving tomorrow, start bringing some strength back to your muscles after the weakening effects of the poison."

She passes the milk over, and I drink it down greedily. It's so fresh it's still warm. After three days with almost nothing to eat, it's the most delicious thing I've ever tasted.

"Thank the gods for your blessings," Gettel says. "When Niklaas carried you in you were curled up so tight, I wasn't sure you'd use your hands again. The poor boy was out of his mind with worry." She smiles fondly, and I can tell she has a soft spot for Niklaas, no matter how sternly she scolded him a few moments ago. "Wept like a man over you, he did. And stayed right by your side until the fever broke."

I pause, letting the edge of the glass slip from my lips. "Really?"

She nods as she straightens the covers. "If that's not love, I don't know what is."

I finish the milk and clutch the glass to my chest. "The love of a friend."

"No, my dear," she says, a secret smile on her lips. "I've

seen the way a boy looks at a sick friend. Niklaas feels the way you do. Just give him some time."

He doesn't have time, I think, not sure what to think, or feel, about what she's said.

It's probably best not to feel anything. I'm not sure she's right about Niklaas. I can't even say for certain that she's right about *me*. I care for Niklaas and admire him, and there are times—when he isn't being impossible—that I'd like to kiss him and keep on kissing until I've pressed my lips to every bit of his ridiculously perfect body, but is that love? And what if it is? Even assuming Niklaas loves me and I return his love, what does it matter? We're both cursed, and he'll be a swan before Nonstyne becomes Harmontyne.

But he doesn't have to be. If Gettel's right, all it would take is a kiss. . . .

My hand shakes as I set the glass on the bedside table. I can't believe I let the thought enter my mind. I can't do that to Niklaas. As frustrating as I find him sometimes, I'd never want him to agree with everything I said. I'd never want to see him empty of his own desires, a slave to my every whim. I'd never want to see him like Thyne.

"Don't fret, sugar. These things have a way of working themselves out," Gettel says, resting a hand on my head.

She has no idea how complicated things are between Niklaas and me, but I nod anyway.

She grins, causing a starburst of wrinkles to form around her eyes. "Now let me help you to a chair by the fire downstairs. I'll put up your hair before dinner. I think you're well enough to join the rest of us at the table, don't you?"

"That sounds wonderful." I toss off the covers and swing

my legs over the side of the bed, grateful to feel the floor beneath my bare feet. I let Gettel help me into a pale blue dress and hold my arm as we walk down the stairs, though I'm feeling stronger than I thought I would. Still, a hand to hold is appreciated. I'm nervous to see Niklaas, anxious that somehow he'll read all the conflicted thoughts racing through my mind on my face.

But I needn't have worried. Niklaas is gone.

The only people in the kitchen are a gray-haired woman Gettel introduces as Baba, her assistant, and a little girl of six or seven with coffee-colored skin and wild brown curls asleep on a giant pillow before the fire, a snoring Hund curled by her side.

"That's my granddaughter, Kat," Gettel whispers as she settles me in a chair a few hands away.

"But you're so young," I say before I think better of it.

"I'm older than I look. Kat is my third granddaughter. The eldest is twelve." Gettel winks before turning to fetch a brush from the mantel, where a hundred different objects, mundane and magnificent, fight for space.

There are brushes and stacks of soap and a giant bottle of honey, side by side with small animal skulls, a vase of exotic feathers, a black-haired doll with shining stone eyes, and a gray rock filled with purple crystals. The rock is the same sort witches are said to leave behind after they steal a harvest. I wonder if Gettel leads raids on the surrounding villages in Frysk and how she happened to be living so far south of the frozen lands the other witch-born are said to call home, but I'm too shy to ask. I don't know Gettel well and I'm too deeply in her debt to risk being nosy or rude.

"Kat is my special helper," Gettel continues as she brushes my hair in long, soothing strokes. "Her mom is . . . away for a time, so Kat is staying with me. She's thrilled to have Hund for a visit. They've been wearing each other out running wild, *helping* with the Evensew preparations." She chuckles. "I'm not sure how much of a help they are. The others are probably glad to have the little menaces out of their hair for an hour or so."

"Is Evensew already so close?" I ask, tension creeping into my neck.

"Tomorrow evening," Gettel says, banishing the laziness from my bones. "I was afraid you would miss it, but now that you're up and about, you're welcome to join us."

"I'd like that," I mutter, mind racing. Gettel continues to chatter about the festival as she twists my hair into a pile of coils atop my head, but I listen with only half an ear. I must have spent more days with the mercenaries than I thought, or lost track of a day while Niklaas and I were traveling or . . . *something*. It can't be Evensew already!

Evensew, the day when the living sew the memory of the dead back into their lives with a festival honoring the ones they've lost, is always on the seventh of Nonstyne. That means Niklaas's birthday is only eight days away. He has only *eight* days, and Jor may not have much longer. Surely the Hawthorne tree will be changing its colors soon.

I would be tempted to tell Niklaas I've changed my mind about his offer if I thought he had a chance of getting both himself and Jor out alive. But if he became a guest in Ekeeta's castle, she wouldn't take her eyes off of him long enough for him to free Jor. He would have to have someone else with him, someone who could journey to the dungeon without arousing suspicion, another warrior posing as a servant or a—

"Prisoner," I breathe as a plan blooms in my mind, flowering as fast as the morning lilies on the west side of the island back home.

"What's that, sugar?" Gettel steps back to survey my hair with a critical eye.

"Nothing," I say, though my thoughts are still racing.

Alone, Niklaas and I would both fail. But if we went together—with me posing as his prisoner, a bribe to convince Ekeeta to grant Niklaas sanctuary from his father—it might work. Niklaas could keep the queen distracted while I find a way to free Jor and myself from the dungeon. And if I can't find a way, Niklaas could risk freeing us knowing he has my staff at his back.

Niklaas is an amazing fighter, and, thanks to my fairy blessings, I'm as good as three or four men. All we'd have to do is get out of the dungeon and down the wall walk to the old dock. We could have a boat waiting behind the rocks, ready to spirit us all away to Malai. We'd still be taking a terrible risk, but at least we'd have a chance, maybe even a good chance. And if we act at the right moment—

"There!" Gettel jabs a final pin into the pile of hair on my head. "Now you look like a princess, sweet pea."

I smile, enjoying the fact the Gettel feels free to call me anything but "my lady." I don't feel worthy of being anyone's ruler yet, but if I can save my brother and convince Niklaas to marry me and keep the ogre prophecy from coming to pass, then . . .

Well, then almost anything will seem possible, including raising an army to take back my throne.

"May I go outside?" I ask, coming to my feet. "I want to find Niklaas."

"Of course you may. Tell him supper will be ready in an hour."

I leap to my feet and hurry to the door, feeling lighter than I have in weeks—anxious and nervous and frightened, but hopeful.

The hope lasts just minutes, the time it takes to find Niklaas prowling back and forth behind Gettel's barn, helping two other boys load casks of beer into a cart, and to convince him to walk with me to the stream where twin willows sway in the breeze.

A breeze that isn't nearly strong enough to sweep away Niklaas's shout when I share the bare details of my plan.

"Not in a hundred years!" Niklaas pants, still breathing heavily from his work. "Not in a thousand!"

We're half a field from the barn, but his volume still turns heads. One of the boys loading the cart pauses to cast a look in my direction, clearly ready to intervene if I need protecting. I wave at him and take Niklaas's arm, holding tight when he tries to pull away.

"Hold still and quit shouting," I mutter behind my smile, "or your friend is going to rush over and defend me from your temper."

"As if you need defending," Niklaas mutters with a dark look toward the barn. But he stops trying to shove me off and covers my hand with his before leading me farther down the bank, away from our audience. "It's *me* who needs protection," he mutters. "From you and your mad ideas."

"It's not a mad idea," I say. "It's dangerous, yes, but—"

"It's too dangerous. You can't risk going to the capital," he says, rubbing his thumb absentmindedly back and forth across the top of my hand. "If you walk into Mercar, you're as good as dead."

"But Ekeeta wants me brought in alive," I say, ignoring the way my nerves prickle when he touches me, even an innocent touch like this one. "You know that."

He grunts. "So she can kill you herself with some crooked ogre voodoo."

"Most likely," I agree. "But that would still give us time. She's not going to kill me on sight. Rituals take time to organize. We would have at least a day, maybe more, before we would need to escape."

"The answer is no." Niklaas pulls his arm away and turns to face me, squinting into the setting sun. "I'm not going to escort you to your death, and that's the end of it."

"Niklaas, please, I—"

"No." He props his hands on his hips. "I almost watched you die once. I can't do it again. I *won't*."

I glance up, taking in his wrinkled forehead and pinched eyes, and wonder if Gettel is right. Maybe Niklaas does love me. Maybe I love him. Maybe this is what love is, being so afraid to lose someone that you'd rather face death than a world without them.

I step closer, my heart beating faster as I reach out, laying my palm on his chest, feeling the warmth of his skin through his linen shirt. "How do you think I feel? Knowing that in eight days you won't be here anymore?"

He takes a deep breath. "It's not the same. I won't be dead, and—"

"But—"

"And I won't be putting the world at risk." He covers my hand with his and pulls it gently but firmly away. "What if you can't escape before the ritual? What if you're the briar-born child Ekeeta needs, not your brother? If you go to Mercar, you're gambling everything, every beautiful patch of land in the four kingdoms, every innocent child sleeping by the fire with her dog . . . everything."

"So what?" I ask, though Niklaas has made sure I'm thinking of little Kat, hating myself for putting a child in even a speck of danger. "Jor is *my* everything. Why should he have to die if there is a chance I can save him?"

"Aurora, he could be dead already."

"No, he isn't! I won't believe that!"

"Then why is Ekeeta so desperate to capture you?"

"I don't know. Maybe she wants to eliminate anyone with a claim to her throne. Maybe she wants to finish what she started and slaughter my entire family, I don't know, but I know Jor is alive. I can feel it." I spin, sending my skirts flying as I pace away. I cover my mouth with my hand, fighting for control before turning back to face Niklaas. "I can't sit here and do nothing," I say, voice trembling. "I have to save him or die trying, and this is the only plan I can think of that might work. I'd rather have you with me, but if you won't help, I'll find someone who will. Or go alone. If I have to."

Niklaas's lip curls. "You're really that selfish?"

"No, I'm *that* willing to give everything for someone I love." I refuse to mind the guilt nudging at my heart, demanding my attention. I shouldn't feel guilty, not so long as I'm prepared to do whatever it takes to keep the kingdoms safe should my plan fail.

"I'll go to Jor and do my best to free him. And if I can't, or if he's already dead and I can't escape, then I'll . . ." I swallow, pushing away a fleeting memory of my mother's filthy dress beneath my cheek, the warmth of her body when I put my arms around her for the last time. "Then . . . Jor and I have both been well trained. We've always known we might be forced to take our own lives before the queen could use us against our people. We know ways to manage it without a weapon. I won't need a knife."

Before I realize he's moving, Niklaas has hold of my good arm with one hand and the back of my neck with the other. "Don't you dare," he says, anger simmering in his words as he leans his face down to mine. "Don't throw yourself away for no reason!"

"It's my brother's life!" I fight the urge to break his hold. I know Niklaas won't hurt me, no matter how dangerous his hand feels wrapped around my neck. "Unlike you, who is willing to give up his humanity to preserve his stupid *pride*."

He clenches his jaw. "I won't marry someone who pities me. I don't want pity, especially from you."

"Why *especially* me?" I stand on tiptoe, bringing my eyes nearly level with his. "What's so terrible about me?"

"Everything," he snaps, releasing me as he backs away. "You're a liar. I don't want to marry a stubborn, reckless liar. I don't want to—"

"Well, what we *want* and what we *get* are rarely the same thing." I will my eyes empty, refusing to show him how much his words hurt. "I'm offering you *life*."

"What kind of life?" he asks, with a shake of his head. "A life spent pretending to be happy? A life spent trying not to get gobbled alive by regret? A life spent lying next to a girl who's as disgusted by bedding me as I am by bedding her?"

Disgusted. The word hits me like a fist in the ribs.

"You said it yourself," he says in a softer tone. "You don't want to kiss me any more than I want to kiss you."

My breath rushes out as I roll my eyes. I don't know whether to laugh or cry or ball up my hand and hit Niklaas as hard as I can.

"I remember how determined you were *not* to have me as your husband," he continues. "I can't help thinking you'd come back to feeling that way. Sooner or later."

He shrugs and stuffs a hand into the pocket of his new navy work britches, loose wool britches that do an excellent job of disguising the well-formed legs beneath. But I know they're there, as I know the rest of his beautiful boy-ness is there beneath his clothes. I hate myself for thinking about it, for admiring any part of this prince who finds me as plain and uninspiring as I always knew he would. I have legitimate reasons for not wanting to kiss him, but for Niklaas it goes no deeper than a lack of attraction.

I don't know why I let myself think the closeness between us might have changed things, that friendship and family feeling and jokes and mutual admiration might make a difference. Nothing makes a difference. Boys like Niklaas only care about whether or not a girl makes their blood rush.

Then make his blood rush, fool. This is no time to give up. Not on Jor, or Niklaas.

My lips part and the aching in my chest becomes slightly more manageable.

Maybe I *can* change Niklaas's mind. The fairy boys always told me I was pretty. I used to know how to dance and tease and flirt and might have had my first kiss sooner if Thyne wasn't so protective of me. That girlish part of me is still there, locked away in a cell I made for her when I realized how dangerous it was for me to attract a boy's attention, let alone his affection or desire. She is still there, trapped in the darkness, but aching to be allowed back into the light. . . .

"Maybe I would have regretted it," I say, my head buzzing with dangerous possibilities. "But I suppose we'll never know."

Unless . . .

How can I even *consider* it? But how can I not, when lives are at stake and Niklaas has so little left to lose? If he's determined to give up, what difference does it make which devil takes him, his devil . . . or mine?

"I'm sorry," Niklaas says with a sigh. "I'm sorry I can't help you, and I'm sorry about what I said. I know why you lied, and—"

"It's all right." I lay a hand on his arm, waiting until he meets my eyes before I add, "I'm sorry, too."

"You were trying to help me," he says. "You don't have anything to be sorry for."

Oh, but I do. Or I will, if Gettel's right and you, my friend, are wrong.

"Let's go back," I say. "Gettel said I'm allowed to eat at the table tonight."

267

"Good. Kat will have someone else to pester with her questions." Niklaas gives me a smile, but it slips from his face almost instantly. "I'm glad you're better. I didn't want to leave until I knew you'd really be all right."

"You're leaving?" I ask, pulse speeding.

He nods. "As soon as I can put my things together and arrange for word to be sent to Haanah that things haven't worked out as we'd hoped."

"At least stay for the festival tomorrow night," I say, ignoring the panicked voice in my head that urges me to steal a kiss right now, before it's too late.

But I must make certain the kiss works. If it doesn't, I am without a partner to help me free Jor, and Niklaas's life is over. Too much depends upon the meeting of our lips to rush, not when even one more day might ensure success.

I know, if given the chance, I can bring Niklaas around. To steal his own words—all I need is for him to be a boy, and me a girl, without anything else getting in the way.

"A party is a nice place to say goodbye." I loop my arm through his and set off toward the cottage, trying not to let on how much I want him to stay. I've learned a thing or two about what makes Niklaas tick, and I know he doesn't find desperation attractive. "And you'd have a chance to prove you can hold your liquor. At this point, I think *I* could drink you under the table."

"You couldn't drink a field mouse under the table." Niklaas laughs. "Well . . . I helped load all that beer into the cart, I guess I might as well help drink it."

"Good," I say. "We'll have a night like we did in Goreman, a night to pretend all the terrible things don't exist."

"All right," Niklaas says, slowing as we near the house. "But only if you'll promise me you won't go running off to Mercar the moment I'm gone. Nothing good will come of you going alone. Not for your brother, and certainly not for you."

I look up into his eyes, with all the force of his will burning behind them, all the frustrating, passionate, loyal, silly, defiant, stubborn parts that make him Niklaas, and doubt I'll be able to do it. How can I risk it? How can I banish everything I love about him?

I *do* love him. I do. No matter how frightening and misery-inducing the realization is, I can't deny it any longer.

"I won't go alone." I wrap my arms around his waist, catching him in a swift, hard hug.

"Easy, killer," he says with a laughing grunt as he wraps his arms around me. "Glad to see you're getting your strength back."

"Are you sure you won't reconsider?" I know I don't need to repeat my offer. And if he reconsiders, then I can, too. I can explain why he can never kiss me, and maybe we can find a way . . . Maybe . . .

"No, but thank you. Again." He rests a hand on the hair coiled atop my head, quashing the last of my hope. "You're a good one, runt. Don't let fear make you do things you know aren't right."

"It's so hard to know what's right." I pull away, staring at the ground. "The line between cowardice and courage can be so . . . thin."

"But you can see it. If you look hard enough." He pats my head like I'm a little girl, but I'm too miserable to be annoyed by it. "Speaking of thin, you're feeling even scrawnier than usual. Let's go fatten you up."

"I've lost my appetite," I say with a sad sniff.

"We're having roast turkey left over from last night," he says in a wheedling tone. "With cheeses and dried fruit and stewed tomatoes and bread with fresh sweet butter."

My stomach growls.

"Sounds like your appetite tracked you down," he whispers, tickling a finger into my ribs. I spin away, laughing against my will.

"Stop it!" I point a warning finger in his direction. "I hate being tickled."

"Oh you do?" he says, a wicked gleam in his eye.

"Yes, I do!" I slap his hand as he reaches for me again and turn to race back to the house, with him close behind. We tumble into the kitchen like children, triggering a warning bark from Hund and an excited squeal from Kat, who is awake and standing on a stool by the food preparation table, up to her elbows in flour.

"Hello, Princess! I'm Kat and I'm making you a pie!" Kat shouts, flinging her hands into the air, sending flour flying.

"You're making a mess is what you're making, pumpkin." Gettel laughs as she grabs Kat's wrists, directing her hands back into the bowl. "Looks like you two had a nice walk." She casts a knowing smile over Kat's head, a smile that says it will only be a matter of time before Niklaas and I both realize we're more than friends.

I hope a day will be long enough.

CHAPTER TWENTY-ONE

NIKLAAS

We stay up late—Gettel, Kat, Aurora, and I—talking and eating, watching Kat's orange kittens torment Hund and eating, praising Kat's rehearsal of the song she'll sing at the festival and eating some more. We graze until I can't stuff another bite in and Gettel forces Aurora to forego a second slice of pie lest she make herself sick after so many days with nothing but milk and bread.

It's close to one in the morning when I say my goodnights and stumble to my makeshift bedroom above the barn. I am asleep almost as soon as my body hits my straw mattress, too exhausted to worry about what will happen when I leave Beschuttz or fret over if I'm doing the right thing lying to Aurora.

But I can't tell her I'm going to Mercar or she will try to come with me. I can't—*won't*—allow that to happen.

I make a mental note to warn Gettel that Aurora may try

to sneak away and to convince the healer to do whatever it takes to keep her safe, even if it means hiring a dozen farm boys to sit on the princess, and then I sleep. I sleep hard, so solid and deep and dreamless it seems barely an hour has passed between the moment I close my eyes on the dark interior of the barn and open them to sun streaming into the loft.

I grimace into the pale dawn light, still so weary my eyes feel full of cotton, wondering what woke me.

A moment later, the wonder is answered with a whisper from the ladder.

"Niklaas," Aurora hisses. "Get up, I need your help."

"With what?" I squint in her direction as she climbs onto the boards.

"I'll show you. Get up," she says, propping her hands on her hips. She's wearing her boy's pants with a lacy white shirt, and her hair hangs in a tidy braid over one shoulder. She isn't as done up as she was last night in that pretty blue dress, but she's certainly looking much more awake than I feel.

"What time is it?" I ask, rubbing at my face.

"I don't know." She lifts a shoulder and drops it. "Before six."

I groan and roll over, burying my face in the pillow. "Go away."

"I can't. I need someone to spar with me before Gettel wakes up and tells me to take it easy."

"You *should* take it easy." I close my eyes and am halfway asleep again when Aurora takes a running leap onto the mattress. I grunt as she lands and hug my pillow tight. "Be gone, woman," I mumble.

"But this is your last day, and my last chance to spar with someone who knows how to fight. Come on, you can nap later." She pokes at my ribs with her bony fingers. "Wake up, Niklaas, wake up, wake up, wake up," she says in a singsong voice, accompanying each "wake up" with another jab to my ribs. "Waaaaake up, waaaake—"

I roll over and tackle her, knocking her flat on the mattress and covering her face with my pillow, muffling her laughter. "I should smother you back to sleep," I say. "Better for everyone. Keep you out of trouble."

"You wouldn't!" she protests with a giggle, her hands finding my bare chest and shoving at the ribs she was prodding a moment ago.

Her touch is cool against my blanket-warmed skin, and surprisingly nice. Familiar but unfamiliar and . . . interesting in a way I wouldn't have expected, making me aware of the fact that there is a girl in my bed, and that we are alone in the barn, and that there is no chaperone around to interfere.

"I can't breathe!" she says, banishing the odd thought with a pinch.

"That's the point." I pull the pillow away, revealing a red-cheeked Aurora, wisps of hair standing out around her face. "You look like you're up to something."

"I am up to something: getting back into condition," she says, wrinkling her nose in a way that I have to admit is cute, despite the fact that she's awoken me from the best sleep I've had in weeks. "Come on, we can practice behind the barn." She sits up, throwing the pillow at my chest before rolling off the bed. "Gettel won't see us from the window, and I've put down straw on the grass to break our falls. First one knocked

273

off their feet three times in hand-to-hand has to give up their scone."

"What kind of scones?" I throw off the covers, wondering if Aurora will be flustered by the fact that I'm not wearing anything but tight long underwear pants Gettel pulled from her son's old things.

But of course she's seen me in much less.

The thought makes my cheeks heat. I've never been shy around a girl, but I've never been nearly naked in front of a girl who wasn't nearly naked herself.

"I'm not sure." Aurora grabs my shirt and throws it onto the mattress without a glance at the nakeder parts of me. "They were still cooking when I snuck through the kitchen, but I think I smelled blackberries."

Blackberry. I shove my arms into my sleeves. "Hand-to-hand, no swords or staffs?"

"I figured that was the only fair way for us to fight." She crosses to the ladder and steps onto the top rung. "Seeing as I possess superior skill in armed combat."

I snort and reach for my pants, suddenly more inspired about this sparring match. "In your dreams, runt."

"In your nightmares," she says with a wink as she disappears down the ladder.

I dress, shove my feet into shoes, and hurry down the ladder to find Aurora already outside the barn, standing on a patch of hay-covered grass. Her hair looks paler in the dawn light, a shining white-blond that trails nearly to the ground.

"You should have put your hair up." I stalk toward her, stretching my arms across my chest as I go. "I fight dirty when scones are involved."

"That's all right, I'm fairy-blessed." She tosses her braid over her shoulder and steps back, making room as I take my place across from her. "But no blows to the face. We don't want you ugly for the festival tonight."

"What are you fairy-blessed with?" I bend my knees and roll my shoulders, waking up my body. "I mean, obviously strength and skill in battle, but is that all?"

A strange looks flits across her face, but it vanishes before I can read it and she is smiling again when she shrugs. "Not much else. Just bravery and mercy." She bends her neck side to side and circles her wrists. "I couldn't hurt a defenseless man even if I wanted to. So don't worry, you have nothing to be afraid of."

I smile, a baring of my teeth that feels wonderfully vicious. But before I show the runt what I learned in twelve years of hand-to-hand combat training with the meanest men in Kanvasola, I have to know—

"Are you sure you're up to this?" I ask. "You were looking pretty fragile while you were sleeping yesterday."

"Aw, Niklaas, were you watching me sleep?" She bats her lashes in an excellent imitation of myself when I'm teasing her. "That's sweet. A little odd, but sweet."

I scowl. "I was worried."

"Well, you don't have to worry anymore. I'm nearly back to normal, which should give you just the *barest* chance to—"

Before she can finish her taunt, I rush her, aiming for her midsection, already visualizing the way I'll sweep my arm back, buckling her knees and knocking her off her feet with one hand as I pin her chest to the ground with my shoulder. I move as fast as a person recently wrenched from their bed can be expected to move, but Aurora is faster. She sees me coming and jumps, shoving her hands into my shoulders and launching herself into the air. There is enough time for my jaw to drop as I realize she's going to jump over me and then her boot is on my shoulder and she's gone.

I spin to face her, but she has already landed and slipped her leg between both of mine. When I turn, I trip, and when I trip, Aurora is right there to pounce on my chest and take me to the ground like a feral squirrel defending its winter stash.

I hit the grass with a grunt as the air rushes from my lungs and pull in my next breath with Aurora's arm across my throat.

"One for me," she says with a gleeful grin. "Do you want me to try the next round with my good arm pinned to my side?"

"Laugh while you can, feral squirrel. I'm ready for you now."

"Is that my new nickname?" She laughs as she pulls her arm from my neck and sits back on her heels, tossing her braid back over her shoulder in a way that draws my attention to the fact that the first two buttons on her shirt have come undone, revealing an intriguing triangle of skin. "I like it. Much better than 'runt.'"

"How about 'feral runt'?" I jump to my feet, mentally vowing not to give her the satisfaction of taking me down again. At least, not so easily.

"That I don't like," she says with mock seriousness. "If you call me that again, I'll have to exact vengeance."

I grin. "Exact away. Feral runt."

This time, she makes the first move, feinting to my right before stepping in tight to the left and hooking her leg around my ankle. She shifts her weight forward as her elbow comes to the center of my back, ready to leverage me to the ground.

Instead of fighting her, I let her propel me forward, tucking my head and diving into a roll across the grass before springing back to my feet. Sensing her close behind, I kick backward, hoping to knock her away long enough to turn around. Instead she grabs my leg and holds it locked against her as she runs forward, bringing the limb up and over my body, flipping me onto my back.

I land with an *oof* of surprise. A second later she is straddling my chest, her arm once again at my throat.

She leans in, bringing her face close to mine before she whispers, "Those scones probably aren't any good anyway."

"Don't count your scones before they're on your plate." I ignore the rushing feeling in my chest as her breath feathers over my lips. "I could still reach three before you do."

She lifts one pale brow, making it clear what she thinks of that possibility.

"How'd you get that scar?" I ask, running my fingertip over the puckered skin near her brow, giving myself a moment to catch my breath.

"I don't remember." She hops back to her feet. "It was the day the queen ordered my mother, my brother, and me imprisoned. I was bleeding when the soldiers threw me into the dungeon, but I don't know how I was wounded."

"You were . . . seven?" I ask, sitting up.

She nods. "I remember almost everything about that time,

but not how I was hurt. My mother said she thought she saw the solider carrying me strike me but . . ." She shrugs and a determined smile thins her lips. "Ready to go again?"

"I've never killed a man." I take the hand she reaches down and let her pull me to my feet. "But if I could find that soldier . . . What kind of monster hits a little girl?"

"The same kind who totes her to the dungeon knowing there's a good chance she'll die there." Aurora's forehead wrinkles. "Now I know Ekeeta was telling the truth about wanting Jor and me kept alive until the long summer of the prophecy, but then . . ."

"She's not going to get her hands on you again." I take her chin in my hand, making sure she doesn't look away. "You promised not to go to Mercar. Remember?"

"I promised not to go alone," she says, gaze sliding to the left.

I sigh, suddenly tired. She's going to put herself in danger. *Of course* she is. I shouldn't have expected anything else. "Then I'd better spend the day making sure no one in this village will leave with you." I turn, but Aurora stops me with a hand on my arm.

"Wait." Her fingers fist in my shirt. "Let's not fight today. We can fight tomorrow morning before you leave if you want, but let's . . . let's have a good day."

"Is it possible for us to go a day without fighting?"

"We had good days on the road, didn't we? We just won't talk about Ekeeta or my brother or your curse or . . . anything that makes us quarrel."

"What's left?" I ask with a wry smile.

"Battle techniques?" She blinks with an innocence I don't

buy for a second. "I mean, you clearly need advice on how to best someone half your size, so I think—"

With a roar, I fling myself forward, tackling Aurora in a combination leap/bear hug that no self-respecting combat instructor would view as anything but laughable. But the ridiculous succeeds where my other efforts failed, and less than two seconds later I have a giggling Aurora pinned beneath me, my hand at her throat.

"One for me," I say, joining in her laughter as I pull my arm away. "But I can't keep my hand on you. It looks too dastardly."

"Dastardly?" she repeats.

"Yes, dastardly." I tickle her the way I did last night and am rewarded with a peal of throaty laughter. "I will fight a girl, but I will not be a dastard."

"Of course not." She bites her lip, regaining control with obvious effort. "I'm proud of you, really. A lesser man would have let me win every round."

"Is that a compliment?" I brace my hands on either side of her face.

"Maybe." She shifts beneath me, making me aware of the places where we touch, where her legs tangle with mine, where her stomach brushes against my ribs as she pulls in breath. "Is that so hard to imagine?"

I look down at her, at her softly parted lips and her eyes the gray of the ocean before a storm, and something shifts inside of me. My pulse escapes its usual haunts, beginning to beat in deep, secret places as I imagine what it would be like to have Aurora beneath me for reasons that have nothing to do with sparring, to feel her skin against mine and her breath hot on my neck as—

"We should get inside." I scramble off of her, heart thudding in my ears as I come to my feet and back away. "That's enough for your second day out of your sickbed."

"But I haven't won yet." She props herself up on her elbows, but makes no move to rise from where she is sprawled on the grass.

"I forfeit." I look at the barn, at the willow trees in the distance, at the horizon full of marmalade, sunrise clouds—anywhere but at Aurora. I'm too ashamed of myself. I can't believe I had *those* sorts of thoughts about her, even for a second. She's like my sister, and the last thing I'd want for my sister is to see her taken in by a boy like me.

Maybe Aurora was right; maybe you do *only know two ways to manage women. Too bad neither method quite applies to her.*

"What's wrong?" Aurora sits up, propping her elbows on her knees.

"Nothing." I force a smile, pretending not to be bothered by the realization that it isn't only Aurora's time spent pretending to be a boy that makes it hard to know how to behave with her. It's the fact that she doesn't fit into the usual baskets. She's not a family member, and she's not a girl I'd have an easy tumble with. She's a little of both, as well as a friend of the kind I thought I could only find in another man. I never dreamt I could have fun sparring with a girl, or making rude jokes, or traveling across country with nothing but two horses and a single bedroll. I've never known a girl who could travel with less than two saddlebags and a pack mule.

But then . . . most of the girls I've known were raised in

Kanvasola, and Kanvasol people expect a girl to be an innocent in need of protection or a temptress in need of a bedding. There aren't many other options, especially for girls too young to be mothers.

"You have an odd look on your face." Aurora cocks her head as she studies me. "Are you sure nothing's wrong?"

"I was just . . . thinking."

She hums beneath her breath. "Don't hurt yourself."

I narrow my eyes. "I'm not stupid, you know. I speak five languages, know the lineage of every royal family in Mataquin back ten generations, and have an above-average grasp of mathematics."

"I'm sure you do," she says in a patronizing tone clearly intended to provoke me.

I smile, determined not to be drawn in. "It's not my lack of intelligence that kept me from knowing you were a girl. I was raised to think girls incapable of certain things. Obviously, I was raised poorly, but that shouldn't be a surprise, considering I had no mother and, well, you know who my father is."

Aurora's grin slips away. "I'm sorry, Niklaas. I was only teasing, I didn't—"

"I know you were." I wave off her apology. "But I wanted you to know that I realize I was wrong, and that maybe I need to change . . . some things."

"What kind of things?" she asks, her eyes searching mine.

"The way I think. The things I expect. Just . . . things." I reach a hand down to help her up. She ignores it, vaulting to her feet with a shove of her arms and a jackknife motion of her body that is impressive. Unnecessary but impressive.

"Maybe you should think about changing a few things, too," I continue.

"Like what?" The look of surprise on her face makes it clear she considers herself above reproach.

"Like accepting help a bit more graciously," I say, waving the hand she ignored in her face. "You don't have to take on the world all alone."

"I know," she says. "Why do you think I was looking for an army?"

"An army you could order to do your bidding." I snort. "That's not the same thing as figuring things out with another person. Working together?"

"I worked with you," she says, her voice getting bristly.

"No, you manipulated me." I cross my arms and stand my ground. "You refused to give me what I wanted until I did your bidding."

She rolls her eyes. "What else was I supposed to do? You wouldn't have taken me to the Feeding Hills otherwise."

"Exactly." I tug her braid and am rewarded with a glare. "And then we wouldn't have had to leap off a cliff to escape from the exiles, and you wouldn't have been shot by ogres or almost died. If you had trusted my judgment from the start—"

"I didn't know you at the start!" She throws her hands up to either side of her head. "I thought you were trying to get out of a weeklong journey, I didn't know that—"

"But you know now." I take her hands. "So will you promise me you won't go to Mercar. Please?"

"How about you trust *me* this time, and come with me?" she begs, her fingers squeezing mine. "Please, Niklaas. Just . . . come with me."

I drop my eyes to the hay scattered beneath our feet. "I can't, I—"

"There you are!" The outraged shout comes from behind me.

I drop Aurora's hands and turn to see Kat, still in her nightgown, standing barefoot in the grass. "I thought you might be out here. Gram told me not to bother you, but I snuck out the back door. I didn't want you to miss breakfast. Baba made scones!"

"Did she now?" Aurora asks in a light voice, slipping around me with a smile.

"She did. And they're fresh out of the oven." Kat skips across the grass to grab Aurora's hand as Gettel comes around the corner of the barn.

"You sneak," Gettel scolds. "I'm sorry, loves, hope she wasn't bothering you."

"Not at all. She saved Niklaas from losing his scone rights in battle," Aurora says, glancing back at me as she's dragged away. "Are you coming?"

"In a minute," I say, catching Gettel's eye. "You go on ahead."

"All right, but you'd better hurry," Aurora says. "I'll keep my hands off your scone, but I can't make any promises for this one." She skips ahead of Kat, making the girl giggle as she has her turn to be pulled along.

I wait until they're out of sight before I turn to Gettel. "I need to talk to you. About Aurora."

Gettel nods. "You want me to keep her safe."

"Yes, but it won't be easy. You'll need help. She's strong and stubborn and—"

"I'm sorry, Niklaas," she says, a sadness in her eyes I haven't seen there before. Gettel always seems to be in a cheery mood, even when bathing fevered patients or cleaning up a mess Hund made. "She isn't meant to stay here."

"You said I could stay. Why not her?"

"Aurora is meant to face the queen." Gettel pulls her shawl around her shoulders, as if chilled by the thought. "The time is nearly at hand."

"But she's too weak. She almost died, how can she—"

"If she chooses wisely, she won't need strength to defeat the queen," Gettel says. "And if she chooses unwisely, all the strength in the world won't matter."

"What does that mean?" I ask, feeling stupid all over again.

"I don't know." She holds out her hands, palms up, and looks to the pale morning sky, as if waiting for wisdom to fall from the clouds. "It's what the magic tells me, and I feel it's true." She glances back at me. "But I can't say for sure what it means. We must trust Aurora will know when the time comes."

"She has to go, then?"

"She does, dear boy." Gettel lays a warm hand on my arm. "I'm sorry."

I want to argue with her, to insist that Aurora facing the queen is the last thing she or Mataquin needs, but . . . I trust Gettel, and her magic. This valley is the happiest place I've ever been, and all the people here love Gettel and trust her with their lives. If she could protect Aurora, I believe she would. But if she can't . . .

"It's all right." I can't deny that I was dreading going alone. Aurora may be impulsive and stubborn, but she's a hell of a fighter and a quick head in a crisis. If she'll allow me to temper her "rush in" with a little strategy, we might have a chance. "I'll go with her. We'll leave tomorrow."

Gettel smiles. "She's lucky to have you."

I shrug and drop my eyes to the ground, not sure what to say.

"She is," Gettel says. "And she knows it. She'll be happy you're going together."

"She'll be happy to have her way," I say with a wry laugh. "I'll go tell her, and maybe we can make it through the rest of the day without a fight."

"Why don't you tell her tomorrow?" Gettel crosses the damp grass, heading back toward the house. "Fairy-gifted or not, she could use another day to heal. I'm afraid she'll drag you onto the road after breakfast if you tell her now."

I chuckle as I fall in beside her. "You know her well, considering she spent her first three days here asleep."

"I know heroes," Gettel says a little sadly. "Heroes are all the same."

For a moment, it's odd to think of Aurora as a hero, but then, just as suddenly, it isn't. Of course she's a hero, a person willing to face extraordinary odds, to rise to any challenge, and to put the welfare of others before her own.

I believed her last night when she said she'd kill herself before she'd put the four kingdoms in danger. I believed her, and it scared me. I've always known my life was going to be cut short, but the thought of Aurora dying before she turns eighteen, before she has a chance to hug her brother again or realize that one failed love doesn't mean her heart is doomed for life, is . . . unbearably sad.

"Will she live?" I ask beneath my breath. We're close to the house now, and I don't want Aurora or Kat to hear.

"I don't know that, either," Gettel says, patting my hand. "So be sure to make the most of every moment you have left."

She disappears into the house, but I pause on the stoop, needing to think, to understand the racing of my heart and the tightness in my throat. I feel panicked, but I'm not sure why. It isn't the possibility of death—that's always been there, from the moment Aurora and I escaped from the mercenary camp—it's what Gettel said.

Make the most of every moment. How do I make the most of my time with Aurora when I'm not even sure who she is, or who *I* am when I'm with her?

"I saved this for you, but just barely." Aurora appears in the doorway with a scone in her hand. "You were this close to doing without." She pinches her fingers together to illustrate the nearness of my escape as she drops the scone into my palm.

"You really are a hero," I say, but the joke falls flat.

"What?" she asks, forehead wrinkling.

I clear my throat. "Nothing."

Aurora tugs at her ear. "Can we start this morning over? With no arguments?" she asks, moving a step closer, wiping her hands on an apron she's tied on over her pants.

"Sleep well?" I ask, smiling as understanding lights her eyes.

"Very well." She lifts her arms over her head and comes onto her toes, stretching like a cat. "I've been cutting apples for another pie to take to the festival. Would you like to help spice them? I know you have firm opinions on pie."

"I have firm opinions on most things," I say, taking a bite of my scone.

"Just one of the things I love about you," she says in a breezy voice, but for some reason the words steal our smiles away. For some reason they make us stand staring for a long, strained moment, until I remember to swallow and Aurora clears her throat and motions me in with a nervous wave.

"Come on," she says. "I'll shave the cinnamon."

I follow her inside, watching her tiptoe across the floor to the cook table in her bare feet, as graceful as a dancer, marveling that this scrap of a girl with the pretty hands is capable of inflicting so much damage on my person.

That unexpected longing rises inside of me again, but this time it isn't simply a longing to touch her, or at least not the way I've known it before. It's a warmer feeling, desire wrapped up in furs to keep it safe from the cold, lust softened like a wine aged for years in gentle darkness. It's not something I've felt before—the need to possess and to treasure so tangled together. It's uncomfortable, foreign, but also . . .

Right. And maybe I don't have to fight it. Maybe I should let it be, and see if . . . Maybe . . .

"Will you get the sugar?" Aurora asks, busy with the cinnamon and the shaver.

I fetch the sugar from the far end of the table and place it by her elbow, hope rising inside me like a ghost from the grave.

Maybe if she knew, maybe if I tell her, and if she feels the same . . .

If she does, everything could be different. Absolutely everything.

CHAPTER TWENTY-TWO

AURORA

Immediately after breakfast, Niklaas is spirited away by a wagon full of men on their way to the festival grounds to set up the stages, dancing boards, benches, and fenced yard for the littlest children to play in while their mothers and fathers enjoy the celebration. He doesn't return until late afternoon, right as Gettel is forcing us all to take a nap in preparation for staying up well after midnight for a second night in a row.

I go to my bed grudgingly, cursing myself and my failure. Some temptress I am. I was gaining ground this morning—I could tell Niklaas was softening toward me—but I couldn't keep my mouth shut and stop fighting with him long enough for softening to become anything more. Still, a twisted part of me relished every contrary word out of his mouth, knowing all too soon he might never disagree with me again.

Or he might defy me until the minute he rides out of the valley tomorrow morning. I can't decide which is worse—to learn he loves me and ruin him, or learn he doesn't and watch him walk away.

"Hold still, I'm nearly finished," Gettel says, pinning another purple-and-white blossom in my hair.

She's been stabbing at my hair for the better part of an hour. My neck is stiff and my bottom numb from the hard seat of the chair, but I do my best to hold still. Gettel has done so much for me—from saving my life to taking in a lovely lavender gown of hers to fit me for the festival—the least I can do is indulge her passion for arranging hair.

"My youngest daughter has hair even longer than yours," she says, a fond note in her voice. "But dark brown and coarse as anything. It would take hours to get it braided or combed out and rolled onto curlers when she was little."

"Is that Kat's mom?" I ask, silently thanking the stars Gettel decided my hair only needed curling in the front. An hour spent fussing with hair, I can suffer. Anything more would have been more than I could bear.

"Yes. I stole her away from her birth parents when she was not quite a year old," Gettel says with a wry smile. "Some of the stories about us witches are true, you know. We do steal children, but only those who need to be stolen. My daughter's parents were thieves by trade and neglected her terribly. I took her away and gave her a kinder life."

"That was good of you."

"No, that was lucky for me," she says. "She was a blessing."

"Is she . . . ?" I pause, not wanting to finish the question.

"Dead? No, but she's . . . lost to me. And Kat." Gettel plucks more flowers from their stems, leaving the blossoms on the handheld mirror on the mantel. "Kat's father supplies the kingdoms of Herth with Elixir of Elsbeth's Rose. He supplied my daughter as well, until she nearly wasted to death. To save her, I was forced to lock her away." She pins another flower in my hair. "There is a tower in the woods beyond the valley. You may see it on your ride out. My daughter has lived there since last spring but still craves the elixir above all else. She expresses no desire to see Kat or . . . myself."

"That's terrible." I can't understand how anyone, no matter how poisoned, could cast their mother from their life, especially a mother like Gettel. "I'm so sorry."

Gettel pats my hand. "I still have hope. One day I will climb the tower and she will be the girl I raised again, I know it." She sets her pins down and takes a long look at her creation. "You should send your mother a message," she says, eyes still on my hair. "She deserves to know where you're going."

"My mother is dead."

"No she isn't, sugar." Gettel smiles and pats my hair like a pet that's performed a brilliant trick. "She's on an island far away, but not so far I can't feel her searching for you. She has great magic, but not enough to find you here."

"She's Fey, my fairy mother," I say, feeling terrible. I haven't thought of Janin in days, haven't even paused to imagine how concerned she must be.

"She loves you, and she's worried." Gettel turns, fetching paper and a charcoal pencil from the mantel and pressing them into my hands. "Write her. I'll have the message sent by falcon first thing tomorrow. Now I'm going to fetch something to give you a little color. Don't look in the mirror until I get back."

I nod and bend over the paper in my lap, but when I put

the charcoal to it I don't know where to start. "I'm sorry" is inadequate, and "Forgive me" will probably come too late. I know there's at least a fifty-fifty chance I will die in Mercar. Janin will know it too.

In the end, I simply tell her that my attempt to secure an army has failed and that I'm going to the capital to free Jor myself. And then I tell her "thank you" and "I love you" and ask her not to blame herself. Not that she would.

Fairies don't feel guilt the way humans do. They live for thousands of years, long enough for the weight of their past mistakes to crush them to dust if they allowed them to. Janin will not regret taking me in and loving me like a daughter and working so desperately to protect me, only to have me deliver myself into danger.

That will be my burden to bear, for however many days are left to me.

"I can get that out now if I hurry," Gettel says, bustling back into the room. "If we're lucky, the master of birds won't have left for the festival just yet."

Gettel tucks the paper into her apron before leaning down to dab something sticky from a pot in her hands onto my cheeks and lips, adding a touch above my eyes.

"I make this to aid in healing, but it's the prettiest pink. It might make your lips tingle, but that will pass." She stands back and claps her hands. "Perfect! Take a look while I give this to Bernard. If Kat comes in, tell her not to eat anything or she'll ruin her supper."

I wait until Gettel is out the door before standing and fetching the mirror. It's a lovely, heavy thing with a silver frame and only gently clouded glass.

It may also be enchanted.

It *must* be, I decide as I stare, slack-jawed, at my reflection. That *can't* be me. That girl with the riot of golden curls forming a flower-dusted frame around her face, with dewy pink cheeks and sparkling eyes that look more lavender than gray. I tip the mirror down, taking in the whisper-thin violet gown that bares most of my shoulders and clings tight to my chest before falling in gossamer waves to my ankles. It is as beautiful as my good gown back home but fits me even better, emphasizing my curves, making me look plush and healthy instead of scrawny and small.

For the first time in my life, I look like a woman. I *feel* like a woman. Tonight I am not plain or boyish, I am as lovely as a girl in a fairy story, nearly as lovely as my mother, the woman whose name for me will always be synonymous with beauty and kindness. She may have cursed me, but she didn't mean to. She only wanted to keep me safe, to prevent me from marrying a man who would betray me the way my father betrayed her. She didn't know what her wish would do to me . . . or to the boys foolish enough to love me.

I close my eyes, remembering the press of Thyne's lips on mine, the ocean and star fruit taste of him on my tongue. I remember pulling away to watch the spark fade from his eyes, sucked away like smoke up a chimney after the fire is put out, leaving nothing but an empty hearth, waiting for me to fill it.

My breath rushes out with a sob. I can't do it. I can't, no matter how—

"Aurora?"

I open my eyes to find Niklaas standing by the fire, wearing a crisp white shirt with a traditional Frysk vest the same dark brown as his riding pants and freshly shined black boots. His patchy whiskers from this morning have been shaved away and his hair cut and combed through with something that makes it shine like spun gold.

He is even more beautiful than usual, so stunning that looking at him would be enough to break my heart . . . if it weren't breaking already.

"Are you all right?" he asks.

I shake my head, my eyes filling.

"Don't cry." He takes the mirror from my shaking hand. "You look beautiful."

My face crumples.

"Well, *that's* not so beautiful," he teases as he pulls me into his arms. "Come on now, stop it. You'll make your face all red."

"I was just . . . thinking of my mother." It's partly true.

"Evensew is for celebrating the dead, not mourning them," Niklaas says, rubbing my back in slow, comforting circles. "Let's go to the festival. We'll sing your mother a song and dance a dance in her honor and enjoy ourselves the way she would have wanted. I want to . . . make the most of tonight, of the time we have left."

He's right. There will be time for tears and regrets and hating myself when Niklaas is spared from his curse and Jor is free.

I pull away with a sniff, wiping my eyes with my fingers, careful not to rub the pink from my cheeks. "You're right."

"There's something I don't hear very often." He winks as he takes my hand, twining his fingers through mine, making me aware of every bit of skin between my fingers, of the way our calloused palms press together in their own timid kiss.

My nerves hum with longing and my heart aches with misery, sending such conflicting feelings coursing through my body that for a moment it feels I'll be torn apart. But just when I'm sure I can't keep holding Niklaas's hand without bursting into tears again, my head steps in and shuts the misery away, shoving it into the dark corner of my mind where the things I can't bear to think about fight and claw and fester.

It will escape to tear at me later, but for now, I refuse to think of it, refuse to think of anything but putting one foot in front of another until this night is over.

I've made my decision. Now I will see it through.

"Ready?" Niklaas asks.

"Ready." I force a smile as he pulls me out the door.

Outside, a wagon half full of villagers—including Kat and Gettel, who share the seat beside the big-armed driver—is waiting. As we emerge, the chatter stops and a cheer goes up. The men and women smile as Niklaas helps me into the back of the wagon, wishing us a Merry Evensew, lifting their candles high in the air.

I take a seat on a hay bale and Niklaas settles down beside me. We are handed candles in honor of those we have lost and light them from the flames of the candles of two little girls sitting across from us, symbolizing that we are all connected in the dance of life and death, and then we are off, trundling down the road to the festival of the dead, where Niklaas's free will will die so that the rest of him may live.

NIKLAAS

She is beautiful, so flaming breathtaking I can't believe I ever thought her merely pretty.

It's more than her hair or her dress or the shine in her eyes. It's the way she smiles, the way our eyes meet across the feast table and words pass between us without anything being said, the careful way she takes my hand as I lead her onto the boards to dance, as if she senses the way things are shifting between us and she's as frightened as I am that somehow we'll drop this precious thing and it will shatter to pieces.

She's . . . magical. Like a dream you try to forget upon waking, something so perfect you have to push it from your head to keep from weeping into your pillow wishing it were real. But she is real, real and warm and in my arms, her breath rushing out as I lift her into the air and set her back down to the beat of the drum.

My hands tighten at her waist and her palms come to rest on my chest, setting my heart to pounding even harder. All around us, men laugh and women squeal as the wild country dance ends with a frenzied fiddle solo that sends couples spinning arm in arm, but Aurora and I don't spin. We stand, staring, lips parted, breath coming fast. The sun has set, but the light is still rosy, emphasizing the color in her cheeks and the copper in her hair, making her so damned lovely it's painful, like someone's slipped a knife of wanting between my ribs.

"Walk with me." I take her hand, leading her off the dancing boards and into the grass, heading for a grove of white-barked ghost gums at the edge of the field where evening is gathering, creating purple shadows beneath the trees.

I expect her to ask me where we're going, to say we shouldn't roam away until the torches are lit, but she doesn't. She follows me, her hand easy in mine. We walk in silence except for the music drifting across the field and the chirp and hum of summer insects that should have died long ago rising from the grass. I take their calls as a sign, an assurance that miracles can happen.

We reach the trees and I turn to Aurora, bowing over her hand. "May I have this dance, my lady?"

"*My lady.*" She laughs. "Have you forgotten who you're talking to?"

"I haven't forgotten a thing," I say, pulling her into my arms.

She stiffens and a wrinkle forms between her eyes. "Niklaas, I—"

"Just dance with me, runt," I say, refusing to let her pull away. "Whatever you're fretting about can wait."

She sighs but doesn't protest as I spin her under the limbs where silver leaves whisper in the breeze, singing along to the blissful lament of "The Last Waltz." The waltz is a traditional Evensew song I've heard dozens of times, but I've never appreciated it the way I do now, when I am on the verge of a moment that will change my life.

Every yearning note wrung from the fiddle's strings vibrates inside me, making my blood rush and my breath ache in my lungs. I have seduced more girls than I can count on my fingers and toes, and I've even imagined myself in love once before, but I've never cared whether a girl said yes or no as much as I do tonight. Knowing that my life depends on Aurora's answer is part of it, but not even close to all. She is already my dear friend, but by the end of the night she might also be the girl I'll spend my life with, the girl I'll make a family with. A family where people love and trust each other, where children are treasured, not cursed and thrown away, and no one has to pretend to be something they're not.

The thought is thrilling and . . . terrifying. Together we could be magical . . . or a disaster . . . or maybe a magical disaster; I'm not sure which. I only know I want the chance to find out if this is real love, the kind that lasts after the first rush is gone, the kind that makes a home a place to find refuge instead of a prison to escape.

"What is this, Niklaas?" Aurora's whisper is so soft I can barely hear her over the rustling of the trees.

"It's called dancing," I say, so anxious that the palm I've placed at her waist begins to sweat. "I think we're pretty good at it." I draw her closer, gaining confidence when she doesn't pull away.

"Niklaas . . ." Her hand squeezes mine. "I have to tell you something."

"What?" My stomach pitches. What if I'm wrong? What if she doesn't feel what I'm feeling? What if I've tricked myself into believing she cares in order to soothe my pride, to make it all right to accept her offer of marriage and save my own skin?

"I . . ." She looks up, the torment in her eyes making me forget where to step.

We stop dancing at the same moment, but neither one of us pulls away.

"What's wrong? Just tell me." I firm up my expression, making sure she can't see how deep it will cut if she says something to hurt me.

I've been covering hurt with a smile my entire life. I can do it for another eight days. After that, it won't matter. I'm sure a swan knows nothing about what it's like to long for a proud father, or a mother who'd lived, or a future without any dark certainties in it and a life without the ending written in stone.

"What?" Impatience colors my tone. "Why do you look so miserable? Please tell me, because I don't understand it, especially when I'm breaking my back to be charming."

She frowns. "I didn't realize it was so torturous for you to be charming."

"Only with you, Princess."

Anger flickers in her eyes, but that's just fine. I'll take anger. Any emotion is preferable to her pity.

"Why? Because I'm like a sister to you?" she asks, dropping my hand.

"No!" I throw up my arms in frustration. "I've been trying to—"

"Trying to forget how nauseating it is to put your hands on me?" Her eyes glitter as she reaches out, slowly fisting her hand in my shirt. "Is that it?"

"I didn't say that." I glance down, eyeing her clenched fist. My head tells me to prepare to be taken to the ground, but my gut tells me something else. It tells me Aurora wants me as much as I want her, and the only reason we fight is because the energy simmering between us needs a place to go. It tells me to take a risk, to quit being a coward and *show her* how wrong she is.

"You didn't say it," she says. "But I'm not a—"

Her words end in a sharp intake of breath as I wrap my arm around her waist. A moment later, my fingers are in her hair, sending pins flying as I fist my hand, making sure she can't pull away and flip me onto my back.

"Stop telling me what I'm feeling," I say, leaning in to whisper the words into the hollow beneath her ear.

This close, she smells like lilac soap and the flowers in her hair, with an undercurrent of something sweeter, like melted sugar, and she feels . . . She feels like a piece of the Land Beyond, like she was made to fit against me, to fill every empty place, to match my strength with her own, tempered by a softness that makes my head spin. I flex the arm around her waist until every inch of her is pressed tight to every inch of me, until I can feel her stomach trembling against mine and her breath in my lungs and there can be no doubt that I'm far from repulsed by her.

She shivers and her arms wrap around my neck. "Niklaas," she whispers. "I . . ."

"Don't talk." I press a kiss to her throat, feeling her pulse racing beneath my lips, its rhythm confirming that her blood is rushing as fast as mine.

"Niklaas wait, I—"

I slip my hand from her hair, trapping her jaw between my fingers as I fit my mouth to hers, cutting her off with a kiss. She moans, a panicked sound that surprises me as it vibrates across my skin, but when I part my mouth, she parts hers, too, her lips gliding over mine with a ragged sigh. She doesn't pull away, and after a moment I regain the courage to angle my head, brushing soft against softer, breath held, then rushing out, warming the whisper of space between her mouth and mine.

A whisper is too much.

I never imagined it would be like this, never thought a kiss could make my body feel as electric as the air before a thunderstorm, make my chest ache and my heart pound and my soul feel too giddy for my body to contain it.

"Are you okay?" she asks, her lips teasing against mine.

"I'm better than okay," I whisper, sliding my hands down to grip her hips. "I'm perfect. *You're* perfect."

And then I kiss her again, soft becoming hard, breath coming faster, until all our hesitation vanishes. She buries her fingers in my hair and I lift her into the air, drawing her up my body until her feet dangle and our lips are even with each other and the kiss grows deeper, until her breath is my breath and her taste fills my mouth and there is nothing but her, nothing but how much I want her.

How much I want to please her, to do . . . whatever . . . it takes . . .

Whatever . . . anything . . .

Anything at all . . .

My head spins sickly. I pull in a breath between kisses, but it doesn't help. The ground is tilting beneath my feet, the wind whipping in from all sides, battering my body until I can't tell which way is up. My heart lurches and my arms tremble, sending Aurora sliding to the ground as I grow too weak to hold her.

"Niklaas?" she asks, panic in her voice. "Niklaas? What's wrong?"

I try to tell her that I'm okay, but my lips won't move, and when I reach for her I stumble and fall. I land in the grass, sticks jabbing into my knees, but I barely feel them. I am outside my body and inside it at the same time, torn apart like a fruit from its peel, my mind and heart and soul screaming though my mouth refuses to utter a word.

I am terrified and ripped and bleeding and broken and then suddenly the suffering parts of myself are gone, tossed away into the far beyond and I am as peaceful as a shell filled with the echo of the sea. I am a vessel, calm and empty, waiting to be filled.

I think that I should be afraid, but I'm not and so the thought vanishes, swept away with the rest of my unnecessary thoughts and feelings. I can't seem to feel anything aside from the overwhelming need to be with Aurora, to serve her in whatever way I am able. To show her that I . . .

I . . . Who am I? I wonder, the notion of self confounding in a way it has never been before. I've always been so sure of who I am, but now . . . I am here with her. She is here with me. That's all that matters. That's all that will ever matter. The thought soothes me, banishing some of the dizziness, making it easier to breathe.

"I'm sorry." Aurora falls to the ground and wraps her arms around me, hugging me tight. "I'm so sorry. Please forgive me."

"Of course," I say, voice still weak, though the world has stopped spinning. "There's nothing to forgive."

"Yes, there is," she says, her eyes filling with tears. "I've done a terrible thing."

"No, you haven't." I take her hand in mine, wanting nothing more than to comfort her, to make her happy. It's all that seems important, the only thing worth living for.

"Yes, I have," she says, then adds in a choked voice, "Don't argue with me."

"All right," I agree, tucking a lock of hair back into the arrangement on her head.

"And don't touch me."

I drop my hands to my lap with a smile. It feels good to do as she asks, so good I can scarcely remember why I ever wanted to quarrel with her.

She shakes her head, her throat working as she fights to swallow. "It's true, then. I was hoping, but I . . . I'm sorry, I'm so sorry, love."

My grin is so wide it feels like it will break my jaw. "I love you, too, Aurora."

"I know," she says, sadness in her voice that I can't understand. I can't understand it, but it makes me sad, too, and when she begins to cry it feels as if the world has been plunged into darkness. I want nothing more than to comfort her, but she told me not to touch her and so I sit and watch, tears rolling silently from my eyes until she finally stops crying and swipes the damp from her face.

"Come now, don't you cry." She brushes the tears from my face with a trembling finger before standing and reaching a hand down to me. "We'll ask the village priest to marry us as soon as the lamps are lit. At least something good will come of this."

I hesitate until she sighs and shakes her head. "You can touch me. I'm sorry, I'd . . . forgotten."

"It's all right." My sadness vanishes as she leads me across the field. I follow her through the tall grass, utterly at peace. No misery can touch me so long as my love's hand is in mine and she is happy with me and I am doing as she wishes.

We hurry past the dancers to where Gettel and Kat are playing juggle sticks with some of the village children. Aurora squeezes my hand as we approach the healer, sending a wave of contentment surging through my body, rushing through the empty space left behind after the other parts of me were cut away, filling me with joy.

I smile as Aurora explains that we want to be married and asks the healer to bear witness to our joining, but Gettel isn't looking at Aurora. She's looking at me, staring with a horrified expression that would trouble me if I cared what anyone but Aurora thought of me. But I don't, and so I smile. I smile until she sends the children away and begins to shout at Aurora, demanding to know what's she's done, demanding she release me from whatever enchantment she's worked upon me.

I move forward, ready to defend my love, but she stops me with a hand on my arm and a softly whispered, "No, Niklaas, don't interfere," and I step back.

I listen as Aurora explains a fairy curse she's under and what it has done to me, but none of it makes sense until she swears that she did what she did so that we could be married, so she could save me from my own curse. Mention of our marriage makes me grin again. I can't wait to be her husband, to be by her side, forever and always.

"You can't marry him now," Gettel says, anger and sadness thick in her voice.

"Yes, I can," Aurora says. "I must! If I don't, he only has eight days left."

"You don't understand, child." Gettel wipes at her eyes, sweeping away tears. "A true marriage can only occur when two souls freely choose to bind themselves together. Niklaas isn't free. He's incapable of making his own choices."

"But he can speak the vows," Aurora says. "He can—"

"Even if you find a priest willing to perform the ritual with him in that state," Gettel says with another sad look in my direction, "the marriage will be invalid in the eyes of the gods."

"Damn the gods," Aurora snaps. "I don't believe in the gods, and even if I—"

"Believe or don't believe," Gettel says, her tone harder than it was before. "There *is* a force that connects us all, binding us together. It is from that force that all magic arises, and the laws of that magic are absolute. Niklaas's curse can not be lifted unless his will is his own."

"That's not true." Aurora shakes her head. "It can't be."

"It is true," Gettel says. "No one knows what it will take to banish a curse better than the one who placed it."

She lifts her arm, touching two fingers to my forehead, throwing open a door in my memory. Images from the night I met the witch in the shrine flood my mind. In each one of them it is Gettel's face that looks up at me, Gettel's voice that assures me there is a way to change my fate.

"It's you," I say. "The witch, the one who took my armor." I know I should be furious for the trick she played on me, outraged by the lies she's told, but any emotion not tied to Aurora's happiness is impossible to muster.

304

"What?" Aurora's eyes widen as she glances between us. "What do you mean? Why didn't he know that before?"

"I banished the memory of my face so that Niklaas would trust me when we met again." Gettel turns to me. "And I took your armor to keep you from being spotted by your father's guards on your way here. My magic told me you would come to me in Frysk, bringing a girl who would break your curse with you. I wanted that for you. That's why I went to Kanvasola. To help you."

"Help him?" Aurora shouts. "You cursed him!"

"If I hadn't cursed him, his father would have found someone else to do it. At least I was merciful. Or tried to be." Gettel rubs her forehead with a shaking hand. "But now, it's too late. Niklaas will be transformed, like his brothers."

"No." Aurora shakes her head. "I don't believe you."

"As I said, it doesn't matter what you believe; it's the truth." Gettel's shoulders slump, and suddenly she looks every one of her sixty-two years. "In eight days' time, Niklaas will become a swan. There is nothing anyone can do to save him now."

"But there must be." Aurora begins to cry again, filling me with despair. I can't help but feel what she feels. It's as if I have no heart of my own, only an echo of her heart, reverberating in the cavernous space within my chest. "I can't have ruined him for nothing. I can't!"

"If only you'd spoken to me, I could have warned you." Gettel pulls her shawl tighter. "He loved you. He would have realized the truth before it was too late. You only had to have faith."

"I wasn't raised to have faith in love," Aurora says, fingertips digging into her temples. "I was raised to have faith in the blood that blessed me and the power in my own two hands."

"Your mother died for love of you, and your Fey mother lived for it," Gettel says, a chill in her words. "I've felt how old her magic is. She shouldn't be walking the ground, but she is, and you are the reason. Her love for you. Her need to protect you."

"But I—"

"My own niece risked her life for yours. I haven't had word from Crimsin since you arrived. She could be dead, her life forfeited to protect her princess and the country she loves," Gettel says, fresh tears rising in her eyes. "And this boy over-came extraordinary odds to protect you, when no one would have known if he had left you in the Feeding Hills to die. If all that hasn't given you faith in love, then you will never have faith in anything, and when you face the ogre queen, you will fail us all."

Aurora sucks in a breath. I can feel how much Gettel has hurt her, but Aurora told me not to interfere, so I stay where I am.

"I'm sorry," she whispers. "I just meant that . . . love didn't save my mother. Love isn't going to keep my brother alive. I thought I had to act, I didn't—"

"Gram! Are you coming?" Kat shouts from the grass near the stage. "It's almost time for my song!"

Gettel holds up a finger. "One second, sugar," she calls over her shoulder before turning back to Aurora. "You may still save your brother, but it will be harder without the true Niklaas by your side. You were stronger together than either of you are apart." She casts a sad glance my way before taking Aurora's hand and pressing it between both of hers. "Go back to the house, take anything you need for the journey. Take my horse and an extra saddle. You'll travel faster if you each have your own mount."

"We'll leave tonight," Aurora says, staring at the ground.

"I think that's best. There will be moonlight enough to find your way. Take the southern road. About three hours out, you'll see my daughter's tower. There is a cabin two fields to the west, where I stay when I visit her. You can sleep there and get a fresh start in the morning." Gettel releases Aurora's hand. "The cabin is warded, but once you leave it, Ekeeta's spies will be able to see you. Whatever your plan, you'd best have it in place by then. She'll be watching."

"Thank you," Aurora says, then adds in a miserable whisper, "I truly am sorry. More than you can imagine."

"I know." Kindness mixes with the sadness in Gettel's eyes as she kisses Aurora's cheek. "But sorry doesn't do anyone any good, least of all our Niklaas." She tucks a flower back into Aurora's hair and squeezes her shoulder, softening the words. "Trust in your fairy gifts. Trust in them and they will protect you. Rage against them, and you will be your own undoing."

Gettel walks away, crossing to the stage where the children are lining up to sing songs in honor of the dead who passed before they came of age. Usually the Children's Requiem makes me sad, but tonight I don't feel anything, can't seem to focus on anything except Aurora and how best to please her.

"I'm still sorry," Aurora says. For a moment I think she's

talking to Gettel, but when I look down she's staring up at me. "Whether it does any good or not."

"This means we aren't getting married?" I ask, squeezing her hand.

"No." Aurora presses her lips together. "You don't want to marry me," she says, and suddenly it's true. I don't want to marry her. I don't want anything that she doesn't want.

"But I can't leave you," I say, an emotion of my own rising inside of me for the first time since our kiss ended. The thought of being without her is crippling. "I don't know who I am without you."

"This is even worse." She pulls her fingers from mine and covers her mouth with both hands, pulling in a deep breath. "It's even worse than with Thyne."

"What's worse?"

She swallows and shakes her head, sending fresh tears spilling down her cheeks. "Nothing. It doesn't matter. It's too late."

"But I can stay with you?" I ask, needing reassurance to quiet the panic inside.

"Yes," she says, sniffing as she reclaims my hand. "Of course. I can't do this without you. I need you to help me save Jor."

I smile, feeling as if the sun has come out from behind the clouds. To be needed, to be led, to please my love—it is all I want. No curse can frighten me with her by my side. "Anything you need," I say. "Anything at all."

But for some reason, my words make Aurora sad again. When she turns to lead me back to the village, her shoulders shake, and the sound of her sobs carries to my ears on the wind. I move closer, tucking her under my arm as we walk, promising I will devote myself to her happiness, but she only cries harder. She cries and cries, until it feels as if her misery will drown us both.

CHAPTER TWENTY-THREE

AURORA

Once, when I was a little girl and still new to the island, I wanted nothing more than to learn to ride the waves the way the fairies did. I would watch them bobbing in the ocean beyond the reef on their sandalwood boards, waiting for a swell, and ache to be beside them, ready to hop to my feet when the perfect wave came and ride it like a bird riding the wind. I could imagine the taste of that kind of freedom, the giddy thrill of harnessing the power of the sea and dancing atop it.

But Janin said I was too little and not a strong enough swimmer. She said I must wait until I was twelve, and no amount of swimming practice in the quiet cove where the babies learned to paddle and float could change her mind.

So one morning, on a cool, rainy day, when not a single fairy was out drifting on the gray sea, I stole the smallest board I could find from the shelter and ran with it into the ocean. I made it out to where the waves were cresting and, after more tumbles than I'd imagined possible, finally caught a wave and rode it . . . all the way into the barrier reef.

I knocked my head hard enough to leave a goose egg, slashed open both knees, and limped to shore with an abundance of bruises and scrapes, feeling terribly sorry for myself and angry at Janin for being right.

"You have to be more careful, Aurora. You won't always get a second chance," Janin said to me later as she cleaned and dressed the wounds on my knees. "Some mistakes are for forever."

"You mean I could have died," I said, wanting to show her that I was brave, that I wasn't too little to handle scary words.

"Yes. You could have died. Or worse." She brushed my sandy, salt-matted hair from my face, her expression so disappointed and fearful that I finally began to feel something other than sorry for myself. "Do you understand, Aurora?"

"Yes, Janin, I'm sorry," I mumbled, tucking my chin to my chest. "I understand."

But I didn't understand. Not then, and not years from that day. Even when I was the mercenaries' captive and feared I had failed my brother and my kingdom, there was still hope of redemption, still a second chance waiting around the corner.

It is only now—with the shell of the boy who used to be Niklaas riding beside me and not a shred of hope of changing him back or saving him from his curse—that I truly understand. I understand and I ache like a rotting tooth that will never be pulled. There is no chance of relief. I have made a forever mistake, and now I will learn what it feels like to pay a price more terrible than death.

"There's the tower." Niklaas points to the thin structure spiraling out of the mist that has settled in this part of the valley.

I glance at it but quickly look away, not wanting to think about the girl held captive there, the girl I was so quick to judge and find lacking, when I am the last person who should ever turn up her nose at another's failings. I am the lowest of the low, and I don't even have Elsbeth's Rose to blame for it. I have no one to blame but myself.

"Aurora? Did you hear me? I said the tower is—"

"Yes, I see it. We should reach the cabin soon," I say, though I feel like I'm talking to myself. A part of me insists there's no point in responding to this not-Niklaas, but to order him to be quiet would be like kicking a dog in the stomach for daring to wag his tail. Niklaas is not who he was, but he doesn't deserve to suffer.

"Good. I'm tired." The real Niklaas would never admit to being tired. The real Niklaas was as defiant of bodily weakness as he was of me.

By the stars, I miss him so much. This is so much worse than I imagined it would be. I would rather see him dead. Worse, I know the true Niklaas would rather *be* dead.

I clench my jaw and grit my teeth, refusing to cry again. I vowed to be done with crying when we left Gettel's cottage. Tears only upset Niklaas, and I don't deserve to cry, not when all of this could have been avoided if I'd only asked for someone else's advice. Janin was right. Niklaas was right.

My pride and my stubbornness are a danger to everyone, poisoning everything I touch.

"Are you tired? Can I do anything to help you?" Niklaas asks.

I suppress the urge to sigh. "No, but thank you for asking. That was kind."

"You're welcome," he says, pleasure at even that small praise obvious in his voice. "Anything for you."

I bite the inside of my mouth, resisting the urge to curse my mother for this "blessing." Mother was innocent; I knew I was walking a dangerous line when Niklaas drew me into his arms to dance. If only I had told him the truth about my gifts. If only I could go back in time and shove him to the ground before his lips met mine.

By the time we reach the cabin, I've replayed how I would save him a hundred times, each one more painful than the last.

"This looks nice," Niklaas says.

He's right. The cabin is a pretty little thing made of split oak logs, nestled at the edge of a moonlit glen. It even has its own miniature barn and a privy with a window in the roof to let in the moonlight. Once Niklaas and I have made use of the privy, we unsaddle the horses, pen them into the two-stall barn, and give them fresh hay.

"We'll water them in the morning," I say, lighting the oil lamp we found hanging from a hook on the cabin's front stoop. "It sounds like there's a stream nearby. We'll be able to see it better in the daylight."

Niklaas doesn't say a word, but I know he agrees with my

decision. He will always agree with my decisions, until the day he is transformed into a swan and the last of his humanity is stolen away.

Inside the cabin, the interior bears signs of Gettel: a mantel crowded with unusual odds and ends, a kitchen nook with pans hung above the cook table by long hooks, and rugs of all sizes, shapes, and colors warming the floor. The coziness of it makes me sadder. Even Gettel loathes me now. Gettel, who I believed incapable of hating a spider hiding in her sheets. But she couldn't bear to look at me another moment and was willing to give away her favorite horse—a mare with a black satin coat so shiny it reflected the moonlight as we rode—to get rid of me. She may be a witch and the one responsible for cursing Niklaas, but I'm the monster, and we both know it.

"Are you hungry?" Niklaas pulls a bag of food from his pack. "I have biscuits and apples and—"

"No, let's get some rest." I set the lamp on the small eating table and tug off my boots. "We'll have to pull a long day tomorrow and be ready to keep moving after only a few hours of sleep if we need to. We have to make sure you're the one to deliver me to Ekeeta. If we're overcome and brought in by her men, our chances of saving my brother will be even worse than they are already."

"All right." Niklaas drops the bag of food and steps out of his own boots.

Our chances couldn't possibly be worse, the real Niklaas would have said. *This is a suicide mission, and you're a fool, and we aren't leaving this cabin until you come to your senses.*

I take comfort in imagining what the true Niklaas would

say until I circle around the wall separating the kitchen from the rest of the cabin to find the small space dominated by a single large bed. It's big enough for three of me and two of Niklaas. Even a day ago, I would have been secretly thrilled by the thought of spending the night with his warm back pressed to mine, but now . . .

"You take the bed." I back into the corner while Niklaas perches on the edge of the bed. "I'll look for extra blankets and sleep in the kitchen."

"That won't be very comfortable, will it?" he asks, but he doesn't rise from the bed, apparently taking my order to "take the bed" seriously.

"I'll be fine. It's more important that you're rested." I open the trunk at the end of the bed, relieved to see several quilts and two knitted blankets inside. "I'm supposed to be your prisoner. It won't matter if I look a little worse for the journey."

"All right, but . . . will you be where I can see you?" he asks, an anxious note in his voice as I fill my arms with blankets and head toward the other side of the cabin.

"I'll sleep by the wall, right here." I point to a spot where I'll be within sight, not surprised by his need to have me where he can see me.

Thyne was the same way. He would beg to be allowed to sleep—just sleep—in the same room with me, saying it made him feel empty when I was out of his sight. Janin said she would allow it, but I refused him every night. I couldn't stand to be alone in a room with him, and knew I wouldn't sleep a wink with him watching, desperate for a chance to please me, even in my dreaming state.

"But I want you to get some rest," I say firmly, feeling like I'm talking to one of the Fey babies back home, the ones I'd warn to stay out of the jungle when walking them back to the cots after a swim. "I'll be unhappy if you don't have a good long sleep."

"I'll go to sleep right now." He peels off his shirt and stands to unbutton his pants.

I turn away, busying myself setting up my pallet and turning down the lamp as he steps out of his clothes and crawls under the covers. I don't want to see him undressed. It would be too strange, to see the body I've lusted after and feel nothing.

Because I *would* feel nothing, the same way I felt nothing holding his hand or allowing him to hug me in an attempt to offer comfort when I was crying. The way I felt changed when he changed, making it clear it wasn't Niklaas's godlike outsides that made me want to be close to him. It was who he was. It was his mind and his heart and his wicked smiles and his maddening advice and the way he'd tease me from laughter into fury and back to laughter within the course of a conversation. It was just . . . Niklaas.

"Good night, Aurora," Niklaas says, grinning at me from his place in the big bed.

"Good night." I force a smile before lying down with my face to the wall and squeezing my eyes shut, praying for the strength to make it through the next few days, to hold together until I save Jor and redeem some small part of my soul.

But I am not strong and I am not sure I'm doing the right thing. I feel more lost than I ever have. I long for Janin. I long for my mother. But most of all I long for Niklaas, mourning him like one of the dead, though he lies right across the room. I can't even bear to think about what it will be like to watch him transform in eight days.

I expect to lie sleepless for hours, but all my crying exhausted me more than I realized. I must have slept, because when I open my eyes, the moonlight is cutting through the window at a different angle and Niklaas is snoring his middle-of-the-night snore, that deep, measured sawing that only comes when he's deeply asleep.

Tears rise in my eyes before I can stop them. He sounds exactly the same, so much like the old Niklaas that for a minute I wonder if . . .

Maybe . . .

I climb silently from my pallet and pad around to the opposite side of the bed in my stocking feet. I pause, letting my eyes adjust to the darkness. After only a moment, I pull his face into focus and my heart turns to stone. My moment of hope was foolish. He hasn't returned to me. His eyelids are too still, his brow too relaxed, and his mouth too soft. Only children are so untroubled, even in sleep.

"You should have a little grit in your jaw," I whisper. "And a flutter behind your lids every now and then." I watch him for another moment, wondering if he will attempt to obey me even while unconscious, but he doesn't stir. He sleeps on, determined to get that good sleep I demanded of him.

"I'm sorry," I whisper, tears filling my eyes no matter how I try to stop them. "I really do love you."

I do, so much more than I realized, more than I've ever loved anyone. I would marry the shell of Niklaas and spend the rest of my life pretending he made me happy if I could. No matter how lonely a life it would be, or that seeing him every day would make me mourn the loss of the real Niklaas all the more terribly.

"If I could take your place, I would." Tears wet my cheeks. "I swear it."

I close my eyes and bury my face in my hands, struggling to regain control, while Niklaas's snore rumbles in and out like a gargling dog. Despite my abundance of self-hatred, after only a moment or two the familiar sound begins to comfort me. Keeping my eyes closed, I pull back the covers and crawl into bed beside him, curling against his wide, warm back, inhaling his Niklaas smell, aching and grieving and dying inside with every breath. Being so close to him is like pressing on a bruise, a bruise at the center of my heart that throbs so savagely it feels like my chest will implode.

Once again, I don't expect to sleep, but I do. I sleep and dream of Niklaas's transformation. I hear him scream, watch his flesh ripple as feathers burst through his skin, smell the blood and sweat and filth left behind as what's left of his human body is abandoned and the swan Niklaas takes to the sky, lost to me forever.

I wake up breathing hard, drenched in sweat, and pull my sticky shirt from my chest with a shaky hand.

"I'm glad you're awake," Niklaas says, making me flinch. I turn my head on the pillow to find him propped on one arm, watching me with a blank expression that's even more unnerving than his childlike grin. "You were having a nightmare, weren't you?"

"Ye-yes." I swipe the sweat from my upper lip with the back of my hand.

"I was going to wake you, but I couldn't decide if you would like that," he says. "So I waited for you to wake up."

"Thank you," I say as I slide off the bed.

"It was nice to find you next to me. So much better than seeing you on the floor."

"I was cold and couldn't sleep." I gather the blankets from the floor and dump them back into the chest at the end of the bed. "I thought it was best if I got warm and was able to rest. At least a little."

"I think we should always sleep together," Niklaas says, proving there is something going on in his mind, at least when it comes to the desire to stay close to me.

"That won't work on the road." I prop my hands on my hips, fixing him with a hard look. The queen's spies will be able to see us soon. We have to make sure we're putting on the proper show.

"You have to remember our story," I say. "I refused to marry you and break your curse, and so you've decided to deliver me to Ekeeta in hopes that she will come to your aid with her magic. You must treat me like your prisoner, someone you hate."

"But I love you," he says, that anxious look creeping into his eyes again.

"I know that, and I . . . love you, too," I say, bringing a smile to his face that sets self-loathing to sharpening its claws on my heart. "But to save my brother we have to pretend to be enemies. From the moment we leave this cabin until we escape the castle with Jor, there must be no kindness between us. Do you understand?"

He nods, but I'm still not entirely convinced.

"Nothing will make me happier than if you are cruel to me until you deliver me to Ekeeta at Mercar," I whisper, crossing to take his hand in mine and stare deep into his eyes. "Be as cruel as you can be. We have to make Ekeeta believe you hate me. Can you do this for me, Niklaas?"

"I'll do my best." He gives me a shy grin. "I'd do anything to make you happy."

"Good." I back toward the door, already needing a moment away from the stranger Niklaas has become. "I'm going to wash up and water the horses. When I get back, we'll decide how to travel. I'll need to be bound so it's clear I'm your prisoner."

"I'll make breakfast and get some rope from the barn," Niklaas says, throwing off the covers and practically leaping from bed in his rush to do my bidding.

I try to take his eagerness as a good sign, but I can't help but worry as we go about our morning tasks, preparing for the journey. It will take four days to reach the capital, and that's if we ride hard all day, swapping our horses for fresh ones when we can, and part of every night. Is Niklaas capable of keeping up an act for that long?

And what about when we reach Mercar? Will Ekeeta be able to see he's under an enchantment the way Gettel could? Ogre magic isn't the same breed of magic as that of witch-born women, but still . . . Ekeeta is powerful and likely to be suspicious. If she asks too many questions, Niklaas may falter and end up in the dungeon right along with me.

I'll have to remind him what to say and how to behave, I think, palms sweating with nerves as we leave the cabin and set out toward the open road, where we will no longer be sheltered by Gettel's wards. *I'll remind him every hour if I have to.*

"Niklaas, I—"

"Quiet!" Niklaas snaps at me over his shoulder, making me blink with surprise. We agreed he should ride ahead, leading my horse by a rope tied to his saddle, since my hands are bound behind me, but at the moment I wish I could see his eyes.

"But Niklaas, I—"

"I said quiet." The hatred in his expression when he turns connects like a slap to the face, leaving a stinging sensation behind. "Shut your mouth, or I'll shut it for you."

I swallow and nod, heart racing as I begin to wonder what mad thing I've done now, ordering a person determined to do precisely as I say to be cruel to me. I know the real Niklaas would never hurt me, but I have no idea what this shell will do in the name of obeying my order to the letter.

"Next time, we'll stuff something in there to keep you quiet," he says.

I shiver, ducking my head to my chest until he turns back around, shocked to find I'm truly afraid. Shocked and strangely . . . satisfied.

Because if anyone deserves to suffer . . .

And suffer I do. I ride for hours without anything to shield my face, until my skin begins to itch, the discomfort becoming torture when I'm unable to lift a hand to scratch my throbbing nose. I'm forced to relieve myself with Niklaas hovering on the other side of the bush, shouting for me to hurry up, and am hauled up from the stream where I kneel to suck down a drink and cool my scorched forehead by a handful of my own hair.

When we finally stop for the night, Niklaas leaves my hands bound behind my back, ensuring I pass the few hours we stop to rest in a fitful sleep interrupted by flashes of pain from my strained shoulders.

He doesn't speak to me at all the first day or the second, not even when we barely outrun a pack of wild dogs or when carrion flies swarm around us for nearly an hour—crawling in and out of every orifice in my head, making me shudder and shake and scream with my mouth closed. Even when the wind picks up and we lose the flies and I beg him to tie my hands in front of my body so I can defend myself if the insects return, he acts as if he doesn't hear a word.

I don't give him an official order to untie me, but I'm not sure it would matter if I did. He has taken my mandate in the cabin so completely to heart that there seems to be no room in his mind for anything but fulfilling his mission and making his mistress happy.

Even if her happiness is to be won with abuse.

By the time we reach western Norvere—racing across a farmer's wheat fields and down into a hidden canyon just seconds ahead of an ogre patrol—my wrists are so chafed that they sting constantly, making me whimper when Niklaas urges the horses into a gallop and I can no longer hold my hands still.

That night, he allows me only an hour of sleep before ordering me to wake up with a nudge of his boot in my side. When I don't move quickly enough, the nudge becomes a rough hand that hauls me to my feet and shoves me toward my horse. Still half-asleep, I stumble on an unseen rock and fall to the ground, bursting the skin on my cheek in the process.

Niklaas doesn't pause to see if I'm seriously hurt, only hauls me up and onto my horse with an order to "move faster next time."

The only good thing about getting so little sleep is that I am spared my nightmares. I'm too tired to dream of my brother's death or the ogre queen or Niklaas's transformation, and Niklaas seems to have forgotten that he is cursed, his awareness of his fate banished by his need to serve me. I am thankful for those things, thankful for every little kindness, even if that kindness is only the absence of further misery.

We ride and ride, day and night, stealing fresh horses three times, until I lose track of how long we've been traveling and measure our progress in how many minutes I'm able to go without crying out in pain.

By the time we reach the coast and begin backtracking to Mercar on foot—hoping to sneak into the city through the aqueducts, putting us inside the castle walls without announcing our presence at the gates—I am weary to the bone, covered in dust, and itching all over from sleeping on the bare ground where the mites could crawl into my clothes. The chapped skin at my wrists has torn open, blood oozes down my palms to my fingers, and a strange heat licks at my wrists. I suspect my wounds are becoming toxic and that I will fall into a fever if they aren't treated soon, but I force my feet to keep moving, refusing to allow weakness to claim me. Not yet. Not when I am so close and my brother's life is in my hands.

My trembling hands, with the fingers swollen into near uselessness from being forced behind my back for so long.

A sob escapes my lips, but Niklaas doesn't order me to be quiet. Perhaps he can't hear me over the wind sweeping in from the ocean. I look up to see if he has turned around only to have the hair escaped from my warrior's knot lash into my eyes and stick to the crusted scab on my cheek where the blood was never wiped away.

What have I done? By the gods, what have I done?

My hope is in pieces, lethal shards that threaten to slice me open if I try to put them back together again. I doubt everything, I trust no one, especially not myself. I am so weary I can't feel my legs, as close to broken as I have ever been, filled with self-hatred and panic and perilously close to losing my connection to the world and retreating into the quiet shadows of my own mind.

I pray my sad state will be worth it. I pray it will be enough to convince the ogre queen to believe Niklaas's story. If it isn't . . .

Oh, if it isn't . . .

I bite my lip to stifle another sob and turn my head, blinking until the hair is swept from my eyes by the wind. When my vision clears, I find I'm able to see the five gently rounded towers of Mercar Castle barely visible above the cliffs.

They look exactly as I remember: eggs balanced one on top of the other, ending in a shape like a conch shell. Inside the shell, there will be ogre soldiers charged with watching the unusually high ocean for intruder ships. If we're lucky, they won't have their eyes turned on the coastal trail, on the rocky path so narrow it can be traversed only by a single rider at a time, so treacherous all but the most sure-footed horse would trip and tumble into the sea. That's why we're approaching on foot, the better to sneak in unseen, two small, human-sized specks against the gray of the cliffs.

The sight of the castle so close gives me strength. Niklaas doesn't have to tug the rope tied to my waist again until we reach the base of the aqueducts. He unties my hands before we begin to climb the stone arches, but my fingers are numb and I struggle to keep up, nearly falling more than once. By the time we reach the top and tumble down into the conduit, where a shallow flow of fresh water streams into the city, I am trembling all over, and too weak to stand.

"On your feet," Niklaas demands, giving the rope at my waist a sharp jerk.

"Please, I need to rest," I pant, spots dancing around his face as he leans in close. "Please . . . I'm so weak. I'm afraid I won't be able to . . . do what we came here for."

For the first time since we left the cottage in the woods, Niklaas's expression softens. "You'll be okay," he whispers. "Gettel told me you won't need strength, and if you need it, then it will do you no good."

"She did?" I try to remember if she said anything similar to me, but I'm finding memories difficult to hold on to.

There has been nothing for me but the ride and the pain and too little sleep for too many days. It seems everything else is a story, told to a different girl, a long time ago.

"She did. You'll be fine." He smoothes my hair from my face with a gentleness that brings tears to my eyes after so many days of cruelty. "I'll sneak out of my room and come get you and your brother late tonight. Just like we planned."

"Thank you, Niklaas. Thank you so much."

"I've done a good job?" He smiles, lighting up with an innocent joy that also makes me want to cry.

But what doesn't? I am broken, a dam with so many holes all you have to do is give me a little poke and I will leak.

"Yes," I half laugh, half sob. "Yes. Very good."

"Do you still want me to be cruel until I turn you over to the queen?"

"Yes," I say, though I flinch as I say it, knowing what it will mean. "Yes, please. You're doing a g-good job."

"Then up you go," he snaps, hauling me to my feet and dragging me along behind him. But even the ten fingers of water flowing through the conduit makes it so much harder to walk. My feet drag, my muscles scream, and my ankles turn as I slosh along. All too soon, I fall to my knees and struggle to get up, only to fall again.

"I can't," I sob, clutching my swollen wrists to my chest. "I can't. Please . . ."

A moment later, the world spins as I'm flipped over Niklaas's shoulder, just as I was in the Feeding Hills. But this time, instead of carrying me to safety, Niklaas will deliver me into danger's wide, hungry maw.

CHAPTER TWENTY-FOUR

AURORA

A field from the castle, the aqueduct splits in seven directions. We follow the middle conduit, Niklaas setting me down and both of us stooping to crawl as the open trough becomes a tunnel of water surging toward the royal garden.

My arms shake and the flesh at my wrists howls as water rushes over my wounds; blackness creeps inky fingers in to beckon at the edges of my vision, but I force myself forward, knowing I could drown if I lose consciousness.

I will my weakening arms and legs to keep moving until I am spit out into the fountain at the edge of the royal garden and break the surface with a gasp. Only then do I allow myself to go limp, rolling over to float on my back, staring up at the explosion of pink blossoms crawling over the castle walls as Niklaas splashes down after me.

"Beautiful," I murmur, confused. How is it the gardens

still thrive? How dare something so pure and lovely bloom in the shadow of evil?

Somewhere in the distance, I hear a woman scream and know we've been spotted, but I make no move to stand. I am too weak, and this is Niklaas's mission now. He must be the convincing captor; I must save my strength.

I must wait and watch and . . .

Despite my best efforts, my eyes roll back and my lids drop, my body demanding rest before it runs to the end of its limited reserves. I am only dimly aware of Niklaas scooping me up in his arms, of more shouts and the sound of swords being drawn, of Niklaas declaring himself the son of the Norvere's only ally and demanding to be brought before the queen to present his prize.

I fight to open my eyes, wanting to be conscious as I'm carried through the castle to refresh my memory of the path to the throne room, but I only manage to crack my lids for a moment before they slide closed once more.

In that moment, I see the gnarled Hawthorne tree at the middle of the garden, its green leaves just beginning to flush at the edges, and know I'm not too late. The tree is not yet crimson; Jor is still alive.

Please let him be alive, please let me save him.

It is my last thought before I fade, sinking into the darkness.

I wake in a bed as soft as rabbit fur, my hair damp and loose and a heavy satin gown tangled between my legs. I blink at the tapestry stitched into the canopy above me—a scene depicting a girl embracing a satyr in a field of flowers—so startled by the luxury of my surroundings that it takes a moment to remember where I am.

And then I do, and try to bolt upright, only to find my arms pinned.

I cry out, whipping my head back and forth to find an ogre woman on either side of my bed gripping my arms gently but firmly in their long fingers.

"Don't move, Princess," the woman on my right, an ogre with warm amber eyes and a brown wig styled in a bun high on her head, says. "We need to finish with your bandages. We'll let you sit up in a moment."

I glance down to see a strip of partially tied linen trailing from my wrist but can't seem to stop myself from trying to jerk away again. My mind can't reconcile this waking with what I expected to find when I opened my eyes.

Where are the chains and the bars? The damp walls and the beetles? Where is the gloomy dungeon light and the stink of fear and the sounds of people quietly weeping in their cells?

"You must lie still." The other ogress—a bald woman with six soul tattoos in a circle above her temple—doesn't ask nicely. "We had to stitch the skin on your wrist. If you fight, it will tear and have to be redone," she says, meeting my glare with cold eyes.

"Where am I? Who are you?" I force myself to relax. I don't know why they're patching me up, but there's no doubt I'll be better off when they're finished. "Why are you helping me?"

"You are in one of the castle guest rooms," the brown-haired ogress says, resuming her work, deftly wrapping the linen around my wrist. "I am Nippa and this is Herro. We are Queen Ekeeta's personal nurses."

"Only the best for the lost princess," the other woman, Herro, mumbles.

"Why?" I ask, heart beating faster, frightened by this show of mercy. What does it mean? What does the ogre queen want?

"The queen is too kind for her own good," Herro says, but I keep my gaze on Nippa and I'm glad I do, otherwise I would have missed the sadness that tightens her expression before she smiles.

Why is she sad? I don't know, but I'm certain it doesn't bode well.

"She is as kind as a queen should be," Nippa says, a note of censure in her tone. "If you're finished, Herro, you may attend to your other duties. I can manage the princess alone now that she's awake."

"Happy to leave you to her." Herro jabs a pin into the bandage at my wrist before rising and departing the room in a rustle of skirts.

"Never mind her," Nippa whispers. "She's unpleasant at times but an excellent nurse. Your stitches are as small and even as any I've seen." She pins her linen in place and smiles. "Are you ready for something to eat?" She motions to a table near the window behind her, where a feast has been laid out. Meats, cheeses, fresh bread, and fruit vie for space on the blue tablecloth, while outside, two castle towers glow pinkish orange in the fading light.

Sunset. "How long have I been asleep?" I ask. If it's been more than a day, Niklaas won't know what to do. We were supposed to free Jor the first night we spent in the castle!

"Six hours, give or take," Nippa says, making me sag back into the pillow with relief. "You took tea with herbs for the pain when we first laid you down. They calm the appetite, but I'm sure you're hungry by now. Shall I help you to the table?"

"No thank you, I can walk," I say, though it still feels mad to be having a polite conversation with a creature that consumes human souls for nourishment. I toss off the covers, glancing down at my far-too-long nightgown as I slide to the floor. "Did you . . ."

"We bathed and dressed you. We knew your wrists and cheek needed tending, but we wanted to be sure we didn't miss any wounds beneath your clothes. We attended to your bites as well." Nippa hovers close as I walk to the table, apparently determined to catch me if I swoon. "You slept like a babe the entire time, poor little thing."

Poor little thing? What in the Flaming Pit . . .

I settle into the chair Nippa pulls out for me, eyes darting around the room. It's magnificent, as big as five fairy cots put together with a bed the size of a small ship at the center and warm wood armoires stationed against the walls like fussing nannies. There is a writing desk pulled before the other window and blue silk curtains that hang from the high ceiling all the way to the floor. Between the two windows, a fire crackles in a white stone fireplace.

It is cold enough for a fire. Does that mean . . .

"Is my brother still alive?" I won't be able to stomach a bite of food until I know, no matter how famished I am.

Nippa hesitates, making my pulse race beneath my skin.

"Is he?" I ask, voice breaking.

"I'm not to speak of such things, Princess," Nippa whispers, "but yes."

"Where is he? Is he in the dungeon or—"

"Not another word," Nippa says in a no-nonsense voice that assures me I won't be getting any more information from her. "You must eat. Start with the broth. Your body will put it to use more quickly than the rest." She plucks the porcelain top off a bowl decorated with pink flowers like the ones I saw in the garden and sets it before me.

I pick it up and drink the broth straight from the bowl, not bothering with the soup spoon lined up beside the rest of the utensils. I don't have time for sipping from a spoon. I have to get rid of this nurse and out of this room, and the fastest way to accomplish both seems to be to honor Nippa's requests.

I finish the broth and reach for the bread, tearing off hunks that I stuff into my mouth and chew as quickly as I can. I follow the bread with slices of cold chicken and cheese and a glass of mixed juices so sweet it makes my tongue curl, but I refuse to touch the cake. I will eat to revive my body, but I won't waste a moment enjoying myself, not when every second is precious and both Jor and Niklaas are depending on me.

Niklaas bribed a fisherman in Nume—using our horses as payment for a boat to be moored near the wall walks after dark tonight, promising the man another fistful of gold when we take possession of the craft—but the boat will do us no good if I can't find Jor. I assumed I would end up in the dungeon within shouting distance of my brother, and it would only be a matter of sorting out how to get us both out of our cells, but now . . .

"If you're finished, I can help you dress," Nippa says.

"I can dress myself," I say, pushing my chair back.

"Of course." Nippa nods. "Your clothes are being washed, but we've found something in your size. It's laid out on the dressing bench."

I keep one eye on my nurse as I circle around the bed, still wary no matter how kind she seems, but when I see what the ogres have found for me to wear, I find it hard to focus on anything else. Instead of the gown I was expecting, there on the pale blue cushions of the dressing bench lie a black linen shirt, black cloak, and black riding pants that actually look small enough to fit me. They must be a boy's pants, and the boots settled on the carpet must be boy's boots as well.

"What is this?" I ask, brow furrowing as I rub the coarse fabric of the shirt between my fingers.

"They are clothes for a night flight," comes a voice from behind me, a voice as airy as a reed flute that casts a net of barbed wire around my heart.

The queen. *The queen.*

I drop the shirt, desperately wishing I had my staff in hand as I turn to face the woman who took everything I love away, who killed my mother and stole my brother, who cursed my life and haunts my nightmares and looms so large and terrible in my mind that I know I will always fear and hate her, *always,* even if by some miracle I am lucky enough to walk out of this castle and live to a doddering old age.

My hands shake and my mouth fills with a taste as sour as nutshells as my eyes alight on the cool white column that is the ogre queen. Ekeeta is only eight hands away, close enough to smell her perfume, an exotic scent like poppy and sea foam with a top note of grilled meat that makes my stomach churn.

She is as beautiful as ever, tall and thin, but with generous curves visible beneath her white gown with the silver trim. Her wig is more elaborate than the one I remember from when I was little—intricate braids coil around her head, creating a crown from which curls cascade down her back in a tumble of gold—but her face is the same. Her skin as smooth, her cheekbones as high and delicate, her eyes as . . .

Her eyes . . .

"Forgive us." She falls to her knees, sending the tears pooled in her eyes spilling down her cheeks.

Nippa rushes to her side: I back away, more startled by her tears than if she'd hurled a knife at my chest.

"We do not deserve forgiveness," she continues, breath hitching. "But still, we ask for it, if only to prove we see how wrong we have been. We have been deceived. Our brother convinced us the souls we consumed would be delivered into paradise, but there is no excuse for the evils we have committed. We should have questioned our brother years ago. We should have sought the truth before so many died in vain."

I shake my head, hands trembling at my sides, itching for a weapon.

A weapon. The knife on the table! If I move quickly . . .

I turn and run, holding up my long gown as I dash to the table to fetch the knife and turn back to Ekeeta, the sharp point aimed at her heart.

But even with half a room and the bed still between us, I know I won't be able to make use of the weapon. Already, my arm wavers, my muscles threatening to turn to stone if I attempt to kill a defenseless woman kneeling on the ground before me.

Damn my mother's curse! *Damn* fairy magic and all the misery it has brought to my family since the day Mother was blessed in her cradle!

"What do you want?" I sob, gripping the knife so tightly my hand begins to sweat, gritting my teeth as I fight to be stronger than the magic, to take the vengeance that is rightly mine. "Where is Jor? Where is my brother?"

Fresh tears as fat as winterberries drop from her eyes. "He is safe. He has suffered, but he will live," she says, wringing another sob from my throat, a sound of pain and relief and mourning mixed together. "We swear he will live. And we swear to aid you both in escaping to freedom tonight."

"What?" I nearly shout the word, so confused it feels as if I've awoken in a world where my dreams and nightmares have married and given birth to hideous children. "What is this? What are you playing at?"

"Quiet." Nippa's whisper is harsh, but with fear, not anger. "These are the human guest quarters and few of our kind come here, but you must not attract attention. If you are discovered, Princess, we will be unable to save your life, or your brother's."

I swallow, my gaze flicking from Nippa's kind face to Ekeeta's tearful one, unable to find anything false in their eyes.

"Explain yourself." I drop the knife to the table where it lands with a dull thud.

"Our brother, Illestros, is five hundred years our elder. He was a powerful priest long before we were born," Ekeeta says, making no move to rise from her place on the floor. "He has channeled more prophecies than any priest since the time before humans roamed the land. His most important prophecy concerns the rise of the living darkness and an age of ogre rule in which humanity will feed the First One's hunger for—"

"A hundred years," I finish, impatient with this story. "I know the prophecy."

Ekeeta nods. "But none of that matters now."

My throat muscles clench. "My mother is dead," I force out, "and my brother and I have lived in exile, only able to see each other for a few weeks each year, because of that prophecy. Jor was taken captive and our fairy friends killed, and I have spent the past three weeks . . . I have risked my life and my *friend's* life . . ."

I squeeze my eyes shut, fighting for control. What if this is real? What if, for some unfathomable reason, Ekeeta truly means me no harm? Then all of this has been for nothing. Niklaas's mind and will and last chance at a human life have been stolen away for nothing. *Nothing!*

"You must listen," Ekeeta says. "There isn't much time. We will be missed if we stay away too long. We regret these things, but we cannot make reparations now. It is more important that we prevent the worst of our brother's plans from coming to pass."

I open my eyes. "You mean the prophecy?"

"The prophecy is not a true prophecy," she says, rising to her feet. "He has lied before, but we didn't want to believe. . . . But now there is no doubt that this divination did not come from our goddess. We know not what Illestros hopes to accomplish with the rise of darkness, but it is not to open the gates to paradise."

I cross my arms at my chest. "Of course it isn't," I say, not bothering to hide my disdain. "He wants the Fey dead and humans so weak they can't fight back. He wants to rule Mataquin and is willing to drive our world to the brink of death to do it."

Ekeeta flinches. "We wish we had seen things so clearly. Our only comfort now is that it isn't too late to set things right."

"Set things right," I echo, acid in my tone. How can she expect me to believe she wants to set things right? She, who assassinated my father, drove my mother to take her own life, and who has made Norvere a place of fear and desperation ever since. "Why this sudden change? After all this time?"

A beatific smile lights Ekeeta's face. "We were in the garden late last night with our creatures. We were lost and afraid and we begged for wisdom, no matter what the cost, and then . . . we felt the goddess moving within us. Her presence guided us to the truth, to peace so wide there is no way for doubt to swim across it."

"You've found peace." I don't know whether to scream or

cry. In the end I laugh, a strained sound that makes Nippa eye me strangely. "How lovely for you."

"We know we are the last soul in the world who deserves salvation," Ekeeta whispers, bowing her head. "But that is the glory of the goddess. Even the most wretched can be made pure if they trust in her guidance."

"And what does the goddess guide you to do?" I ask, glaring at her with undisguised hatred. I hate her still. I might even hate her *more*.

How dare she? How *dare* she come to her enlightenment *now*, when my mother is dead, my brother scarred, my dear friend and first love both robbed of their senses, and myself cursed to a lifetime of regret? How dare she talk to me of peace, when I know it will *forever* be beyond my reach?

"The goddess does not wish for death or pain or for one people to destroy another," she says. "Human, ogre, Fey—we are all one in her eyes, and paradise will come to each of us, in its time, in its own way. The only genuinely holy quest is to nurture peace in our own hearts and do our best to love each other."

She lifts her arms, as if offering an embrace. I instinctively cringe away. Her words about love and unity are all well and good, if she means them, but they are still coming from the mouth of a monster.

Which reminds me . . .

"Your new peace will make mealtime difficult," I sneer, enjoying the way her skin pales at mention of her voracious appetite.

She presses her lips together and breathes sharply through her nose. "We shall no longer feed upon the souls of man, and shall ensure that our brothers and sisters make the same promise." Nippa comes to stand at her elbow in a silent show of solidarity. "Ogres can be sustained by simpler foods. We may perish sooner, but better a hundred years of life lived in love than a thousand in fear and greed."

I shake my head numbly. She means it. I can tell. She's going to stop killing, and she's convinced at least one other ogre to do the same. So . . .

"Then you'll let us go?" I ask, finally daring to hope our escape may be far simpler than I've dreamed. "My brother and . . . and me?" I almost let Niklaas's name slip but stop myself. I can't let her know Niklaas is my ally. If I do, and this turns out to be an elaborate trick, I will have ruined our last chance at escape.

"We can't let you go; our brother would never allow it," Ekeeta says, "But we can help you escape. We will send Nippa to you as soon as darkness falls. We will fetch Prince Jor and meet you at the docks. You will have our fastest ship and two of our trusted guards to sail it. Thank the goddess, it was our personal guard who found you in the fountain this morning. They will keep our secrets and aid you well."

"We won't need the guards." The fewer ogres involved, the better. I'm sure Ekeeta's brother isn't the only ogre who will loathe the idea of giving up living for centuries and ruling the world. "Jor and I can sail a small ship together."

Ekeeta's long fingers tangle in front of her. "Hopefully he will be able to sail. We sent healers, but some of his wounds . . . We're afraid some of them are deep."

I clench my jaw. "I can manage on my own. He's alive. That's all that matters."

It isn't all that matters, and she can be damned sure I'll have my vengeance if she's broken my little brother, but for now his life is enough. I can wait to plot my revenge—and devise a plan to reclaim my kingdom—until Jor, Niklaas, and I are safe on Malai.

"But I want Niklaas of Kanvasola on board when we set sail," I say, realizing how I might save Niklaas without giving our connection away. "He betrayed me and doesn't deserve his freedom. Tie him up and leave him below deck. The Fey and I will dispense the punishment we see fit."

"The prince will be punished soon enough," Ekeeta says. "His eighteenth birthday draws near, and there is nothing we can do to lift the burden of his curse."

"Then I will have to dispense justice quickly." I meet her tearful glance with a cruel one, imagining it is she who will be my prisoner. "Have him stowed beneath the deck of the ship. No one betrays me without paying for it."

Ekeeta nods. "It saddens us to see cruelty in another when we are so recently free of it, but . . . we owe you that much."

"You owe me everything," I spit, so angry I begin to shiver with it. "My throne, my family, my heart. You owe me more than you can *ever* repay. And if I'm cruel it is because of *you*."

Ekeeta watches me, eyes shining with a mix of tenderness and sorrow that makes me wish I could strike her, if only to slap that stupid expression from her face.

Her lips part, but she wisely decides against speaking to me again and turns to Nippa. "Stay with her. If I'm needed, send Herro. I'll come straightaway."

Nippa curtsies, bowing her head so far to her chest she develops an extra chin. "Yes, my queen. Blessed be, my lady."

"Blessed be, my friend." Ekeeta touches a light hand to Nippa's shoulder and leaves without a backward glance.

I'm glad. I don't want to look at her a second longer. I hate her so much I can taste it, like cork-fouled wine filling my mouth, destroying my ability to recognize any flavor but its bitterness. I stomp around the bed, tearing off my gown as I go, not caring if Nippa sees me naked. She's already bathed me. It's not as if we can be on more intimate terms.

"Is it not more extraordinary for one so lost to be found than it is for one who never strayed in the first place?" Nippa asks, plucking my gown from the floor and folding it as I pull on the boy's pants—which fit as perfectly as I suspected they would—and reach for the black shirt.

"Yes," I say in a falsely pleasant voice, working my buttons with trembling hands. "She should be given a medal for finally realizing it's wrong to go about killing people as if they are grouse."

Nippa frowns. "I know your heart is kinder than that. Even half of your mother in you is enough to make you three times the person your father ever was."

I pause in pulling on my new stockings. "You knew them?"

"I knew your father when he was a young man, and, after your mother moved to the city, I would attend her when she was ill." Nippa sets the gown on the bed and begins spreading up the covers. "I came here as a junior nurse when the queen was married to King Radord. She lost so many babes during those years." Nippa tuts beneath her breath. "Little ones born of a human and ogre union rarely survive, and when they do it is often only for a few days. Ekeeta would hold the babes, rocking them until the light went out of their

341

eyes. It made her . . . frail, easy prey for Illestros and his allies. Her brother convinced her the only way to end her torment was to allow him to poison King Roland."

"He killed my grandfather *and* my father?" I ask, not wanting to think about Ekeeta rocking her dying babies. She has destroyed too many lives for me to have pity for her suffering. "Is he the one who ordered the executions of Mother and the others loyal to my father, as well?"

Nippa nods. "And ogres, too." She opens the armoire across from the bed and pulls out a sliding shelf, revealing a brush and comb set and a bowl full of ribbons.

"My sister died for refusing to swear allegiance to the new rule," Nippa continues, handing me the brush and a blue ribbon and watching as I pull my hair into a swift braid. "She made me swear to go along with the takeover and . . . everything else. She believed one day our queen would see that Illestros had led her astray and need allies. Those who've been in hiding are glad that day has finally come."

"After ten years." I shove my feet into the black boots.

"Better than twenty," Nippa says, clearly a pragmatist. "Better now than after our world has been plunged into darkness. I believe your mother would have agreed. She wasn't the sort to hold on to anger."

"I'm not so sure about that," I mumble as I tie up my laces. If Mother hadn't held onto her anger at Father, then she wouldn't have wished for me to possess a heart no man would dare defy and Niklaas's and Thyne's minds would still be their own.

"I am. She had such a kind soul. She was the only person

who could bring out your father's gentle side. I only ever saw him smile in her presence."

"Will you tell me about them? My father, especially?" I ask. "I remember my Mother, but I—"

I stop, head swiveling as a terrible howl breaks the silence outside. I hurry to the window, with Nippa close behind, coming onto my tiptoes to see down into the garden.

What I see makes my gorge rise.

"Goddess," Nippa murmurs, hand flying to cover her mouth.

Three floors below, on the east side of the royal garden, ogre soldiers are busy in the animal pens. A company swarms into the neatly ordered holdings, slitting throats and shattering cages, claiming a life with every slash of their blades. A few birds manage to escape their enclosures and take to the air, but dozens of vultures, crows, and other birds I can't name are not so lucky. Feathers fly and wings go limp as the animals fall and are trodden into the dust by black boots.

In the dog and wolf pens, teeth flash and claws scratch, but it is steel that sends blood spraying onto the grass, onto the stone walls, onto the uniforms of the ogres who have set about killing the queen's pets with a single-minded rage.

What could these animals have possibly done to deserve such a fate?

It isn't the animals; it is their mistress this is meant to harm.

"We have to go. Now." I grab the sleeve of Nippa's brown dress and pull her from the window. "Where is my staff?"

"The guards took it," Nippa says, clasping her hands

together, terror and misery mixing on her face. "Why are they doing this? What's happening?"

I ignore her and turn, scanning the room for anything I might use as a makeshift staff, but there is nothing. I snatch up the paring knife, deciding it will do until I can steal something better.

"Our plan has been discovered. Take me to my brother," I say, motioning for her to follow as I dash to the door. "If we hurry we can—"

My words end in a growl of frustration as ogre soldiers appear in the doorway, swords drawn. I rush at them, knife slashing in swift diagonals, puncturing chain mail and nicking ogre flesh, but it's only a matter of seconds before I'm disarmed and my arms wrenched behind my back. There are too many of them and I am still weak. Too weak even to resist as they haul me from the room.

I hear Nippa cry out behind me, but I know a plea for mercy from me will only make things worse for her.

I am the enemy, and it seems I'll have my chance to suffer for it, after all.

CHAPTER TWENTY-FIVE

AURORA

The golden hall leading to the throne room is even more magnificent than I remember. Floor-to-ceiling windows as tall as Gettel's cottage line the walls, granting an unparalleled view of the city on one side and the castle grounds rolling down to the sea on the other. In sharp contrast to my dreams of a crumbling Mercar, the city is in excellent condition—every whitewashed building standing tall and strong, every shutter straight, every street so clean it's hard to imagine horses ever travel them.

There are no horses now. No people, either. It's as if the citizens have sensed the darkness building inside the castle and have shut themselves up against it, though the evening is warm and the setting sun makes the city glow a glorious pink, like roses dipped in honey.

It is beautiful, so beautiful it makes me ache all over. The light, the sea, the elegant lines of the castle my ancestors commissioned after the last fairy war—they paint a picture that fills me with such bittersweet longing I'm tempted to close my eyes against it, but I don't. I focus, sealing this last glimpse of Mercar away in my heart.

Janin was only a girl when the last fairy war ended, but she remembers the celebration to christen the new castle, the way humans and fairies celebrated with dancing in the streets and midnight swims and feasting that went on and on until people collapsed on the grass to sleep off the effects of too much meat and wine.

I imagine the streets filled with laughing people. I imagine pleasure ships floating in a peaceful sea, waiting to take the adventurous out for a swim with the giant turtles. I imagine so hard that, for a moment, I swear I hear music—fairy pipes and fiddles calling all to dance—but then we arrive at the throne room and my paper-thin imaginings are burned away by the reality of a bonfire lit before an ogre altar and a scaffold of pale wood against the wall behind.

Niklaas and Jor stand atop the scaffold, their hands tied and nooses looped around their necks, already trussed and ready to die.

"No!" I scream, tears springing into my eyes.

Niklaas calls out my name as I'm dragged across the room, but Jor doesn't waste his words.

"Don't do what they ask, Ror!" he shouts, turning his face as the soldier next to him grabs the back of his neck. "Let me die, it's all right. I love you, I—" His words end in a pained cry as the soldier forces a rag into his mouth.

My brother is as thin as I've ever seen him, with bruises on his face and a filthy, patchy beard that makes Niklaas's look perfect in comparison, but he isn't broken. He is as strong and good as ever, and willing to die for what is right.

But by the stars, how can I let him? How can I watch him hanged? How can I let my brother, my best friend since the day he was born, the boy whose baby tears I wiped away, who has trusted me with his hopes and dreams and fears and whose hand has always fit so perfectly in mine, die, if there is anything I can do to spare him?

And Niklaas . . . *Niklaas* . . .

Gods, goddess, any good force that might be listening, give me the strength to do what's right, to save them if I can and to make their deaths noble if I cannot.

But how can I? *How?* I would rather die myself. I would rather suffer torture for a hundred years than see either one of them lost.

By the time I'm shoved into a chair in front of the flames, separated from the scaffold by the fire, altar, and a number of armed guards, I'm crying so hard I can barely see. The world blurs, turning the priest's robe to a smudge of white.

"You may still save the ones you love, child," the priest says, his voice so deep it vibrates my bones. "If you do as I bid you."

I sniff hard, focusing on the dagger in his hand, following his arm up to his shoulders, and on to his eyes. It is Illestros, Ekeeta's brother, the priest who terrified me as a child, and the puppeteer behind the ogre queen's cruel reign.

His gaze is even more predatory than I remember.

"What do you want me to do?" I glare at his oiled head, wishing I could strip the skin from his bones, piece by piece.

"It is not what I want, but what the goddess demands," he says with a cruel smile.

I shiver. Illestros is no servant of the goddess. He isn't even deluded like the fanatics who burn people they suspect of being witches; he is simply evil and greedy and willing to do whatever it takes to convince those who follow him to commit the necessary atrocities. The goddess is nothing more than a tool, an instrument of manipulation he twists in the hearts of his people.

"Release her." Illestros nods to the ogres pinning my arms behind me.

I wrench free, rubbing at my shoulders but making no move to rise from my chair. There are at least a hundred men in the room: five priests, the rest soldiers. I am fairy-blessed, but even on my best day I wouldn't stand a chance against these odds, and today is far from my best day. Walking to the throne room was enough to have my heart beating faster. I am a shadow of myself, weaker even than the animals slain in the garden.

You will not need strength, and if you need it, it will be too late. Gettel's warning echoes in my mind, giving me some small hope that my weakness won't matter.

"What must I do to save them?" I ask. "I want them both spared."

"That is within my power, so long as you do as you're told," Illestros says. "You will await my signal. When I raise my cup above the altar to begin the ritual, you will drive this knife into my sister's heart."

He motions with his free hand, and a moment later, Ekeeta, her arms bound and mouth gagged with a strip of her own torn dress, is shoved onto the stones before me. She kneels as she did in the bedroom, looking up at me with eyes that beg me not to do what her brother demands.

"You want me to kill your sister," I echo.

"Yes." Illestros holds out the dagger. My fingers reach for it, wrapping around the hilt without my conscious permission.

I imagine it, the way it would feel to drive the dagger into Ekeeta's heart, to destroy the woman I hate. It should fill me with savage anticipation to have the justice I've hungered for finally within my grasp. Only minutes ago, I was aching to destroy her, or at least I thought I was, but now . . . with the reality of Ekeeta helpless before me . . .

I don't want to kill her. I don't want to kill anyone. I just want to take my brother and Niklaas and go home.

"It is the only way to open the gates to paradise," Illestros continues, "and she's done her share of killing your kind." He fists his hand in Ekeeta's wig and pulls it away, revealing her bare skull and so many soul tattoos I can't begin to count them.

My jaw drops. The markings spread across her skin like a rash, old and new crowded together along every inch of her skull until they spill down her neck and crawl beneath the collar of her dress.

"She has glutted herself in preparation for this day," Illestros says, "but she was willing to betray the humans' sacrifice to spare her own life."

So that's the reason for her change of heart. Ekeeta must have known she was destined to die.

"She deserves death," Illestros continues. "Yours will be the hand of justice."

I shake my head. "No, I . . . I can't."

"You are gentle, then, like your brother." Illestros hums

beneath his breath. "I understand, but I will tell you, his gentle ways earned him no mercy from my sister. She whipped him. Whipped him and set beetles free to infect his wounds. They have likely laid eggs. When they hatch, the young will burrow from his flesh, causing great pain. Perhaps it's better for him to die quickly."

He turns away, leaving me with the dagger—knowing there is no risk in leaving me armed when I'm surrounded by guards—and circles around the fire, bowing to the other priests before climbing the steps to the scaffold.

The platform is elevated, allowing everyone in the room a clear view. I realize this method of execution was likely chosen for that exact reason, but then Illestros stops beside my brother and I lose the ability to think of anything but Jor's life so close to being lost. A single push and he will fall through the hole in the boards and choke to death and there will be nothing left to do but mourn.

I look to Jor, but his eyes are closed. He is prepared to die. I should let him. I should honor his wishes, respect his bravery and his willingness to sacrifice himself for our people, but I can't. I can't sit by and watch my brother and Niklaas be killed. I am weak and selfish, and I don't want to live to see a world without them.

"Don't do this!" I beg. "Please! Kill me instead!"

"Impossible," Illestros says, his calm voice carrying clearly across the room. "In order for the prophecy to be fulfilled *you* must kill the queen. You are the briar-born child with fairy blessings."

The prophecy fulfilled. I can't help him plunge our world into darkness, but I can't let him destroy my brother, either.

I can't think straight; I don't know what to do. I need more time, time to think of a way to—

Illestros lays his hands on Jor's shoulders and I scream, "Wait! I can't kill her! I'm blessed with mercy. I can't kill someone who isn't fighting back."

"Can't? Or won't?" Illestros shoves Jor, sending him stumbling forward. My brother falls through the hole in the planks with a terrible choking, gasping, suffering sound and I scream as if the rope grips my own throat.

I surge toward the scaffold but make it only a few steps before I'm captured by guards who grip my arms, ensuring I can do them no damage with the dagger in my hand.

"Give Ekeeta a knife and I'll fight her," I shout as Illestros descends the dais and Jor writhes at the end of the rope and my soul dies a little with every passing second. "I'll win! I'll kill her and win, I swear it, but please—"

"Kill her now and Reende will pull the boy up." Illestros takes a cup from an awaiting priest and holds it above the altar, meeting my eyes across the flames. "Kill her, child. It isn't too late."

The guards release me and I turn to face Ekeeta, the knife clutched in my sweating hand. I take two frantic steps toward her, the dagger lifted level with my eyes, ready to slaughter her like a pig if that is what it takes to save Jor, but as soon as I tense to drive the blade home, my muscles seize with such force that my spine arches and my breath freezes in my chest.

I fall to the ground, knees slamming into stone as the knife goes skittering across the floor. I scramble after it, panting against the pulse of angry magic burning beneath my skin.

My hand closes around the knife and I spin on hands and

knees to see Jor still moving, but just barely. "Please! Pull him up!" I scream. "Give me time!"

"There is no time." Illestros lifts his arm and crooks two fingers. On the scaffold, a soldier moves closer to Niklaas.

"No!" I wail as I crawl back to Ekeeta.

She has fallen to her side on the stones, knocking the gag from her mouth. She cries out as I flip her onto her back and lift the dagger, but I can't understand her. I can't hear anything over the hurricane of terror swirling inside of me, the howling of magic fighting to do as it was bidden, to honor its rules as stubbornly as anything born of the natural world.

But it is not natural to allow your brother to be murdered. I can't do it, I won't! I will kill Ekeeta, even if it kills me.

And it might. My body feels ravaged by lightning, every inch of my interior scalded and raw and my head on fire, filled with smoke and wailing so loud I don't realize I am screaming until I thrust the dagger down—shoving it into Ekeeta's beating heart—and the world goes silent.

So quiet. Quiet as the center of a storm, as the breath before dying.

I gasp as I sag to the ground, but it's as if there is no air left in the room. I roll onto my back, clawed hands clutching at my chest as the lightning storm within me rushes out to sea, streaming from my body, leaving me alone and friendless and empty as a pocket. Emptier. Within only a few moments, there is not even an echo of magic left inside of me, only a weak, whimpering, sweating husk of a girl.

A girl mortal in every way.

The magic is gone. I have betrayed the laws of my fairy

blessings, and now they have abandoned me. I know it as sure as I know I am a murderer and a fool.

"Jor," I moan, rolling onto my side, clutching my aching core with both hands. I look up, but I can't see the scaffold from the floor. I can't see anything but the fire and the shadows it casts. I don't know if Jor is alive, I don't—

"Please . . . listen," Ekeeta whispers from my other side.

"Jor!" I cry out in a strangled voice, but there is still no answer, only shouting from the scaffold and footsteps thumping back and forth across the boards.

"Aurora, please." Ekeeta gasps, a liquid sound that makes my stomach roil.

I roll over, tears streaming from my eyes, hating myself for what I've done even before I see the black cloud filling the air around the ogre queen, spreading out like ink in water. The blood pouring from her chest is turning to black smoke that swirls away, swept up on some unfelt breeze to hover above the room like an ominous cloud.

The living darkness. Ekeeta is *becoming* the living darkness, and I've made the transformation come to pass. I can feel the magic shivering in the smoke, the same magic that once pulsed beneath my skin.

Fairy blessings can only leave a person in blood. I've known that truth since I was a child, but I didn't stop to think that the blood might not have to be my own or that a murder would serve as well as a suicide.

"I'm sorry." I touch Ekeeta's cheek. It is still whole, her eyes full of life though she is dying. Bleeding, dying . . . murdered. "I'm so sorry."

"It's all right," she whispers. "I forgive you."

I sob as she lifts her hand to my cheek, mirroring my caress. I'm surprised to find her hand still warm and her touch so gentle and . . . human.

She smiles and I cry even harder. "It's all right. The . . . Fey army . . . at the gates . . . told my guard to help them."

"What?" I ask, hope and grief twisting inside of me.

"I tried . . . to tell you." She sips in air with a labored rasp. "They will . . . break through. I . . . only wish . . ." She swallows with obvious pain. "Forgive me?"

She doesn't have long, soon she will die and I will have committed murder—real murder, not an accident made while defending myself—and the entire world will suffer for my failure.

Our failure. Hers and mine. We are both wicked and selfish; we were both weak when we most needed to be strong. She is my enemy, but she is also . . . my sister.

"I forgive you," I say, meaning it with my entire heart. "I forgive you for everything." I bite my lip, tasting misery salty on my skin.

"Yes . . . that is . . ." She doesn't finish. She drifts away like a ship sinking to the bottom of the sea. Her hand falls from my face. She dies. She dies and I am alone on the floor before the fire as the ogre soldiers charged with guarding me suddenly rush away.

Perhaps they're going to fight the Fey army Ekeeta said was at the city gate. Perhaps they're simply terrified by the black cloud filling the room. I don't know. I only know that I am lost.

I roll onto my back, feeling stronger than I did a moment

ago, but too scared to sit up. It will be too late now. If Jor wasn't cut down, he will be dead. I can't bear to see it, can't bear to know that I have committed murder, squandered the gifts my mother died to give me, and cursed the world, and haven't even managed to spare Jor in the process.

I lie broken on the stones, staring up at the swirling black smoke, watching as the cloud begins to thin, going gray in patches until I hear—

"Aurora!" Niklaas shouts from the scaffold. "Some help!"

I bolt into a seated position, the room spinning as I come onto the balls of my feet.

I look to the scaffold to see Niklaas and my brother—my brother! Alive! Still alive!—fighting off the ogres surging up the stairs. Niklaas stands at the top of the steps and Jor defends from behind. My brother is obviously weak, but he's managing to help keep the ogres at bay. Somehow he and Niklaas have both acquired swords and are doing a decent job of defending themselves, but even with many of the ogre soldiers running from the room, they are still outnumbered.

Spinning, I search the ground for a weapon, but there is nothing . . . nothing but the dagger still plunged into Ekeeta's chest.

Wincing, I grip the hilt in one hand and give the dagger a tug, and then another tug and another, but it barely moves. Finally, I fist both hands around the hilt and haul at it with all my strength until it pops free with an awful sucking sound and I fall onto my bottom, breathing hard.

Breathing hard, simply from pulling a knife from a motionless body.

My gifts really are gone. Completely gone. I am as weak

as any smaller-than-average, too-skinny girl of seventeen. Weaker. Now that my gifts are gone, I'm keenly aware of the stinging, aching wounds at my wrists, of the way my heart labors as my body struggles to recover from the exhaustion and deprivation of the last five days. I am not the warrior I was. I'll be lucky to take down a single man before I lose my own head.

Then better make your man count.

I turn, fist tightening around the hilt of the knife, strength rising inside of me as I find Illestros with my eyes. He is alone now that his soldiers are either fighting on the scaffold or fleeing the room. He leans over the altar, his hands braced on the glass, his head bowed. His is the one death that might stop this. He is the leader, the priest, the prophet. If he dies, the remaining ogres may lose their center and falter in their fight, giving Niklaas and Jor the chance to escape before Jor grows too weak to hold a sword.

I creep forward on shaking legs, circling the fire to approach from over Illestros's shoulder one careful step at a time, hoping my luck will hold and I will continue to escape the other ogres' notice until it's too late.

The soldiers are busy with Jor and Niklaas, and the priests have run to the window, where they seem to be trying to guide the graying cloud out the window with palm leaf fans, but I don't spare them more than a second of my attention. I keep my focus on Illestros's narrow back, judging where I must plunge the blade to strike a mortal wound, knowing I'll have to shove the dagger with all my strength if I hope to hit his heart.

I cannot hesitate. I cannot falter. I take a breath and hold it, inching forward though my head screams for me to hurry, to run at him and have it done.

I am five steps away . . . three . . . two . . . close enough to see Illestros's ravaged face in the altar glass as I lift the dagger, close enough to hear his sigh when he spies my blade's reflection and turns to face me.

"So you will kill me," he says, arms hanging limp at his sides. "Now that your blessings are gone you can kill without hesitation. Does that please you?"

"Call off your men and I won't hurt you." I try to firm up my muscles, to keep my raised arm from trembling.

"I could take the knife. I know you're weak," he whispers. "But I won't. I'm ready to die. The ritual has failed."

He points one shaking finger to the ceiling; I glance up to see the black and gray mass transformed, the oily smoke replaced by feathery white clouds that grow thinner by the moment.

"Your fairy magic was the fuel and your hatred the spark to set the new beginning in motion," Illestros continues, voice breaking. "The darkness should have risen. I should be on my way to ruling a world where my people once again dominate cattle like you, but instead everything I've worked for is lost, and she is dead, and it is for *nothing*!"

He's telling the truth. His pain and rage are too real for it to be a lie. For some reason, the ritual has failed.

I realize that there will be no living darkness, that the people of Mataquin will be spared, and relax for a fraction of a second, just long enough for Illestros to lunge for my throat.

I scream as his hands wrap around my neck, but the sound emerges as a gurgle, too soft to be heard over the shouts of the men behind us. I try to jab the dagger into his chest, but he spins, slamming my head into the altar, sending the weapon flying.

"You did this," he hisses, his sharp teeth bared behind his thinned lips. "What did you do? What did you say to her?"

"I forgave her," I manage to gasp before his grip tightens.

"And I suppose she forgave you, her own murderer," he growls. "She knew your hatred played a part. She ruined everything. She deserved to die. She was weak. Weak!"

I kick at his legs and dig my nails into the skin at the backs of his hands until I draw blood, but his bony fingers only squeeze harder.

"You stole her death," he spits. "And now I will steal everything you love. I will kill your brother and every fairy foolish enough to fight for a worthless child like you."

My pulse pounds behind my eyes, white light flashes at the edges of my vision, and my ears fill with the echo of my suffering heart, drowning out the sounds of Niklaas and Jor still fighting on the scaffold.

I am fading, dying, but I will not give Illestros the satisfaction of knowing I died miserable and afraid. There are so many things I would do differently, but I am not worthless. I've made mistakes, but I didn't fail. I was the girl my mother wanted me to be. In the end, I honored the most important gift she gave me. I was merciful. I wish I had been merciful enough to spare Ekeeta's life, but at least I let her die in peace. I released my hatred before it was too late. I forgave Ekeeta and helped save my people, even if I can't save myself.

I close my eyes, and spread my arms, ready to meet my

death with the same bravery Ekeeta met hers, when my fingers brush against something cool and heavy.

The cup. The gold cup Illestros was holding above the glass . . .

I curl my fingers into a fist, drawing the stem of the goblet into my palm and squeezing tight, willing myself to remember my training, to remember where to strike for the greatest effect, before bringing the chalice down on Illestros's skull with enough force that it bounces off his head with a *gong* that rings sweetly in the air.

He groans and his grip loosens. I twist free, air rasping into my raw throat as I stumble away.

Evasive tactics seem to work well without my fairy gifts. Now it's time to see what else I can do.

I spy the dagger on the ground and snatch it up, spinning to face Illestros as he staggers toward me. I'm injured and no longer blessed with strength, but I'm as well trained as an ogre soldier and likely better trained than a priest. And so I hold my ground, waiting until the last moment to sidestep, driving my shoulder into Illestros's gut as I hook my foot around his leg, sending him to the ground as easily as I toppled Niklaas in our sparring match.

A moment later, I'm atop his chest, dagger at his throat.

I dig the blade into his flesh, knowing I must pull it across the thin skin and commit my second murder, but before I can strike, familiar hands snatch me beneath the arms and pull me away.

"Wait!" Niklaas plucks the dagger from my hand, keeping it trained on the priest blinking on the floor. "He'll be more useful alive. I killed five of his men, and the others have run. He's the last ogre left."

"What?" I ask as Niklaas kneels, rolling the priest over and tying his hands with rope he must have snatched from the gallows. "Why did they run? When?"

"Just a few moments ago," Niklaas says, double-checking his knots. "A messenger brought word that the fairies had breached the last of the castle's defenses. With their queen dead, I guess the ogres didn't feel like sticking around to defend her throne."

"Where's Jor?" I glance about the room, finding it deserted save for the ogres lying dead on the stones near the scaffold. "Where is—"

"I'm here," comes a voice from behind me, making me jump.

I spin around, taking in my brother's blood-smeared clothes long enough to be certain none of the blood is his own before throwing my arms around his neck. "You're alive! I'm so glad you're alive," I sob against his filthy shirt.

"You too." His arms go around me, hugging me so tightly he lifts me off my feet. "For a minute there, I thought we'd both . . . You stopped it somehow, didn't you?"

"Yes. The ritual failed. The kingdoms are safe."

"Thank the gods." He pulls in a ragged breath and hugs me even tighter. "Still, you shouldn't have come, Ror. You should have let me die. We both knew it might come to that someday."

"I couldn't," I say, voice muffled. "I just couldn't. I'm sorry. Can you ever forgive me?"

"Of course I forgive you," he says. "I can't say I wouldn't

have done the same if it were you with the rope around your neck. It would have been easier to die than watch them kill my Ror."

I pull back to look into his face, relieved to see his eyes clear and his gaze strong.

"You'll be all right?" I whisper.

"I will. And so will you." He sets me back on my feet, forcing me to tilt my head back to meet his eyes. He's so much taller than he was last winter. He's still a beanpole, but he only needs a few inches to be as tall as Niklaas.

Niklaas. I was so frightened and worried that I didn't stop to think when he starting issuing orders, but now . . .

My arms go limp, sliding from Jor's neck as I turn, slowly, cautiously, afraid to hope. But as soon as I see Niklaas standing with his arms crossed and that brooding, relieved, enraged expression on his face, I know.

"You're back," I breathe, tears springing to my eyes.

At this rate, I may never stop crying, but that's all right. My brother is alive, the Fey have taken the castle, and Niklaas is himself.

"Yes," he says, the word forced through a jaw so tense I can see the muscles twitch at either side of his face. "But I remember everything. Every flaming thing."

"I'll keep watch for the Fey and let them know the ogres are bound for the boats," Jor says, obviously sensing that Niklaas and I should have a moment alone.

As much as I hate to let my brother venture an inch from my side, I know he's right. Niklaas should be able to lash out at me with the full strength of his fury, without worrying about offending the innocent.

"M-my fairy blessings are gone," I stammer as Jor hurries away, my eyes darting from Niklaas's feet to his shoulders, finding it impossible to meet his staring-through-my-skin look head-on. "They left me when I . . . I . . . killed her." My face crumples, no matter how hard I try to fight it, and I know it will be a long time before I can speak of the terrible thing I did without weeping.

"I saw," Niklaas says. "I watched you beg for your brother's life, and all I could think about was how lost I'd be if you weren't alive to tell me what to do."

I swallow hard, forcing myself to stop blubbering. "I'm sorry, I—"

"You knew what would happen if I kissed you," he says. "That's what happened to that fairy boy, isn't it? He kissed you and it stole his damn mind away."

I bite my lip and nod, heart sinking as Niklaas curses beneath his breath and lifts his eyes to the ceiling. "I am sorry," I whisper. "You have no idea how sorry."

"I have an idea," he snaps, shooting me a look so sharp it makes me flinch. "If you weren't sorry, you wouldn't have made me hurt you on the way here, would you?"

"I just wanted to make sure we were convincing."

"No, you were punishing yourself, and using me to do it. When I think of all the . . ." He runs a shaking hand over his mouth and lets out a jagged breath. "That's what I hate most. You made me brutalize a girl half my size, a girl I . . . cared about." He shakes his bowed his head. "You turned me into a monster."

"No, Niklaas," I say, knowing I can't let him live with

guilt that is all mine. "It wasn't your fault. You weren't in control, you—"

"It doesn't matter." He props his hands on his hips, but keeps his head bowed, as if he can't stand to look at me. "I've spent my whole life trying not to be my father, and with one flaming kiss you made me as bad as he ever was. I would have killed you if you told me to. Killed you. Or worse."

"No, Niklaas," I say, remembering his moment of gentleness on the aqueduct. "You would never have—"

"Oh, I *would* have. If I believed it would have made you *happy*." His lip curls. "It almost makes me glad I won't be human much longer. I won't have to look at that new scar on your cheek and remember I was the one who put it there."

"Please, Niklaas . . ." I press my lips together, fighting tears as I realize the meaning behind what he's said. "You don't have to do this. You have your free will again. We can . . . we can be married."

He sighs as he turns to walk away.

"Please!" I cry out, stopping him. "I know you hate me, but don't throw yourself away because of it. I want to help you, I want to marry you. I—I love you."

I lose the battle against the tears shoving at the backs of my eyes, but I don't feel as bad about it this time, because when Niklaas turns back to me there are tears on his cheeks, too.

"No, you don't," he says "If you did, you wouldn't have lied to me again and again, and you never would have used me the way you did."

"Niklaas, I didn't—"

My plea is cut short as a shout rises from the hall outside, a cry of celebration and thanksgiving so loud it shakes the walls. Moments later, fairy warriors stream through the throne room door, Jor carried along at the center of a group of mountain Fey hugging him too tightly for his feet to touch the ground. I see faces familiar from my visits to the mountains and then even more familiar island faces, men and women as dear as family, who rush to gather me in their arms, passing me from one hug to the next until I end in a soft, familiar embrace that sets me to weeping like a baby all over again.

"Janin!" I wrap my arms around her and cling tight. "I can't believe you're here. You must have been outnumbered ten to one. How did you ever—"

"Your letter came with a note from the witch woman who helped you in Frysk. She said there was a growing resistance movement within Mercar and gave instructions on how to find them. I sent spies to meet with their leaders yesterday," Janin says, rocking me back and forth the way she did when I was little and needing a long hug. "They sabotaged the gates and fought with us. Hundreds of them. And some of the ogre soldiers fought for us, as well. The other ogres weren't expecting an attack from the inside. They didn't last an hour."

"I'm so glad you weren't hurt," I mumble against her shoulder, never wanting to let her go. "Can you forgive me?"

"There's nothing to forgive," Janin whispers into my hair. "You did what you thought was right. I couldn't ask for more."

"I shouldn't have left without telling you where I was going."

"I shouldn't have tried to keep you from trying to save your brother," she says, pulling in a breath and swiping tears from her cheeks. They are more wrinkled than I remember, but her silver hair is pulled back in the same tidy braid and her face glows with a happiness I haven't seen there in a long time. "You should have been able to use your fairy blessings as you saw fit."

A hopeful cry leaps from deep inside me. "My gifts are gone," I say, able to view the loss with excitement now that Niklaas is free. "Thyne should be himself again."

"Thyne is himself again."

I blink. That voice. Thyne's *real* voice. It's like a piece of my innocence restored, a part of myself I thought I'd lost forever falling back into place.

I shift my gaze to find Thyne standing behind his mother, his chestnut hair bound in a warrior's knot and new armor sitting on his slim shoulders, and cry out with joy. He *is* himself! His green eyes shine with mischief, and his smile is as arrogant as ever.

Janin steps away and I fall into Thyne's arms, shocked by how slight he feels after growing accustomed to Niklaas's hugs.

"Glad to see you alive, scrapper." Thyne presses a sloppy kiss to my forehead. "Guess it's safe to kiss you now, right?"

"I'm so sorry, Thyne, I didn't—"

"I know you didn't. It's all right." He laughs. "But I confess I'm glad to go back to being your brother."

I smile up at him, relieved that he feels the same way I do. Our kiss was a mistake. We were never meant to be more than friends, but we will always be family. He is so many things to me—a brother and teacher and friend and first hero all in one—but he was never the boy I love.

That boy is slipping out of the throne room with a group of Fey soldiers, no doubt bound for the docks and a fight with any ogres who remain there.

I move from Thyne's arms, intending to follow Niklaas, but Janin stops me with her fingers at my elbow.

"Stay, Aurora," she says. "You are a queen now, and your life too important to your people to risk it fighting battles that are already won."

Queen. I hadn't stopped to think, but she's right. Ekeeta is dead, and I am heir to the throne. This castle belongs to me. This city, and every soul in it, is mine to command. I suppose the thought should fill me with satisfaction, or triumph, or some similar emotion, but all I feel is a great weight settling on my shoulders, nerves clawing at my insides, and a terrible, creeping certainty that I will find a way to do everything wrong.

"Will you help me, Janin?" I ask as the rest of the Fey fan out across the throne room to douse fires, dismantle altars, transport our prisoners, and . . . dispose of the bodies. "I want Ekeeta to have a proper burial. She'd changed. If not for her, the prophecy would have come to pass."

"Of course," Janin says. "I'll make the arrangements."

"And, Janin," I say, stopping her before she can move away. "Can we put together an advisory council? With elders from the mountain Fey and the island Fey? And some of the resistance leaders from the city, and there's an ogre I trust, too, if she's still in the castle." I take a deep breath, silently hoping Nippa is alive and well. "Her name is Nippa. She said there are other ogres who opposed the priest's plans. I don't want them punished and I . . . I'm going to need help. I can't do this on my own."

Janin smiles and her blue-green eyes shine. "You will be a good queen, Aurora," she says, catching my chin between her fingers. "Never doubt it."

By the time I've sorted out who should be imprisoned and who should be freed, found Nippa and had her attend to the fresh wound on Jor's neck, and helped the Fey clear the throne room of the dead, it is dark and a group of curious human men in servants' uniforms lurk in the doorway.

I learn that they are the lamplighters, wanting to know if business should continue as usual now that nearly every ogre in the castle has fled.

"Yes," I say. "Please light the lamps and let the rest of the staff know they are safe. No one will be harmed. Anyone who wishes to stay is free to; anyone who wishes to go can go."

"Why in the good lands' would we want to go, my lady?" The man who speaks is old enough to be my grandfather, with a full gray beard to prove it, but his smile is as giddy as a child's. "Long live the true queen of Norvere!"

The rest of the men take up the cheer, making me blush. I'd expected my people to be grateful to be spared the fear of losing their loved ones to the ogres' hunger—the ogres only consumed criminals, but their version of what classified as a "crime" ranged from murder to stealing an apple from a cart—but I hadn't expected such an unabashedly enthusiastic reception.

My father wasn't a beloved prince, and my grandfather's choice of an ogre for his third wife left many of his subjects feeling betrayed, but apparently my people are ready to treat me as my own person, a person they believe will right the wrongs of the last ten years and before.

I still don't feel like a queen, but I swear at this moment to do everything I can to be worthy of my people's faith, starting with providing them with a brave and good-hearted king. I will persuade Niklaas to marry me. Even if I have to promise never to speak to him again after we say our vows. I will save his life, and my own, because I can't imagine living my whole life without him.

It can't be too late.

It is my last thought before I fall asleep in the corner of the throne room, curled up next to Jor on a blanket someone brought when we refused to leave the makeshift war room or each other, filled with gratitude for my brother's life and determined to make things right.

CHAPTER TWENTY-SIX

Four days later

NIKLAAS

What do you pack for your final night of human life?

A brush? Rosemary ash? A flask full of barley liquor and a hammer?

Every item I pick up, I drop. Finally, I leave the clothes and supplies spread out on the bed beside my pack and cross the carpet to the window to stare down at the garden, stabbing at the open wound festering on my heart one last time before I go.

She's still there, sparring with Thyne. They've been at it for nearly two hours, his hands wandering over her body as he adjusts the angle of her staff or steps in to give her a boost when her boneless monkey flips bring her head too close to the ground. Aurora is determined to regain as much of her former fighting skill as possible without being fairy-blessed, and her dear old friend *Thyne* has been all too eager to help.

He's just waiting until I'm gone, until the sorry oaf Aurora pities so much she's begged him to marry her ten times in the past four days has turned into a bird, and then he'll offer his shoulder to cry on and his hands will be free to wander wherever they like.

I saw the way she looked at him that night in the throne room, the way she threw herself into his arms with a sound like she was dying of pleasure to be there. She loves him. She might love me, too, in her way, but I would never be happy sharing her.

Even if I could trust her, even if I could forgive and forget . . .

But I can't. Every time I think of the way I kicked her awake with my boot, I want to be sick. I hate myself for the way I treated her. Janin assured me it was magic no man could overcome, and that the darkness hidden in fairy blessings is the reason the Fey stopped gifting human children, but it doesn't matter. I still hate myself, and Aurora, and *Thyne.* I've barely said ten words to the ass, but oh how I hate *Thyne.*

Imagining that fairy bastard with Aurora in his arms, kissing her tears away with his girly-soft lips makes me want to punch something.

So I do, slamming my fist into the wall beside the window hard enough to split my middle knuckle and send blood oozing from the busted skin. I stare down at the damage, but I can barely feel it, let alone work up the energy to fret about it.

What does it matter if I'm hurt? This body will only be mine for one more night.

A night I won't be spending here. The fairies, aside from *Thyne,* are good people, and Jor has become a friend, but

I can't stay. I won't share my transformation with anyone. I will find an inn, bar the door, open the window so the swan I'll become can fly out of it come morning, and do my screaming and writhing in private.

"Niklaas? Can I come in?"

I turn to find Jor at the door, looking quietly concerned. He's a quiet sort of boy, a thinker and a planner and a considerer of things. He will be a good foil to his sister's rash, hurling-herself-into-trouble mode of living. She may have a council of advisers and seem to be slowing down to think now and then these days, but she's still Aurora. Still impulsive and as stubborn as a stone mule.

"Come in." I force a smile as I cross to the bed and begin shoving my things into my pack. I am determined to keep up a happy front; I won't ride out of this city boohooing into Alama's mane.

Aurora kept her promise to retrieve my horse. I'm not sure how she managed it, but Alama and Button arrived yesterday, delivered by Crimsin and a group of young exiles who fled the Feeding Hills after Aurora and I left and have been in hiding in the borderland woods ever since. Aurora was thrilled to learn Crimsin was alive, and Crimsin more than eager to start her new life in the capital.

She was surprised to find I'd turned down Aurora's proposal, insisting I was in love with Aurora before I even knew she was a girl, a statement I found laughable and uncomfortable-making at the same time. But after an hour spent telling me how stupid I was, Crimsin didn't waste any more of her time with me.

Which is fine. No one should waste time with me. I'm

too far down the deep, dark well of my own misery to be fit company.

Jor stands watching me pack, observing in his quiet way until I sigh and look up.

"Yes?" I ask.

"You're leaving." He sounds more broken up about it than I thought he'd be.

We've had fun exploring the castle together the past two days since his wounds became less painful, but I know he hates how miserable I've made Aurora. I've been avoiding her when I can and making a swift departure from her pleading eyes and offers of marriage when I can't. Nothing she, or any of the emissaries she's sent to win me over, says is going to change the way I feel. There's no point in dragging out the fight.

"When did you decide to leave?" Jor asks.

"I figured it was best," I say. "Spare everyone the spectacle and the aftermath."

"We never asked to be spared, but I know by now nothing can change your mind once you've made it up. I guess all that's left is goodbye." Jor plucks my comb from the bed and tosses it into my pack. "I don't like goodbyes."

"Then we'll shake and be done with it," I say, holding out my hand with a wink.

Jor scowls at my palm. "She's always been my best friend." He doesn't bother clarifying which "she" he's talking about. We both know there's only one "she" as far as the two of us are concerned. "I know her better than anyone in the world. I was telling the truth when I—"

"I know." I shove my spare shirt into my pack, though I

doubt I'll need it. "I'm glad you're sure she loves me, but I'm not, and I'm the one who matters."

"What does she have to do to convince you?" Jor asks. "She's already sent a company to retrieve your sister from Eno City, and promised to take care of Haanah for the rest of her life. She did that out of love for you."

"She did that because she is a decent person and knows my father is a monster," I say, clenching my jaw, refusing to think about never seeing Haanah again. I won't be here when she arrives. I'll never hug her again, never get to tell her how sorry I am for failing and leaving her alone without a single decent family member left in the world.

"I disagree," Jor says, "but even if you're right, what about the way she's begged and pleaded and written half a dozen letters to try to change your mind? You don't know how strange all that is. Aurora doesn't beg. Or write love letters. Or cry. Before now I could count the times I've seen her cry on my thumbs."

"She feels guilty." I shrug. "She'll get over it."

"No, she won't," he says with quiet assurance, not accusing me of anything, but not letting me off the hook, either.

"Maybe she won't," I grumble, closing up my pack. "But that's her problem. I told her it's stupid to let guilt eat her up over things like this. Sometimes you break people and sometimes you get broken. It's the way life is."

Jor sighs. "You're as stubborn as she is."

"Impossible." I grin as I swing my pack over my arm.

"It's not funny." Jor crosses his arms over his thin chest. He's a gangly kid—all arms and legs and knobby elbows—but I've never been tempted to tease him about it. Jor is a sensitive soul, so intensely earnest it would be no fun to tease him. He wouldn't get all red in the face and fight back the way Aurora does.

The way she did . . .

"No, but there are worse ways to go," I say, refusing to think about Aurora, to miss her smile and her laugh and the easy way it was between us. "Come on, now." I extend my hand a second time. "Shake and wish me luck."

Jor grudgingly takes my hand. "Good luck."

"And good luck to you," I say, giving his fingers a squeeze. "You and your sister are going to do great things for this country. I truly believe it."

"Will you at least tell her goodbye?" he asks. "I think she deserves that."

"Why don't you tell her goodbye for me?" I'm already moving toward the door, the thought of being forced to face down Aurora making me want to run for the stables.

I can't see her again, I can't or I might weaken and say yes. I might agree to marry her and spend the rest of my life jealous and angry, doubting that I'm the one she wanted, fearing she took me as her king for all the wrong reasons. It would sour me from the inside out, kill all my dreams of a happy family before they could be born. I'd rather become an animal than settle for the farce of a human life.

I don't want to pretend to be happy anymore. I wanted the real thing. I wanted someone I could love, someone who would love me back with no lies or curses or compromises getting in the way. I can't have that with Aurora. There are too many things standing between us. It's best if I leave and neither of us looks back.

"Tell her I hope she's happy with Thyne."

"She and Thyne are friends, Niklaas," Jor says. "They never—"

"Fine, fine. Thyne or . . . whoever. It doesn't matter. Just . . . tell her to be happy." I drop my gaze to the carpet, not wanting Jor to see how much it hurts to think of Aurora with someone else. "I want her to be happy enough for the both of us."

"Niklaas, I— Niklaas, wait!" Jor calls my name a third time, but by then I am out the door and down the hall, breaking into a run toward the stables, where Alama will be waiting to leave on our last ride.

AURORA

I sprint for the stables, arriving as the master of horses is leading Button into the yard to be saddled. I silently thank Jor for sending word to get the horse ready before he came to fetch me and run faster, pushing my tired body to nearly fairy-blessed speed.

"Thank you," I pant, snatching the bridle from the horse master's hands.

Ignoring his startled protests, I swing onto Button bareback and urge my horse out of the yard with a dig of my heels, grateful I'm still wearing my sparring pants.

Not that it would matter. I would ride Button bareback in a dress or naked if I had to. There isn't a second to waste. Jor said Niklaas left out the city's main gate headed north ten minutes ago. I have to reach him before he turns off onto another road or checks into an inn. I can't lose him. *I won't.*

"Hee-yup, go, go!" I shout, leaning low over Button's back as he surges through the gates, his canter becoming a gallop as we leave the city.

My every muscle tenses, straining for a sign of Niklaas on the road ahead. But there is nothing, no one, only fields of freshly cut wheat and the tree-lined dirt road warming to a ribbon of rich brownish red in the light of the setting sun.

The sun is setting. If I don't find Niklaas before it rises . . .

I grit my teeth and clench the reins, so angry and frantic that there is no room inside me for the despair I know I'll feel if I fail to reach him in time.

I won't fail, and I won't take no for an answer, not this time. I'll make him marry me at knifepoint if I have to.

I squint into the wind, refusing to let it bring tears to my eyes. For the first time in days, I don't feel like crying. I feel like wrestling an insufferable fool to the ground and beating the stupidity out of him.

How dare he? How *dare* he leave me? How dare he throw his life away?

Deep down, I didn't believe he'd do it. I thought he was only making me suffer until the last moment before he relented. I expected him to tell me to fetch the priest at dinner tonight and to be unhappily married to a boy who hated me by morning.

But instead, he's done *this*. He's run away. Run away and left me and, *by the gods,* right now I hate him as much as I love him.

I hate him. I love him. I hate him. There's so much feeling

raging inside of me I honestly don't know if I want to kiss him or throw a punch at his stubborn jaw. But when I reach the crest of a hill and see him a field ahead, his shoulders straining the seams of his Kanvasol shirt, his hair shining in the radiant light of his last human day, my anger is banished in a rush of relief so powerful it feels my chest will burst.

"Niklaas!" My shout is rough and raw but loud enough to carry across the space between us. I *know* he's heard me, but instead of turning back he digs his heels into Alama's side, sending her racing down the road away from me.

Away! He's running away! Again! Without even looking back!

With a howl of rage, I kick Button harder than I mean to and he launches down the road like a blade from a knife-thrower's fingers, so fast the air whistles in my ears and my heart lurches and for a terrifying second I think I'll fall. But then I tilt my torso forward and find my seat, leaning into the wind, hovering over Button's back as he closes in on Alama.

Closer, closer, until we're so close I could reach out and touch Alama's tail as it flies out behind her. She is fast, but Button is faster and carrying less weight.

Soon he'll be carrying no weight at all.

I'm so livid I don't stop to worry if I still have the agility to pull off a stunt like the one I'm planning. I simply grip Button's mane in both hands to steady myself and pull my feet beneath me, crouching on the horse's back for a bare moment to take aim before launching myself at Niklaas's shoulders.

Time slows and I hang in the air for a second that seems to last an eternity. I realize I'm going to make it, but just *barely,* and then I'm landing on Alama's back with a giddy cry, snatching handfuls of Niklaas's shirt and clinging tight to keep from sliding off, while the startled horse screams and dances to the side of the road.

Unfortunately Niklaas isn't holding on quite as tight. When Alama rears onto her back legs with an enraged whinny, he's thrown from his saddle, carrying me to the ground along with him.

We land in a tangle on the grass, my legs pinned beneath his and enough of his weight on my chest that when my breath rushes out with a groan, it doesn't want to rush back in again.

"By the Land Beyond, what's wrong with you?" Niklaas growls as he rolls off of me. "Are you mad?"

I want to demand the same of him, to demand that he tell me what kind of cowardly bastard runs away without even saying goodbye, but I can't pull in a breath. All I can manage is an evil glare as I curl onto my side, clutching my fist to my chest, willing my wretched lungs to breathe.

"You've probably broken something," he shouts, his voice as rough as his hands are gentle as he curls his fingers under my shoulders and pulls me into a seated position. I lean over my legs, while he rubs my back, helping coax the breath back into my body. "Can you breathe?" he asks. "Can you talk? Are you—"

"Yes," I finally manage to wheeze.

"Well, where does it hurt, you fool?"

"In here." I jab my thumb at my chest as I turn to face him, ignoring the twinge in my shoulder that sends nasty shivers shooting down to my hip. I'm hurt, but not badly, not nearly as badly as I'll be come morning if I don't force Niklaas to see reason.

"Your ribs?" he asks.

"My heart, you insufferable idiot," I shout. "I love you and you're determined to do away with yourself, and I *hate* you for it!" I shove his shoulders with both hands and all my strength, sending him falling back onto his ass with a startled grunt.

"You hate *me*?" he asks, anger creeping into his tone. "Well, I hate you, too! All you've ever done is lie to me and deceive me and—"

"Risk my life for you and worry about you and tell you how beautiful and wonderful and funny you are," I say, tears creeping into my eyes though I'm hot all over and not feeling inclined to cry, especially not now, when it looks as if Niklaas might actually be paying attention. "And laugh with you and fight with you and listen to you, and love you, even when I was sure you'd never love me because I'm not pretty enough or girly enough and my chest is too small."

Niklaas scowls. "You're flaming beautiful, and you know it."

"I do not!"

"Well, you should, you thickheaded thing, but it doesn't matter," he says, scowl deepening. "It doesn't matter that I can't stop thinking about the way you looked in that dress on Evensew, or the way we— None of it matters. I can't trust you."

"Oh, come down from your holy mount!" I shout. "You lied to me, too. You lied about your curse and you—"

"No, I didn't! I didn't tell the truth, but I didn't—"

"And you lied about other things, too." This time, when I shove at his shoulders, I follow him as he falls onto his back in the grass until I'm lying on top of him with my lips inches from his and my fingers tangled in his hair, until I can feel his breath rush out and his arms come around me in spite of himself. "You don't find the thought of kissing me repulsive."

"Aurora . . ."

"And when you kissed me in the grove," I rush on, breathless all over again. "I never . . . I never dreamed a kiss could be like that."

"Like what?" he asks, one hand dropping to grip my hip, sending a jolt of electricity surging through my body.

"Like opening a door to the most beautiful place I've ever known." My lips drop closer to his, heart racing from being pressed against him, from feeling his warmth through my clothes and his strength coiled beneath me. "Like coming home and a wild adventure, all at the same time. Safe and dangerous, and I . . . I finally felt . . ."

My breath rushes out on a jagged sigh.

"I didn't feel alone," I say, voice breaking as I confess the one thing I've held back, the one thing I was afraid to share in the letters I've written him the past four days.

The only thing scarier than feeling so alone is fearing you'll always feel that way, that no one will ever see you for all the things you are, and the things you're afraid to be, and the person you want so desperately to become. But Niklaas did, he saw me, he knew me better than anyone, even Jor. I know he did, if only he can remember.

"Even with people I love, I've always felt like a piece that didn't fit. I was fairy-blessed but not a fairy, human but with gifts that made everyone expect so much more of me. I've always felt alone," I whisper, forcing myself to keep going no matter how anxious this confession makes me. "Ever since my mother died. I'm always lonely . . . except . . . except when I'm with you."

"What about Thyne?" he asks after a moment, the flash of pain in his eyes making me realize how much I've underestimated his capacity for jealousy.

By the gods, if I'd known, I could have sent Thyne to convince Niklaas that there is absolutely nothing romantic between the two of us.

"Thyne is like another brother to me. I love *you*, Niklaas, no one else, not in that way." I trail my fingertips across his cheek, willing him to see how much I care. "I love you. If you don't love me back anymore, tell me and I'll let you go, but don't run off to die because you doubt me."

And then I kiss him, and after only a moment he kisses me back and I learn there is something better than a first kiss with Niklaas. There is a second kiss. There is his hands in my hair and his tongue slipping past my lips and his muscles flexing beneath me as he rolls us over in the grass until he hovers over me and my legs wrap around his hips and my fingers dig into his back and our kiss becomes so deep it feels like we're the same being, the same aching body, the same full heart, the same pulse that races beneath the skin.

We kiss until the sun sets and the air grows cool, but I scarcely notice the creeping in of the autumn twilight. I have never been so warm, so dizzy, so drunk on another person.

All my lines are blurry and the world has narrowed to his lips and his taste and his hint-of-a-beard rough against my skin and the delicious smell of him and the even more delicious way his hands roam over my body, touching me everywhere I've been dying for him to touch, making me more breathless with every moment, until I pull his shirt from his pants and run my hands up his bare back and down his chest, summoning a rumble from his throat.

"Stop." He pulls my hands away, pinning them to the grass above my head.

"Why?" I lift my head, bringing my lips to his, drawing him back into another kiss with a sigh of satisfaction.

"We're on the side of the road," he mumbles against my mouth.

"I don't care," I breathe, shifting beneath him until he groans. "I don't want to stop." I slip my tongue out to flick his upper lip. "Don't stop, Niklaas. Don't—"

"And this is why you drive me mad!" he shouts, retreating so fast that I curl into a seated position like a rolly bug discovered beneath a rock. "You never think!"

"I do t-too," I stammer. "I just—"

"You could have killed us both!" he shouts, jumping up to pace back and forth in the grass. The sun set a good fifteen minutes ago, but there is still plenty of light left to see how irate he's become. "You're not fairy-blessed anymore, and even if you were, Alama and I are not. You can't go jumping from horses without a second thought. You're the queen, by the Pit, and people are counting on you!"

"I know people are counting on me, but—"

"But nothing!" he shouts, making me flinch. "You have to be more levelheaded."

"I'm trying, but you don't make it easy!"

"You think it was easy pulling away from you?" he asks, stooping to shoot me a look that makes me shiver with wishing he were back in my arms, doing all the things we both so clearly enjoy. "But I did it, because you don't deflower a damn queen in a field by the side of the road."

"Deflower?" I ask, my lips stretching into a smile. "What am I, a petunia?"

"Don't smile," he says, his own lips twitching. "This isn't funny."

"Oh yes it is." I laugh as I stand, tucking my shirt back into my pants as I turn to search for Button. "I was the one who started this. If anyone was deflowering anyone, it was *me* deflowering *you*."

"I was deflowered long ago, Your Highness," Niklaas says.

"Yes, I know, I haven't forgotten what a successful whore you were." I spy Button and Alama grazing by the side of the road a half a field away and turn back to Niklaas. "Maybe I should run to the nearest village and find a boy or two to experiment with. I mean, if the deflowering business is such a burden, I—"

"Don't you dare," he says, snatching me around the waist, pulling me into his arms and up his body until my feet dangle off the ground, muffling my protest with his kiss.

His kiss . . .

There is nothing better, nothing in the whole world.

"I could get drunk on your kisses," I sigh against his lips.

"*My* kisses," he says, arms tightening around me. "No one else's."

"Does this mean you'll do it?" I ask, pulling back to look him in the eye.

"Deflower you?"

"Marry me," I say, then add in a whisper. "Then the other. As soon as it can possibly be arranged."

He shivers and I smile because I know he wants me as much as I want him and that we've finally found our way to each other and everything is going to be all right and then he says—

"No."

—and my heart plummets.

"Why not?" I demand. "You love me, I know you do."

"I do, more than I've ever loved anything," he says, setting me on my feet. "A frightening amount considering I've only known you three weeks."

"Then why?" I ask, positively sick to the bone. I can't lose him, not when I was so certain . . . so sure. "I swear I will never lie to you again, even if we live to be a hundred. Even if it's kinder to lie than to tell the truth."

"Even if my breath stinks?" he asks, a teasing glint in his eye that makes me hopeful. "Or my gut starts to spill over my pants?"

"I'll tell you," I say. "I swear it. Immediately."

"So if I ask you a question right now," he says, humor leaving his voice, "you will be bound to tell the truth?"

"I swear it on my mother's memory."

"If it weren't for my curse, would you still be considering getting married?"

I pause, but hurry to speak when I see distance creep into his eyes. "No, I wouldn't. I won't even be eighteen until spring. I would rather wait, but—"

"But nothing," he says, turning to walk away. "I won't force you—"

"No one is forcing me to do anything! Let me finish!" I grab his arm, digging my heels in until he stops. "But you don't have a year or five, so we'll do it now, and I will never regret it because I know I'll never love anyone the way I love you."

"How can you know?" he asks, looking down at me with obvious skepticism. "You're only seventeen. You've only kissed two people, and both of them—"

"Unlike some people, I don't need to sample every beer in the tavern to know which one I prefer," I say, propping my hands on my hips, not bothering to hide my frustration. He wanted me to be honest and at the moment he is honestly the most frustrating boy in Mataquin. "And we don't have another week for me to spend praising your humbling good looks and your sweet heart and your bravery and on and on until your vanity is satisfied."

"My vanity?" He rolls his eyes, but I see the tension easing from his expression and know I'd better get him to a priest before he finds something else to fret about.

"Yes, your vanity," I say, tucking my hand into his arm and leading him toward the horses. "Now, you're going to get on your horse and come back to the castle and we're going to be married and tomorrow you'll wake up and you won't be a swan and I won't be alone and neither of us will regret a damn thing."

"Well, I suppose somebody has to keep you out of trouble," he says, stopping to pull me into his arms. "Thank you."

"For what?" I ask, lacing my fingers around his neck.

"For being so wretchedly stubborn. I was pretty sure it was the only thing I didn't like about you." He laughs beneath his breath. "But anyone else would have given up on me the fourth or fifth time I said no."

"I guess you'll have to add it to the list of things you love about me," I whisper, standing on tiptoe to brush my lips against his, sighing as my entire being lights up. It's like being filled with fairy magic but better, because this is magic we make together, Niklaas and I, something that was born and nurtured between us that can never be twisted or tainted or stolen away so long as we're willing to fight for it.

And I will always fight for him. Always.

I feel shot through with light all the way back to the castle, all through the ceremony, and late into the night as Niklaas and I set about deflowering each other with as much tender enthusiasm as I had expected. And it is beautiful and right and by the time I drift to sleep in his arms, he is truly a part of me, a treasure I will hold close for the rest of my life, the greatest blessing, fairy or otherwise, I have ever known.

NIKLAAS

I open my eyes to sunlight flooding through unfamiliar yellow curtains, bathing the bed in gold, and for a moment I can't remember where I am.

And then I hear her sigh and turn my head to find Aurora propped on one arm, watching me wake up, and it all comes rushing back—the breathless ride back to the castle, the wedding in the garden with the last of the autumn roses tucked into Aurora's hair, going to bed with my best friend and learning I've been doing it all wrong, and needed to be deflowered after all.

Last night was what love is supposed to feel like, terrifying and beautiful and so close you're afraid you'll lose a piece of yourself, but you don't. You gain a piece of the person you love instead, a piece that makes you stronger and happier than you could have imagined possible.

Thank the gods she came after me; thank the gods I had the sense to let myself be saved or I never would have known.

"Good morning," I mumble with a smile, reaching lazy fingers up to brush her cheek, needing to touch her. "How long have you been awake?"

"Since before the sun rose." She leans into my touch. "I wanted to be sure . . ."

"Aw, you were worried about me, you tender-hearted little thing." I grin as I roll over, pushing her back onto the pillows.

"Of course I was, you idiot," she says, fighting a smile as she punches my bare arm, proving that marriage isn't going to make her go easy on me. "I have important business to attend to. I don't want to spend the rest of my life cleaning up swan droppings."

"Is that all?" I lean close enough for our noses to brush. "The only reason you're glad I'm still human?"

"Well . . . I love you," she whispers, her fingers threading through my hair, pulling me even closer. "I suppose there's that."

Before I can tell her I love her, too, she's kissing me, and one kiss leads to two, which leads to a challenge to prove love is as much fun in the daylight, and I never have been the sort who can resist a challenge that involves a beautiful girl.

A beautiful girl who loves me, who makes me feel like I've finally come home.

"Let's never sleep apart," I whisper later as we lie curled together, drifting back to sleep in the pale morning light. "I want to wake up with you every day."

Aurora sighs. "You really are sweet, you know."

"It's true, Your Highness. I am very sweet. You should always love me," I say, pressing a kiss to her bare shoulder.

She laughs. "I think that can be arranged."

ACKNOWLEDGMENTS

First, big thanks to the usual suspects—to Michelle Poploff and Rebecca Short for their editing prowess, and to the entire team at Delacorte Press for their excellence. Thanks to my family—to Mike for love above and beyond, and to Riley and Logan for laughs and love and the joy of being Mama to two such extraordinary people. Thanks to friend and critique partner Julie Linker for her keen eye and unflagging moral support, to Jennifer Redstreake-Geary for her delicious artwork, to the Debutantes of 2009 for community of the best kind, and to my mother and father for all those trips to the library. Last, thank you to my readers: your enthusiasm and support mean so much; I am honored to tell you stories.

ABOUT THE AUTHOR

Stacey Jay is the author of seven previous books for young adults, including *Of Beast and Beauty* and the popular companion novels *Juliet Immortal* and *Romeo Redeemed*. She lives in a cabin by the river in Northern California with her winemaker husband, two sons, her beloved sewing machine, an electric ukulele, and all the stories still making their way from the ether to the page. Learn more at staceyjay.com.